What people are saying about

ZORA AND NICKY

"I love this woman! She puts into print what many people are thinking but few confess. Unflinchingly honest and bold as brass, this story brings our modern struggles over race and religion down to a personal, relational level. While reading Claudia's novel, I broached the subject of interracial dating with our college-age kids and found out just how relevant these issues remain. Clearly, Claudia Mair Burney knows her stuff. *Zora and Nicky* isn't safe, but it's good."

—LIZ CURTIS HIGGS, BEST-SELLING AUTHOR OF BAD GIRLS OF THE BIBLE

"*Zora and Nicky* is a great book—Burney can really write, and I'm thrilled about this title. It really brings prodigals to life, and there are SO many out there whose faith hasn't yet become their own—but rather mimics their parents'. If you like your tension high and your writing well done, order it up. I'm impressed!"

—KRISTIN BILLERBECK, AUTHOR OF WHAT A GIRL WANTS AND SHE'S ALL THAT

"*Zora and Nicky* is far more than a love story, far more than a study in racial contrasts, far more than just a good read. It is a manual for living a life of honesty and relentless pursuit of wholeness in Jesus, disguised as a novel that glides effortlessly between stirring, lyrical, and hilarious. *Zora and Nicky* challenges our understanding of what it means to live the Christian life; you can't read it and not be changed."

VIOLETTE BETWEEN

"This is the best read l   ia Mair Burney is an
accomplished novelist,   ir heart away long
before they have finishe⌐ ⌐⌐⌐⌐g you their story."

—PHYLLIS TICKLE, AUTHOR AND LECTURER,
RELIGION EDITOR (RET.), PUBLISHERS WEEKLY

ZORA AND NICKY

A NOVEL IN BLACK AND WHITE

Claudia Mair Burney

David ⓒ Cook®

transforming lives together

ZORA AND NICKY
Published by David C. Cook
4050 Lee Vance View
Colorado Springs, CO 80918 U.S.A.

David C. Cook Distribution Canada
55 Woodslee Avenue, Paris, Ontario, Canada N3L 3E5

David C. Cook U.K., Kingsway Communications
Eastbourne, East Sussex BN23 6NT, England

David C. Cook and the graphic circle C logo
are registered trademarks of Cook Communications Ministries.

This story is a work of fiction. All characters and events are the product of the author's
imagination. Any resemblance to any person, living or dead, is coincidental.

Unless otherwise noted, Scripture quotations are taken from the King James Version of the
Bible. (Public Domain.) Scripture quotations marked MSG are taken from *THE MESSAGE*.
Copyright © by Eugene H. Peterson 1993, 1994, 1195, 1996, 2000, 2001, 2002. Used by
permission of NavPress Publishing Group.

The song lyrics on page 17 are from "Get Away Jordan." The lyrics on pages 48 and 389 are
from "Let us Break Bread Together." The lyrics on page 312 are from Fred Hammond's song
"Let the Praise Begin" from the album *Hooked on the Hits*, Verity Records, 2003

LCCN 2007939850
ISBN 978-0-7814-4550-4

The Team: Andrea Christian, Lisa Samson, Jaci Schneider, Karen Athen
Cover Design: The DesignWorks Group, Jason Gabbert
Interior Design: The DesignWorks Group
Cover Photo: © Masterfile Royalty-Free / Masterfile

Printed in the United States of America
First Edition 2008

1 2 3 4 5 6 7 8 9 10

012508

A NOTE FROM THE PUBLISHER:

Zora and Nicky is a comedy/tragedy of errors about two subjects held sacred in America: race and religion.

Like many of us, the characters often have more questions than answers. There are times when they are plagued by doubt, emptiness, and loneliness; times when they feel separated from love—from God. If we are honest with ourselves, we have known these feelings.

Zora and Nicky is about our longing for love and the sometimes dark places it can take us. It addresses the reality of a broken world full of broken people who have distorted images of love. Ultimately, these pages paint a beautiful picture of a God who pursues us in our brokenness and forms us in His love.

This novel doesn't offer pat answers or simple solutions. It is simply a story, and like all good stories, we begin to see our own lives reflected in the pages. We trust that the underlying message will point you toward hope—toward God.

Thank you for reading,

Don Pape
Publisher

But we have this treasure in earthen vessels.

2 Corinthians 4:7

My beloved friends, let us continue to love each other since love comes from God. Everyone who loves is born of God and experiences a relationship with God. The person who refuses to love doesn't know the first thing about God, because God is love—so you can't know him if you don't love. This is how God showed his love for us: God sent his only Son into the world so we might live through him. This is the kind of love we are talking about—not that we once upon a time loved God, but that he loved us and sent his Son as a sacrifice to clear away our sins and the damage they've done to our relationship with God.

My dear, dear friends, if God loved us like this, we certainly ought to love each other. No one has seen God, ever. But if we love one another, God dwells deeply within us, and his love becomes complete in us—perfect love!

1 John 4:7–12 (MSG)

ACKNOWLEDGMENTS

I am so blessed to have this opportunity, Holy Trinity, One in Essence, and Undivided, Father, Son, and Holy Spirit. Thank You, thank You, thank You. Without You I am nothing. I could do nothing. All this is for You.

Thank you, my beloved and ginormous family. This was a tough one. I'll make good on the bribes, except for the Porsche, Ken. I was just playin'.

Hi again, patient Claudia Mair Burney readers who wondered where I disappeared to. I'm back! Thanks for waiting for me, and welcome newbies!

I have a literary beloved community. They're my first readers, cheerleaders, mentors, and advocates. You include: Mary, Lisa, Lori, Stacia, Heather, Diane, Paula, Donna, Mark, and Bethany. And God bless you, Ragamuffin Diva friends, who patiently endure my blog absences while I write novels.

Steve, my *Zora and Nicky* evangelist, what a wonder you are. Thanks for believing in my Anne-Lamott, you-know-what first draft. And John Juan Blase, you were a wonderful Nicky. I owe *you* a cheeseburger.

I am deeply indebted to Lisa for being more than a BFF and bringing her servant's heart to me as my editor this time around. You taught me not just how to make a fine book but how to give hospitality Jesus-style. I learned more in this short run than a girl is entitled to from her literary crush. Thank you.

I will never be able to repay the grace and kindness of Don and Terry, who not only rescued me from a dark night of the soul but made many dreams come true with this book. You showed me that my Father is very, very, fond of me. Now if I can only get a pair of patched pants!

I am grateful to have been blessed to work with a remarkably gifted editor and sassy *broad*—and honey, God don't make broads much anymore. I am very proud to know you, and work with you, Miss Andrea Christian.

Chip MacGregor, the Holy Spirit got it right when He chose you as my agent. Your guidance has been impeccable. Thank you, lovely, quiet, and patient Patti, for sharing him with this neurotic writer.

Fancy Pants, aka Brennan Manning, my hero, you changed my life with *The Ragamuffin Gospel.* You inspire me, delight me, and I adore you, and it's pretty obvious from the pages of this book.

Robert Benson, I discovered *The Body Broken: Answering God's Call to Love One Another* as I put the finishing touches on this manuscript. Reading your book was a quiet "amen." And sometimes it was a hearty one. Your vision is woven in these pages too.

A few good friends will always grace the pages of my acknowledgments. They are my sustenance: Evette, Gail, Gina, and especially Carly, even though you're my sister. And my David C. Cook "Girls" (insert our secret *alternative* name here), *Good morning!* Love you.

Maybe I didn't say your name. If you have contributed to this book in any way and I've failed you here, it doesn't mean that I am not most grateful for your contribution. In the words of our hero Nicky, it simply means I suck. Forgive me.

Finally, the team at David C. Cook is far too large to name, but I must give a wildly enthusiastic shout-out to El Presidente Cris, man-in-demand Dan, everybody's right hand Denise, and all around wonderful, amazing people: Melanie, Kate, Theresa, Annette, Christina, and Amy, and so many more who work quietly behind the scenes with this dream team, making a sistah (and her book) look *good*. Real good.

GOD bless you and keep you,
GOD smile on you and gift you,
GOD look you full on the face
and make you prosper.
Numbers 6:24–26 (MSG)

Love is of God.
Mair

CHAPTER ONE

ZORA

I used to imagine myself as a tiny shoot on a tall brown tree, the gnarled roots of that tree tangled and twisted beneath the black earth. Our roots run so deep, my family can trace its origins back generations. To my great, great, great grandfather who followed the drinking gourd all the way to freedom. To slave ships with lyrical names that belied the horrors taking place in their wide bellies. To the shores of the west coast of Africa where one of our own returned, a single, dark, shining prince, unfettered by imposed forgetfulness, refusing to relinquish his name.

We are a tree with roots and long-limbed branches reaching skyward—a tree with tiny green shoots like me, emerging from something solid and substantial. When we are in season, we scent the air with our bright, fragrant blossoms.

But this Sunday morning I feel alienated from the dignity and hardiness of my ancestors. I don't feel like a Psalm 1:3 sistah—a tree planted by the rivers of water, that bringeth forth her fruit in her season. Her leaf also shall not wither; and whatsoever she doeth shall prosper.

And that was just the King James Version. Don't make me pull out my *Amplified Bible* and quote that Scripture three times fast.

Sometimes I long for that old-time religion that's good enough for me. No, I take that back—I long for it all the time now.

I scan the sanctuary. I need God to speak to me today. For *real*. That's one reason I'm sitting in the third row. Besides being Daddy's "amen" corner (the reason I sit here most Sundays), the first three rows make up what we call Prophet's Row on the sly. In this esteemed section, you're more likely to get "a Word" from God. I've received them on several occasions; I was told three different times that the Lord had a husband for me, and one prophet went so far as to say that he'd be a godly man with a pastoral call. I stopped sitting there for six months after that.

Once, a prophetess visited us at Light of Life Christian Center and said God told her to give a woman in our congregation the silver fox coat right off her back. I know the recipient: Ms. Pamela Darden, a squat, obese woman with a widow's mite, a bad wig, and three hefty daughters. Not one of the Darden women can keep a man, even if they shackle him to their bedposts, and it has nothing to do with their weight. They possess an air of quiet desperation, only it refuses to stay quiet and they end up making a big stink of their manlessness at every opportunity that arises.

The Darden women don't have much, and Ms. Pamela, the breadwinner, still takes care of her grown daughters while they "wait on the Lord." But Ms. Pamela remains faithful. She tithes and gives offerings far above her means, grasping for the promised but ever-eluding hundred-fold return on her investment. She's like a compulsive gambler tugging on the sleeve of a one-armed bandit like it was God's own. Just one more silver fox coat. Or maybe a house. Or maybe help my girls get a job, God. Send me a Word, and money, money, money. *Puh-leese, Lawd.*

I'm feeling you today, Ms. Pamela, every desperate Puh-leese, Lawd, puh-leese, Lawd, puh-leeeeeeese! I actually admire your crazy desperation. It takes courage to be that honest with God. That needy. My parents groomed me to not need anything.

Trade ya.

And Ms. Pamela, I've been watching you. I know you got behind in your car note, scrambling to pay all those online dating service bills your girls stuck you with when they believed more in Match.com and eHarmony than their mama's hard work. I know if you thought somebody needed it, you'd give them the silver fox right off your back. I know you've lived a hard life, and you've had more than your share of boyfriends after your husband left you, and you're still a little twisted from it. You still love rather freely, only now you love for Christ alone. It's *how* you love for Him that's so extravagant. You show up for whoever needs Him, with whatever you can give. That widow's mite of yours goes farther than the fattest wallets of some of our wealthiest members, including Daddy. You love Jesus like you don't have a bit of sense.

God bless you, Ms. Pamela Darden. God help you in this place.

Service hasn't started yet, so I step away from my chair over to the second row where Ms. Pamela and her daughters sit now. They don't sit in the third row anymore, upgrading, probably, to sit closer to "the anointing." I hope that works out for them. I tap Ms. Pamela on the shoulder. Fortunately, she's at the end of the row so I don't have to step over her daughters, Tessa, Vernice, and Noelle.

I reach out to give her a hug. For all the hard edges of her life, her face, at least in church, is only softness and light. She takes me in with her warm brown eyes and draws me into cinnamon-colored big mama arms. Gives me an embrace scented with baby powder and rose water. There is a bit of hope for me to hold on to in that squeeze.

There's this facade I'm forced to endure, that everybody loves *The Bishop's* daughter, whether they do or not. And then there is Ms. Pamela, who actually loves me.

"How you doin', Miss Zora?"

"I'm good, Ms. Pamela."

God will forgive me for that lie if He forgives all the liars here who claim they have faith, healing, and prosperity when they're riddled with doubt, sick, and broke day after day. At least I hope He will.

"How are you this morning?" I ask her with sincerity, not trying to gauge whether or not she's outconfessing, -believing, and -receiving me.

She clears her throat, the resulting rumble a frightening death rattle that forces my hand to my own throat. "Girl, I'm healed in the name of Jesus," she says.

Which means she's sick. She wheezes instead of breathes, follows it with a raspy cough that sounds as if her lungs are about to come out of her throat.

"Are you okay, Ms. Pamela?"

A breathy, "I'm healed by the stripes of Jesus."

She can barely get the name of Jesus out before she's seized by a coughing fit.

"Have you seen a doctor?"

"I have faith." Another coughing fit.

I think she's going to have an asthma attack with that faith.

She takes my hand and squeezes it. "Just touch and agree with me in prayer, baby."

She releases my hand. I've touched her, but I don't agree. I'm about to tell her that I will take her to the hospital. I'll take her right now, but then she smiles at me.

"Worship is about to start. You better go take your seat. Remember what happened to me in that seat? Don't want to miss your blessing."

Worship? We're not about to worship. We're about to start singing the *Songs of Faith* that our worship leader must have seen on a late night TV infomercial after he got tired of watching reruns of *The X-Files.*

I shuffle back to my seat, praying diligently for Ms. Pamela's healing. I pray that somehow I can forget the craziness of the conversation we just had. She's going to die of pneumonia. What is she doing? What am I?

I want to fly away from here, and I'll put her on my back and fly her out with me.

One of these mornings bright and fair
I want to cross over to see my Lord.
Going to take my wings and fly the air.
I want to cross over to see my Lord.

Now that's a real song of faith.

Don't you go singing Negro spirituals, Zora. Don't you do that during the ridiculous *Songs of Faith.*

We are fifteen hundred strong this morning, and that's just the first service, an ocean of people standing in front of their chairs—not pews. It looks like a conference hall in here, with a cross. We don't do *church.* We are a *Christian Center,* and I'd like to know who thought of that. I mean, once upon a time, the black church really was a *center* of life, civil and social justice, and community change, along with worship. But that sure isn't what's going on here.

We worship—a generous description—in decidedly uninspired spaces, complete with every amenity, including a coffee bar and a bookstore and gift shop, which sells a multitude of booklets with titles like "Victory in the Tongue," "Confess Your Way to Health," and "God Prosper Me." A concession stand even sells overpriced junk food, just like a *conference hall!*

I remember visiting my grandfather's church—a real church—as a little girl and holding a hymnbook that I was too young to read. I remember hearing the old folks singing songs they didn't have to look at the pages to know.

But the songs I'm hearing now aren't *my* songs of faith. These songs make my eyes roll back to the whites, and I can't believe we've actually adopted the unforgettable ditties—now flashing before me in PowerPoint letters as big as my head—for *worship*.

At least we have a bangin' choir that responds with great swelling voices to whatever our Kirk-Franklin-wannabe music director yells at them: *Come on! Come on! Nah! Ha! Uh, uh, here we go nah!*

Should I even complain? Aren't these songs musical reminders, as if we need it, that God wants us to prosper and be in good health, even as our souls prosper?

Isn't that what God wants?

Oh, for a rousing chorus of "Go Down, Moses."

Let my people go.

We need a Moses in the house, all right, instead of these forked-tongue prophets of prosperity, their gold-weighted backs permanently curved toward offering baskets, reeking of new money

and the ache of unrelenting hunger. It always strikes me as odd how
these self-appointed messengers of God always pronounce *blessings*
on us, mostly material ones. Not one of them has said, "Hey, deacon,
you need to stop sleeping with the secretary." Nobody tells the youth
group that God has a problem with the abortions half the girls use as
birth control.

Now mind you, Light of Life Christian Center wholeheartedly
condemns these unfortunate lifestyle choices, as LLCC's PR materi-
als clearly state. But people have a way of being human. And humans
have a way of sinning. Besides, who around here has time to teach
anyone about living holy when we're all chasing abundance and a life
of no lack, especially when the evidence of our *blessedness* is stuff?

And we have stuff. Lots of stuff. And we have prophets with
promises of new cars and houses we'll build from the ground up. Our
dirty deeds remain hidden, obscured by all the glorious things we've
amassed.

I wish just *one* of the songs on the screen inspired the kind of awe
that would make adulterous deacons and aborting teenagers fall
right on their faces. I want to fall on my face too, not so much
because I'm a sinner, and I am—though we aren't allowed to call
ourselves sinners. We even changed the words to "Amazing Grace"
and made ourselves "someone" instead of "wretches." I almost
fainted when I found out the real lyrics said *wretch*. No, I want to
fall down before God because it has to be amazing to love and revere
Him that way.

Holy, holy, holy. Lord, God almighty. That's how they do it in
heaven.

We aren't a fall-on-your-face church, though if the choir is doin' its thing we can shout the paint off the walls. We don't have to fall down though. That isn't necessary. We don't even have to get our expensive clothes soiled by getting slain in the Spirit anymore. We are little gods. We confess not our sins, but promises, and we shall have whatsoever we say.

Jesus' word to the *church*—not the Christian Center—in Laodicea in the book of Revelation?

Because thou sayest, I am rich, and increased with goods, and have need of nothing; and knowest not that thou art wretched, and miserable, and poor, and blind, and naked.

But I *am* rich, Jesus. My parents are crazy paid. I have everything I need, want, desire, and more. I drive a Lexus. I have the perfect, Denzel Washington look-alike boyfriend. My Kate Spade handbag cost more than my salary pays in a week—the salary I earn at my daddy's church. I'm a Black American Princess, black Ivy League educated, who wants for nothing except everything Jesus is talking about in these verses.

"I counsel thee to buy of me gold tried in the fire, that thou mayest be rich; and white raiment, that thou mayest be clothed, and that the shame of thy nakedness do not appear; and anoint thine eyes with eyesalve, that thou mayest see."

That's not the kind of thing I tend to buy when I go shopping, Lord. I don't know where to buy gold tried in the fire. Can you purchase white raiment with a platinum Visa? Is that eyesalve available at Nordstrom?

"As many as I love, I rebuke and chasten: be zealous therefore, and repent."

Did you just say, *"Repent"?* Like John the Baptist?

Sorry, Lord. We never get that kind of prophecy around here. The people won't give a good love offering for "a Word" like that. Repent implies we are wretched, miserable, poor, blind, and naked, and that does not jibe with our statement of Faith, with a capital *F*.

Oh, God. I can't stand another moment in this pseudosanctuary country club. I need to go to a hospital for the spiritually ill.

My bad. We aren't allowed to be ill at LLCC. Sickness is evidence that you don't have enough faith. Isn't that right, Ms. Pamela? Keep confessing until you drop dead.

What's gonna happen to you, Ms. Pamela? What are we going to do? I've got to help us.

The singing finally stops. Daddy tells us to hold up our Bibles. We do this every Sunday. I repeat the words I know so well, Bible held high above my head.

"This is my Bible. I can have what it says I can have. I can be what it says I can be."

I can have what it says I can have.

Gold tried in the fire. White raiment.

I can be what it says I can be.

"As many as I love, I rebuke and chasten."

I can be rebuked. I can be chastened.

Daddy starts in on Genesis 1:28. Blessings. Fruitfulness. Multiplying. But I keep hearing Jesus talking about wretchedness, misery, and blindness.

I've gotta get out of here.

I stand up and step away from the chairs and Prophet's Row, and walk right down the center of the aisle, Daddy's voice fading from my hearing. I can sense the Plexiglas podium growing smaller and smaller behind me, as do all his ideas about taking dominion over every living thing that moveth upon the earth.

Can he discern, with all that divine revelation he claims to have, that my heart has splintered into a thousand pieces?

In the April-sweetened air, I let myself hurt for the Laodicians I've just walked out on, and for the Laodician I've let myself become. I reach my black Lexus without comfort, praying for God to send Ms. Pamela a Word from Him, and God, please, please, please, let it be, "Go outside so Zora can take you to the emergency room."

Please, God. That ain't much to ask for.

NICKY

An old rugged cross made of maple wood that my great, great grandfather carved is the focal point of our altar at True Believer Gospel Tabernacle, and now my dad stands in front of it at the pulpit, red faced and earnest, like his father before him, and his father before him, and his father before him. This is the legacy of the Parker men.

Blah, blah, blah.

The cross is about the coolest thing we've got going. Everything goes downhill from there. From the synthetic blood-red carpet—I don't have to tell you whose blood the color is supposed to represent—to the crushed-velvet cushioned pews—a really bad idea, might I add—to the corny stained-glass windows done by the biggest drunken hack in town. I mean, if you gotta do stained glass, the least you could do is get a real artist to do it. Trite stained glass is just *wrong*. Visually, we're a mess.

And don't get me started on the message.

I know the sermon Dad is preaching so well I could give it myself, and have given it, in fact. Nobody noticed when I repeated it, either. It sounds like every other sermon he'll preach—the same phrasing, same inflection, same modulation. Truth be told, he's already recycled this exact sermon three or four times this year, and it's only April. I don't think the tree huggers had that in mind when they admonished us to reuse, but it seems to work for Dad. For us.

I look behind me, my gaze roaming around the congregation. The people look pleased as punch. I wish somebody—anybody—would shoot me in the head. The thought of my blood and brain matter flying in my dad's red face holds my interest more than his sermon.

Man, I have to stop watching all those forensic shows, but they make for great story possibilities—nothing like violent death to heat up the battle between good and evil. I always think in story. Not that anybody ever encouraged that. My parents almost burned me at the stake when I suggested the Bible is literature. I fancy myself a novelist, though God knows I'm more blocked than a nursing home population without prunes. But what I'm *not* writing interests me more than Dad's sermon. And it looks like, based on the earnest faces around me, our members are wolfing down his every word like starving dogs begging at the master's table.

I'm gonna blow. Big projectile vomiting, which I hope lands on my dad. Or maybe on the hackneyed, stained-glass scene of the anemic-looking good shepherd.

However, providence is with him. Dad, that is. Maybe with the anemic good shepherd too. Instead of regurgitating like my dad is doing, only in a different way, I decide to think about God. Now, I *could* just fantasize about what I'll do to my girlfriend once I marry her—okay, I plan on getting a few favors once I put a rock on her finger. The mere thought of Rebecca, fair and unsullied, stirs the cauldron of lust constantly brewing in me. I ponder God for two seconds, Rebecca a full five minutes, and my ex, the stunning Brooke Bennett, for a good while longer.

I still think of Brooke fondly as a gorgeous version of the rich young ruler whom Jesus told to sell all he had and give it to the poor. Brookie wouldn't walk away heavy hearted and still rich as sin. She'd hit her knees and wash Jesus' feet with her tears. I know this. Innocent Rebecca would drop dead on the spot if she knew exactly *how* well I *know* Brooke, and how well she knows me. God, help us.

I met Brooke at Berkeley, I the prodigal son, and she a Bible thumper with a social conscience. Suddenly Bible Boy, who I'd heartily abandoned, returned with great zeal, and I tried my best to impress her with my advanced Scripture brainwashing, er, memorization. Brooke had me strung out like she was meth and I was in need of a thorough intervention.

By some miracle, I talked her into moving in with me and being my lover. Jesus promptly talked her out of it. I'd have married Brooke. I would have, but she loved Jesus more than me, as well she should have. She ended up joining some kind of Jesus-freak community and became a sprout-eating hippie nun who makes her own clothes. But sometimes I miss her.

A lot of times I do.

I really should have married her instead of making her. But maybe I did God a favor. After I deflowered her, she stopped *thinking* about giving to the poor and actually gave them everything she had. I deserved her hasty departure. And no, I don't actually think I did

God any favors, not at all. I wouldn't know how to do God a favor if He wrote it on my calendar accompanied by fiery angelic visitations. My best effort to serve Him has me sitting on the front pew, wishing someone would kill me rather than force me to endure one more sermon that moves nothing in me but my gag reflex.

I can't take one more minute of the lies I sit through Sunday after Sunday.

I get up and walk out, passing our pew dwellers without looking at them. Who cares if I disappear? If I vanish into thin air—personally raptured—right in front of them, nobody will notice. On second thought, Rebecca will. She's made it her job to scope me out during services, probably to see if my eyes stray to any female over age eleven and under fifty. She'll see me shuffle out, but will she be able to read the defeat branded like a scarlet letter on my face?

What of the words of Jesus, written right there in the New Testament, in red?

"If a man have an hundred sheep, and one of them be gone astray, doth he not leave the ninety and nine, and goeth into the mountains, and seeketh that which is gone astray? And if so be that he find it, verily I say unto you, he rejoiceth more of that sheep, than of the ninety and nine which went not astray."

You have to forgive me. I think in the King James Version, having heard "it's the *only* true word of God that exists" drilled into me from the time I was a fetus. I don't care what translation of the Bible I use; all of them say a real shepherd goes after one lost sheep. Even the bad stained-glass shepherd is good enough to carry one of his straying sheep.

What of my dad, the shepherd, Reverend Nicholas Aaron Parker

Sr.? The man I'm named after. The man I can't seem to do anything but disappoint with every choice I make that isn't *his* choice. He's supposed to be all about the Bible.

"How shall I choose a career?" "Just go to the Holy Bible," he'll answer.

"How do I choose what I'll eat for lunch, Dad?" "The Holy Scriptures," he'll say, beaming.

"Should I wear the red polo shirt, or the blue- and yellow-striped one?" "Search the Scriptures, my boy."

Okay, it isn't that extreme, but man, it's close. Didn't he read the story of the good shepherd? He commissioned those awful windows for heaven's sake! Why didn't he know when I fled for California to pursue a degree in literature, which he found worthless, that I found *life?* Why didn't he know I waited, bleating and moaning in grief, the saddest sheep of all? Didn't he know I needed him to come for me?

I swing the door open and storm out, and nobody grabs my legs while I drag them across the steps of the vestibule. Nobody says, "Please, Nicky, don't go."

Don't go.

A few minutes later, I'm sitting in my black Chevy pickup, reading my contraband *NIV Men's Devotional Bible,* and I read, thinking of a Jesus who may actually want me enough to leave His ninety and nine to find me no matter where I stray to. I can't even concentrate on the words, I feel so twisted inside.

A tap at my window.

It's Rebecca. I roll the window down. "Hey."

"Hey, are you okay, Nicholas? I saw you walk out. Are you feeling all right?"

I look at her, seeing what my mom and dad see: a good girl. Pretty. Perky. Blonde, blue-eyed. Jesus loving. A True Love Waits girl. Someone they can groom into a good pastor's wife. Someone so much more malleable than myself.

And I like her. She's one of the sweetest people I've ever met. She's the freakin' bridge between me and my parents—the only thing I've done right since coming home to fix things with my father, like God told me to.

God, what did You mean? How do I put things right with him? Do I have to marry her? I don't want to marry her.

"I'm okay, Rebecca."

She stands there. She wants me to open the door. I don't want to open the door. I want her to go away, but she'll stand there until Jesus returns if I don't. I decide to stop acting like an animal, and actually get out of the car and go open the door for her. Get her seated in the truck. Close the door behind her. Get back in.

I wonder if she'd leave with me. I don't think she would.

When we're settled in, I risk asking her, "Do you ever wish you could run away?"

"From church?"

I don't say all the expletives before the word *yes* that pop into my head. I don't even say yes. I just watch her.

"Sometimes I wouldn't mind leaving home, but I love church. I love your dad and your mom. I love it here. I love this building. And the people. The old folks. The babies in the nursery. I've been here since I was eleven and your dad knocked on my door *himself* to see if me and my brother wanted to take the bus to Sunday school—the *pastor!*"

She's says *pastor* like it's a big freakin' deal. When she was eleven and he was knocking on her door evangelizing, I couldn't get him to have a conversation with me. The *pastor!*

She means it. That's the worst part. Or maybe it's the best part. I'm not even sure. She wants this life at Tabernacle. That's why my parents love her so much, because she shows up at the potluck with her casserole. And she shows up for the antiabortion rally. And for the women's breakfast, and basically every time the door opens.

Rebecca doesn't want to run away from church.

"Did you enjoy the sermon?"

Say no. Please say no.

"I didn't hear all of it, but it's very good."

Rebecca is good about recycling. She's a regular spiritual environmentalist.

Cut it out. She doesn't deserve that.

She reaches for my hand. I let her take it. I never let things go further than this, except in my thoughts. I wonder if I should just kiss her. Just surrender to this life. I don't even know what I'm holding out for. Kiss her. Fall in love. Go to seminary. Be the good son. You can do it, Nicky. That's why you're back home.

You're not a writer.

Ouch. It kills me to think it.

Rebecca must see me wince. "You sure you're okay?"

I don't even speak. I just nod.

"Why don't we go back in? It's almost time for communion."

"I'll be there in a few minutes."

I see her out of the truck like the good boyfriend, even though I suck to high heaven. Oh, what I wouldn't give to be Anglican today.

I've been sober since I left Cali, even though I don't go to meetings. My dad would be appalled if he thought I went to Alcoholics Anonymous. But dear God, if we served real wine instead of grape juice, I'd take the leftovers out of those tiny plastic cups and tie one on today. Then seek out the rest, served up straight from the bottle.

Jesus, help me. Help me.

CHAPTER TWO

ZORA

I'm at a strange white woman's Bible study. Linda welcomes me into her cramped apartment, and I see books instead of walls. The volumes, dust, and stale air conjure the spirit of my girlhood like a roots woman casting spells, and for a moment, I imagine I'm sitting on the floor of a used bookstore, twelve years old, some treasured tome in hand. Toni Morrison's *The Bluest Eye* or Zora Neale Hurston's *Their Eyes Were Watching God*. A buck fifty taking me on a voyage where I travel by words instead of planes and trains, boats and automobiles. The thought of that comforts me now.

'Cause sistah girl don't feel no other comfort in this place. I walk toward the sectional sofa where the others wait, and I'm feeling fragile as glass and just as transparent. I think the four of them can see inside of me; they can look right through me at the disheveled room inside my head, books stewn all over the floor and debris piled up, now invisible to me since I've let it go for so long.

Their smiles welcome me, greetings to the new girl. The *black* girl. I wonder when it will begin. When will they thrill and inspire me with their insipid stories about the one black person they know? When will they ask me, subtly or not, if my long hair is a weave? When will they tell me how pretty they think I am without saying "for a *black* person," even though we both know that's what they mean?

I grin wide at them like I own the whole world, conscious of keeping my back straight—invisible book, something big, maybe the collected poems of Langston Hughes, balanced precariously on my head. I shake hands with a firm, decisive grip.

"I'm Zora," I shoot at them. I make an effort to remember their names. I think of Mama and Daddy telling me I have to work twice as hard and twice as long to get an equal measure of success among them. I wonder what I'll have to bone up on to prove myself when all I want to do is listen, soak it all in, and maybe add something to my heavenly bank account with the zero balance.

They are an odd lot, this group. Young and older.

Older man, Richard, maybe in his late sixties. White hair, and a shock of it, sticking straight up. He is frail, but his big blue eyes teem with a delightful mix of wisdom and mischief. Baby-blue button-down shirt with a few buttons open. Crazy throwback windowpane pants. He wears a crucifix attached to a leather cord like somebody hip loves him. He reeks of cigarette smoke. Richard caresses a well-worn, obviously loved black leather Bible.

I wish I had a Bible that looked like that.

White boy so pretty he can pull off having a girl's name. He must make his parents proud. Nicky. Heaven help me, he's hot as *fire*. Blue eyes that make me think of sweet raspberry popsicles and September birthstones, and that subtle sense of sadness because the season will change so soon, and before you know it, it'll be cold again. Nicky's sapphire eyes make me think of that.

A graphic T-shirt stretches across a broad chest that will make some white girl—blonde—very happy one day, if he isn't making her grin already. Those blue eyes of his widen just slightly when he sees me. They flicker up and down my frame, and a smile he probably can't help affirms his appreciation.

Oh, yeah. Go Zora, go Zora.

No Zora, no Zora.

I'll buy myself a first-class ticket to hell before I consider him for *anything*. I don't care how good he thinks I look. Or how good I think *he* looks. I don't do white boys. Uh-uh.

But is he ever *fine*. And, watch yourself sistah Z. Is that a hint of a smile, acting completely of its own accord, spreading across your mouth? And pretty boy notices.

I make sure not to sit by him.

Billie. Platinum blonde in her forties. Maybe. She's too cool to let the cutie get to her. She probably has a stable of boy-toy bucks to choose from. Her hair is a wild mane of crazy dreadlocks with rainbow colored tips. I've never seen anyone like her. She's flung a black leather motorcycle jacket across the back of her chair. Her white tank top shows off impressive, though feminine, muscle mass. Tattoos of a flowered vine snake up and down her right arm. The Virgin Mary in Technicolor on her left. Nice tats. I sit between her and Linda.

I met Linda at LLCC several weeks before I walked out. This brave white woman came alone to visit us. "Just wanted to fellowship with my brothers and sisters in Christ."

I'd looked at her like she was high. I didn't particularly mind her being with us; she was a curiosity to me. I asked her why she chose to visit us, and she said she'd watched Daddy on television.

She didn't seem to have the hysterical "speak the Word tick" afflicting most Word-Faithers. When I shook her hand and asked, "How are you?" she didn't spout off fifteen pages of Scriptures she'd memorized. She didn't even say, "I'm blessed." She said, "Fine, thank you. How are you?" I wanted to kiss her for that alone.

"Welcome." I actually had a sincere smile for her.

"I'm happy to be here." She had an easy way of speaking, almost lazy. Coarse red hair she couldn't handle. Freckles all over. Wise hazel eyes, but a child's zeal for life. Something about her that put you at ease. Skinny and terribly unfashionable, she'd never fit in at LLCC, and I liked her for that, too.

We chatted for ten or fifteen minutes, and for the first time in God only knows how long, I didn't care I wasn't being politically correct, a good pastor's daughter working the crowd. I learned in that short time that Linda took Sundays to visit churches, and during the week she hosted this small Bible study in her home. Whosoever will, let him come. She pulled a card out of the long, Little-House-on-the-Prairie jumper she wore. She'd done the calligraphy herself on the card she gave me.

I tucked the card away in my Coach handbag and promised I'd visit her Wednesday-night Bible study one evening. Now, here I am, as thirsty and as bereft of God as the Samaritan woman at the well. I just want a drop of God. I want Him to come to me in a way He isn't allowed to at LLCC.

Knock me on my face, God.

I stop. My mother will institutionalize me if she gets wind of such thoughts flying around my head. You have everything. *Everything,* Zora. You don't need to be knocked down.

Linda asks me to tell the group more about myself. I hate this part. I take a deep breath and start my spiel.

"Like I said, my name is Zora. Zora Johnson. My father is the pastor of Light of Life Christian Center in Ann Arbor. It's a pretty big church, and I work there." God, please don't let them ask me what I do.

Linda says, "That's a coinkydink." And I think how very Linda-like it is that she says *coinkydink* rather than *coincidence*. "Nicky is a PK too."

Poor Nicky. His ears and cheeks turn pink, and he looks down. I feel his pain. I smirk at him, and he shifts on his part of the sectional.

He shrugs. Looks embarrassed. "My dad is the pastor of True Believer Gospel Tabernacle. It's a big—"

"I know that church! I voted for Reverend Nicholas Parker when he ran for governor the first time I ever voted." I'd just turned eighteen.

Nicky Parker's fine-as-wine mouth hangs open. I love surprising people by doing something completely opposite of their expectations. I'm black and female. I'm not supposed to vote for a white Republican man with no concern for the poor and a rabid antiabortion agenda.

Surprise!

He seems to pause in thought for a moment. Runs one of his hands across his mouth, long fingers like a musician's. Fingers that look soft-tipped and capable of magic. I shake the mental image of him touching me with those hands.

"You voted for my dad?" he says, as if he's never heard anything so absurd in his life.

"I know I don't look like a Republican, being the wrong color and all—"

"No, I'm not surprised about your color. I know plenty of black Republicans. You look *smart* however. I mistook you for a thinking person."

Now my bottom lip almost hits the floor. When I can speak again, with the precision of an orator, I say, "Excuse me?"

I sound so much like my mother it chills *me* more than it does him. Nicky keeps on swingin'.

"I said, I mistook you for a thinking person."

"Are you suggesting people who want to see abortion abolished are not thinking?"

"No, I'm saying that people who were historically subjugated and choose to ignore my dad's despicable policies, including his thinly veiled racism and capitalistic interest in doing away with welfare—which by the way, he feels is a crutch for lazy African Americans—are not thinking."

"Mr. Parker, are you suggesting that because I'm black, I should, without question, vote for Democrats based on what we perceive as their support, nominal at best, of America's—specifically black America's—poor? Did it occur to you that I may believe abortion to be murder? Genocide to be precise."

He opens his mouth to respond, but Linda halts our discussion. "My dear brothers and sisters in Christ, I believe it's time for us to pray."

The four of them pull out a thick book, one I don't have until Linda walks across the room and digs a volume out of a big box full of assorted books sitting on her dining room table.

She presents the copy to me with a grin, like she's giving candy to a little kid. *The Divine Hours, Prayers for Springtime.* Biker chick tells me what page to turn to. It's almost 7 p.m., and they seem to be sticklers about the time. We sit in silence in those few minutes, and I'm glad no one rushes to fill the space with conversation. I'm still salty with Nicky Parker, and I try to calm myself. I close my eyes, drinking in the pause before we'd contact heaven, greedy for it, consumed by my need for the simplicity of not running my mouth for a change.

How did my life get so noisy? How did I get so noisy?

How did I mess up everything but manage to look so fly on the outside?

Time passes too quickly, me more aware of wanting to be quiet than actually being quiet in mind and heart. Linda stands, facing east. Everyone else does too, and I clumsily find my feet beneath me and face where the sun rises with them.

Linda speaks one word: *vespers.*

Something about the word holds infinite appeal to me. I've heard it somewhere but don't know its definition. My mind associates it with religion. With God. I want to ask what vespers means, but Linda calls us to prayer, and we all quietly obey. Her voice rings out like a song.

"Praise God, from whom all blessings flow; praise Him, all creatures here below; praise Him above ye heavenly host; praise Father, Son, and Holy Ghost."

Wow. I haven't heard those words since the last time I visited my grandfather's church. In my mind I hear the voices of those old timers, singing their old, old songs, their faith more ancient than their deeply lined brown faces. They are part of a *massive* tree, planted by an *ocean*. I remember one service, years ago, where they sang, "Let Us Break Bread Together on Our Knees," and the words, "When I fall on my knees, with my face to the rising sun, Oh Lord, have mercy on me." Those words did something to me.

I cried when I sang it, gripping the hymnbook with my little girl hands. In that moment I became one with my ancestors, and for the first time, I became keenly aware of my roots and my place on that tree. A tender green shoot. Branches surrounding me, raised like brown arms lifted to the sky in praise. The old folks touched God on their knees for generations, and those ancient souls of my distant past—having nothing, enslaved, their own gods, language, and culture stripped away—embraced the God they'd been given, the suffering Jesus, and they begged the One, who many of them believed to be the white man's God, for mercy.

The tree got bigger in Granddaddy's church that day, even though for the most part I forgot about them. Now, saying the words to the doxology elevates me again in those high branches reaching for God.

Linda requests God's presence.

"Show Your goodness, O Lord, to those who are good and to those who are true of heart."

I may not be good, but can't You see I'm true? At least I am with You. In Your presence I'm naked and ashamed, the chief of Laodiceans. Look at me, God. Wretched, miserable, poor, blind. But let my dull eyes catch a glimpse of You in this darkness.

Something in me breaks. Whatever it is, once safe, protected by the stony layers of my heart, splits wide open. I try to stop the grief flooding out of me in breaking, cascading waves, but I cannot.

I hear only snatches of the greeting Linda gives to God. I've already greeted Him, and He's been kind enough to speak to me in return, shattering what was hard and cold. Heaving sobs burst from my belly. From my very core.

The group reads the words of a hymn, but I've been seized by the power of a great affection. That's what the old folks used to call being born again. I literally throw myself to my knees, my face on the floor, my butt in the air. My heart in God's hands. All decorum gone.

I'm just Zora, naked with God.

And nobody in the group seems to mind. I hope.

NICKY

She walks into the room like freakin' Nefertiti, looking just as good. No, better. She's tall. I'll bet she can look me in the eye with very little effort, and I'm six-foot-two. She shakes hands like a man. Works the room like a politician, and I know politicians well.

Zora, the Queen of Sheba, and I can just see her rocking King Solomon's world. Zora, the Shulamite woman, dark and comely.

Okay, I know this is going to sound totally white, but I've never seen anybody with skin like hers. She is the darkest person I've ever seen in real life. Her skin is luminous. Like it's glowing. I've always heard that saying, "The darker the berry, the sweeter the juice." Well, her juice must be something else, and God help me, I just want a little taste. It looks like God stained this beauty with blackberries—all those purple, blue, and red undertones lying beneath that rich brown. Holy cow, she really is colored! She's a freaking masterpiece of tones. I can't stop staring at her.

And she's a firecracker.

Doesn't shrink and fold when I insult her, and man, why did I insult her? I guess I think she's too cool to vote for my father. *I'm* too cool to vote for him, and she's way cooler than me. I don't mean to insult her; it just comes out like that. But she stands up to me, no doubt dismissing me as a silly bleeding-heart liberal.

And she's right.

I hate her instantly, while simultaneously falling deeply in love with her.

And, God have mercy on my sex-deprived soul, she starts praying. Real down and dirty praying, and the next thing I know, she's on the floor with her three-dimensional rear end coming right at me.

I try not to look. God knows I try, but He made the gross error of making me a man, and we're visual. The sight of her literally drops me to my knees.

I think bad thoughts to distract myself: people I love dying, children in Africa with AIDS, national tragedy—anything to sober me, but nothing, and I do mean nothing, compares to the rewards I receive from swiping a few more lust-filled glances at her.

"Lord, help me, please, please, please."

I have to marry her.

I start counting the cost of her engagement ring. The Rock of Gibraltar, princess cut, on a platinum setting. How will I be able to afford Zora? I can tell she ain't no cheap date. I'll have to get a real job, or three. Maybe teaching. Of course teaching! What else will my worthless bachelor's degree in English literature and creative writing make way for?

Oh, man. How many people will come to our wedding? Like four? Will her family disown her with the same aplomb my family will disown me with? Will we have to serve chitterlings at the reception, and why are they called "chitlins" when the word is *chitterlings?* With three syllables, not two.

And do I even like soul food?

Already this is too complicated. I have to stick with Rebecca, who possesses none of the Shulamite's charms. None! She never fights with me. She's submissive, and we aren't even married! And don't get me started on the differences between both their untouched-by-me assets.

Think of Jesus. Think of Jesus. Think of Jesus.

I've changed. I'm not a total dog anymore. My animal nature no longer rules me. Not much. Okay, not *as* much. Come on, God. I've conquered a goodly amount of the flesh and even my sinful mind most days. Have mercy! I'm a good boy with Rebecca, who I'll ask to marry me, just as soon as I banish Zora's—

I have to get out of Linda's apartment. Maybe fresh air will act as a cold shower for me. Maybe I should drive home. *Now.*

Yeah. I'll drive home and save my soul. *If thy right hand offend thee, cut it off.* If Zora's glory offends, or pleases me more than words could adequately express, cut it off. And since I'm no psycho wanting to take a hacksaw to that masterpiece of God's creation she carries on her backside, I have to get out of Dodge. *Fast.*

I'll miss the Bible study and sharing, but I have a fighting chance at salvation if I leave now and if she never returns, which I figure she won't.

I practically back out of the parking space in front of Linda's apartment on two wheels, ungodly fantasies riding shotgun with me all the way back to Detroit. If I were the type, I'd pray in tongues, but the proper Southern Baptist, political Parkers don't encourage that kind of demonstration.

I race home doing my own version of praying without ceasing. I say the Jesus Prayer all the way to my hovel, an abbreviated version I hope my heart catches on to a little faster because of its lack of pretense.

Lord, have mercy, Lord, have mercy, Lord have mercy!

Lord, have mercy all the way down the freeway until I reach downtown, exit on John R., and find myself in front of my building.

Don't let her come back, Lord.

Hear my prayer, O God. Incline Thine ear to me, and if You will, have mercy!

CHAPTER THREE

ZORA

Thursday morning, I sit at the computer in my office at the LLCC, chiding myself about my complete meltdown at Linda's Bible study. Mama would have been appalled at my display. *I'm* appalled! My face burns every time I think about it.

I should be working, but instead my gaze wanders about the room. The offices stand in stark contrast to the impersonal environment of the sanctuary. Everything in the room looks gold and gilded. It reeks of "kingly." Lots of damask fabrics and rich tapestries drape the windows. Massive desks and plush upholstery, with *Egyptian* art accents of all things! Once a white preacher visited and didn't know if he should rebuke Daddy for the Egyptian art or commend him for being culturally proud. It was hilarious.

I design LLCC's esteemed newsletter that goes out to ten thousand Word-Faithers in the tricounty area. I am what Daddy calls Light of Life's Visual Arts Director, which means I make things look pretty around here, specifically all the print media we send out. I should be grateful for this job—and I am—but in truth, it takes me away from my true passion: painting.

Daddy has a little difficulty honoring me as an artist. He thinks I'll make more money as a graphic designer. I hate to admit he's more right than not. But it's just as well. I haven't put paint to canvas in a year. An excruciatingly long year that eats away at me every day, hour, minute, and second. But Daddy confesses—as in fires off Scriptures machine-gunlike toward God or whoever is listening—that I'll be blessed one hundredfold for contributing my talents to the ministry. A one-whole-hundredfold return on my investment of twenty-five hours a week (and of course, I get weekends off). That's like, twenty-five hundred hours' worth of blessings. Who am I to complain because God needs clip art and public domain-photos skillfully arranged?

Easy, Z. Back to work now, God help me.

Daddy wrote an article using Isaiah 40:31 as the Scripture reference. "But they that wait upon the LORD shall renew their strength; they shall mount up with wings as eagles; they shall run, and not be weary; and they shall walk, and not faint."

I wish that sounded remotely like me. Guess that goes to show who's an eagle and who's a big, black, nasty crow.

But even crows fly.

The thought of flying takes my mind right back to the Bible study. I haven't stretched my shiny black wings to their full span and cleaved the night air in how long? Maybe I stopped soaring around the time I stopped painting. That awful Bible study! It did something to me.

I'm never going back there. It's too painful. And yes, I know I begged God to do exactly what He did for me, but it's one thing to ask God to devastate you. It's another to have Him do it. And in front of white people! They probably thought of me as some savage African. Might as well have brought the drums and the half-naked dancers! All that excess. What was I thinking going there?

Makes me think about being in Atlanta that first week of college.

The weather still nice, me and my girls from school went swimming. I wore my long hair natural, like I do now, and I *don't,* contrary to popular opinion, wear a weave. But even if my hair grew down to my butt, it would shrivel up to a four-inch afro when it got wet. So there we were hangin', my sistahs in their weaves, and me in my 'fro looking like a fierce Angela Davis in the sixties. We're swimming to our heart's content when I heard it.

Some white people in the water talking smack.

It was a public beach. Late in the evening. The only lifeguard, a black kid about our age, was way up in his lifeguard chair paying absolutely no attention to us. The white people were laughing. Rude enough to point at me. They said I looked like a blankety-blank monkey. They called me the "n" word and the "b" word and then strung the two together. They went on a tirade about my nappy hair. Oddly, they singled me out. Spared my synthetic-hair-enhanced friends. They called me a savage and told us, the only blacks in the water that time of day, to go back to Africa.

Go back to Africa? Guess they forgot it was them who came and got us in the first place.

We stepped out of the water to go tell someone from management—well, I did. My girls bounded out ready to rumble. I talked them into keeping the peace. Yes, indeedy, I'm a regular Dr. Martin Luther King Jr. Got the emotional scars to prove it. We finally got the lifeguard's attention, but by that time the hecklers had gone.

The lifeguard gave us a knowing smile. Must have noticed my northern accent. "You're in the South now, sis."

It ain't much different in the North, bro.

Daddy says racists are everywhere. Even in lily-white liberal Ann Arbor. And a lot of them don't know they're racist, but they can't help it, the racism slips out. The way the white woman clutches her purse in the presence of a brotha. The nervous white guy who sweats as his eyes dart around an elevator full of black people. Those tests psychologists have done, flashing the image of a black person in front of a white person. The physiological changes that register. Changes that mean they're seeing something they don't like.

Racists that don't know they're racist.

And then there's the blatant stuff. The persecution you get driving while black. Being profiled at every turn. Followed around in the boutique when you have enough money to buy whatever high-end items they have. In pairs if you want two of them! The assumption that you are a thief, even in a convenience store—especially there. Indignities chip away at your soul, unrelenting, until you're angry and don't even know why anymore, until you look up, and so much of you has been chipped off you realize you've been turned to ash.

I slam my fist on the gold marbled desk. I shouldn't have gone to that Bible study. I trusted Ms. Little-House-on-the-Prairie with her whack modest clothes. Maybe I should have done a background check first. Show of hands, does anybody here think I'm a savage? What about a *noble* savage? Or how 'bout we keep it churchy? Does anybody go to an Assemblies of God church? At least they'd be familiar with my Pentecostal extremes. Biker chick with dreadlocks, do you ever attend Women's Aglow meetings? She's got to be okay. She's got dreads. Probably listens to Bob Marley. He'll take care of her white guilt. Old guy who'll kill me from the second-hand smoke emanating your shirt, could you in your wildest dreams go to a Word-Faith church? There are a lot to choose from. Please, please, please say yes.

In their defense, none of them shunned me—not to my face. They all seemed a little sympathetic after my big display of God affection.

Bible study began without another hitch, but I still sat there wishing I could disappear, even though my soul felt light and airy. I flew away with God, if even for a few minutes, to somewhere high, and bright, and clear. And white, black, or green, they let me go there.

This is too complicated. I curve my back into the thick throne-like upholstered chair. With wheels! I need to stick with my own kind. And God, don't make me think about Nicky Parker and his buttons-up-all-the-way-to-the-top conservative church. Didn't he practically tell me his father was a racist? Nicky, the bleeding heart liberal, fled the scene as soon as I got started.

I stab at a few keys on my keyboard, deciding not to use the eagle-in-flight photo. I punch at a few more to bring up another picture, an eagle sitting on a rock high atop a mountain. It had to get up on that rock somehow. *Flying.*

I chide myself again. I can't think about flying anymore. Besides, suddenly Nicky fills my thoughts. I stop beating the computer keyboard long enough to stretch my limbs and allow my thoughts a leisurely few moments of him.

Nicky, with the eyes like a Bahamian beach, where the ocean is so blue against the blazing sun that it hurts to look at. Nicky, who needs a haircut, but the way he wears his shaggy do makes him look wonderfully wild-headed. Nicky, with the Republican dad, who gets mad at black women he thinks are too smart to vote for his own father. Nicky, full of mysteries, with hands that look like they can make music.

Okay. I've lost my mind.

Even if he does think I'm cute, and he does, he obviously can't deal with Mother Africa here. And who cares? It's not like I ever have to see him again.

But there's something about him. Something a little sad and empty that I recognize in some ways. What's he doing at that kooky Bible study?

What was I doing there?

I go back to battering my keyboard.

I should have been done with the stupid newsletter on Tuesday, but I've avoided coming into the office since Sunday. I didn't want to deal with Daddy about my walking out, or worse, have to think about the fact the Daddy never noticed I left.

I'm unraveling like a ball of yarn, more and more of me coming undone from the perfect circle of symmetry I believed myself to be. I thought I was worthy for God to use. Now knots, tangles, and frays mar what I believed to be my usefulness. I think about the songs at Granddaddy's church. Sing that one I love aloud.

> *When I fall on my knees*
> *with my face to the rising sun,*
> *O Lord, have mercy on me.*

A clear-toned baritone voice joins, and his voice soars around the room like an eagle, finally crashing through the ceiling to be free. I stop singing to listen. I love Daddy's voice.

"Let us praise God together on our knees. Let us praise God together on our knees." I join him and we repeat the refrain. *"Lord, have mercy on me."* And we sing it again.

Daddy plants a kiss on the top of my head. "I can't believe you remember that song, baby."

"I do remember it, Daddy, and all those visits to Granddaddy's church. That old spiritual touched me in a really special way."

He shrugs. "I guess. But I don't miss the old songs, or the old ways. I don't miss being a lowly worm before God."

I miss it. My parents groomed me to be successful. The top. The best. I didn't have to be last, they've always told me, even if it meant I had to work twice as hard as those born with privileges they didn't have to earn. I miss being the last God would exalt in the end. They had something I don't, and I know it.

But Daddy isn't really talking about the old *ways.* He's talking about the old *man,* and the condemnation his father heaped on him like white-hot coals. He means he doesn't miss *him.*

"Sometimes I think the old folks had it better," I say.

Daddy laughs. "Better? We're the ones free in Christ. We prosper, and they groveled. We're the head and they were the tail, only they weren't really the tail. They were the head, too, but didn't know it." He sits at the edge of my desk, and for a moment, sitting amid all that gold, he looks more like a TV preacher than my daddy. He gives me his million-dollar smile and a shake of his handsome head. "I don't miss that, Zorie, and you shouldn't either. You have what they couldn't. What they fought and died to see, but didn't."

I nod, wheel a few feet away from the desk and take a long look at him, but I don't necessarily agree. I figure when it comes down to inheriting the kingdom of God, the last will be first like the Scriptures say. Daddy seems to conveniently skip these texts in his arguments for prosperity.

I take a deep breath. I'm not up for sparring today, not that I've gone to battle with Daddy about this or anything else. No, I'm a perfect daughter. Just *perfect.*

"I'm almost finished with the April issue."

"Good girl. You and Miles are coming for dinner tonight." He's not asking.

I can't take both Daddy *and* Miles tonight. "I'm really behind. I'm going to take this home and work on it tonight so you can get it to the printer tomorrow. Sorry I'm late with it."

"Don't worry about it, baby. Get somebody else on staff to finish it. With something like that, it doesn't make any difference who does it anyway."

"I suppose you're right," I say through clenched teeth. "Anybody on our team can do this work. *Anybody!*"

He doesn't even catch my sarcasm. He doesn't ask why I walked out of church Sunday either. He just clipped my wings a little bit more just now, and he doesn't see the blood on his hands or on me.

He knocks absentmindedly on my marbled desk. "See you at dinner tonight, baby."

"I'll be there, Daddy."

And I will because I'm a good girl. I do what I'm told. Daddy's little princess. I fold my wounded wings inside myself.

Maybe I'll go back to Linda's Bible study. Maybe one more time, and that's it.

NICKY

I sit in my company's big, stinking white truck that says VendCo LTD, bored out of my mind. It really is big—practically a semi. And it does stink, of stale diesel fuel, and Ron, the unwashed freak who works the shift before me and reeks of weed and patchouli.

The truck is pretty much stocked wall to wall with Tom's potato chips, pretzels, and other assorted snack foods. I personally loathe the entire product line, which just goes to show, it doesn't favor *me*.

Is it normal to want to lie down in front of the truck I drive to deliver snacks to vending machines? Let said truck drive back and forth over me a few thousand times until I'm out of my misery? Finally. And a miserable day it's been. More so than usual.

I can't get her out of my mind. And I don't just mean that luscious … oh, oh, don't make me say it. I'm worse than I thought I'd be. Lust is one thing, but I want to know her.

I'm in trouble. Big trouble.

I Googled her. Thank God for Google, and thank all the saints, the prophets, the angels, and the apostles deep down in my Southern Baptist soul for MySpace. The beautiful Zora Nella Hampton Johnson, according to her profile:

Is twenty-two years old.

Comes from one of the most prominent African American families in Ann Arbor.

Studied African American studies at Spelman and graduated at the top of her class.

Loves gospel music, rhythm and blues, and hip-hop. Favorite album of all time, Fred Hammond's *The Inner Court.*

Is a BAP.

Spends too much money on Kate Spade and Prada.

Loves the book *Their Eyes Were Watching God,* and gives a shout out to her namesake.

Is a praise dancer at Light of Life Christian Center. A dancer. And

an artist. A painter. Calls herself dreamy. I'll call her that too. For the
rest of my life.

And God help me—and I mean that in the most destitute way—
she posted pictures of herself. A dozen of them! Not pictures of her
sticking out her ample rear end or—not quite as ample, but nice anyway—breasts like most of the MySpace ladies—if you can call them
that. Pictures of Zora dancing. A lithe beauty with her lovely arms
extended and those endless legs poised gracefully, about to do a
pirouette. Zora smiling. Zora reading a book. Zora holding a paint
brush in front of her grinning face, a streak of blue paint forgotten
at the tip of her nose. So freakin' gorgeous that I reach out and touch
the computer screen.

I got it bad.

She blogs that she wants to spend the rest of her life finding out
what Jesus meant when He said, "Blessed be ye poor." In another
blog she said she wanted to be naked before God.

Naked!

I spent a lot of time reading that one. And rereading. And rereading. And now I can't stop thinking about her. What's worse is that
my route is over now, and I gotta go face Linda.

Linda, of extraordinary discernment. Linda, who can see right
through my crap and call me on it. And she does it in love.

Now, I know all about people allegedly doing things in love. My
father preaches in love, so he says. He's lacerated every poor unfortunate soul he's drawn to our church in love. I'm telling you, Dad
makes Jerry Falwell look like a raging hedonist. The King James Bible
is his sixty-six-book arsenal of weapons of mass destruction. I've seen
the sin-weary flee our church so fast after his fiery "You're going

straight to hell for even thinking of that" preaching that Jesus shook in the stained-glass windows.

But Linda, she really does love with that double-edged blade—the Word of God. She wields it like a master swordsman.

I shuffle into the office of the vending company. Linda's running the front desk as usual. I eye anything but her—the walls, a weird blue color, which are badly in need of painting. I check out for the gazillioneth time a few bad posters supposed to inspire us to do our best. *If you can believe, you can achieve.* Blah, blah, blah. I look at the front desk, a huge countertop covered with yellowing Formica that's old as God. Linda brightens the place up with her smile, even though everybody laughs at her crazy, old-fashioned clothes. She's unfazed. She believes in modesty and lives it. And she lives love. Just wants to bless her brothers and sisters in Christ whenever she can, she says.

She smiles at me. And I can't help but smile back.

"Hey, brother Nicky."

"Hey, Linda."

"Missed you at Bible study."

I challenge her, though it's useless. "I came to Bible study, Linda."

"You know what I mean. Did something bother you?"

"I just had to go. I didn't want to interrupt you with the new girl," I say, as if I don't know everything I possibly could find out about "the new girl."

She looks through me like I'm made of Saran Wrap. "That Zora sure is pretty, isn't she?"

If my flaming red cheeks don't give me away, my grin will. "Is she?"

Linda laughs. She knows she's nailed me. "I think she is. Maybe you didn't notice. At least not her face."

Wicked, wicked woman.

I throw my hands up. "I noticed her face too." I fold my hands across my chest. "I noticed everything, Linda. That's the problem. You know me. You know I'm trying not to be that guy." I am that guy, but I'm trying not to be.

She stands. Rest her hands on the countertop. "So why'd you leave? You didn't leave any other time a nice-looking young woman came to Bible study."

"I've only been going a few months, Linda. Not many nice looking women have come, no offense to beautiful you and Billie."

"But some have."

"None like her."

"Why don't you tell me about that?"

I roll my eyes, thrust my hands in my pockets. "There isn't anything to tell. Let's just say she aroused certain passions in me. Ponder that statement awhile, just so we're really clear."

"I think God can handle that, Nicky."

"I can't handle it."

"But what if she comes back?"

"She won't."

"Why not?"

I laugh because what I'm going to say sounds absurd even before I let it out of my mouth. "Because I prayed she wouldn't."

Linda cracks up, and I don't think I've ever seen her laugh like that. Her whole face opens wide, and something akin to music spills out of her mouth. She hits the countertop with one gentle hand.

"We'll see about that one," she says, wiping away actual tears.

This time it's me that puts my elbows on the countertop. "I'm not the defiler of virgins anymore. For the last three years I've forced myself to be Mr. Upright. I've never even kissed Rebecca."

She looks at me askance.

I backpedal. "Okay, maybe I think about what I'd like to do to her when we get married."

Another searing gaze.

"Okay, engaged. But there's no guarantee I'll try any of that stuff once we are."

She cocks her head to the side, those wise eyes knowing.

"Okay, give me a minute. I'll clean that up too! My point is, the old Nicky would have had Rebecca horizontal by now, and gone on to the music director's daughter and six more handmaidens of the Lord. Or I'd be back out in the world doing what prodigal me did best. But I've never touched Rebecca."

Linda shakes her head at me. "I don't think this is about Rebecca. You don't touch her, but you don't seem to talk about her either. You don't tell me cute Rebecca stories at lunch. You don't bring her to Bible study. You don't seem to feel anything for her. But you felt so strongly about Zora you got up and walked out of Bible study."

"It's lust. I'm feeling lust. Big, sweeping, all-encompassing lust."

"I'm glad, because at least you're feeling instead of walking around like a corpse."

"I don't want to feel lust, Linda. Lust is bad for me. God doesn't like lust."

"Then fight it full on, with the whole armor of God. Don't scamper away from it like that'll make it go away. It won't. I don't want to lose you, Nicky. God is doing something in you. And something happened for Zora last night too. I'd like for her to come back to us so we can see what else God does. I don't want to lose her either, Nicky. Do you understand what I'm saying?"

I nod. "Yeah, you're saying to me, 'Stop praying amiss.'"

"I'm praying for you, Nicky. You can beat this."

I mumble thanks and stand upright, a posture my slouching spirit doesn't share.

The whole armor of God, huh? I have no more ability to put that on than I have to grow a third eye in the middle of my forehead.

I'm in trouble, but Linda is right. I have to fight it full on. I'll start with the computer. No more myspace.com/blkandsassy.

It's a start.

CHAPTER FOUR

ZORA

Dinner at my parents' house. Oh, joy.

The gang's not all here. Mama is present in the living room as resident queen. It's a weeknight, which means their cook—they actually have a cook, a *servant,* and she's black, ironically—doesn't have to work as hard as she does on Sundays. Weeknight dinner is a relatively casual affair.

I'm wearing a Spelman sweatshirt, some Levi's, and my Coach sneaks. I know Mama wants to kill me for this hookup because dinner isn't really casual. It's never casual. She looks sophisticated as ever in her pink cashmere sweater, pearl earrings, straight black skirt, and silk hose—she wears silk hose or none. Her feet are shod with a pair of black leather mules made of butter-soft calfskin, and *mercy!* I'd smile at her while taking them right off her feet if she didn't wear that itty-bitty size five-and-a-half.

Her oval unlined face nearly glows she's so radiant. Mama's skin, a golden color, reminds you of a peach that needs to sit a few more days in the sun to sweeten, and she's got a mane of fiery auburn hair she doesn't have to chemically straighten to go with that peachy skin. Our family is a regular rainbow coalition. Daddy and I dark, my chestnut brown-toned twin brothers in the middle, hale and hearty men, and Mama and my little sister Zoe, fair-skinned maidens. God doled out the hair texture haphazardly. The twins got wondrous multi-textured heads that can't quite decide what they want to be. Zoe got hair like Daddy, and she never forgave God that trespass. Let's just say, I got a flat iron and the best of both. Hair not quite as confused as the twins' and not quite as willful as Zoe's "If only I'd been born in the seventies" afro.

Daddy sits down on the couch and begins small talk.

Daddy does not love Mama. I think over the years he's grown used to her. He may even be fond of her. But he doesn't look at her like a man should his woman. She lives the nightmare of being a trophy wife every day of her life, but I'm not supposed to know. It isn't hard to see, though. To make up for the lack of love in her life, she buys everything she needs, wants, doesn't need, and doesn't want. My sister, brothers, and I benefit immensely.

Mama wears a mask of perfection I have seen slip only on few occasions. Sometimes, when we're at the table and she asks Daddy a question, he ignores her. Doesn't even glance in her direction. Sometimes the mask slips and a bit of sorrow clouds her hazel eyes. She fitted all of us with our own masks of perfection. Mine grows heavier every day. And I'm afraid it's going to fall right off my face, and soon, if I'm not careful.

I've gotta be careful. Careful, Zora.

Daddy wears a white button-down shirt with navy linen slacks. He has on a silk striped tie, elegant and understated. He's blessed with the good looks of a movie star. Or is that a curse? I'll have to ask my mother about that. Hershey's chocolate-bar-brown skin and perfect teeth that startle you they're so white against his dark skin. And he doesn't bleach them either. He's just naturally beautiful. Dark and comely. He exudes a manly wildness that on occasion I see and love in other men.

Nicky?

Don't start, Zora.

If you didn't know Daddy well, you'd never know about the scars. Some of them physical. Some of them soul scars. Daddy's back reminds me of the Mississippi slave, Gordon. They show his pictures in a lot of slave books, whip marks slashing a story on his broken body.

To make him into a religious man, Granddaddy brutalized him. The stern apostle did not spare the rod. But Daddy refused to be broken. He lives his life by *faith*. When he speaks, his words have *power*. Death and life are in the power of the tongue, and Daddy speaks life. He's the beloved that the apostle Paul—not his father, the wanna-be apostle—wished above all things would prosper and be in good health, even as his soul prospers.

And I can't blame him. I can't fault him for wanting life when Granddaddy held it at arm's length away from him while giving it liberally to the people in his congregation.

Can I blame Granddaddy? Maybe he thought the best way to get his message across to the charmed boy with good looks was to beat it into him. I don't know. I only know I feel the same pressure Daddy must have felt, even though my parents pamper me rather than batter me. I feel bribed instead of beaten to conform to their image, an image increasingly hard for me to understand.

Miles joins in on the fun. My boyfriend. My perfect "other" handpicked by my parents. All year he'd labored with the youth ministry, Faith Afire, in order to sidle up to Daddy hoping he'd win enough approval to ask me on a coveted date.

And dates with me certainly are coveted. Daddy has every romantically inclined male and a few questionable females in church deathly afraid of me. Nobody, and I mean that, asked me out at church from the time I was old enough to date, with the exception of the family, not the young man, the *family*, who approached Mama and Daddy to ask if their son could escort me to the debutante ball where I was introduced to society. And what a cheeseball he was. Don't make me think about him. I gotta eat.

I guess no social life was a mixed blessing. It saved me from the storm of raging hormones that tore my best friend MacKenzie's house down. There are worse things than twenty-two-year-old virgins who've never been kissed. Not that I didn't get lonely.

Now, Miles is good looking. A Morehouse College man, two years older than me with good teeth and clean nails. You can tell a lot about a man by his teeth and nails. He's great with kids—having put his time in at children's church before going on to Faith Afire. He earned an engineering degree and is already working in his field. He makes good money and, in a few years, just may be able to afford me without Daddy's help. He's got an "I'm hotter than Denzel Washington" thing going on that the sistahs at LLCC drool over. He's a perfect gentleman. Only holds my hand and sometimes kisses me on the cheek. If he's got "experience," he hasn't shared that with me. I assume just after his ordination to be one of our associate pastors, Miles Zekora and I will taste the first of the fruits of sexual love on our wedding night.

And my name will be Zora Zekora.

I don't know if I can live with that.

He thinks my painting is a nice hobby. Is it any wonder that I don't care that he's never kissed me? I used to care. He used to be the biggest crush I ever had. He used to make my heart soar, just the thought of him. Tonight I'd rather be home putting together that newsletter *anybody* with a brain could assemble.

Don't think about these things, Z. Eat. Listen. Don't say much. You don't know what'll come out of your mouth, girl.

WE'RE GETTING READY to be seated at the hub of our family, the opulent dining room table. She may not cook anymore, but Mama knows how to sit down together as a family. Despite our failings, we've always eaten together. The dining room is beautifully furnished; a handcrafted, endless mahogany table that seats sixteen is the focal point of the room. Mama has each place set with bone china and fine linen napkins—with an African flair, of course. The room has been featured in an issue of *African American Metropolitan* magazine.

My brothers, the twins, James and John, don't live at home anymore. They make their living as wildly successful stockbrokers and have taken a bite out of the Big Apple, lucky dogs. They offered to take me with them and look after me while I went to art school. I'd been accepted to Parsons. *Parsons!* MacKenzie and I dreamed of Parsons since we were little girls waxing poetic about color. And now she's going in just a few days, God bless her, but Daddy would have none of it for me, for all his big stinkin' faith. Mama either. It was Spelman or "you're on your own." Many a day I wish I'd have chosen on my own, but they forbid my brothers to help me. Worse, I couldn't even study art at Spelman. It wasn't practical, they said.

My baby sister Zoe is away at school. She, too, chose Spelman—if you could call what she had a choice. Only her choice of premed is acceptable to Mama and Daddy. At least she's got that.

Just chill, Zora. You've got food to digest, girl.

I really shouldn't complain. I don't even live at home—a coup for me. But because I live in town, I try to have dinner with them as often as I can. Tonight, it's the usual suspects: Mama, Daddy, Miles, and me. My parents won't count the cook, whose name is Betty, by the way. Betty Grace Way.

Miles pulls out the chair to seat me. Whispers in my ear, "Why didn't you dress for dinner?" This seemingly innocuous question is full of disapproval. My father is grooming him well. And as if he were my father, I defer. I try to charm him on the strength of my grin.

"It's a casual night." It comes out with more bite than I intended. "Baby," I add to soften it.

My mother chimes in. "There's casual, and there's unacceptable. We're eating, Zora, not playing basketball."

"I'd rather play basketball," I mumble.

She gives me "the look" as I sink into my chair and Miles scoots it up to the table. "Zora!"

"I'm sorry, Mama."

Miles regards me with what actually looks like a thoughtful gaze. "Are you all right?"

"I'm wearing jeans and a sweatshirt to dinner. *Clean* jeans and a *clean* sweatshirt. I feel like you all are treating me like I've committed the unpardonable sin."

Miles sits down across from me. "No one is judging you, baby. I just wondered why you didn't dress."

"Why do we have to dress when it's casual? Why do you have to clean up before the housekeeper comes? If you do the cleaning yourself, why do you even need a housekeeper?"

The three of them stare at me. Betty saves me from their comments. She ambles into the room, a heavy, dark-skinned sistah who can cook like God can bless. And my family treats her like the hired help. Our very own mammy.

I gotta get out of here.

Betty places a heaping bowl of collard greens and bacon in front of us that makes me salivate. She looks at me. "Your favorite, baby girl."

My mother rebukes her. "Please refer to my daughter as Zora."

Betty gives her a curt nod. "I'm sorry, ma'am."

"You'd better not, Betty," I say. "That 'baby girl' thing may be why I always get the biggest piece of pie."

For a moment our eyes lock, and Betty's brown eyes flash a subtle thank you.

"You get that big piece a pie 'cause you're a bag a bones. So skinny you disappear if you turn side-a-ways." And probably just to let my mother know she heard her loud and clear, she adds, "Zora."

When Betty walks out of the room, I challenge Mama, something I rarely do. "I don't see anything wrong with Betty calling me an endearment. She's been working for us for years. I'm crazy about her."

It's Daddy who responds. "Betty is a wonderful woman and an excellent cook. We simply don't want her to get confused about her role around here. We've had some experiences we don't want to repeat when we've blurred boundaries."

Which means they've treated people horribly and it turned into a hot mess. Now, Betty has gone to our church forever. But when she's at work for us, she becomes the help. A hot mess!

"Seems to me like boundaries get blurred all the time around here."

Daddy put his fork down. "Excuse me, Zora. Do I need to ask for the keys to that Lexus until you can learn some respect?"

"It might take a long time for me to learn some respect so, yeah, I guess I'll need to give you the keys to my car."

"It's my car," Daddy reminds me. "I believe I pay for that Lexus, *baby girl.*"

My mother graduates to phase two of "the look," which is more stern and menacing. By now I'm good and tired of them treating me like a surly teenager.

Or am I acting like a surly teenager? I don't even know.

I only know my face burns so hot I can hardly stand it. I can hardly breathe. Betty comes back into the room with a bowl of buttery mashed baby red potatoes. She must feel the palpable tension in the air. She scurries out of the dining room to get the next portion of food.

Miles tries to play peacemaker. "I don't think you'll need to take the keys to the Lexus, sir. Zora is just stressed, that's all." He gives me one of his Denzel smiles, complete with the Hollywood caps. I think I should be happy I've got this good, handsome man having dinner with my parents and asking me if I'm okay. I try to breathe. I try hard.

"I have a lot of work to do," I say when I can speak.

Daddy waves away my comment. "I told you, Zorie, you don't have to worry your pretty head about that. The newsletter will get done. That's why I have a visual arts staff."

I try very hard to keep my voice even. "It's *my* job to do the newsletter. It's my job to do most of the graphic design at LLCC, or at least it used to be, Daddy. It's what I get paid for."

He winks at me. "Being the bishop's daughter has its benefits."

I bristle at the word *bishop*. Nobody made Daddy a bishop. One day he told us God had elevated his position. Deacons suddenly became associate pastors—as did my mother—and Daddy was suddenly a bishop. He didn't have to answer or explain. We simply held a lovely service in his honor, and we gave him outrageous gifts and offerings.

"I prefer to do my work myself," I say.

"Well, I prefer if you enjoy the leisure that I've paved the way for you to have, in the same way you enjoy your Prada and ... who is it, Mother?" he asks Mama.

"Kate Spade."

He nods briskly, approving of her answer but not mine.

I have no recourse. Daddy pays my salary. Daddy pays for my car. Daddy gives me gifts. Daddy pays for the gifts Mama gives me. Everything in my life belongs to Daddy. I'm Daddy's girl in ways I never realized.

I stand up. Miles stands up, ever the gentleman, looking confused. I fish in my handbag for my car keys and plunk them on the table. In fact, I toss that Kate Spade designer bag on the floor. He paid for that, too.

"Thanks for the use of your car, Daddy. Thanks for everything, but I think I'm going to choose *on my own* like I should have done instead of going to Spelman."

He bolts up from his chair. "Zora Nella Johnson, just what do you think you're doing?" I noticed he didn't include my mother's maiden name before Johnson.

I don't answer him. I'm too busy leaving. He may not have noticed I walked out on him at church, but now I've made my statement. This time there's no doubt he knows Princess Zora has voted herself off the island of abundance.

NICKY

I'm at Barnes and Noble with Pete, my best friend. Had a little church business to attend to in Ypsi and rewarded myself for being civil to my dad with a trip to the bookstore nearby. Pete and I have been buddies since the third grade. His dad has been a deacon in our church forever, and Pete and I were always getting into a world of trouble together. We're not so much alike. We never were actually.

I've always loved to read. You have to make Pete read. I'm blonde. He's dark haired. He tans. I wilt in the sun. I'll admit it, I get the ladies' attention. Pete's the guy in the movie destined to be cast as "best friend." Yeah. He's got that vibe, but he works it. He charms the ladies, and in a while has them thinking he's Tom freakin' Cruise. Tonight he's trying his game on the barista at the Starbucks inside of B&N. She's grinning at him while I peruse the latest issue of *Writer's Digest.* There's an article about jumpstarting your novel, and I'm thinking I probably couldn't jumpstart mine if I had the cables *and* the juice—or even the beginnings of a decent story.

And Dad wanting me to go to seminary is weighing on me. Maybe because he's so freakin' impressed at how good my undergraduate degree has been to me, the way I've racked up credit card debt buying writing books. He scoffs at any mention of an MFA program, especially since I'm so blocked I can hardly write my name, and he's nuts about my stellar job supplying disgruntled workers like myself with potato chips and pretzels.

God, please let Pete slip some arsenic in my latte.

Then again, the way things happen for me, it'd probably only make me sick. Let him shoot me. I've already got the gun thanks to my NRA-loving grandfather. Better yet, I'll just shoot myself. Pete won't have to go to jail, and I won't have to go to Southern Baptist seminary.

Pete returns with my poison-free latte and a venti mocha for himself. He's got the newest Jay-Z CD under his arm.

"Nick, you think I should get this, man?"

"I thought you had it."

"I did, yo. But I ended up giving it away."

Pete says "yo" in just about every other sentence. I have no idea where he picked up the habit, but I wish he'd take it back.

"Pete, if you want it again, buy it."

"I don't wanna spend the money on it twice, yo."

"Then don't get it."

"But I like it."

I try not to strangle Pete. "Then get it!"

"What's eating you, yo?"

I turn my head away to keep from unloading any more of my discontent on him, and that's when I see her.

Zora, the Shulamite. Sitting at a table alone, shoulders rounded and looking as broken as she did at Bible study last night. I can't believe how my heart pounds just looking at her. I grab my latte just to give myself something to do and take a long drag. It's hot and burns my mouth. I end up spraying Pete by accident.

He leaps up, disgusted. "Nicky, what is up with you, man?"

I look over to see if she heard. And, sure enough, at the sound of my name Zora searches the café and finds me. Our eyes lock, and I can't tell if that's a smile or a grimace on her face.

She probably grimaced.

I stand. I can't very well act like I don't see her *now.* I force my feet to move, one in front of the other, until I make my way to her table. Once again, my eyes meet hers.

She's been crying. Oh, Dreamy. What happened?

I don't know if I should shake her hand or what, so I stick my hands in the pockets of my jeans.

I nod a greeting, and she pretends she doesn't remember my name.

"Hey you, is it Nicky?"

"Yeah. And your name is …"

"Zora."

"*Zora!* That's right."

And your mother's name is Elizabeth, and your father's Jack, and your first puppy, a Shar Pei, was called Diamond. I learned all that on MySpace. "How are you?"

"I'm good," she lies.

And here comes Pete. "Hey there." His grin can't get any bigger.

He nudges me. "Aren't you gonna introduce me?"

I say no with my eyes, but he ignores my signals. He thrusts his hand out at her, and she takes it. She leaves no trace of the sorrow I just saw. She's a good politician.

"I'm Zora Johnson."

"Pete Greene."

"Nice to meet you, Pete."

He turns her hand over and kisses it. Then the clown bows from the waist until he almost hits his head on the table. "The pleasure is all mine, lovely Zora."

I lose all semblance of patience with him. "I'll see you at the table in a minute, Pete."

"I'd like to stay and chat with you and *Zora*." Not a yo to be heard.

"We don't want you, Pete."

Zora snickers, but at least I made her smile. She's all grace and kindness. "You're both welcome to join me."

"Pete doesn't want to disturb you." And to Pete: "Could you go keep an eye on our table? *YO!*"

I irritate him, but he doesn't want to punch me in the face in front of Zora. He does another goofy bow for her. "Milaaaaaady," he says, and saunters away.

Zora laughs. "That Pete is quite a character."

"Quite."

I sit down. Pete can wait. "Look. I won't beat around the bush. I can see you were upset, though that was a good save. I don't want to pry, but if you'd like to talk, I can be a good listener."

She gives me a shy smile. "I don't know, Nicky. The last time I cried you hightailed away from me at warp speed."

I can't stop the blush creeping to my cheeks. I stare at her like a deer in the headlights, and she calls me on it.

"Say something, Bambi."

I'm totally flustered. "I don't know what to say."

"How 'bout you don't feel comfortable with black people being so"—she crooks her fingers into quote marks—"'expressive.'"

My mouth opens. I can't even respond at first. I sputter like an idiot until I finally get out, "Is *that* what you think?"

"Maybe. You're the one who said your father is a racist. Like father like son, Nicky?"

Okay, she might look like the Queen of Sheba, but wait just a minute. "I'm nothing like my dad."

"Why'd you run?"

What? I'm supposed to tell her? Another verbal seizure. "I can assure you that wasn't the reason."

"What was it?"

I hate this woman, but I don't want to lie to her. Did I mention I hate her? Regardless of how I feel, I'm not gonna let her brand me a racist just because she's in a mood.

"Maybe," I lie, "I wish I could be that"—I imitate her gesture—"*'expressive.'* Maybe I've been walking around like something from *Night of the Living Dead* and I see you wallowing on the floor with all that ..."

Luscious, round ...

She looks impatient. "With all that *what?*"

"All that, uh, *feeling.*" Real smooth, Nicky. "I'm ... I just mean, you definitely stirred something in me." Now that's the truth.

Her eyes search mine. "For real?"

"For real. It was *difficult* for me to process all that was going on inside of me, and that's God's honest truth." I drum the table with my fingertips while she stares at my hand. "Look, Zora, I'm a PK;

you're a PK. At birth we get a cross, a Bible, and a mountain of issues. Don't let my issues concern you. All of us go to Linda's Bible study because it's safe. You can find God however you find Him there. It can look like however it looks, and if for you it looks like being on your face ..." *with your glory coming at me* "so be it."

A stray strand of hair sweeps across her cheek, and God help me, I can't resist, I brush it back behind her ear. She recoils.

Stupid, stupid, stupid, Nicky.

I bolt back away from her. Can't even think of how to save face this time. I touched her face. Can I *be* any more intimate? I could! Which is why I need to stay as far away from her as possible.

"Nice to see you again, Zora. God bless. Feel better."

I try to run again. Fast. But she calls my name, and I can't help myself, I turn back around, and I just fess up. "Sorry about the hair thing, Zora. I don't know what—"

"No problem."

An endless pause, and then a miracle of an olive branch. "Nicky, I was wondering ... can you give me a ride home? I've got, uh, car trouble."

"Is your car outside? Maybe I can look at it for you. Do you have road service?"

"Never mind."

"Wait. I'm sorry. I was just—"

Pete appears out of nowhere and rescues me. "We'd *love* to give you a ride." He still hasn't uttered a single yo, which annoys me even more, since obviously this verbal hiccup is reserved for me alone.

"Right this way," I say.

Gonna be an interesting ride.

* * *

PETE DRIVES. IT'S his truck. I hate that Pete drives. He controls the CD player and blasts his new Jay-Z CD with no regard as to whether Zora is a fan or not. He prattles on and on about how much he loves "Hova" until he starts in on Beyoncé.

I know we're treading dangerous waters. Pete watches BET. *Loves* BET. Pete thinks Jay-Z's super sistah "B" is the pinnacle of woman-hood—black, white, or otherwise. I'm praying as if my life depends on it that he won't use the *other* "b" word, even though I know he's easing up to it.

"Do you like Beyoncé, Zora?"

I try to distract him. "Do you like Wayne Newton, Pete?"

He disses me. "I'm talking to Zora, Nick."

"Maybe Zora doesn't want you to interrogate her all the way through your who's who in hip-hop list, *Pete.*"

"I wanna know what kind of music she likes."

"Then why don't you ask her that, and you can stop name dropping every black artist you can think of whether or not you actually listen to them?"

Zora laughs. "Relax, Nicky. I think he's kinda cute."

I don't even want to think about how jealous this makes me feel. And I'm never jealous of Pete. Pete, who is *always* jealous of me, laps up her words like a cat at a milk dish.

His voice goes about forty octaves lower in what must be an attempt at sexiness. "I think you're cute, too, Z."

He's really starting to irritate me. "Did she say you could call her Z?" He ignores me, and horror of horror, he says it. The "b" word.

"I think you're *bootylicious,* Zora."

I think my heart stops. I'm gonna have to be resuscitated.

Zora's voice turns into ice water and pours into both Pete and me, even though she only addresses him. "You don't know me like that, Pete. Back up."

I groan audibly. Words fail me. I wrestle with homicidal urges. I watch a lot of crime shows. I know how to kill Pete a number of ways. I reach all the way across Zora—saying excuse me, of course— and bop Pete in the head like I'm Little Bunny Foo Foo.

We reach Zora's apartment, and Pete actually tries to get out of the truck with us.

I give him a stare so completely cold I can rethink my career options and go into cryogenics. Fortunately, *this time* he takes the hint. Zora's kind enough to take my hand as I help her out of the truck.

I walk with her to the front door of the apartment building, a building much nicer than my own, surprised she has to use the buzzer.

"You do live here, don't you?"

"Yes, I do."

"Don't have your keys?"

"Don't have my purse with me."

"I see," I say, not seeing. Don't women have purses, no matter how small, surgically attached to them at all times?

Her gaze goes downward.

"Zora?"

She lifts her head, and her eyes meet mine.

"Are you okay?"

She shakes her lovely head. "I've got daddy trouble."

"I know all about that."

"Thanks for the ride, Nicky."

"I'm so sorry about Pete. He's ... retarded."

"He's like a *lot* of white people I meet."

My heart drops to my feet. I'm embarrassed. "I hope not all white people you meet strike you that way."

"No, not all. But too many."

"Maybe we can talk about that sometime."

"No, thanks."

I know I shouldn't push, but I do. "Why not?"

"I'm not interested in rescuing you from your white guilt."

Man! She's not a tongue biter. "Are you always this—"

"Honest?"

"I was actually thinking *rude*." Probably shouldn't have said that.

"Only to bleeding heart liberals who think a conversation is going to change the world."

"It's a start."

"Start with someone else."

A tinny voice explodes through the speaker.

"Who is it?"

Zora pushes the intercom button and shouts, *"It's me."*

"Who?"

"It's Zora, Mac. Let me in."

"Where yo' keys?"

Zora yells. "Let me in, MacKenzie."

A buzzing sound pierces the air. Zora snatches the door open. I don't want us to end our time together this way. It's selfish of me, and maybe I do want to assuage my white guilt. Or maybe I just like her. Since I'm not the one whose people were slaves, I decide to make the peace offering.

"Daddy problems do get better." I don't know when, but it has to be true.

"I hope so."

For a few moments, we're silent. She's still holding the door open. Finally, she smiles at me. "Thanks for the ride."

"You're welcome. Again, I'm sorry about Pete. He's in love with Beyoncé. He'll never get close to a woman like you again, and he went nuts."

"It's no problem. You didn't have to smack him, you know."

"Yeah, I did."

"Jealous?"

Is it written on my forehead? I try to look cool and give some Clint Eastwood-like icy gesture, but end up jerking like I've got Parkinson's. Oh, man. She spares me the humiliation of saying something about my unfortunate gesticulations.

I try to cover my ineptitude with a shot of meanness. "Why would I be jealous of who Pete is interested in? I've got a girlfriend."

I know it's a mistake before I even say it, but I feel like it's my last defense. She's won every battle tonight. I just want one win.

A tiny hint of disappointment flashes on her face. I know this. I am a *master* at reading women. She's attracted to me. And I just blew it. Never mind that I really do have a girlfriend. Before I can even deal with how disappointed I am, or what a jerk I've been to her, she recovers.

"Of course you do."

"And I'm sure you have a boyfriend and were just humoring Pete to be sweet."

She leans close to my face. "Wouldn't you like to know?"

She sweeps through the door like the diva she is and nearly bumps into a wide-eyed grinning spitfire, hands on her ample hips, who has to be MacKenzie.

And I have her approval.

MacKenzie's, that is.

CHAPTER FIVE

NICKY

Why did I move to Detroit? It takes Pete forty-five minutes to drive me home and all he talks about is Zora, spending an inordinate amount of time on the subject of her butt.

I want to kill him.

I don't engage him. And that's difficult. We do this. We talk about breasts and booty and have done it since we were twelve. And never have I had a more magnificent rear end to wax eloquent about. Only I can't. It's not right. I feel dirty just listening to him, and that this feeling is new to me is what's making me most uncomfortable of all! Not that Pete noticed.

He makes gestures indicating size. He rolls his eyes back. I have to elbow him in the ribs so he doesn't wreck the truck.

"Okay, Pete. I get it. She's amazing."

"I'm not talking about *her*. Maybe she *is* amazing, but before I can get to that, man, oh, man—"

"Pete, if you say one more thing about Zora's butt …"

He looks at me, confused. "What's the matter with you anyway, yo? Usually you'd be leading the praise here."

"Maybe I'm tired of disrespecting women."

"Since when?"

"What do you mean *since when?* I've been celibate for three years."

"And we've had many conversations about a good butt in that time, yo. It's that weirdo lady you been going to Bible study with.

She's influencing you, isn't she? Her and her skirts to the ankles. No makeup. Does she even comb her hair or use deodorant?"

"Yeah. She combs her hair and uses deodorant, Pete."

"That your type now, Nick? Untouched for a reason, yo?"

"I don't appreciate you talking about Zora *or* Linda. Okay? Say another thing about either one of them and I'm gonna bust you up. Say 'yo' again and I bust you up. I mean it, Pete."

He shrugs. "Whatever. I don't know why you're so sensitive. Looks to me like Zora is like any other *sistah.*"

I don't like how he says *sistah.* It feels wrong. Like he hasn't earned the right to say that word. "What do you mean she's like any other one?"

"She's got the tight jeans showing off all that tail, because she wants the world to see it. She loves it. And she loves me lovin' it. Just look at the videos. Black chicks are totally into showing their stuff."

I want to hit Pete much harder than our usual horseplay allows. "What kind of racist crap is that, man? What? White women don't wear tight clothes? Why are you singling out black women?"

"C'mon, Nicky. The videos on BET and the ones on MTV are totally different. It's the culture, man. They give it up more than white women. They do. It wasn't a white girl that made up the bootylicious song. And personally, I like that. And I like that song. And I like Beyoncé. And I like Zora. You got her phone number? Because if you're not interest in hittin' that, *I* am. I hear sistahs are wild in bed."

Hittin' that? He's with a black person for an hour and he wants to throw around the vernacular. "You're a Christian, Pete."

He laughs. "Oh, you can judge? What were *you* when you talked all those sweet sisters in the Lord into your bed? What were *they?* You nailed, like, half the youth choir when we were in high school, man. And the cherry on the top, no pun intended, was your declaration, 'Once saved, always saved.' Didn't tell Reverend Parker about that, did you? But I said then, and I say now, 'Amen, Nicky!' "

I don't say another word to Pete, because everything I want to say is so angry that I honestly believe we'll come to blows and it'll end our lifelong friendship. I sit there, stewing in my own juices, until he finally pulls up in front of my building, and I storm out of the truck, slamming the door behind me.

But in all truth, Pete is holding up a full-length Nicky mirror, and I see myself with such startling clarity that it shocks me. I hate the self I see in Pete.

He yells something to me. I don't listen. I just keep going, trying to run as far away from myself as possible. By some mercy he doesn't follow me.

ZORA

MacKenzie puts me in a headlock that I think she mistakes for a hug. Before Nicky's even walked away she's whispering, *"Giiiiiiiiiiiirl,"* in my ear. "Where you get Halle Berry's white boyfriend?"

I chuckle. He does sort of look like that Versace model Halle's been seen with. What's his name, Gabriel Autrey, Aubrey? Who knows? He's fine—and so is Nicky "Save the Negro" Parker.

Okay. That was uncalled for, like most of my attitude these days. When Nicky walks away, Mac lets me breathe again.

"He's just some guy I know."

"Girl, that white boy looks good enough to chew on."

"He's taken."

She puts her hands on her hips as if he's standing in front of her and she's getting her flirt on. "I'll take him too."

"You can have him." We start walking up the flight of stairs to our second-floor apartment.

"Why didn't you ask him to come in? Don't tell me he's all walkin' you to your door and you're not trying to holla."

"I'm not trying to 'holla.' I have a boyfriend." A boyfriend that's afraid of my father, who's paying part of his salary *too*. But who's counting paychecks?

"Girl, I heard white boys are freaky. I'll bet he can teach me some things."

"I doubt that, Mac."

"What you sayin?"

"I'm saying you know a lot already. Don't you?"

"Look, don't be salty with me just because you ain't ready to go international. Girl, it's a'ight. I'll go before you. I'll make the way plain. I'll go to that mountaintop, though none go with me."

She starts preaching like my granddaddy, and I smile despite myself.

"Where's yo' key?"

"At my parents' house. Along with the Lexus."

"You mean you ain't even got Lexi? I thought you was just frontin' 'cause you didn't want that white boy to know how paid you are."

We reach the apartment, the door is open, and I'm welcomed in bohemian BAP paradise. Truly. I live in high style, thanks to my parents' money, B. Smith, MacKenzie, and our collection of design books. I've achieved an eclectic-influenced, though always

African-inspired, visionary style for our little apartment. I love all things black couture. Everything is class, culture, and refinement with a whole lotta funk thrown in for good measure.

I kick off my shoes and sink into my buttercream-colored leather sofa with mudcloth accents. MacKenzie and I designed the pillows with Ashanti gold weights for charms.

"Oh, Mac. I had dinner with Daddy, Mama, and Miles, and it turned into a nightmare."

"It had to turn *real* bad if you came back here with a *white* boy."

"Can you stop calling him that?"

"Well, he *is* white."

"Yes, but you're saying it like that's some kind of personal defect."

"Shoot, girl, it *is* a personal defect. That boy ain't got enough melanin."

I look at her, and she's dead serious. "You know you're out of your mind, right, Mac?"

"I'm just saying. I'm not the one that came from the Caucus Mountains. Some people got melanin. Some don't. He don't."

"What is up with you, Malcolm X? Why you gotta be dissin' him because of his skin color? Would you like it if he was with his buddy talking about me being a jungle bunny?"

"He probably *is* talking about you to his buddy. He's probably telling his buddy how bootylicious you are."

I laugh.

"What?"

"Mac, his friend said I was bootylicious all in my face, like he knew me like that."

"That's what I'm talkin' about. They talk about us, and we talk about them. It's like Earth, Wind & Fire, sings, baby, 'That's the way of the world.'"

"The world is a very bad place to be. What if he's nice? He stood up for me, you know."

"Honey, *he* ain't nice. Look at him. He ain't gotta be nice. He's got 'bad boy' written all over him. In fact, I don't want to know anything nice about him. I want to know the bad stuff. The *nasty* stuff."

"You're just saying that, Mac. Why don't you stop frontin' like you're so cool with all that sex and deal with your brokenness?"

Mac snorts. "What *brokenness?* I like sex, Zora. I like men. You haven't had a taste yet. Come back to me when you do, and then we can talk. In fact, come back to me when that white boy turns you out. I got a feelin' he gon' be the one. 'Cause you *know* that's what he's sniffing around you for."

"He's not sniffin' around me. I asked him to give me a ride home. I saw him at Barnes and Noble. I walked over there after I walked out on Daddy."

She fakes coughing. "Shut up! You did *not* walk out on *The Bishop.*" MacKenzie starts strutting around with her chest poked out with such a dead-on imitation of my father I'd be mad if she wasn't my best friend forever. She uses his pet Scriptures in an exaggerated male voice.

"Turn your Bibles to Genesis 1:26–28. God gave Adam total dominion over the earth. If you're going to exercise your dominion of creation and over your enemies you need to activate God's Word in your mouth. *Activate* it."

Then she really gets silly, jumping up and down. "You got to *activate* that Word. Like that stinky pink stuff you put in a perm. Pour it in yo' mouth. Let it burn up yo' doubt and negativity. Activate that Word and enjoy the soft curls of salvation. Halleluuuuuuuu-yah!"

We both crack up, and she sits down next to me. "Did you really walk out on him?"

"Without my car or my purse. He said everything I have is his. And he's right."

"Heifer, you better call him and apologize."

"I don't know if I want to do that."

"Oh. Okay, you trippin'."

"I'm serious, Mac. I'm tired of being chained to his pockets."

For a moment she's quiet. "You don't know what you sayin', girl."

"I do know."

"No, you don't know. See, you ain't had no hungry days in yo' life, princess. You ain't had to worry about where you gon' stay, cause yo' mama done left with some niggah and you don't know where she is."

"Don't use that word, Mac."

"Look, just cuz you got you a white boy don't mean you ain't down no more."

"I've never liked that word, no matter *who* is using it, and I don't have a white boy."

"We got a *right* to use it. Take that junk back and turn it on them. Make it something other than what they said we was."

"Is that what you just did? Because it didn't sound like you used it as a term of endearment just now."

"I ain't trying to argue the merits of the 'n' word right now, Zora. I'm just saying. It's a blessing to have the help you have. If you didn't have yo' rich-as-sin daddy, you wouldn't have been able to help me out."

"You're on your way to Parsons, Mac. This weekend. That little piece of change I squirreled away here and there for you. That was nothing."

"Girl, you trippin'. You had my back all my life. I wouldn't know there was a Parsons School of Design in this world without you."

"You would have figured it out, Mac."

"That ain't likely. So you really left him the Lexus? When you gon' call and be like a Hallmark card commercial?" She sniffles with all the melodrama of a silent movie queen, though I doubt Mac has had a conscious moment of silence since she emerged from the womb. "Daddy, I'm so sorry."

She pretends to be my daddy. "Baby." Then she mimics me, again with wonderful funny gestures of flinging herself toward an invisible father. "Daddy." Then an exaggerated him toward me. "Baby."

She gets serious on me. "You got a perfect life, Zora. You don't go walking away from all those blessings just 'cause you mad."

"I know. I mean, I don't know. It's not like I meant to disrespect him. It's just ..."

"What?"

"I want to paint."

"Did he say you can't paint?"

"He thinks it's a hobby. So does Miles."

"Welcome to being a woman. Listen, you gotta deal, girl. Painting ain't nothin' compared to the security you got. Paint, Zora. Paint without permission, even if you don't go to Parsons with me. But don't lose your support system. You are a black woman. You at the bottom of the pile, baby. I know they say the black man is at the bottom, but who be the ones stuck with the babies when Raheem an' 'em gone on to pursue they rap career? You know how hard it was for me to get all this together to go to school. You know more than anybody. Call yo' daddy and tell him to bring Lexi back. Then again, wait a few days so Halle Berry's boyfriend can give you rides again. What's his name?"

"Nicky. As in Nicholas Parker, son of Reverend Nicholas Parker."

"The abortion guy?"

"You guessed it."

Her face collapses in disappointment. "Dang."

CHAPTER SIX

NICKY

Can't sleep. It's three o'clock in the morning.

I keep thinking about how I drove all the way to Ypsi just because Dad thinks if I don't darken the doorway of his church every time he opens the door, the wrath of God will descend upon me. Or maybe he thinks I'll change my mind and not let him turn me into Nicholas Parker, which is who I am and who I'm not at the same time.

My family never calls me Nicky. Well, they did, but stopped when I was twelve. I like being called Nicky. They say it sounds childish. That's what I like about it. It reminds me of my best days. Days when we went to Lake Superior in the summers. Days of picnics and cook-outs and the promise that everything good would stretch out before you like grains of sand. Like Abraham's promised sons, so good, so numerous you can't even count 'em. This was before my first kiss and first sexual encounter. Before I was a grown man with a bachelor's degree and a head full of poems flitting around like blinking fireflies too free to place in a glass jar. Before I started pushing freakin' potato chips into machines.

I want to sleep here in the silent darkness of my room, but I keep thinking about Zora. All kinds of crap. About when I met her and it was *me* being unnecessarily rude, trashing her because she voted for my dad. But I didn't like it when I felt she tore into me for no reason.

Who am I kidding? I don't attack my father's supporters. I lit into her because she stunned me. Because I *felt* something when I looked at her, and it scared me. Linda was right. In *two minutes* she got more out of me than Rebecca has in the six months I've dated her.

Whether or not I want to admit it, I knew then if I gave in just a little bit to the feelings she stirred in me, my life would change. The conversation with Pete will be the first of many talks like that, and all of the ugliness of the people around me—all the ugliness in *me*—will come to light, just like it's doing tonight.

Some things are better left in the dark.

Not only is she in my thoughts, my body burns for her like it's taken to heart everything Pete said, and I hate that about myself.

I'll never be able to take her home. So I think maybe I should let myself imagine bedding her. Relieve myself of that particular pressure, and be done with it.

This is craziness. I pick up the phone and call Richard from our Bible study. He's a friend of Bill—he knows what it's like to have a temptation and need somebody to talk it out with. Richard, a writer, used to be an AA sponsor before he started drinking again. He always said he wasn't afraid of a call in the middle of the night.

I read his book when I started the Bible study. It's called *Good News for Rascals, Rebels, and Whores*. I had to laugh at the title because I'm certainly a rascal. Come to think of it, I'm a rebel and a whore, too. Richard's book is one long, clear grace note to the imperfect, and I can hear its sweet and mellow tone through the noisy discord inside of me. And I'm still trying to process what he's written.

Dialing with a little fear and trembling, I feel ridiculous calling him up to say I want her so much I could burst. Literally. But who else am I going to talk to about this? Linda? Or Pete?

He answers after three rings. Wasn't even asleep. Richard's got the coarse voice of a man who smokes too much and drinks even more, but the colossal mess loves Jesus more than anybody I know.

"Rich." God knows I feel like I want to cry just to think I can unburden myself.

"Nicky?"

"Yeah, it's me, man. I needed to make that middle-of-the-night call."

"You want to drink?"

"No, I want to masturbate."

I'm glad he can't see my face, but he has to hear the shame. It plays like white noise when the TV set stops broadcasting and no voices are left to drown out the pain. "I'm sorry. I'm so embarrassed, but I need to talk about this to somebody."

"If it makes you feel any better, you know a lot more about me than I know about you. My books lay my life out for the world to see. Everybody knows my crap that bothers to read 'em. If you tell me some of yours we'll balance the scales of the universe."

I take a deep breath and decide to plunge deeper into the scary waters of honesty and confessing our faults one to another. Man, I miss AA meetings sometimes. Richard has been the next best thing. He doesn't go anymore because he feels guilty he's still drinking, but I'm so grateful for his conversation. I need this. I miss it.

But this isn't about taking a drink.

"Remember the new girl that came to Bible study yesterday? Zora?"

"I remember her." There's a smirk in his voice.

"What?" I say, heat rising to my face.

"Nothing. I'm waiting for you."

"You're laughing at me."

"No. I was laughing at you at Bible study. I'm just listening now, my friend."

"Richard!"

"Oh, come on, Nicky. That was the funniest thing I've seen in ages. You should have seen how flustered you were around her. Let an old man have some laughs."

"Glad I could help. I saw her tonight."

"I hope it went better than last night for you."

"It did. I didn't end up tearing out of the parking lot doing ninety."

"So what happened?"

"I don't even know, Rich. That's the thing. We just seem to clash."

Richard hacks a cough into the phone. I wait until he's done. "My friend Pete was with me, and he gets all jungle feverish when he meets her."

"Jungle feverish?"

"Yeah. It's that movie by Spike Lee. It's about a black guy that has an affair with this white woman. Jungle fever is supposed to be that thing where white people think black people ... well, you know."

"I'm not sure I do, Nicky. Tell me."

"Oh, come on, Richard. You know."

"Do I?"

"You're doing this on purpose."

"I just want to know what white people think. What's jungle fever?"

"It's when white people think black people are, you know, kinda wild in bed."

He's quiet for a moment.

I'm glad he can't see how embarrassed I am. I can't imagine what he's thinking. "Rich? Have you seen that movie?"

"Yes, I have, Nicky."

"You suck, Richard. Why did you make me tell you all that?"

"I'm just listening, son. Why don't you tell me what you're feeling?"

"Pete really ticked me off. And he wasn't even subtle."

"Go on."

"And then I thought about what a racist jerk I've been because I wasn't a stranger to that thought."

"So you get home, and then what?"

"And I can't stop thinking about her. Now, could you tell me how I can get her royal highness out of my head?"

"Are you sure that's what you want?"

"I have a girlfriend."

"Are you sure that's what you want?"

"She probably has a boyfriend, too."

"Are you sure that's what you want?"

I resist the urge to throw the phone across the room. "Uh, Richard. I'm sensing a theme here. What's your point?"

"What's yours, Nicky?"

"I already told you."

"I'm not so sure you did."

I'm frustrated now. I didn't call to talk in circles. That's what I get for inviting the geriatric crowd into my life.

"I think there's a lot going on here, Nicky. But we'll get to that. Let's go, first things first."

"Okay."

"What if I told you I thought she was pretty hot too?"

"Richard, are you some kind of pervert?"

"Yes, but that's beside the point. I'm getting to something here. We all feel, Nicky. I see a good-looking woman, I might think for a moment, 'I sure would like some of *that*.' It's a thought. It passes. We all get tempted. You. Me. Even Christ was tempted."

"I'm not Christ."

"You're jumping ahead, Nicky. Stay with me."

He waits for me to interrupt, and when I don't, he continues. "It's not a sin to be tempted."

"Feels like it is."

"That's a trick of the Enemy of your soul, son. Look at the Christ's temptation. You don't see Him with His tunic in a knot because He was tempted. No, He dealt with the temptation, each one, until it passed."

"Again, I'm not Christ."

"Then why didn't you just do it instead of calling me?"

I don't say anything.

"Nicky, I think you called me because you want me to remind you that you don't *really* want to sin."

I don't say anything.

"And perhaps you want me to remind you that it's okay you're feeling something that maybe you aren't ready for because that beautiful girl walked into the Bible study, and you're so attracted to her you don't know what to do with yourself."

"Was I that obvious?"

"Nicky, Billie, Linda and I, we're all a lot older than you. We've been through life. Billie and I have had particularly hard lives. Kid, it was pretty obvious."

"Man, I'm so freakin' embarrassed. Do you think Zora noticed?"

"Probably, but you're a good-lookin' kid. She didn't miss that. But she only had eyes for Jesus last night."

My heart pounds when he says she noticed me. I feel like a kid all right—a desperate, very excited one. "You think she finds me attractive?"

"Yeah, Nicky, but before you go all Romeo on me, remember you're a rascal, and we both know it. So we're going to do whatever it takes to keep both of you safe."

"You don't think I'm safe for her?"

"You're not even safe for *you* tonight. I don't say that to condemn. I know you love Jesus. If you didn't you wouldn't be on the phone with an old cuss like me."

"So what do I want?"

"You tell me. And how's about you give me your no-bull answer? What do you want, Nicky?"

"Man, she's so beautiful, Richard."

"She is, but that doesn't tell me what you want. Go on."

"What if I only dig Rebecca because it's easy? I certainly don't have to lie here wondering if I'm a racist when I think about her. I lie here thinking I'm a jerk, but not a racist."

"That's definitely easier."

"What if my white guilt is why I'm attracted to her?"

"I don't think white guilt is driving you, Nicky. Come on. Dig a little deeper."

I stare at the phone. The old fart is making me work. "Okay, what if, God help me, it's not just lust I'm experiencing, but I really want to *know* Zora? How smart she is? What makes her laugh? What makes her feel? I want to see her dance, Richard. I want to see her paint."

"Do you think you're afraid of intimacy?"

"Richard, I can't even begin to figure out how to be intimate with a woman. I know sex. I don't know intimacy. I'm afraid I don't have any self-control, and if by some miracle we end up together, I'll probably disappoint her."

"Like you disappoint your father?"

"Yeah. Maybe even more than I disappoint my father."

For a few moments we're quiet, then he breaks the silence.

"You're affected by her, Nicky. You're digging into your big ol' box of manipulations so you won't have to deal with the crap that's coming up in you. Zora came into your life and, without even knowing it, threatened your self-imposed exile. Now you want to use sex, and it doesn't matter if it's masturbation or sex with her or somebody else. You're really trying *not* to feel. You want to blunt how vulnerable you are. And how ugly some of the stuff inside of you is. It's scary to think maybe you can be *involved* with a woman. I mean really involved, Nicky, in a way that will change you. Like maybe you could love somebody. And she's a black woman. That can really shake up your narrow little world."

"I'm a sinner. A rascal, rebel, and whore. I don't know how to love."

"Say that last part again."

"I don't know how to love."

"Now, Nicky, tell me what you really want."

I finally know what he's been getting at. "I want to love."

That statement hovers in the air like something alive and big, and I feel a little courage seeing it. "I want to *be* loved too, but I'm so messed up."

"That's also why you called, Nicky. You don't want to be full of the racist crap we've all got. If you did, it wouldn't have bothered you what Pete said. By your own admission you've thought the same thing yourself. But you can't sex the darkness inside of you away."

"What am I gonna do, Rich?"

"Normally, I'd tell you to go read your Bible, but for right now, I want you to do something physical. I want you to engage your body in a different way than you wanted to. I'm going to give you a bodily prayer. Read the Scriptures after you do what I ask, okay?"

"Okay."

"First I want you to get quiet. Lie face down on the floor with your body in the shape of the cross, and don't get up until the urge to do something that doesn't reflect the love of God passes. The love of God will deliver you. If you think, 'Whatever happens, I'll err on the side of the love of God,' you'll be all right. 'Does the love of God want me to masturbate? Does the love of God want me to defile Zora?' It's kinda like those weird rubber bracelets, only you're asking what would love do."

"What if I fail, Richard?"

"A righteous man falls seven times in a day. Get up again, or in this case, lie down on your face again. Just like Zora did. And you don't have such a nice silhouette, so it shouldn't distract anybody."

I smile, even though he can't see over the phone. "All right. I'm gonna try it."

"Trust God. Have a little faith."

"I will."

"It only takes a mustard seed. Those are tiny."

"That's all I got. Tiny faith."

"That'll do. Night, Nicky."

"Good night, Rich."

I get off the phone and sit up on my bed. This is what I get for hanging around weird old former Catholic rascal-rebel-whores who have faith.

I stand. Stretch. Sit on the bed again. I don't want to lie on the floor. I've got hardwood floors, and it's gonna feel bad. Relieving myself would be a lot easier, but then how would I feel? Guilty. And what if I ever see Zora again? I'll feel all weird, as if she could know I had nasty thoughts about her. I'll probably never see her again, after I called her rude like that. Then again, she'll probably think I'll never want to see her again now that I know what she really thinks about the white people she's met. But this isn't so much about Zora. It's a God and Nicky thing.

It's a God and Nicky thing.

Before I can change my mind, I drop to my knees. I stay there for a while. Just thinking—or rather, avoiding.

Finally, I lie down. I stretch my arms out and one goes under my bed. I saw something like this in the movie *Luther,* and even then something in me admired the idea of stretching out in your own cross. I felt drawn to it. And now, here I am. Still, I feel silly. My dad would have a quadruple bypass if he saw this. In fact, he wouldn't even need the bypass. He'd just fall dead of a heart attack on the spot.

I lie like that for at least an hour-and-a-half, ticked off at Richard for making me do something so dumb and ineffective, but I don't get up.

Oh, but at dawn, as the light eases through my miniblinds, something begins to change. Suddenly my cross, my awkward position, my cold skin, my discomfort gets lost, absorbed into the cross of Christ. His nailed-on, outrageously beyond-awkward position, and His whip-split flesh become my meditation. I ruminate on His nakedness and humiliation. My little cross of sexual temptation—all my little crosses—is nothing. *Nothing!* Except to Him, who loves me so much that every little thing I bear in this life matters. Enough to die for.

I don't think of me anymore. I don't think of Zora. Jesus soaks Nicky Parker's games in blood and love. It's as if that blood and love nourishes the fallow ground in my heart, and suddenly everything inside begins to green and bloom.

He makes a garden filled with roses. Crimson-colored roses for me to run in, even though there are thorns big enough to pierce your head.

CHAPTER SEVEN

ZORA

Friday morning. After a fitful sleep, I awaken to the sound of five rapid-fire raps at my door. That is his warning. I know that knock. I hear his key twisting inside my lock. My father is coming in.

I stumble out of my room to the door, righting pajama bottoms twisted around my waist. I try to prepare myself to face him. It can't be too bad. This is my daddy. But I did make him angry. No one challenges *The Bishop,* especially not his little girl.

But this is Daddy.

He swings the door open, perhaps expecting I'd still be sleeping. He looks a little surprised to see me standing there near the door. He comes inside, walks past me, and seats himself on my sofa. No greeting. He's obviously not here to extend social graces.

He glances around at a room he's seen a million times.

The sapphire blue walls. The Sankofa symbols I stenciled onto the borders in a cream color, the same as my leather sofa. For Word-Faithers, we Hampton-Johnsons are a particularly culturally aware bunch. Funky, hip Cheryl Riley furniture, all contemporary and afrocentric. The fine art prints—Daddy thinks the originals are too expensive and not worth it. Gilbert Young, Cynthia St. James, Romare Beardon. Everybody I wish I had the courage to be like. MacKenzie has life drawings and renderings she's framed and displayed. Just a few. Painting and drawing aren't her thing; she's more of a furniture design diva. I'm the one who paints and draws. In theory.

I do not showcase my art. I don't have a single painting of my own displayed in my apartment. Not one drawing. My easel and paints hide away in my closet like you'd keep the clothing of a loved one who died out of sight.

Daddy sits on the sofa like he owns it. Which he does.

It's not his fault I haven't displayed my work. I'm grown. I can paint if I want to. Can't I? I try to choke back anger rising like the tide inside of me. Or is that grief?

Wait a minute. I've got everything. Look around you, Z.

Isn't this everything? Even MacKenzie said I need to be thankful for these blessings. I should apologize.

But I say nothing.

It feels like a snake is coiled tightly inside of me, and if I open my mouth, it will hiss, strike, kill. And I can't guarantee exactly what or who will die.

God help me.

Daddy hasn't lost his words. "Don't you have something to say to me, Zora?"

"Mama stopped by last night. She brought me my purse and talked to me."

"Then I believe you have something to say to me."

But I don't. My mother wore me out with her recriminations. I'm silent.

He stares at me. I try to remember how badly my grandfather treated him. I think of the road map of misery trailing scars across his back. I try to dredge up every psych class I've ever taken. Tell myself he's only this controlling because he's had so many losses. I try to think of him like the little boy he was, just being himself and having his father try to beat the Jack Johnson out of him. Beat him like a slave.

Slave.

Slave.

Slave.

Daddy doesn't beat me. My daddy doesn't beat me.

I still can't speak.

"So, you're just going to stand there and stare at me?"

I clear my throat. I don't know what's wrong with me. I'm perfectly capable of speaking. I just do not wish to be manipulated. "No, sir."

"No, sir, what?" he barks like a drill sergeant.

"No, sir."

"I said, 'No, sir, what?' What do you have to say to me, Zora?"

I start to feel hot. Sweaty. For a moment it feels like I can't breathe. No, sir, what? No, sir. Yes, sir. No, sir, boss. Yes, sir, boss.

I wonder, do I bow my back and widen my eyes, shuffle my feet? Uh, no, suh. Uh, yes um, massa. I's sorry I's offended you! Suh! Massa.

This is your father. A black man. Don't be like this, Z.

I press my lips together, still not knowing what's wrong with me.

Daddy stands up. "You want to act like you're mute. That's fine with me. I can get quiet too. But before I do, I'm taking my stuff. You want to be on your own? You do that, Zora. You are on your own. And your mother, your brothers, your sister, none of them can help you, or I cut them off. Do you understand?"

"Mama came by last night. We talked."

"Then you should have apologized."

I want to say, "I didn't do anything," but I can't seem to get the words out of me.

My heart thunders inside me. I hope he can't see through my baggy pajama pants how my legs are trembling. I didn't know it was possible to feel so angry. I want to tell him to take his stuff, and then tell him what to do with it, but I can't bring myself to do that any more than I can apologize for wanting to own my own life.

I don't understand. All I wanted to do was finish the newsletter. Skip dinner. Dress in jeans and a sweatshirt.

Maybe this is my answer. Maybe this is Jesus' capsule course on poverty. The thought of that takes a bit of the sting away.

Daddy's rage is so completely controlled it startles me how casual he sounds. "I've got some of the men from church and a moving truck with me. I'm here to get all my things since you don't want to honor your father. You can keep what's on your back."

The words confuse me, as if he'd spoken in Swahili. I can keep what's on my back?

He holds his hand out. "Give me your jewelry, including your promise ring."

This *is* another language. I was to give my daddy this ring back after I gave my husband my virginity. This is the ring I put on in tears, promising my daddy I would not as much as kiss a young man until I was on the altar letting my daddy pronounce me my husband's wife. This ring kept me through high school. It kept me in college when I was away from home, aching and throbbing with need and loneliness. I would tell myself those nights I fought alone against my own body, fingering that band of gold on my finger, "I promised. True love waits." And I meant that.

I don't understand this.

But I take off my promise ring. I put it back in his hand the same way I put it on my finger, with tears in my eyes. I guess promises are made to be broken, just like the world and all those fast heifers at school said.

I give him my gold hoops. I take the cross off my neck and give it to him. It's like an out of body experience. Suddenly I'm not inside of me anymore. I'm watching myself put my treasures, my maid's ornaments, into his hand. And it's strange and surreal, as if I'm a ghost, something dead, watching what used to be me going through the motions.

He storms past me and knocks me so hard that I fall to the ground. He doesn't even look back.

I'm glad the lease is in my name. At least he can't take the apartment.

Two of the guys I go to church with walk in to help my father strip me of my dignity. They refuse to look at me. I grew up with them. Mike Gregory and Timothy Jones. I used to have a crush on Tim. They work with solemn efficiency, and for a man who hardly gets his holy hands dirty anymore, *The Bishop* throws himself whole-heartedly into this project.

Everything they walk out the door with cuts like a slash across my back.

No, this is different. He's not treating me like he was treated. This is just stuff. This is not a beating. These are not stripes across my back like the lashes he got.

They take everything that Mac hasn't packed for her move. They take all the furniture. The art. My easel and paints and brushes from the deep recesses of my now empty closets. They take my toothbrush!

Everything they think belongs to me, until nothing remains but Mac's boxed-up belongings.

MacKenzie, for all her talk, is at least her own woman. Her things are hers. She doesn't even have credit card debt. Nobody can repossess her life.

I'm amazed at how quickly my life disappears. Nothing left but the pajamas on my body, some papers, business cards, and a handmade card in calligraphy that dropped out of the spring purse Tim emptied when he was taking my makeup.

I WALK IN and out of MacKenzie's room. She's ready to fly away on her own, black, shining wings. She gave away her furniture to a single mother who had a three-year-old baby, a man in prison, and a whole lot of nothing. I think about what her room used to look like before she boxed up what she'd take with her to Parsons. A little lived in, but mostly neat. MacKenzie had cute furniture, but it was cheap. I joked with her that it was mortal, and when it died it would turn to dust. *Sawdust* that is. She could only afford prefabricated furniture kits you had to put together yourself, that you'd better not dare put a teacup on. Another artist friend of ours, Shanna, calls that kind of furniture "Shanghai surprise."

I wonder if Mac thought my jokes about her furniture were funny, while I sat in the living room on my Cheryl Riley originals. Oh, Lord. And now it looks like the Grinch stole *my* Christmas.

My knees feel week. I realize that hours have gone by since I woke up and I haven't eaten a thing. I walk on shaky legs into the empty kitchen. My dining room furniture is gone, not as fancy as my mother's, but a scaled-down version by the same designer. All my linens with the Adinkra symbol embroidery that went with the stencils on the walls are gone too. I'm grateful I didn't rent a house, because maybe he'd have taken the stove and refrigerator too.

Thank God I had the good sense to get the lease in my name. He'd tried to cosign for me, or get the lease in his name, but I persevered. He can't take my apartment. But he has my job. And my car. And all the credit cards. My clothing. My computer.

My résumé is in my computer. Not that I can go job hunting. What am I going to do in my pajamas? I don't even have any shoes. And what about interview clothes? Clothes, period?

I don't want to think about the implications of any of this. I want to call MacKenzie. She'll help me through it. I've helped her.

I go back into her room since he took my phones. I pick up her old-fashioned princess trimline, and a feeling of heaviness overcomes me. Didn't Mac tell me I needed to apologize? She practically idolizes this apartment. She's going to flip her weave when she finds out *The Bishop* came in and took everything I own. I put the phone down.

It feels like my blood sugar has gone down. I'm not usually hypoglycemic, but the stress of the day, my nerves, and no food has wreaked havoc on my body. Once again, I walk from MacKenzie's room to the living room. I sit down, cross-legged on the floor. I'd read my Bible but he took it. And the thought of that makes me laugh. The Bishop went so far in punishing me for my sin of disrespecting him that he took my Sword of the Spirit.

How am I supposed to speak the Word? How am I supposed to

find the victory in my mouth? Ha! I'll bet that to him the only victory in my mouth are the words, "I'm sorry, Daddy."

I wonder how many slashes across his back before he said "I'm
sorry" to Granddaddy? I wonder if he had to say the actual words, if
he had to concede his defeat in the exact way Granddaddy specified.

Maybe if I showed up at church in my pajamas and put my arms
around his neck, just held onto him, maybe he'd circle my waist with
his arms and that would be *I'm sorry* for both of us.

What would that mean for our lives? Would he have Mike and
Tim come back bearing my things with a smile? All is forgiven? As if
I'd ever forget that the two guys I've gone with to children's church,
to youth group, to singles group, sold me out like two overseers on a
plantation.

"Miss Zora gon' fly away, Massa Jack. She gon' cleave da' air an fly
away."

What's the matter with me?

I lie down on the floor and tell myself I'm thinking crazy. I
shouldn't have gone to Spelman. I definitely shouldn't have majored
in African American studies. If I'd gone to Parsons, I wouldn't be
lying on my empty floor thinking about slaves and overseers and
wings I don't seem to have.

All that black stuff. It just makes you angry. Sometimes I think
it's better not to know it. Any of it. But even the most ignorant of us,
the straight-up hood rat with no education at all, gets it. It's in us like
a mourning song that we can't remember all the words to. Like an old
spiritual that wounds and heals at the same time. Even the hood rat
can hear the ghosts howling in the trees where the brothas hung.
Smell the blood and sweat in the soil down South. Hear the wails of

the ancestors in the waters of the Atlantic Ocean. God, we hear it, and it makes us angry, and it comes out in our rap music, and our ghetto violence, and our hopelessness. It comes out when we bite back our rage and smile at every Mister Charley we work for, and it comes out when we bite off the head of every Mister Charley we work for.

In so many ways, we are still caught in the same drama that others created for us so they didn't have to work so hard. We are still house slave and field slave, trying to be that talented tenth. We're still giving ourselves brown-paper-bag tests, and hoping whitey approves of us. And sometimes, we take on all the attributes of our oppressor, whatever color he is, because in the end, humanity is basically evil, and it hasn't a thing to do with our skin tone.

We'll turn on a dime if the price is right.

I need to call somebody. I need to get out of here. I need to get out of this headspace.

I glance around the room. My eyes land on the fallen papers and Linda's card.

Not a chance I'll call that white woman. I'll sit here and lose my mind first, God.

CHAPTER EIGHT

NICKY

I glance at the caller ID and answer the phone, complaining from the first word. "Come on, Linda. I'm entitled to a day off now and then. You should be glad I'm having a Jesus day."

"I am glad. I don't mean to interrupt you and the Lord, but Jesus needs a favor. Someone we know needs help."

"He didn't tell me that. He didn't say anything about favors or helping anybody, and I've been chatting with Him all morning."

"He's saying it now."

"Aw, man, Linda. Can't you just let me be an uninvolved, marginal Christian? I don't want the kind of demanding Christianity that actually has to help others. I don't *really* want to be Jesus for people."

She laughs. "It's Zora. Would you be Jesus for Zora?"

I close my eyes. Try to breathe deeply. Pause and wait for my heart to take the elevator back up to where it's supposed to be.

"Tell me you mean another Zora, and not the one who had me laid out in the shape of a cross all night."

"Laid out in the shape of a cross, huh? Sounds very Richard. You'll have to tell me about that later. Anyway, I'm thinking she's probably the same Zora. How many other Zoras do you know?"

"You suck, Linda."

"I wouldn't ask you, but I can't leave here today. We're short of people because somebody called off work so they could let Jesus love on them. Now Jesus needs to love on somebody else, and Billie can't get away from the house, and Richard didn't answer his phone."

"Richard is probably asleep because he was up half the night with me. Don't you know any other Christians, preferably better Christians than me?"

"Can you just go take her some clothes?"

For a moment a delightful image of Zora sans clothing fills my head. Of course Linda the prophetess knows.

"Nicky. Grow up. Something happened, and she's lost everything."

"What do you mean she's lost everything? Did her apartment building catch on fire or something? I saw her last night and she was fine."

"She told me about last night, including the fact that she saw you, and it goes right into why she doesn't have anything today."

"What happened? You mean seeing me is part of why she lost everything?"

"Don't be ridiculous. Everything isn't about you. She can tell you herself what happened. Will you take her some clothes?"

"Where am I supposed to get women's clothes?"

"Be creative, Nicky. I don't care where you get them. What's most important is that you help your sister in Christ in need. More than anything, she needs your presence. This is the kind of incarnational living we talk about at Bible study. Be Jesus for *her*, not just Nicky, okay? I know you can do this."

"Didn't I tell you I didn't want to be Jesus for anybody? Especially her! I can't, Linda. I have ... thoughts. Feelings about her that aren't squeaky clean, if you know what I mean. I don't want to end up flirting with her or something, especially if she's vulnerable."

"Nicky Parker. You're a better man than you realize you are. I'm sure you can put your adolescence to the side long enough to hand her an outfit and tell her you're sorry for her trouble."

"You're wrong there. I can't help her. I'm sorry. You'll be off of work at five. She'll have to hang on until then. She has a roommate, MacKenzie or something. Maybe she can help her before you can get to her. I can't."

"She wears a size eight. Clothes and shoes. You only have to remember one number. You can handle that. Thanks a lot."

She hangs up on me.

I call her back. "Linda, I'm not going over there."

She tells me she doesn't have time to engage me if I'm going to keep acting stupid. What am I supposed to say to that?

I'm not going. I told Linda I'm not going, and I'm not going. And that's that.

HOW DO YOU dress a Black American Princess?

I have no idea.

I find myself at the fifth store in the mall. The *mall!* And I want to give up. First of all, the only place I have interest in shopping for Zora is Victoria's Secret, and I'm thinking that's not what Linda has in mind. I go to the place where my mom shops, Eddie Bauer, and then I realize my *mom* shops here. Bad idea. I call Rebecca, and God, was that ever a colossally bad idea. I ask her where she buys her clothes, and I can hear the delight in her voice. She thinks I'm about to up the ante, and now I gotta get Rebecca something too. Then I'm appalled to find out that she shops where my *mom* shops. I get terrifying visions of the life that is set before me: my father's life, complete with pot roasts, the 'burbs, a four-door sedan, and recycled sermons nobody realizes are recycled.

Kill me now, God. Please.

I go into Macy's. I'm sure not going to be buying her any Prada or Kate Spade—I don't care what her MySpace page says—but maybe I can find something nice that I, the pretzel-machine guy, can afford. I go through rows and rows of clothes. Lovely, incredibly expensive clothes that make me want to smoke a joint I feel like such a failure in life. I will never, ever be able to afford that woman. I end up getting depressed by exactly how much the pretzel-machine guy *cannot* afford. Finally, I go back to Eddie Bauer and pick up a necklace I hope Rebecca won't think is engagement jewelry and head back to my truck, not only defeated but steaming mad at Linda.

Mad or no, Zora still needs some clothes. I take one more trip to downtown Ypsilanti and go to Puffer Red's. That's the spot for urban chic in Washtenaw County, and when I say urban, read "black." All the rappers that come to town stop into the boutique and get their picture taken with Red, and they really do have the coolest clothes and shoes. Pete introduced me to the place when he first began his—forgive me for saying this—*wigger* stage. Don't make me explain the term. Please don't.

I realize I've seen Zora twice. I have no idea what she wants to wear. Both times she wore jeans. I head over to the denim, and the first thing I see is a brand called Apple Bottom. *Apple Bottom?* I start having visions. Really, really good ones of Zora in Apple Bottom jeans. I stand there an inordinately long time caressing the hanger until I realize I look like some kind of "off the rack" freak.

Gonna be a cross for a long time tonight.

A long time.

I can't buy her these jeans. Pete's freakin' voice rings in my head about *sistahs* wanting their bodies to be seen. I don't want to think about what Zora's motivation is for wearing jeans. Maybe it's the same as my own. Jeans are comfortable. Easy to wear. But my brain feels stained by the thought.

I let the hanger go. I can't do this. I knew I couldn't and tried to tell Linda. My anger rises like bile to my throat, and I think it will explode out of my mouth. And I don't care. I'm gonna let Linda have it.

I pick up my cell phone and punch our work number. The kindness in her voice as she answers the phone shames me.

I pause, and she waits, as if she knows it's me. I sigh into the phone. "Linda. I have no—"

"Go to Janelle's."

"What?"

"Janelle's. It's a boutique. It's on Washtenaw by the K-Mart in Ypsi. Do you know where that is?"

"Yes."

"She's a nice lady. A sister in Christ. She'll help you."

"How did you know what I was going to say?"

"The Holy Spirit. Now get going. You've wasted enough time. *Victoria's Secret!*"

"I didn't go in!"

She laughs.

I stare at the phone and hang up before God can tell her anything else about me.

* * *

I GET TO Janelle's, and despite what Linda said, I still feel like I'm spinning my wheels. Nobody is in the store. I see all kinds of church lady suits in pastel colors. If they were egg-shaped, I'd feel like I walked into an Easter basket. Immediately I think Linda has steered me in the wrong direction. This doesn't look like a place a Black American Princess shops. It doesn't even look like a place Linda shops. Thank God for *that*.

I start yanking hangers around the racks, looking at clothes I doubt Zora will wear. I think about the Apple Bottom jeans. And all the racy little halter-tops I've looked at today. I think about the Eddie Bauer twin sets and black pencil skirts. I think about the dizzying array of skirts, blouses, slacks, capris, and I have no freakin' clue what to do.

I just want to please you, Zora.

She doesn't know. She doesn't know that it's taken me hours because I want to get just the right thing. That I want to get that dazzling smile out of her. She has a dimple, just on one side. And she wears CK One, the same freakin' Calvin Klein unisex scent I wear. Her skin looks like blackberries, and she glows from the inside out. She'd be gorgeous in white. A dress she can twirl in when she dances, but how practical is that?

I feel a presence behind me. I turn and see an older black woman. I notice her eyes first. Black as obsidian. Crinkled, crow's-feet-marked eyes full of wisdom and laughter like I imagine Jesus' are now. Not before. I use to imagine Jesus with stern brown eyes of judgment, but now His eyes are loving.

She's the color of café au lait, and her face is covered with brown freckles. I never see black people with freckles, so the sight of them startles and delights me. I like her.

"Can I help you?" she says.

I nod. "I need help, badly. I've gotta get something for my woman."

"Something for your woman, you say?"

For a moment I don't answer. The question takes me by surprise. Janelle smiles. "Is that what you said, sweetness?"

"I'm sorry, what did I say?"

"You said, 'I've gotta get something for my woman.' At least that's what it sounded like you said."

I scratch my head. "Did I? I meant to say for *a* woman."

"Out of the abundance of the heart the mouth speaketh."

"It would appear that you're right." I shake my head. My slip unnerves me. "She's not my woman." I chuckle. "Right now, it'd be good if I can just figure out an outfit for her."

"That's a big step, an outfit."

I laugh. "Oh, no. We're not at the buying-clothes stage or anything. We're not even at the *friends* stage. There's a need. I'm not sure what it is, but I hear it's bad. Like 'she's lost everything' bad."

"The poor thing."

"I want to get her something until we can take her shopping. The people in our Bible study. At least I think so. I'm Nicky. My friend Linda sent me."

"I'm Janelle. I figured you were Nicky. Linda called me and told me you were coming. I don't get many handsome twenty-something young men in here."

She makes me blush, and I notice she didn't call me white. "Thank you, Janelle. I'm not even sure exactly how much I should get. I really don't know the plan. And I don't have much money. I can use my credit card, but I don't have much credit, either. Student loans."

"That's okay, sweetness. We'll go easy. We don't always get the plan, but we still have'ta act, don't we? You say you think she lost everything? Linda didn't say much to me. Just that you were coming."

"Yeah. I don't know the details. I just need to tide her over until we all meet or something. I don't know. I've been at the mall for hours." I throw my hands up. "I'm. Just—" I thrust my hands into the pockets of my jeans. "Lost."

I look at her. "You don't sell Apple Bottom jeans, do you?"

She seems to laugh with her whole body. "No, baby."

"Do you sell other clothes like that? I don't want those. Well, I do, but Linda would kill me."

She chuckles. "I can't imagine Miss Linda hurting a living soul. How 'bout you tell me about your young lady?"

My heart races to think of her. "She's beautiful, Janelle, and complicated. In the way the horizon is beautiful and complicated at dusk and dawn. She's a dancer and a painter." I imagine those MySpace pictures, and the thought of them takes my breath away. "And she's smart. Sassy. She's an Ella Fitzgerald scat, or a Thelonius Monk melody. You know?"

Janelle shakes her head at me. "You've got it bad, Nicky."

"Can you tell?"

"I'm afraid so. Is she African American, sweetness?"

"Yes. And she's totally not into me."

Before Janelle can address my dilemma, I throw this out there before I can change my mind. "Can you find something modest for her?"

She smiles and nods like I've pleased her.

"Not like old lady modest or, forgive me for saying this, even *Linda* modest. And please, Janelle, don't even show me something Eddie Bauer white-lady modest like my mom would wear. Zora is ... a *sistah*."

I didn't mean it like Pete. I meant it in a good way. I said it with respect. "I want her to look like Zora, the artist, the dancer, the *sistah*. Not somebody else's image of who they think she is, and that includes me."

I hesitate, not knowing how to say this next part without sounding crazy. I look at Janelle. Those kind black eyes gaze into mine. "Janelle, if she were, like, to pray, lying prostrate, with her ..." I gesture toward my rear. "You know, in the air a little bit ... I don't know. What kind of thing could she wear so that her, you know, so she'd still be okay to pray like that around ... me? And it not drive me crazy. In a *bad* way."

Janelle cracks up like Linda did when I said I prayed Zora would never come to Bible study again. She even gets a few chuckles out of me she laughs so hard.

I ask hopefully, "Can we try something in white, too? She's darker than you. She'll look good in white, with the contrast against her incredible skin. Don't you think?"

"I know just the thing."

She leads me to a rack of markdowns. And right there, at seventy-five percent off, hangs a white wrap, three-quarter-sleeve shirt. On the same rack, Janelle finds flowing black bottoms that I think are a skirt at first. She calls it a split skirt. I call them pants, but they're beautiful, and Zora will look fantastic. Both are size eight.

I save so much money with the sale prices I can buy her a spring dress that's not on sale. It's a gauzy number, but not sheer. White. And the skirt is made for twirling in. I buy her big silver hoops because Janelle says all bohemian types love those, and I finish the look with a simple sterling silver cross and the some underthings I hope she won't think are too personal, but rather a necessity. I even try to keep my head out of fantasyland. Impossible while buying Zora bras and panties, but I tried just the same. Janelle gives me fifty percent off a pair of black leather ballet flats and a throws in a few more unmentionables for free to help with Zora's losses, whatever they are. We pray together for Zora, and she sends me on my way.

I don't call Linda to report on how well I did. Somehow I have a feeling the Holy Spirit has told her all about it.

CHAPTER NINE

ZORA

I know I'm losing my mind. I tried to find Mac's Bible without success. I doubt if Mac can find her Bible. I don't want to raid her boxes, especially since my things have been pillaged.

The feeling of being violated fills me with indignation. I want to stretch out having everything taken from me for as long as I can. Oh, I'm in solidarity with my ancestors now. And every violation I feel today is in remembrance of those for whom a simple apology would never suffice. Ever.

I think of all the Scriptures I have memorized, and only one brings comfort. Over and over Jesus' words in the Gospels play in my mind. "Blessed are the poor in spirit." And again where He said, "Blessed are you poor." Something like that. I meditate on them. My only deviation, in snatches, is to actually think on those poor. Those poor in spirit. And then back to the Scripture.

I try not to think about myself. I try not to think about Daddy.

I don't cry.

I have no idea how long I lay on the hard floor like that. But I'm sore from the assault the ground puts on my body. At some point I hear someone buzz my buzzer. It surprises me. I'm rarely home on a Friday morning. Or is it afternoon? Maybe it's Miles. I think it is. Miles is going to help me stop thinking about slaves and masters and overseers and Daddy. He's going to talk some sense into me. 'Cause I've lost it, and all I can think of is the poor.

I don't even ask who it is. I buzz him up, wishing he could fly up the stairs instead of walk. I run into the bathroom but I can't do a thing with myself. Funky tank top. My hair nappy at the roots. I can't even brush my teeth. Not that I'd have time to. Not now. I rinse my mouth and wipe my teeth with the tank top and smooth it back over my pajama bottoms. I hear Miles knocking, and rush to let my sweet boyfriend in.

Only it ain't Miles. It's Nicky Parker.

I'm so flustered I can't get my mouth to work, and he's leaning at my doorjamb.

"Hey," he says with an easy grin. Like my whole life hasn't fallen apart.

When I find my voice, I blast him. "What are *you* doing here? Did Linda send you? I knew I shouldn't have called her. What are you supposed to be, my great white hope?"

Nicky looks stunned. He bolts up from his leaning position. "Great white hope? Didn't you call *Linda?* Did it occur to you that *she's* white too? Or am *I* the only white person you've taken it upon yourself to torture with your 'hate whitey' crusade?"

"At least Linda is nice."

"What? I'm not nice? I've been at the mall for hours for you. With my own money, mind you. And I don't even know what's going on with you. I took a personal day off work, for *myself,* Zora, and that is a rare and beautiful thing, by the way. I've spent it shopping for *you* because I heard you had trouble in Black American Princess land. So you'll excuse me, but I think I'm pretty darned nice, especially since you're so freakin' salty."

Okay. Man at mall cuts across all racial and cultural boundaries. But did she have to ask *him?* I look a hot mess, and he's looking all fine, especially when he's mad. And he argues with me. Miles never argues with me. I thought his speech was over, but no.

"You know, if you ever come back to our Bible study, and you *should,* since apparently you *need* it, you'll find that we happen to think Christians should bear one another's burdens. We love each other the way Jesus says we should. It doesn't matter what color we are."

"All of you are white."

"*You're* not white, angry *black* woman. And I'm here bearing *your* burdens." He thrusts a beautifully gift-wrapped box at me. "Here are some clothes. And shoes. And even some other stuff that isn't necessary—but just *nice.* Linda calls it being missional, and intentional, and incarnational. I don't even understand all those terms, Zora. But when she says we need to be Jesus for one another, I get that. That's pretty concrete."

I stand there looking at him until he fusses some more.

"Take the box."

"I don't want it."

"Why not?"

"Because Jesus wouldn't be standing here yelling at me."

"Jesus would probably take a switch to your behind."

He runs his hand, with those delightfully long fingers, through his hair. It looks like he's done that gesture several times today, probably at the mall. For me. It falls back in soft layers around his face. It's a little sun kissed in places, blonder in some spots than others. Nicky is crazy fine, and he's standing so close I can smell CK One. I used to have a bottle before *The Bishop* confiscated it. I haven't even asked Nicky in.

He tucks the package under his arm.

He takes a step back like he's going to walk away, and then steps up to me again, as stealthy as a lion. But he doesn't roar this time. His voice is soft.

"Zora, I'll tell you the truth. I didn't really want to do this. But I honestly want to be Jesus' hands, and feet, and heart, even if that means I have to go to Briarwood Mall. And Puffer Red's."

I smile when he says he's been to Puffer Red's.

"And Janelle's. I don't know what happened to you, but I can see your apartment is empty, and you're in your pajamas, and you don't look like yourself. Linda said you're in trouble. Will you take this package from Jesus, and not turn Him away because He happened to come to you looking like a ticked-off white man today?"

Again, he stretches the package out toward me. I take it this time.

"Come in, Nicky."

He hesitates.

"Come on."

He follows me inside. I don't make a show out of what's left in here. Nicky notices my work on the walls.

"Did you paint in here?"

"Yep."

"It's beautiful work, Zora. What a rich blue color."

"I love this color. It looks just like your sapphire eyes."

I shouldn't have said that.

He actually laughs. "You mean you *like* my eyes? Me, the blue-eyed devil?"

"Okay. You get three cool points for knowing some early Malcolm X. But why don't we cool it with the militant stuff? I'm sure you've had your fill for now. So have I."

I sit on the floor. Beckon him to do the same, and he does.

We both sit cross-legged. He seems to look everywhere but at me. I tease him for avoiding my gaze. "You must really like that paint job."

"I like more than that." And then that sweet baby turns red on me.

"Didn't mean to let that one out, did ya, Nicky?"

"No, but if you'll forget about it, I'll pretend you didn't say I have sapphire eyes."

Oh, yeah. There's definitely something wild and sweet about him. I like him despite myself. He finally looks at me.

"I feel a little nervous around you, Zora. Nobody has challenged my white guilt like you do."

"I can't turn off the militant in me sometimes. I wish I could."

"I can't say I understand that, Zora. But who am I to judge you for it?" He points to the ceiling. "What's that symbol that looks like a bird? I've seen it before."

"It's Sankofa. It means go back and fetch it."

"I don't understand. Is it like, some kind of flying thing? Some kind of freedom thing?"

"In a way. You see how its head is turned? It's looking back, behind itself. Its lesson is that what we've lost is in our past, and only in going back can we truly go forward. So maybe there is a kind of flying lesson. Maybe we have to fly back to where things began. Flying back, looking back, maybe they're the same thing, just going at different speeds."

He looks uncomfortable. "I don't want to look back at anything. I definitely don't want to fly back to my past. I'd just as soon leave everything behind me right where it is."

"Sounds like you have a reason to go back. Maybe you left something important there."

"It'll have to stay."

For a few moments we're both quiet and then he continues. "I mean, it seems like my whole life is one big Sankofa. I went to UC Berkeley, far away from Reverend Nicholas Parker Senior. And you know what? After a while, I missed him. I'd burned all the bridges I could, and I had no idea how to get back home again."

I look into his eyes. He's telling me his prodigal son story, an abbreviated version, but the pain of eating with the pigs is still in his eyes.

"Talk about wanting to come back to your past to get what you lost. I wanted to make amends. I felt like God said to me, 'It's time to put things right with your father,' but I suck at it. I should have just let it be."

His words jar me. Put things right with your father.

Not today, Lord.

Nicky gets quiet on me. I guess it's my turn to give my own father story. "I guess I'm the prodigal daughter today. I don't even know how all this happened, Nicky. It's so weird. Daddy invited me to dinner. Just a quiet night with him, my mama, and my boyfriend. I didn't even want to go. And the next thing you know, he's cut me off from all of his financial support. He came here early this morning with a moving truck. And he's taken what he's helped me buy, which is everything. He's taken everything away from me."

"That sucks, Zora."

"It really does suck. And I can't decide if it's a blessing or not, because I keep praying that Jesus will show me what the Scripture means—"

"Blessed are the poor in spirit."

My heart quickens. "Yes. Yes! That's it."

"That's a dangerous prayer, Zora. He may show you exactly what it means. And you may not like it."

"Though He slay me, yet will I trust Him. I know that my Redeemer liveth."

He takes a deep breath, like he drank in the Scripture. "I like a King-James-only girl, even though you totally fused two different Scriptures. And does your dad know you think God slayed you? I don't think he believes in that."

He's so silly, I laugh.

He nudges me. "Can I take you out of the screaming blue abyss here, pajama girl?"

"I'd like that very much." I touch the beautifully wrapped box beside me. "So what's in the box?"

"I'll surprise you. Open it in the bathroom, though. I can't bear to see it if you're disappointed. If you hate it all, lie like a rug."

I laugh again. He really is sweet.

"Nicky?"

"Yeah, Zora."

"I'm sorry I was mean to you."

"Don't worry about it. I was a little snippy myself. You forgive me, and I'll forgive you. Now go get fabulous and let's get outta here and break bread together."

What he doesn't realize, is that we've just broken bread. Maybe not on our knees like the song I love says, but cross-legged on the floor, he gave me a bit of his bread of sorrow, and I gave him a bit of mine. Now, I'm ready for a little milk and honey for our journey. I stand up and look at him still sitting there, and his face, so open and vulnerable, looks so beautiful that he takes my breath away.

"Remind me to sketch you one day, Nicky."

He grins at me. "Are you an artist, Zora?"

"Yeah. I am."

I walk into my bathroom with the box in my hands, singing, "When I fall on my knees with my face to the rising sun, O Lord, have mercy on me."

And for a moment, I feel hopeful. That is until I realized that all my towels and washcloths are gone. Along with the shower curtain.

I determine that God is with me despite my nightmare morning. God may have come in the skin of a really cute white guy, but He came bearing gifts, and if I ever needed to receive anything from God, in all the years that receive, receive, receive had been drilled into me, it's today.

Nicky said he practiced incarnational Christianity. This is from You, Lord. From You.

Oh, God. I hope You have good taste.

Now see, there I go. Already I've got it all wrong. Do the poor get the luxury of fine taste? Nicky spent his money on me. This isn't even a taste of real poverty. He didn't come here with a pair of his sweats and an old T-shirt for me.

God, when will I ever get living for You right?

I take a deep breath. I try to imagine the sunshine of Nicky's face as I untie the gossamer white ribbon holding the box together. He'd had it wrapped in a simple floral paper printed with daisies. Wildflowers. I like him a little more for that.

God, don't let whatever is in here be hideous. Supernaturally make me like it if You have to. I've had so much disappointment today. Can You just not let this be something Britney Spears would wear?

I decide to close my eyes and feel around. You can tell a lot about a man by the fabric he chooses.

First I touch paper. I make my way past it and feel cool cotton beneath my fingers. It's a gauzy fabric, and already my fingertips tell me my body is going to at least like the feel of it against my skin.

I take a chance and open my eyes. It's white. It's amazing. A dress as simple and lovely as an India.Arie song. It's something the singer would wear, in fact. I ain't gon' be no Britney today. It's got a sweetheart neckline, and three-quarter sleeves. I could wear it to church and to a picnic, and with heels I can take it to the dance floor. It's perfect.

For a moment I feel so happy I hold the dress to my heart.

Thank You, Jesus. And thank you, Nicky Parker.

There are other treasures in the box. Big sterling silver hoops and a simple cross to go with them. Oh, somebody must have trained him well. He knows a sistah's heart. Black palazzo pants and a white wrap, three-quarter sleeve T-shirt. How could he understand me so well? These aren't just clothes I'd pick myself, these are clothes I'd pick since I've met Linda. Her modesty, even though, God help me, I don't want to dress like her, well, it touched me. And I've wanted to cover myself a little more. Just with a bit more style than Linda. And he's captured it beautifully.

Wait. Does he think I'm immodest?

I think about the other two times he's seen me. Well, I certainly wasn't modest all over the floor when we first met. What did I have on that night? Jeans. Tight jeans. And last night at the bookstore? More tight jeans, though I doubt if he found the sweatshirt immodest. And his friend, saying I'm bootylicious …

He's gotta think I'm immodest.

Should I ask him? Should I be mortified?

I sit on the countertop. His friend has jungle fever, and Nicky thinks I'm a stank ho. He's over here being Jesus so he can tell me in a nice way that I'm a ho.

All of a sudden this is all too much for me. All my clothes gone. All my stuff gone. This guy I just met having to come and rescue me. Me wondering what he thinks about all of this. About me. My father. An ocean of sadness and confusion pours out of me and I begin to sob into the white dress.

He hears me. He knocks on the door.

"Are you okay, Zora?"

"Go away."

"You can't send me away. I'm the great white hope."

"That's not funny, Nicky."

"You hate everything I got, don't you?"

"Waaaaaaaaaaaaaah."

"Aw, man. I suck. But I tried. I really did, Zora. I can't afford you. And I just didn't think I should get you Eddie Bauer or Apple Bottoms."

"*Apple Bottoms?* You were thinking of getting me *Apple Bottom* clothes?"

"Okay. I'll admit it. The name compelled me. Would you have rather had Baby Phat?"

"Waaaaaaaaaaaaaaaaaaaaaaah."

"Zora, you're really damaging my self-esteem here. Cut me some slack. I've never shopped for a black woman."

"You're damaging my self-esteem, you wretched man. *Apple Bottom!* You think I'm bootylicious too, don't you? You're just like Pete."

"I'm not. Okay I am, but, not really. Yes, I am, but in a different way."

I hear him make a groaning sound. It sounds like he's banging his head against the door.

"Zora, listen. What I mean to say is, you do have a nice butt."

"What?"

"Okay, that sounded worse than I meant it. It sounds awful, but please bear in mind I'm of the male species, and we tend to be visual. It's a biological flaw."

"Get away from my door. You're perpetrating the myth of the black whore."

"*Myth of the* ... Zora. I don't even know what the myth of the black whore is."

"Liar."

"All right. Maybe I know it, but it's a *myth*. Aw, man. Zora. Can you tell me exactly where I went wrong?"

"No, I hate you." I cry like a babe in arms, only I'm not in anybody's arms.

"May I come in there?"

"No."

"Please."

"No."

"Do you still have your pajamas on?"

"Yes. And don't you come in here."

He opens the door, outraging me.

"You're just going to barge in here anyway? Just do what you want. You're such a *white* man!"

He looks around the space and laughs. "Wow. Your bathroom is, like, red."

"I like to experiment with color."

"It's really cool."

"What do you want, Nicky?"

He walks up to me. "I'm sorry, Zora. I didn't mean to make you cry."

"Do you think I'm a ho?"

"Excuse me?"

"I said—" I try to compose myself, which is impossible. "Do you think I'm a stank ho?"

"No, you said ho first. Plain ol' ho. Let's not add anything, okay?"

I guffaw through my tears. "You're silly. You're a silly, silly man."

"Why would I think you're a ho, Zora?"

"Why did you buy these clothes in particular? They don't look like anything you've seen me wearing."

"I got the clothes I thought you could wear and be as perfectly beautiful as you are. That's all. I assure you, Zora, between the two of us, Nicky is the ho. Just ask Richard from Bible study. He'll tell you. He wrote a book about it."

He gets another chuckle out of me. "Richard wrote a book about you being a ho?"

"No, he wrote a book about God's grace to people like me. It's called *Good News for Rascals, Rebels, and Whores*. You'll have to excuse us. We white folks say 'whore' instead of ho. Except the rappers. And the ... wiggers." He winces.

"Did you just say *wigger?*"

"I did. Forgive me."

"Okay, you're stupid. You know that, right?"

"When you say stupid, do you mean lacking intelligence, or funny? You know we white people have vastly different meanings for the same words."

"You're funny. You may be stupid too, but you're funny."

"I made you smile."

And then I bawl again.

"Oh, Nicky. I don't have a job now. What am I going to do? The rent is due in three weeks. I don't have any savings. My parents gave me everything, including my job."

"I guess you're going to have to trust your heavenly Parent." He takes my hands in his. "I don't have any easy answers, Zora. But I really believe in this incarnational Christianity thing. And God really is with you. Not just in us, your friends, Zora. He's with you."

He squeezes my hands. His hands move to caress my face. Nicky wipes my tears with the backs of his thumbs. I was right. He does have magic hands, and I close my eyes and feel myself surrender to his tenderness.

His hands make their way to my hair, and I pull back.

"What?"

"Don't touch my hair."

"Why not?"

How can I tell him it's because my hair is coarse and his is straight, and there's too much painful history between the two textures? And that's just one thing among way too many. I can sum it up in a rhyme from my childhood that is a perfect commentary of life in America between the races. *If you're white, you're all right. But if you're black, step back.* After all these years I still haven't discovered how to be happy I'm nappy. And I'm not alone.

How can I explain to him that I refuse to chemically alter my hair because I like to think I appreciate my natural hair texture, yet I use a flat iron to straighten it and hot curlers on it every day? That I feel conflicted because as much as I appreciate natural styles, my mother and father would be embarrassed by me in an afro. Or that it still stings to think about that swimming incident in Atlanta. How self-hate that didn't start with us gets absorbed so deep into the skin you can't tell its origins or endings. Or if it's even self-hate at all.

"Just don't, Nicky."

"But I like it. It feels like a really soft kind of wool. Why do you straighten it?"

I push him. "None of your business. Stop playing."

He's reveling in it. Having himself a good ol' time.

He can't understand this anger surging in me. *They* made us feel the brunt of their hatred of our hair texture. Our black skin. Our thick lips.

"I like the way you feel, Zora. Let me touch you."

The truth is, I like the way he feels. I like his boldness. And I like him liking my hair. I actually believe him when he says he likes the way it feels. At least I want to. I've never met a man that affects me like Nicky Parker. He's so ...

Sexy.

Dear God, is it because I feel so vulnerable? Is it because Miles is too afraid of offending *The Bishop* to run his hands through my hair? And here's an irony. My nappy roots would probably offend Straight and Narrow "Why didn't you dress for dinner?" Miles. I know I should stop him, but I let Nicky Parker's hands continue to roam around the wild terrain of my head. He makes me feel free and easy as a bird in flight.

I think I moan.

"Oh, man," he says. "You're going to get me in so much trouble, Dreamy."

It's like my heart hiccups. I always call myself dreamy. And he does it. This amazes me, and I'm so touched. Nobody calls me dreamy. Spacey, yes. But that's not a compliment.

He leans forward so slowly. His blue eyes locked with my brown ones. "You are stunning."

Suddenly, I can't breathe. I can't think. I part my lips expecting his mouth to descend up mine. With the pad of his thumb he traces my lips. I don't think my heart could beat any faster and just when he makes his final move I screech, *"Don't!"*

He snaps back like a rubber band yanked him. Moves away from me and shoves his hands into his pockets.

We avoid looking at each other. A few endless moments pass. Finally he makes idle talk.

"So, what kind of shower curtain went with all this red?"

"You don't want to know."

"Oh, but I do."

"It was zebra. I know it sounds horrid, but I made it work."

"I'll bet you did."

"I had some African art on the wall. It was pretty fabulous in here."

"Sounds like it."

"Don't try to kiss me again, Nicky."

"Why, because we white people have no lips?"

"Not funny. You just can't. Okay?"

"I won't."

"And we shouldn't go out together."

"I just want to get you out of the house. That's it. I promise. Consider me terribly embarrassed now."

"I don't do white boys."

"So I gathered."

"You have a girlfriend."

"You have a boyfriend. He sucks, obviously."

"Why do you say that?"

Now he looks at me. He has the nerve to look like he's annoyed with Miles. "Why isn't he here for you?"

"He's our youth pastor. He's still tethered to my father's pocket and approval."

"Sounds like you need to consider getting another boyfriend."

"I just did."

A smile creeps across his lips. He cocks his head to one side and looks at me with those sapphire eyes, one eyebrow raised.

He caught me while I was down. I need to put a stop to this little flirtation before it goes any further. "See what I mean, I'm not thinking straight. You start massaging my hair, and I lose my mind. I need to stay clear of fine white boys with magic hands until I get right."

"So, how 'bout we have Ethiopian food, Queen of Sheba? Is that African enough for you? There's a great place downtown. The Blue Nile. In fact there's one downtown Ann Arbor *and* downtown Detroit. You can take your pick, urban girl."

"I'm not going out with you."

"Plain ol' American soul food it is, then. But you'll have to pick the place. Hey, why do black people say *chitlins* instead of *chitterlings?*"

"You're a mess, Nicky."

"But Jesus loves me. You'll know that when you read Richard's book, even though you're not a whore." He looks me up and down with a mock critical eye. "Maybe you're a rascal."

When he's got me grinning again, he takes my hand. Electricity, no, *fire* surges between us, and he doesn't even hide that he feels it too. We stare at each other, his eyes full of mischief. He pulls me off the cabinet.

"You're definitely a rascal. Get dressed, Dreamy. There's an abundant life out there to be had, even if we are poor in spirit."

"Did you hear what I said? I'm not going out with you."

"I heard *everything* you said. I'll be sleeping in the shape of a cross for the next week because of it."

"Sleeping in the shape of a cross?"

"It's like your shower curtains. You don't wanna know."

"But I told you about my shower curtains."

"Which means you're terribly indiscreet. How can I trust you with my crosses?"

I get myself dressed, thinking I do want to know about him sleeping in the shape of a cross. I want to know more about Nicky Parker than I'd like to admit, no matter how indiscreet the details.

CHAPTER TEN

NICKY

Zora nixes the idea of both Ethiopian and soul food. In fact, she refuses to let me buy her anything else, which is good, because I already went way over budget anyway.

I'm determined to feed her, though. She leaves me no choice. I take her to Oasis of Love. The restaurant Billie helped found in downtown Ypsilanti.

Predictably, she's never been here.

"What's this place? Didn't I tell you I don't want you buying me anything else?"

"This is different. It's really a charity. The meal is going to be seventy-five percent off because I get a discount for volunteering, and you get a discount for being poor and destitute. We'll eat like royalty for, like, four bucks."

She laughs, the sound of it my own oasis. She waters all my dry, thirsty places.

"It looks like a restaurant. Not a charity."

"That's the whole idea."

She looks around at all the southwestern colors. Soothing oranges, beiges, pinks with a little aquamarine blue. I watch the artist in her take delight in the desert theme. The Mexican textiles.

I watch the revolutionary in her delight in the multicolored faces sitting at the table. I let the poor-in-spirit Zora love the obvious brokenness of some of the people sharing crowded tables. Here, they can eat out in an upscale restaurant they'd never be able to afford for a little of nothing. It's a way to give people back their dignity. Often kids come here who have it tough at home or who have no home. It's a safe place. A few whispers to Bill, the manager, and you don't even have to pay the little of nothing if you don't have it. You'll wash a few dishes. Or sweep the floor. Bill thinks in the end people feel better about themselves if they contribute in some way. But he doesn't turn anybody away because they don't have money to eat.

While Zora takes in the vibe, I tease her.

"Order whatever you want, baby. Money is no object."

She laughs. "How many times have you been able to say that on a date?"

"Never." I reach across the table and take her hand. "Is this a date?"

"Not if you've got a girlfriend. Remember her?"

I remember all right. As does Zora, and now that Pandora's box is open, God help the both of us.

"Tell me about her. What's her name?"

"Rebecca."

"Rebecca what?"

"Rebecca Taylor. What's your boyfriend's name?"

"Miles."

"Miles what?"

"Miles Zekora."

I peruse the menu, but I'm a writer. I do things with words. I can't help but put her name with his. "If you marry him your name will be Zora Zekora."

"Shut up."

"That sounds like a character in *The Lion King*." And then I crack up. I end up laughing so hard that she starts laughing too. She kicks me underneath the table.

"You know you can't stay with him. Not just because he's a jerk. You won't be able to live with that name, Dreamy. What does the Lion King do?"

"Stop calling him that. When he's not youth pastoring, he's an engineer."

"He makes good money?"

"Yes."

"Very good money?"

"Very good."

"He's an even bigger jerk than I thought. How can he let you go through this and not totally take care of you? What a fool."

"Let's talk about you, Nicky. What do you do?"

"Put snacks in vending machines. And now I must go kill myself."

"Stop it. There's nothing wrong with that. Didn't you go to college?"

I laugh. "Yeah. I did go to college. Berkeley! That's what makes me an even bigger loser. Maybe God can kill me right now, and I won't have to commit a sin by committing suicide."

"I don't have a job at all, Nicky. And before that I did 'clip art and stock photo arrangement' for my daddy. Now that's a loser. Tell me, what does Rebecca look like, besides blonde and stacked?"

She totally sees how shallow I am. "That's it."

"Is she tall?"

"No. Not like you are. You can almost look me in the eye. How tall are you anyway?"

"I'm five-ten. So she's short and submissive. Cooks well. She's a Republican. Wants the suburban house. The two-point-five kids.

The minivan. And to be a pastor's wife. She loves Kay Arthur Bible studies."

"Hey, it's Beth Moore Bible studies. Get it right."

"I stand corrected."

"You're kinda spooky."

She shakes her pretty head. "You know, I'm really disappointed. Couldn't you surprise me just a little?"

Her words cut into me. In her little description, she's just told me what my life with Rebecca is going to be, and both of us are bored to death with it already. "I'm disappointed too."

I look down at my menu, almost too depressed to order now. I don't even want to think about what must be going on in Zora's mind. I can only imagine how shallow I sound. How hollow and dead.

Unfortunately, Zora has no respect for the dead.

"How often do you bring Rebecca here?"

"I don't. I tend to keep my Bible study people separate from my True Believer Gospel Tabernacle people."

She cocks her head. "Why would you do that?"

"I dunno. I need Linda, Richard, and Billie to be something else. Something my dad and the Tabernacle people can't be."

"I know precisely what you mean. Only I don't have people like that. Except Linda. And now you."

I like the way "And now you" sounds.

We order our food. She gets some chicken dish, and I have the same. But that Pandora's box of Rebecca and the Lion King she opened brings discomfort and tension with it. We both pick at our food.

An hour ago, I was so close to her I had my hands in her hair. I almost kissed her. Would have if she hadn't stopped me. Now there may as well be a million miles between us. Me and my milk-toast life-to-be. What did it have to do with her? And what was I thinking saying her name would sound like a character in *The Lion King*? I didn't mean that to sound racist, but she probably thought it was. Maybe she was just too tired to challenge me on it.

I wish I knew what to say to her. I'd rather have her razzing me than this awful silence between us. But she surprises me and speaks.

"What is it, Nicky?"

"What's what?"

"That thing you want that nobody gets?"

I know exactly what she means, but the fact that she asks unnerves me.

"What are you talking about, Dreamy?"

"You want to do something, but nobody in your life honors it. What is it?"

"How do you know I want something like that?"

"I know things. It's like you said, I'm spooky."

"I want to write."

"Are you a writer, Nicky?"

I hesitate.

"Are you?" she insists.

"Yes."

"What kind of things do you write?"

"All kinds of things. Novels. Poems. Essays. Psalms. I just write."

She smiles at me. And there is more generosity in that smile than in all the meals Oasis serves in a year. She gives me a single word blessing. The same one God uses again and again in the beginning of Genesis.

"Good."

I smile back at her. "Good."

Then the grief I can hardly contain begins to spill out of my mouth in too many words.

"Or I *should* be writing those things, but I don't. I don't write anything anymore. I'm blocked. I haven't written anything for at least six months, and that, a little villanelle, sucked. I haven't tried anything serious in two years, Zora. I just think about writing and miss writing and buy writing books and *Writer's Digest* and wonder why I spent all that money to go to Berkeley when I knew I wouldn't have begun to get what I needed without an MFA, and anyway I'm going to be Nicholas Parker Senior only with a junior behind my name. I don't even believe in Nicholas Parker. And why should I? He never believed in me."

I just disclosed *way* too much. I laugh to shake off the embarrassment I feel. "Sorry. I don't seem to know who I am anymore."

"Same here." Her gaze goes to her hands, and then back to me, but her eyes seem softer somehow. I find a gentleness in them that moves me. She cradles her chin in the palm of one hand, while her elbow rest on the table. She sighs, looking like a little girl. "Sunday morning I walked out in the middle of my father's sermon. Suddenly it just became unbearable, and I left."

"You left?!"

"Yeah. Awful isn't it?"

I can't believe how in sync we are. How in the freakin' world?! "You left this past Sunday, in the middle of your dad's sermon?"

"I did."

"You said it suddenly became unbearable?"

"Yeah. I couldn't stand it, Nicky. Not for another minute."

I put my elbows on the table. I lean so close to the table I almost knock my water over. "Why not?"

"I don't know now. I got sick of it. Sick of me. I feel like I don't know anything now."

"I'm so with you. You have no idea."

This time she reaches across the table and takes my hand, and I've rarely felt so needy. She holds it for a long time.

God, is it possible that somebody in this world can understand me?

"Miles isn't going to like this Zora Zekora."

"Neither is Rebecca of Sunnybrook Farm."

But she keeps holding anyway. Then she gets an idea. She lets me go, which I don't like, and she stands up.

"Where you going?"

"Just wait."

She glides away in her white dress and I can't take my eyes off her. I feel guilty. I don't feel the things I feel with Zora when I'm around Rebecca. Oh, I feel some pleasure watching Rebecca walk to and away from me. But Rebecca doesn't tick me off. She doesn't mystify me. She doesn't make me wildly happy or bring me to the brink of tears all in the space of a few minutes. Rebecca doesn't peer effortlessly into my soul. And when she takes my hand in hers, I don't feel like I'd want to go on a little bit longer just because of it.

Zora comes back with a paper placemat and a pencil in her hand.

"What are you doing? You're not going to make me write you something are you?"

"Not yet, but you should prepare yourself. I'm demanding."

"I can see that."

"I'm going to sketch you."

"Oh really?"

"Really. Now just get comfortable." She sits down and right away gets going.

"Do I have to stop talking?"

"No, I'm actually good. But you can't look down at it. I want your eyes looking somewhere else."

"Can *you* keep talking?"

"I'm talking aren't I?"

"So can I bombard you with questions?"

"Ask away."

I ask her silly things like what her favorite color was in the first grade. Who her first crush was.

She asks me to tell her about my first kiss.

"That's off limits. Tell me about yours."

"Off limits."

"Fair enough."

She asks me about the things I wrote about in California. I end up yakking about mountains and what it's like to stand at the ocean and not see an end to the water on the horizon. I tell her about sand dollars and my hair turning blonder, and she smiles at me when I say that. Then I tell her about Lake Superior when we used to go away for the summer. Back when I was innocent.

It takes her a long time to sketch my portrait, but I have a lot of

Lake Superior stories to fill up the time. Finally she's finished, but she doesn't hold it out to me.

I reach for it.

"No," she says.

"Let me see it."

"I can't."

"Why not? You made me sit here boring you to death for what, a half hour? And now you won't let me see?"

"Nicky, I haven't worked in a long time, either. It's been a year for me."

"I won't judge it. I promise. I just want to see it."

She gazes at me with her doe eyes, and I can tell I'm going to have to pry it out of her grip. I try to do so with kind words.

"I'll bet it's lovely. I'll bet it's earthy and wild, like you."

"You're the one who's wild."

"Nah. I'm as tame as they come. I'll bet it's as phenomenal as the woman who sketched it. Do you know that poem by Maya Angelou, *Phenomenal Woman*?"

She laughs. "Do *you* know it, white boy?"

"I don't have it memorized, but I read it in college. You'd be surprised at the subversive literature I've read just to tick my father off."

"I guess I would be. What about *Phenomenal Woman*?"

"You gotta know that's what you are. So, give up the sketch, Dreamy."

And she does. It's a striking likeness of me, but it's not me now. I mean, it's me, but it's a different me. She finds the me who's twelve years old. Nicky full of innocence and freedom. Nicky with Lake Superior sand between my toes, and the freshest lake water in this whole freakin' country glistening on my skin. Oh, she doesn't sketch all of that. Just my face. My hair in need of a hair cut. This cocky "It's all here; everything I need is in me" expression on my face. She finds everything pristine and good in me, and it's right there in my eyes, staring back at me. I haven't seen that Nicky in so long, tears come to my eyes.

I shove the sketch back at her. "Doesn't look like me."

Her mouth opens, but she doesn't say anything.

"Let's go."

"Nicky, are you o—"

"I said let's go."

She stands up, and I'm surprised she doesn't protest. I want her to protest so we can fight, but she doesn't. She just goes along.

We get into my truck, and neither of us breaches the silence stretched between us. I want to tell her I'm sorry, but she's exposed my soft center, and I can't stand it. I'm glad I didn't take her far from home. Only fifteen minutes of discomfort before we say good-bye.

I pull up to her apartment, and she says, "I'll let myself out."

"That's not necessary. Wouldn't want you to go around saying white boys don't open the door for you."

She doesn't take the bait. I open the door for her, and she steps out, but I can tell I've hurt her feelings, and not just with that comment. But I don't know how to take it back.

I walk with her to her apartment door, and she has to buzz several apartments before someone buzzes her in, which reminds me …

"How are you going to get into the apartment?"

"I'll ask the super to let me in."

"Will they charge you?"

"Probably, but I can probably get them to give me another key. For a price, of course."

"Do you need some money?"

"I'm not going to take anything else from you, Nicky. Thanks for everything, but this is it for us."

I just nod. I think she's right.

Then the craziest thing happens. Something literally falls out of the sky. An earring. And it lands at her feet.

We both look up. I start laughing because it's so freakin' weird.

"Maybe it fell from somebody's balcony," she says.

I pick it up. A circle of gold. Absolutely perfect. Smaller than the silver pair Zora is wearing. Thicker in width. Beautiful. I decide to give her a final offering. Why not? It literally fell at her feet anyway. "For you, the dreamy rascal."

She refuses it. "No, thank you. I think you've given me quite enough. Besides. What am I supposed to do with one earring?"

I don't know, but I've got the weirdest feeling she's supposed to do something with it. It feels surreal and absurd, but what she says next sobers me. "I don't want to see you again."

"Okay."

"Bye, Nicky."

"Bye, Zora."

I thought that was my last offering to her, but when I get home, I'm thinking in poetry. Can't write my name most days but she pulls a poem out of me in a single afternoon. I even get enough courage to scrawl it down on a piece of paper. Maybe I'll mail it to her.

An earring falls,
From lowly Jesus' ear.
we find this treasure
full of holy whispers.
Listen.
Love is whispering secrets
in this
sad and silly
poem.

ZORA

I should have taken the earring, just to feel him put it in my hand. Let his magic fingers graze my palm. That would have meant our time together wouldn't have ended like it did, and I would have had something of him to keep. A simple touch. His fingers brushing mine. Now I feel stupid because I'm longing for him, and I don't have the earring, or the memory of his touch—anything, much less the drawing.

What a fool I've been. I let that white boy get to me. He played me the whole time. I thought his friend had the jungle fever, but it was him. Have a little fun with the natives. I almost let him kiss me. My first kiss would have been from a white boy who wanted to see what it's like to take a walk on the wild side.

I thought about what he said, Zora Zekora sounds like a *Lion King* character. Never mind it's true. What gives him the right to say something so racist?

I didn't feel like it was racist when he said it. I just thought it was funny then. And now, I don't know. That's why I stick to my own kind. White people have a way of being racist in ways they don't even realize. And I have a way of knowing it. Sorry, Dr. King. Sorry, Rosa Parks. Integration didn't do what you thought it would. There's a lot to be said about voluntary segregation.

I wander inside of my building, feeling hurt as thick and palpable as fog hovering around me.

Don't you cry, girl. What's so disappointing? Once again you've been proven right? That's why you stay away from them. It's simpler that way. You don't have to explain anything. Your hair, for instance. Why you use a flat iron to straighten your hair. Why your hair products are different. Why you hate it when white people say *nappy*. Let them try being four hundred years in a strange land without the right kind of comb. Before a Madame C. J. Walker came along to tell us how to look more like them. Let's see what they'd look like if we took their stuff.

Man. I gotta stop thinking like this.

The supervisor isn't in the maintenance office. He isn't in the rental office. Where the heck is he? Of course it's Friday evening; people disappear like the Rapture took place. I miss the convenience of my cell phone.

My mind goes right back to my blacks-only tirade, but I know racism is not what's bothering me at all. I felt like we were beginning to enjoy each other. Every race thing I threw at him, he took. I went out of my way to call him "white boy," and he dealt with it just fine. But he takes one look at my work and *blam*—a wall goes up. And it's worse than with Miles. At least Miles thought my work was *nice*. Not good obviously, but nice enough to make a hobbyist out of me.

I think again about that earring Nicky held out to me. A perfect circle, and he offered it to me. Sometimes I wonder if signs and wonders don't follow us. Not big miraculous ones, but little ordinary wonders, if we only have eyes to see them. A golden circle falls from the sky at the end of a miserable day. Why did he offer it to me, even after what happened? Did he think it was as beautiful as I did?

Why did it fall at that moment? What could it mean?

Maybe it's some sign for us to hang on to the good from the day. There was some good. There was him playing in my hair.

Was that good? He called me Dreamy. Or was that just a line? I don't know.

I finally go back to my apartment. All I can do is wait for MacKenzie. I sit with my back against the door until I fall asleep.

It's Linda and Billie from Bible study who wake me up instead of Mac.

I rub the sleep from my eyes.

"Linda? Billie?"

Linda greets me with her smile, her red hair all wild over her head. Billie winks at me. "Hey, baby." They've come bearing their own gifts. Bags and bags of them.

I clear my throat, but I still end up croaking out, "What time is it?"

Billie glances at her watch. "It's almost ten. Sorry it took us so long. We had to kick Nicky's butt."

I smile, though I try hard not to. "Why did you have to kick his butt?"

"He told us how the day went. Did he really try to kiss you?"

"He didn't do it."

Linda, the gentle, looks annoyed. "All I asked him to do was bring you some clothes."

"You sent, Nicky. That's all I gotta say," Billie quips.

She helps me up. "We would have come ourselves. Some things are woman to woman, but Linda and I couldn't get away, and we didn't want to send someone you didn't know at all."

"He was really sweet sometimes."

"Oh, I'll bet he was. You couldn't get inside?"

"No. I didn't see the super, and my roommate must not have come in."

"Let me have a look." Billie steps over to my door and digs through her massive leather hobo bag. She finally exhumes a sharp instrument of dubious origin and proceeds to successfully pick my lock.

The whole thing cracks me up. "Billie, you got skills."

"You don't want to know, baby."

We take the bags into my apartment. Billie whistles. "He really cleaned the joint out, didn't he?"

"He let my roommate Mac keep her stuff. It was packed up. She's going to design school tomorrow. Maybe that was a no-brainer for him."

Billie shakes her head. "What a gentleman."

Linda shoots a look at her.

She shrugs. "Sorry." She doesn't mean it. "So, was he awful?"

"My daddy?"

Billie laughs. "Sorry, baby. My transitions can be rocky. No, was Nicky awful?"

"Yes."

"I'll bet he was."

"And sometimes, he wasn't."

She seemed to understand. "I'll bet he wasn't." Billie looks at me. I don't know what she's been though with her wild tattoos and crazy platinum rainbow-tipped dreads, but she looks like she knows a few things.

"He's young," she says. "There are a lot of things I can say about Nicky Parker, but I can tell you this: he's a doll, baby. He really doesn't mean any harm. That's why we opened up a can on him."

Linda adds, "That's enough about Nicky. I promise you that won't happen again. Zora, we were honored that you came to join us Wednesday. We'd like for you to come back. We'll keep Nicky in line."

Oh, no. They've put me on the spot.

"I appreciate all that you've done for me, Linda, but I wasn't planning on coming back."

"Why not? It seemed like the Lord really met you there."

Billie starts taking stuff out of the bags. They've got all kinds of food and necessities for me. A few gift certificates from Meijer. I can't believe their generosity.

"God did meet me, Linda, I just don't know if your Bible study is right for me."

"Why not?"

I don't want to tell them it's because I'm the only black person, because honestly, did that make a difference? Did God withhold His blessings from me because four white people were in the room with me? Not at all.

Billie takes my hand in hers. "Tell us how you're feeling, Zora. We can take it."

I didn't know if I could take saying it. "You've been very kind to me. I know you don't know me from Adam, and you've brought me necessities and groceries."

"This isn't all," Billie says. "I run a house of hospitality for home-less women. I don't have new clothes, but we've got some really nice used clothes. You're welcome to come by and get whatever you need."

"Nicky got me a few things for now. I don't feel right about asking for anything else."

"You didn't ask, baby. You shouldn't have to."

I can hardly find my voice because I want to cry so much. "Thank you."

"Come back. Nicky just has a crush you. He's a little stupid, but it'll pass."

"I don't know."

Linda takes my other hand. "You need some friends, and despite his failures today, he tried to be that, too."

"We were having a great day, and then he just shut down."

"He didn't tell us that," Linda says.

"And that's telling," Billie says. "Maybe you touched a nerve. I don't know, baby. I just know none of us are finished with you. At least we don't want to be. I know it looks like you don't know who to trust right now, but let the fruit tell you what kind of tree you got."

I thought about what she and Linda said. Daddy has a church of thousands of members, but not one has come to help me, not even Miles. I can't even say they probably don't know, because news spreads like wildfire at LLCC. And here I am flanked by two crazy white women. Didn't the Scriptures say "By their fruit you shall know them"? Just like Billie said?

"Maybe I'll come back. I don't know how the rest of the week is going to go."

They give me a group hug and let me go.

"You won't regret it. I promise you," Billie says.

But I had regrets already, the main one being a six-foot-two rascal who calls me Dreamy.

ONE O'CLOCK IN the morning, and MacKenzie's finally coming through the door, exhausted and content in that way people look when they've put their old life right in the best way they know how, and they're about to move on to the new one.

I stand up to greet her.

Mac scans the room. She opens her mouth, but no sound comes out. She walks from room to room like she's in a daze. Finally, a wide grin spreads across her face. She gathers me in a hug.

"You're going with me!"

Oh, God. I know she didn't mean to break my heart just now, but she did. Lord, Lord, Lord. I'm not going with her.

"I'm not going anywhere."

That snake, once a little garter snake in this garden of my heart, coiled, ready to strike, has grown now. A wily snake. I pull away from her embrace. I repeat myself just so we're both clear. "You're the one going off to Parsons to be fabulous. I'm staying here."

Concern and confusion war on her face. "What happened here, Zora, where's our stuff?"

The serpent in me hisses. *Our* stuff?

"Unfortunately, it's not *our* stuff. Daddy decided it's *his* stuff, and he took it."

"Zora, I told you to call him!"

"And say what? I'm sorry I want my own life?"

"Yes. If that's what it took. What's wrong with 'I'm sorry'? People say it all the time."

"It's just stuff. He didn't take anything I can't get back."

"Without yo' Daddy you can't afford that stuff. Girl, you had it goin' on. And you want to beef with him now? Call him and tell him you sorry and ask him for yo' Cheryl Riley hookup back."

"I don't want to do that, Mac. I just want to be who I am."

She takes my hand. "Z." Squeezes it. "You listen to me, girl. We girls. We go back a long way. I don't have to tell you that. You look out for me, and I look out for you. I know you don't always agree with the choices I make, but princess, I don't always agree with you."

I nod my head. I'm listening. Or I'm trying to.

"Who you are is a spoiled brat, Zora. Most of the time, you ain't thinking about nobody but yo'self, and right now, you ain't even doin' a good job with that."

Is this what my best friend thinks of me? The person who I've been helping make her dream—my own dream—come true? She thinks I'm selfish?

"I don't think that's fair of you to say, MacKenzie."

She releases my hand. "I know what you thinkin'. You thinkin' of how you let me live here. How you helped me with school. How you gave me your cast-off clothes when we was little. But I'm thinking about how small your life is, Zora. How you haven't really had to reach out and get your hands dirty. Partly because your parents never encouraged that, but the other part was because, why bother when everything is yours already? You haven't had to serve anybody. Not really, sweetie."

"I've always been your friend, Mac."

"You have. The best way you knew how. But it ain't perfect, Z. You are not the perfect friend. You got a lot to learn about being a friend. And I'm telling you this because I *am* your friend. I've lived with nothing most of my life. It ain't good. It forces you to make choices you wish you didn't have to make. If I had something I'd have a preschooler right now. You have something. Hold on to it."

"You can't use your mama making you have an abortion as an excuse for all the bad things in your life, Mac."

"And you can't hide behind yo' daddy because you afraid to grow up. Paint if you want to. You don't have to give up everything in yo' life. You had a closet full of paint supplies. What's really the problem here?"

"I'm not afraid to grow up."

"Keep telling yourself that, Zora."

"Mac, I know you're mad, but don't say something you'll regret."

"What I regret is not saying this to you a long time ago. I'm not *The Bishop*'s daughter. I didn't have nobody quoting Scriptures over me since before I took my first breath, but I know enough about the Bible to know there's something in there about the wounds of a friend being better than the kisses of an enemy. I'm gonna say this one more time, Zora. Put things right with your father."

Put things right with your father. Isn't that what Nicky said?

"But Mac. I've been praying that Jesus would teach me what it is to be poor."

She starts laughing. She collapses onto the floor she laughs so hard, and she wipes tears from her eyes. "Zora. Honey, you didn't have to pray for that. I been telling you all my life what it's like to be poor. I guess you wasn't listening."

"I thought I was listening."

"I don't think so, girlfriend. Look. I'll stay. I'll help you get this together."

"No. You can't stay."

"*The Bishop* is even more stubborn than you, Z. I can't leave you in this apartment with nothing. You won't last the week."

"Jesus is going to teach me how to be poor."

"Oh, Lord, there goes my scholarship."

"Mac, you aren't giving up your scholarship."

"Maybe I can get another one."

"You can't."

"What do you know about poor, Zora?"

"Nothing. But I know Jesus. At least a little bit. Can you trust me with Him?"

I sit down on the floor with her. I don't feel so full of self-righteous fury anymore. I know with all my heart that MacKenzie just offered me her widow's mite. I think about all those dreams. All those hours we spent when other girls played Barbie, and we used reams of paper drawing all our dreams. She would have given that up until I felt ready to make a stupid phone call.

I so don't deserve her.

This time I go to her for the hug, and she doesn't withdraw her love like my father withdrew his possessions. She takes me into her big bosom like she's the mother she didn't get a chance to be. In this, she lets me be a little girl.

"I'm so sorry for not seeing how hard things really were for you."

"Girl. How were you really gon' see that? Shoot. I ain't sure I wanted you to see it all. Not really."

She rocks me until that snake inside falls asleep.

"What am I going to do without you, Mac?"

"I'm always gon' be your girl. You remember that. You promise me you gon' remember that I'm always here for you. We girls. A'ight?"

"A'ight."

We hug for a good, long time.

CHAPTER TWELVE

NICKY

She keeps calling me. I'm not supposed to resent it when my girlfriend calls and wants to get together, but I do. It's the freakin' call I made to her from the mall. She's expecting a gift. Which I have for her. And now I have to give it to her.

What am I talking about? She's my girlfriend. She calls me. I'm supposed to call her. That's a problem, because most days I don't want to call her. And man, she's hanging in there with me. That stupid necklace I bought is probably the most hope she's had for us in weeks.

I finally decide to do something decent for a change and go to her house for dinner.

I get to her house Saturday night. It's a modest, black-and-white A-frame near Eastern Michigan University. Her father is disabled. He got hurt on the job years ago and ended up losing a leg. Her mother teaches at one of the elementary schools. Rebecca's family is just under middle class, so I'd be a real upgrade. Well, not me personally. The Parkers would be.

My dad thinks she's great. She's kind. Earnest. Virtuous. I mean, she really is one of those Proverbs 31 types. Very pretty. You can totally see her on the cover of *Today's Christian Woman*. She's a photo op waiting to happen.

Frankly, I thought she was cute and had a nice rack. I'd spent a long time being alone, and I wanted a warm body to pass the time with. Not that I've felt her warm body.

Don't get me wrong. It's not that I don't want to feel Rebecca's warm body, but I came home to put things right. As it was, Brooke Bennett broke my heart. I didn't need to be distracted by sex. And upon the prodigal's return, a lot of the handmaidens of the Lord I'd slept with before had fond memories of our trysts, and after a few painful slips—broken heart and all—I settled uncomfortably into celibacy. I've learned to steer clear of women. If it means steering clear of feeling, so be it. I've even learned to compartmentalize body parts for pleasure viewing.

Pete had me right. We've discussed many a fine rear end in the past three years. Many a fine pair of twin fawns. That's a good way to avoid having to love. Including Rebecca. But even if I didn't love her, I certainly wasn't going to let sexual desire blindside me. It was my way of staying safe, technically pure.

Her mother answers the door, grinning at me. Maggie Taylor is a robust, mildly garish middle-aged woman living vicariously through Rebecca, her only daughter. I'm certain that every time she looks at me she sizes me up for the tuxedo I'll wear when I take her Rebecca down the aisle to wedded bliss.

Oh, God, help me.

"Hiya, Nick," she says. She kisses me on the cheek and spots the Eddie Bauer box. "Oh, my. Now what's that you've got in your hand? Is that for my little girl?"

"Hello, Mrs. Taylor." I step into the house and glance at her husband. "Mr. Taylor."

He gives me a curt nod. The man hates me. He would shoot me dead on the spot if he could. I know he has a gun. He can't chase me down, but he can shoot. All the men at my church hunt. They love guns. They are the scariest bunch of NRA-lovin', Charleton-Heston-venerating … don't make me think about it.

No wonder Zora hates me. She probably thinks I'm just like them.

Don't think about Zora.

I hold the box up. "I have a little something for Rebecca." Thank God it's bigger than a ring box. But they can tell it's jewelry. Mrs. Taylor will be counting the days to our engagement now.

Rebecca comes to the door. "Hi, Nicholas."

"Hi, Rebecca."

Why doesn't my girlfriend call me Nicky? Why don't I call her Becky or something?

I hand her the box.

"For me?" she says, grinning.

I grin back to keep something sarcastic from coming out of my mouth. She really is very pretty. A really nice girl.

I sniff the air. "Something smells nice. What did you cook?"

"I made your favorite. Pot roast."

I smile. She takes my hand and drags me into the kitchen so we can be alone. Her mother almost cheers; I can just tell. Meanwhile, her father plans my death.

What makes her think pot roast is my favorite food? Did my mother tell her that? My father? I grew up eating pot roast. All the time. I was in pot-roast hell. When I was in California, I tried to eat everything imaginable other than pot roast.

"Thanks, Rebecca."

But it does smell good. She actually makes a fine pot roast. What's one more when I've had millions anyway?

She stands by the sink, and I'm next to her. She opens the box, and unlike Zora, Rebecca doesn't cry. I chuckle thinking of those tearful brown doe eyes, and her asking, "Do you think I'm a ho?"

I bought Rebecca a fake pearl necklace. They didn't have the real deal at Eddie Bauer. They only had costume jewelry. Not that I would have bought her real pearls anyway.

"Nicholas, it's beautiful." She looks up at me with pale blue eyes, and she's so happy, I feel horrible. It isn't beautiful. I paid twenty bucks for it, and I didn't even want to. I spent a lot more on Zora, and took more time and thought doing it. I would have spent even more on Zora if I could have.

"I love it," she says. And what's worse, she does.

I take her hands. It occurs to me that I rarely even hold her hands. "Rebecca?"

"Yes, Nicholas?" Her eyes are shining. She's full of expectation, and I don't want to disappoint her.

"Do you really want to be with me?"

"I do."

"Why?"

"I just care for you. I pray for you all the time."

"You don't really know me."

"We can get to know each other."

"We've been dating six months, Rebecca."

"You've been a gentleman."

"I've been a coward."

"It's okay."

I could end it right now. I could tell her that she's one of the nicest people I've ever met, and that she makes a mean pot roast. I could

tell her she's gorgeous, and she has a nice rack, but I don't feel anything for her. I think about my father. And my mother. And how
disappointed they'd be. And I think about Dreamy, who can see right
inside of me. Who asked me what my thing was that nobody got, the
first time we were alone together.

You've got some sense of humor, God.

I do something I've never done. I lean down, and I kiss Rebecca.

Her lips are soft and welcoming, even though I surprised her. I
shouldn't, but I part her lips with my tongue and deepen the kiss, and
she allows me. We stand in her kitchen, kissing over pot roast, and I
pray that I feel something other than my mouth on hers, but I don't.
I felt more just wondering if I should kiss Zora.

I let her go. She's so freakin' happy she squeezes me.

"I love you, Nicholas," she says.

And I lie. "I love you, too, Rebecca."

She holds my hand. "Dinner's almost ready."

"Rebecca, I want to be a writer."

She looks up at me like she's got this all figured out. "Well, I know
you went to school for that. And I know your father thinks it's nonsense, but personally, I don't think there's any reason for you not to
write."

For a moment, I feel hopeful. "Really?"

"Of course. You can be just like Max Lucado: a writer *and* a
pastor."

"Like Max Lucado. Right."

She smiles at me. Gives me a peck on the lips.

I feel sick to my stomach. "I'm going to go in the living room and
sit with your dad."

"Okay, honey bunny."

She just called me honey bunny. Honest to God, I hope that crazy man blows my head off.

ZORA

I'm lying in the middle of what Nicky called the screaming blue abyss with my head on the box he gave me. It's been my pillow all night. Just before dawn MacKenzie crept into the room and kissed me on the forehead. I pretended to be asleep. I couldn't bear to say good-bye to her.

God, I couldn't bear it.

Maybe I am selfish. Okay, I am. I should have helped her load the few boxes she had left into her car, but I couldn't. I'm too sad. I was afraid I might beg her to stay with me because I'm still not ready to make that call, and I don't even know why.

I want my friend. I don't have another one.

Jesus, have mercy on me. This is the worst time of my life, and as much as I've been trying to forge a solidarity with the poor, I have no idea how to really do that. What's going to happen to me? I have no idea how I'm supposed to grow up, or how I'm supposed to deal with my father.

I just lay here with my head on a box, while my thoughts scream and wail at me.

Sometime after noon, I hear a knock at the door. It's not MacKenzie because she's gone, and—if she's smart, and she is—she's not coming back.

It's Miles. Finally.

I open the door. "Who buzzed you up?"

"I came in with someone else." He gathers me in a hug. It feels good to be in his arms, or at least in somebody's arms. "How are you, baby?"

"Take a wild guess, Miles." I step out of his embrace.

How are you, baby? What kind of dumb question was that? He knows MacKenzie went off to *art school,* and all my stuff is gone.

He whistles. "You really pissed The Bishop off."

"Thanks for your insight."

"Don't be sarcastic. It doesn't suit a woman of God."

"Pardon me, Bishop Junior."

"Zora, I came by here to see if you're okay. I didn't come for your attitude."

Man. He really *is* Bishop Junior.

"Does it look like I'm okay, Miles? And why weren't you here yesterday to see if I was okay?"

In fact, why are his hands empty today?

"I thought I'd give you some time to cool off."

"I'm not the one so angry that I stripped somebody of all their stuff."

"He was making a point. One I think you needed to be reminded of."

"I don't really think I need any reminders, seeing as all my stuff is gone, but just to be nostalgic, tell me, what point is that, Miles?"

"Zora, you seem to be having a problem with authority."

I stare at him. We're alone. There's no audience for him to impress. Daddy isn't around. So now I'm really scared, because this means he's bought into, and actually believes, Daddy's hype.

"What authority are you speaking of, Miles?"

"Zora, you've been in church all your life. It's just like with church. When you're a member of a church, there's a headship. Christ is the head of the church, and in our case, Bishop is the head of Light of Life. In the home, Christ is the head of the husband, and the husband is the head of the wife and the children. Zora, you are an unmarried woman. Right now, you are under the protective covering of your father."

"I don't even live with my father, as you can see."

"That's not his choice. And I don't think it makes a difference."

He takes my hand. Says something he's never said to me before. "I love you, Zora. I know this isn't the best time to talk about this, but you know I want to make you my wife one day, and if you agree, when we get married, you'll come under my covering."

He slips his arms around my waist. I'm completely horrified.

"Baby, you need to know your place. I don't mean to sound chauvinistic, but it's your God-given place. There's nothing wrong with being where God wants you to be. I'm a man of God. Your father taught me to be a man of God. You're under his authority, and you need to submit to him. You had no business walking out on him like you did, and I support what he's doing. Out of love, baby. Rebellion is as the sin of witchcraft. You need to call your father and apologize."

Rebellion? I think Nicky missed one! Apparently I'm not just a rascal! I'm a rebel, too. I'm definitely going to have to read Richard's book.

I start screaming at Miles. "Apologize for *what?*"

"I think you need to calm down, baby."

I try. God knows I do. "Will. You. Just. Tell. Me. What. I've. Done. That's. So. *Wrong?*"

"You disrespected the man who supports you."

"Define support. In fact, define *disrespect.*"

"He gave you a job. Is lavish with gifts. Money. Anything you need. And all he asked you to do is watch your tone with him."

"He doesn't give me *anything* I need. Because I *needed* to go to Parsons, not Spelman. I *needed* to do some meaningful work without him hovering over me and telling me that what I do, *anybody* with some clip art and a PC can do. And you know what the real problem is, Miles? He's right."

"I see what this is about. You're upset because Mac went to the school you wanted to go to. You're having a tantrum."

"This is about so much more than that. And if I'm having a tantrum, what is he having?"

Miles turns away. Looks back at me. "Zora. Don't do this. You have it so good. Don't you see what we can be together? Where is your vision, baby?"

"I want to paint."

"You paint, Zora."

"I want it to be my life's work."

"You're not meant to be a painter, baby."

"I am, Miles."

"You're not that good at it, baby."

I feel like he's just slapped me across the face. I can't even form a reply.

Miles doesn't even notice my jaw drop; he just keeps talking. "And here's another thing for you to think about: if you were really a painter, nothing—including me or your daddy—would stop you from painting. What you are is scared of growing up. You're having growing pains, baby. You weren't groomed to be a painter. You were made to be a pastor's wife—just like that prophet who came to our church told you that time. He was right, baby. I knew it. You'll be just like your mother: beautiful, classy, godly, magnificent. We're going to be everything I wished—that my poor mother wished—I could be when I was a little boy. You should have seen her, Zora. Every day, without fail, that woman prayed over me. She confessed God's word over me. I'm just like you, Zora, the hope of my parents, only without the advantages you had. But that never stopped my mother from having faith. She believed that I had a call of God on my life, and now, I'm going to see the fruits of all those prayers. I'm so close. Your father wants me to be his son-in-law. And I want to do that. I want to be a good man. I do, Zora. Listen to us. We'll take care of you, but you can't be in rebellion."

His arms feel strong. Arms like my father's. Miles holds me like my daddy does.

"You don't have to worry. Because as soon as your daddy lets you go, I'm going to take over. I'll be Daddy. And Daddy Miles is gonna take good care of you."

I don't like the way that sounds. Something about it scares me.

"That sounds incestuous, Miles."

"I promise you'll like it."

Miles is trying to comfort me. I just turn and stand in the corner. He says I don't want to grow up. I'll prove him right. I turn around and stand there facing the wall while he rubs my shoulders and begs me to call my daddy, *The Bishop.*

I want him to kiss me. Finally. I want this big, chauvinist pig to take me in his arms and be my hero. Make everything feel better— take me off into the sunset on his white horse. That's how vulnerable I feel. *Miles,* who's been a jerk since all this happened, looks good to me. But he doesn't do any of that, lest his actions get back to *The Bishop,* whose covering must still apply, despite all evidence to the contrary. Miles just rubs my arms, though he stands closer than usual. I can tell he wants to do more, but he restrains himself. He leaves me with these parting words: "Rebellion is as the sin of witchcraft."

He leaves me standing there in the corner, mute and chastised like a little girl.

For a few hours, I sit on the floor in my apartment, truly empty except for the box of clothes Nicky bought me and the food and necessities Linda and Billie provided. More hours pass, and I try to sleep but dream about a big plantation, only the slave masters are black and they're all people in my life. Ms. Pamela is in the field with me, and she's dying, but we keep getting whipped, and we have to keep going. I'm so scared. I don't know how to keep her from dying, and I start feeling sick too. I start coughing and thinking I'm going to die, me and Ms. Pamela right here on this plantation.

I wake up, and I don't know how I'll endure all the silence. All the nothing around me. It feels like the blue walls are caving in on me. The Sankofa bird mocks me. I don't know what I'm supposed to go back and find. I don't know what I've left behind.

I have to get out of here. I think maybe if I just go to the mailbox I'll feel better. Maybe. Please, God, let that small thing, because it's all I've got, help me feel better.

I get up and go to the door. Open it. My door is covered by a huge canvas. It's almost as tall and wide as I am. And there's paint. All kinds of paints.

Maybe Miles has come through. Maybe this is his way of showing me he's with me. He's going to support my desire. Maybe I can be The Bishop's wife one day and paint on this amazing canvas. Miles has provided everything. This huge canvas. Oils, watercolors, acrylics. There are brushes and pads, paper, charcoals, and pens. It makes me so happy that I laugh and laugh.

He's taped a note on bright red paper where I can see it. "Zora" in big, bold letters with a smiley face.

Wait a minute. This isn't Miles's handwriting.

My heart pounds. Did MacKenzie do this? She couldn't. She had to use everything she had to get to New York. Even if she could sacrifice something, she'd never be able to do this. Besides, it's not her handwriting either.

I tear open the envelope. That snake in the garden of my heart, I can't find it anywhere. But I feel a butterfly. A tiny one, released from its just-born wings, now freed from its dark chrysalis. Fluttering. Fluttering. Fluttering.

Inside is a poem about the earring, and after the poem this note: "Okay, so it looked like me. What else can you do?"

I'm not the dreamy one. Nicky is. He must have written the poem right after he left me.

I don't get you, Nicky Parker. But I like you. I like you way too much.

And what is this thing emerging between us?

You've gotta be kidding me, God.

I spend a few hours sketching on that enormous canvas. Little children. I don't know why children. I think they're going to be of every color. Some of them are holding hands.

Maybe I'll just paint Dr. Martin Luther King's dream right there on that canvas, where it's safe.

NICKY'S SUPPLIES HAVE given me a bit of freedom. And what do you do with freedom? I have no idea.

I think maybe I should go to Meijer to get a flat iron for my hair. For all their kindness, Linda and Billie didn't think of what I need for my hair.

I still don't have any cash, but I can walk right down Ellsworth to get to Meijer by way of what MacKenzie calls Pat and Turner: pat your feet and turn the corner. It's late, but Ann Arbor is pretty safe. I don't normally walk around at night, but I don't think much will happen. Ellsworth is a major street. There's a sidewalk I can walk on, and traffic. I don't have a cell phone, but I can pray. I think it'll be okay. I want to do something to my hair. It's getting pretty ratty. I want to look pretty. Maybe just get some cheap lipstick. I don't want to buy any MAC. Just something so I can look decent the next time I see him.

Oh, man. I'm plotting to see Nicky.

Well, what's wrong with that?

I take the gift certificate, fold it up, and for lack of any other place to put it, stick it in my bra. Lord, have mercy. Necessity is the mother of invention, indeed. I miss you, Kate Spade. Truly.

After about a mile, I'm thankful for all that dancer's training. Today was dance-team practice. Today I would have been dancing for Jesus at LLCC. I'm thinking of twirling right here by the side of the road, on Ellsworth, in the dress Nicky bought me, a dress that looks like it's just made for dancing. But I don't. I just keep walking. That's right. Keep walking, Zora.

I wonder if I'll ever dance for Nicky. Maybe I will. In this dress.

That's so silly. What's wrong with me? I've never wanted to do a personal dance for Miles, and he's my boyfriend.

I'm about halfway to Meijer when a car—and not a very nice one—slows and comes to a stop beside me. Oh, man. Maybe I was wrong. Maybe this is some crazy person who's going to hurt me. MacKenzie would never let me walk out in the middle of the night just because Meijer is open twenty-four hours.

The window rolls down. I'm about to sprint when I hear a familiar voice.

"Miss Zora!"

Good grief! It's Ms. Pamela. My hand flies to my chest.

"You almost gave me a heart attack."

"Girl, whatchu doin' out walkin' the streets this time a night?"

"I'm just going to Meijer to get a flat iron."

"Girl, if you don't get in this car ..."

I slide into her ancient Honda Accord. I don't think I've gotten in a worse car since Mac had an old beat-up Escort. Most of the time if we rode together, we took my car. It happened to be getting serviced once or twice, and we had to roll out in hers. I didn't appreciate her Escort's performance and was quite vocal about it.

How did she stand me all those years?

Ms. Pamela and I bump and shake the last mile to Meijer, and it feels like it's the longest trip I've ever taken. She's still got the cough. I'm still concerned.

"Did you ever make it to see a doctor?"

"I had The Bishop lay hands on me and anoint me."

I don't want to say anything disparaging, and not because *The Bishop* is my daddy. I want to honor her faith. I think about the dream of us being on the plantation. Both of us slaves. Aren't we both trying to cling to Jesus, despite some semblance of oppression? And me, what kind of oppression is somebody dreaming up a life for me? A life of affluence? Yeah, Zora, how hard is it going to be as that kind of slave?

Maybe I should ask my mother.

Oh, girl. Don't you start that. Not tonight.

"Ms. Pamela, I'm glad you got prayed for. I'm just wondering if Jesus doesn't think it might be wise to see a doctor, too."

"You know, your daddy always preaches whatever is not of faith is sin."

He must be the chief of sinners then, because maybe he should have a little faith about letting me live my life. It was him standing in the way. Right?

Wasn't it, Z?

"I don't think it means you have less faith if the doctor took a look."

"Maybe I'll go. Tessa thought I should go. Maybe."

Every breath seems to be a struggle for her. She's hanging in there, but she doesn't sound right. "I'll go with you. I'm not doing anything but trying to get something to do my hair with. We can just turn the car around and head to U of M's Emergency Department."

"Naw, baby. I think the Lord sent me out. You been on my mind."

"What?"

"I was just wantin' some lemons to make me some lemon and honey tea. Had it so strong, but Tessa said she was tired and my other baby, Vernice, she sleep. My other baby out on a date."

It's one in the morning. Their mother is half-dead, and the no-working heifers won't get up to get her some lemons. The other one is out with some clown from MySpace probably. Yeah. They really are tired.

"So you had to get up yourself?"

"But I think the Lord sent me. I been thinking about you. The Lord lay you on my heart. People talk, honey."

"People at our church do."

"I heard your daddy and you having some problems."

"Apparently, I'm the only one with the problem. The sin of witch-craft. That's what I heard they're calling it."

"I don't know 'bout that. I just know sometimes girls come to a certain age, and it's hard for their fathers to let them be women. And it's hard for the girls, too. They want to be women and little girls at the same time. It can be confusing sometimes. My girls, their father ain't been around for years. They missed so much. But I had a daddy. I think I know what you're going through."

"Did your daddy take all your stuff because he was mad at you?"

"I didn't have much for him to take. But he tried to control me in other ways. He was just scared that if he lost control, everything would fall apart. That's all."

"I can't imagine *The Bishop* being scared."

"The Bishop didn't take your stuff, honey. Your daddy did. I'm not saying I agree with what he did. I'm just saying sometimes daddies make bad decisions because they want their little girls to stay little girls as long as they can. And little girls have to become women. Don't they, honey?"

"I suppose they do, Ms. Pamela." All except those morons at your house.

But I don't say that.

We get to Meijer, and Ms. Pamela buys her lemons and more groceries for me than I know she can afford. I believe she is the world's wealthiest widow who knows how to work the heck out of a mite.

Blessed are the poor in spirit, theirs is the kingdom of heaven? I see what You mean in this child of God, Jesus. I pray God really does give her back one hundredfold what she forces me to take.

She still won't let me go with her to the emergency room, even though she insists on taking me home. I leave her with this:

"My daddy would have taken me to the hospital by now."

I spend a long time in prayer. Before morning dawns, liberally gifting us all with new mercies, I ask again and again with my miserly faith for God to heal her.

CHAPTER THIRTEEN

NICKY

I almost knocked on her door. The problem is, if she'd have let me, I would've gone in. And since I was in such a kissing mood, I would have given her the kiss I shouldn't have given Rebecca. The one that really belonged to her. The one that would have been full of feeling. Too much feeling.

I can't go around feeling things.

Not for Zora.

I just left the stuff at the front of her door. I'd said enough. Too much. The poem. The art supplies. The note. I tried to leave my feelings at the door with the gifts.

I ended up taking those feelings right back home with me.

ZORA

Sunday morning. Every Sunday morning, barring deathly illness—which we weren't allowed to have, and fortunately, we never did—I was in church. Mostly black churches, and whether those churches had organs or praise teams, whether they had choirs or a quartet of barber-shop-style warblers, whether there was a dance and flag team or old ladies shouting out their press-and-combed hairstyles, I worshipped with my people, and I did this with great love and reverence.

Today I want to go somewhere else. I want to go to True Believer Gospel Tabernacle.

The day is sunny. It's unusually warm, in the seventies. God, what a precocious April You've allowed. Nature coming alive in this cold Midwestern land before its time. What a gift this is to me. You know I don't own a jacket, much less a coat right now.

I put on the white dress again. And oddly, I don't grow tired of it. To me, it's like the clothing of the Israelites as they walked toward the Promised Land. That one outfit that takes you where God wants you to go. Even though he gave me another one, even though Billie offered more, this is my Promised Land dress, and I want Nicky to see me in it again.

Maybe, if I can get him alone, I'll dance for him in it.

I put on the "last all day" lipstick I got last night. I want to add just a few brushes to my lashes of the Wet n Wild mascara that cost a mere ninety-nine cents. My mother would die if she saw this makeup. But it's all I can afford. I just want to look pretty for him.

When I'm ready, I head out the door. Once again, I take Ellsworth, but I keep walking past Meijer and Target. I used to look down my nose at these very ordinary stores. I didn't remember that until now.

I was a Nordstrom girl. Macy's. Saks. MacKenzie was so right about me. Oh, girl. I am so sorry.

I keep walking past the Wal-Mart. I *really* wouldn't have been caught dead at a Wal-Mart. MacKenzie loves Wal-Mart. Did I make her feel bad about her things? God, exactly how insensitive have I been through the years? Prancing around with my little Kate Spade and Prada bags and more designer clothes than I'd care to name, like it would never end, and in truth, even now it doesn't have to. All it takes is a call, and I can get it all back. For the cost of a phone call.

I think about Nicky Parker coming all the way back from California to put things right with his father. How far had he gone? He said he was a rascal. He probably did more than mouth off at his father. And how far had he strayed from his heavenly Father's commands?

How far have I? I mean, really?

I don't know. I can't tell where it began. Was it Thursday at dinner? Sunday when I walked out of church? Was it before then when I began to wonder if there was more to life than *believe that ye receive them, and ye shall have them?*

I watch the cars whiz by me—beat-up cars driven by folks with not so much money, and shiny new cars with smug drivers with lots of money. And now I'm walking instead of flying carelessly by in my black Lexus. Everything can fall apart in an instant. Or it can all become clear in a single moment seen through the eyes of grace. Things change that quickly.

Will Nicky's girlfriend be there in their lily-white church? Will she be the perfect model Barbie doll—or worse, Bratz doll—I think she'll be? Does she love him? Is he going to marry her and have perfect white babies that will grow up to have his smile and eyes like sapphires?

Maybe I shouldn't go. I should let Nicky Parker be so he can have a great life with blonde, pretty, nice Rebecca.

But, I argue with myself, *I should say thank you.*

And it's Sunday. I don't have any place to go. I want to do something different. It wouldn't be different going to another black church. And God, I don't want to be alone today.

NICKY

Honest to God, Rebecca is surgically attached to me. I don't have to wonder if she'll notice if I walk out this Sunday. I'd definitely have to drag her out of the door with me today. And all I can think about is Zora. Wondering what would have happened if I'd knocked on her door last night. My stomach leaps around inside of me just thinking about it. I don't hear a word of Dad's preaching, as usual.

What am I doing?

I called Richard again last night when lying in the shape cross did nothing to banish Zora from my thoughts.

He laughed at me. "It's not a formula for success, you idiot."

And I thought it had worked so well that first time.

When I told him about kissing Rebecca, he groaned. "Tell me you just gave her the kiss of peace."

"Unless the apostle Paul was in the habit of putting his tongue in the mouth of the faithful, it wasn't the kiss of peace."

"Nicky, kissing Rebecca isn't going to keep you from falling in love with Zora."

"Whoa, whoa, whoa, Richard! Wait just a minute. Who said anything about falling in love?"

"You're not falling for her?"

"Of course not. It's lust."

"Keep telling yourself that, Nicky."

"It's just lust. It is."

"Right, Nicky. I'm going to bed now." And the old dog hung up on me. Which is just as well.

"I'm not falling in love."

"Excuse me," Rebecca stage-whispers.

"Did I say something?" I whisper back.

"I think you did."

"No, I didn't."

"You said you're not falling in love."

"Why would I say that?"

"I don't know."

"Shhh," I say. "Dad is preaching."

Oh, man. I'm talking when I don't know I'm talking now. The next thing you know I'll be hallucinating. I'll look behind me at the door and I'll see Zora walking into the sanctuary in her white twirly dress.

Just to show myself how absurd the idea is, I look behind me and—

"OH NO!"

"Nicholas!"

I put my hand over my mouth. I'm freakin' hallucinating! I thought I just saw Zora come in and sit on the back pew. And she's in the white dress.

Aw, man. I'm crazy. I'm really crazy. Maybe Richard is right. I'm falling in love, and it's making me insane. I knew she was going to get me in trouble. I didn't know I was looking at putting in some time in a straitjacket.

"What are you looking at?"

Oh, no. Now Rebecca is going to see that I'm crazy, too.

She looks toward my hallucination. "Is it that black woman that just came in?"

I grab her arm. "*You* can see her too?"

She leans into me. "Nicholas, what is the matter with you? Of course I can see her."

I don't look back. "A young black woman in a white dress is in our church?"

"Yes." Rebecca whispered. "What is going on?"

"I have no idea. Black people don't come to our church. She doesn't come to our church, even though she voted for him."

"Do you know her?"

I give a noncommittal grunt halfway between a moan and something else. I don't know what.

"Was that a yes?"

"She goes to my Bible study."

"What Bible study?"

"The one I go to on Wednesday night."

"You go to a Bible study on Wednesday night? I thought you had to work."

"Rebecca! You are talking incessantly during Dad's sermon. Can you just be quiet? Please!"

I start shaking my leg. I do that when I'm nervous. I also drum my fingers. Between my shaking and drumming, I'm turning into a freakin' one man band, and it feels like my father is never, ever going to stop preaching. It also feels like Rebecca is never going to take the vice grip off my arm. Did I mention that I have to puke? I'm not just having puke fantasies today. I gotta hurl. I will never pray something interesting happens at church again, I promise, God.

The heat rises into my face. "Excuse me."

Rebecca starts to get up with me.

"I'm going to the john, Rebecca."

"Oh."

Oh, God. I really am going to be sick. Why, oh, why do I sit at the front of the church? I go past a thousand freakin' pews, and I can't look at her. I know Zora sees me walking away. I know Rebecca is watching me. My father is probably watching me. God, Jesus, the saints, and the devil are probably watching me, and they're probably all placing bets. And who knows what I'm going to do?

I go into the bathroom, hyperventilate. Pace back and forth. Hyperventilate. Pace. Then take a deep breath. As calmly as I can manage I take my cell phone out of my pocket and call Richard. By some miracle he answers.

"Richard?"

"Hey, Nicky."

And now a dumb question to kick-start what surely will be a dismal conversation. "You didn't go to church this morning?"

"I thought I'd stay home and seek the Lord." His speech is slurred. Richard is drunk, and I don't think it's with the Spirit.

Dumb question number two. "Richard, are you drunk?"

"Yes."

"Man, please tell me you aren't drunk when I'm having a crisis."

"What's going on this time, lover boy?"

"Zora is here. And Rebecca is here, and she's in love today. And in case you didn't hear me, Zora is here."

"You've got two gorgeous women. Sounds like you're having a really good day."

"I'm afraid I'm not."

"You more pathetic than I am, Nicky, and that's real pathetic."

"I know. And what's worse, you're the person that I talk about this with. And even worse, God won't kill me."

"I wish I could help you, but I'm a little intoxicated, and not quite at my best. Go with God, my friend."

"Oh, that's helpful, Richard. You know what? I will never buy another of your books."

"Let me know how you get out of this, and I'll start buying *your* books."

"Richard, I need you."

"I'm sorry, my friend. I know I'm a disappointment to you. But I'm not going to be much help right now."

"You suck, Richard."

I hang up on him.

I can't stay in the bathroom for the rest of the day, but I stay there until I hear my father close out the service. Finally, I take a deep breath and surrender myself to my fate.

I make my way back into the sanctuary and see Zora scurrying away from the back of the church. I can't help it; I have to go to her. I know Rebecca needs reassurance, but I don't have any for her. She's surrounded by people who love her, but no one is here for Zora.

I notice not one person has spoken to her. No one has welcomed her to our fold.

"Hey, Dreamy." I gather her into my arms. I don't want to admit to myself how right she feels there. I want to freeze us. Keep us right there for as long as I can.

As if on cue, Rebecca appears. "Aren't you going to introduce me to your friend, Nicholas?"

Man! Rebecca has her arm in mine before I'm completely disengaged from Zora.

She's a trouper, that Zora. She extends her hand. "You must be Rebecca. Nicky has told me all about you. I'm Zora."

"That's funny. Nicholas hasn't told me anything about you."

They give each other the most insincere smiles imaginable. I stand there with my own completely mystified expression—quite possibly something between a grimace and a good likeness of Edvard Munch's silent screamer—and notice my parents hightailing it from the front of the church so fast they nearly knock down a few members to get to me.

I'm telling you. They would have nothing to do with me if Zora wasn't there. Especially my dad, who claps me on the back. My, my, isn't everybody touchy feely today?

"Nicholas, you have a guest today?"

"This is my friend."

I don't want to introduce her. I just want to keep her to myself.

"Her name is Zora," Rebecca says.

Zora, the good politician, stretches forth her mighty hand again. "Reverend Parker, it's a pleasure to meet you. My name is Zora Johnson. I voted for you when you ran for office the very first time I voted."

He actually recognizes her. "Are you the Reverend Jack Johnson's daughter, Zora?"

"Yes, sir. I am. I'm honored that you remembered."

"Of course. You and your father came to several of our antiabortion rallies. How is Reverend Johnson?"

"He's Bishop Johnson now. And uh, he's …"

I have to rescue her. "He's *prosperous!*"

Zora tries to suppress a smile. At least I hope that's a smile she's trying to suppress. "Anyway, I know you guys would love to stand here yakkin' but I'm sure Zora has to go."

"Actually, I have nothing to do. At *all.*"

Wicked, wicked woman.

My father is pleased as punch. "Well, Zora, why don't you come to our home for dinner? We'd love to have you."

Not with my grandfather. Might as well ask her to a Ku Klux Klan rally!

"You know, Dad, Zora probably is vegan. And we're probably having *pot roast.*"

Mom and Rebecca already look uncomfortable, no doubt wondering if Zora has strange leftist sociopolitical leanings because of the vegan thing, even if she is antiabortion. Will she pull a can of red spray paint out from under her skirt and write *meat is murder* on the Crock-Pot?

Zora reassures everyone. "I'm not vegan. Remember we had chicken at that lovely restaurant you took me to yesterday? What was it called, The Love Nest?"

"That's not what it was called."

I do *not* look at Rebecca or my parents. I wonder why Zora wants me killed.

"Pot roast it is," I say.

I tried to warn her. She deserves whatever happens. At least that's what I tell myself.

CHAPTER FOURTEEN

ZORA

I walk into that sea of white faces, and it is almost okay because really, there's only one white face in the whole crowd I'm looking for. And when his eyes finally meet mine, he doesn't look happy to see me.

He sits all the way in the front. I figured he'd be near the front, but in the very first row? A good son. I don't even sit in the front row at LLCC. She sits with him. She almost sits on his lap, she sits so close. Even from across the crowded church, I can see she's everything he said she was.

She loves him. Almost worships him. She'll be a good wife. Perfectly acceptable.

I try to concentrate on the message, but I want to leave. It's almost over, though. Reverend Parker is preaching. There can't be too much left. I can't even concentrate because all I can see is that tripped-out look on Nicky's face and him putting his hand over his mouth.

What is he trying to keep from saying? I feel so excited about the prospect of him seeing me I can't hear past my own heartbeat.

Not much later he gets up. He walks right past me. I should get up and disappear while he is wherever he went, but I sit here frozen in place. The only black person in the entire building. He doesn't come back into the sanctuary, and I watch his girlfriend looking for him. Looking at me. She must be wondering who the lone black woman is who's gotten her man's attention.

You don't have a thing to worry about, honey.

I decide to go ahead and bounce. Reverend Parker is closing the service out. I leave the sanctuary, thinking I can get out of here before anybody has to deal with the discomfort of having to greet me. And I find myself in Nicky's arms.

He smells like our cologne. He's holding me, and it feels so good that I bury my face in his neck and just stay there, thinking everything I thought was all wrong, because he calls me Dreamy, and he is welcoming. He's the guy who writes me poems and buys me art supplies.

Then Rebecca swoops in to break up this little party.

Before I know it, the inquisition starts, and Nicky breaks into a sweat. His parents descend and oh, Lord. This is awful. I shouldn't have come. And now, for the rest of the day I get to live through *Guess Who's Coming to Dinner?* What have I done? I just want to be with Nicky so bad. I can't think straight, or talk straight. Everything keeps coming out of my mouth all wrong. The look Nicky gave me when I called that restaurant by the wrong name let me know that this was not going well.

Logistics have to be worked out, which Nicky apparently has a pathological need to control.

"Okay. Rides. Zora, how did you get to church this morning?"

"I walked."

"You walked?"

"From my apartment." I look at his parents. I've done pastoral politicking all my life, but I'm a nervous wreck. Too much information shoots out of my mouth. "It's pretty far, but I really wanted to see Nicky."

Nicky makes some kind of humming, groaning sound.

But I keep going. "Nicky knows where I live, right off Ellsworth and Shadowwood. He came over last night."

I probably shouldn't have said that. Rebecca's face collapses. She finds her voice. "He was with *me* last night."

Nicky's father raises his eyebrows and looks at Nicky. "You must be *exhausted*."

Oh, no. That's not how things happened at all.

"No, Zora is probably exhausted after all that walking. She walked about seven miles to get here, Dad. And I think that's extraordinary. Why don't you ride with me, Zora?"

"I'll ride with you," Rebecca says. She loves him. She really does.

"I think you should drive your own car, Rebecca."

I look at her face. Man, is she brave. I'll bet she's not certain of anything having to do with this man. Maybe she never was, but right now, I'll bet everything is beginning to crumble because this strange black woman showed up. And she sees it happening. And how is she going to stop it? He should let her ride with us.

I try to reassure her. I feel sorry for her. "I think it would be great to ride together. I'd like to get to know Rebecca more."

"You can talk with her during dinner." Now he's politicking. He wants to talk alone. I shouldn't have come.

Rebecca says, "I don't see why a little ride to your parents' house would make a difference."

Nicky tries—and fails—to charm her with his smile. "That'll be inconvenient, honey bunny." I can tell his parents are mortified at our little triangle. So am I. "I'll need to take Zora home later, and then we'd have to pick up your car."

Rebecca puts one hand on her hip. "I'm sure that won't be too much for you to do for your *girlfriend*."

"It would be today, Rebecca. Like Dad said, I'm exhausted."

Nicky runs those longs fingers through his hair. He takes a deep breath and grabs hold of my arm. "Let's go, Zora. And Rebecca, just drive your own car like you do every freakin' Sunday. Okay?"

He practically drags me to his truck, saying absolutely nothing.

NICKY

I seat her inside my truck and get in myself. The space feels oppressively small. My eyes look at everything but her face, where I know I'll see a myriad of emotions far too deep for me to process right now. I just want to get her out of here.

Zora's falling in love too. Nobody walks seven miles to church unless they love Jesus or somebody in that church, and she could have loved Jesus in any number of churches. At least that's what I tell myself. I want to think she's falling in love with me. The thought fills me with a deluge of hope so extravagant I can hardly breathe.

I'm quiet, and so is she, but I can't hold my need to hear her voice for long. After a few moments, I speak, but keep my gaze toward the windshield, as much as I want to look in her face. "Long way to walk, Dreamy."

"I'm a dancer. I could do it."

"Why here? Lots of churches closer."

"I wanted to see you."

"Why?"

"To say thank you."

It's still not what I want, but I'm gonna keep fishing until I'm closer. "Is that all? You didn't have to walk all that way to say thanks."

I'm surprised at how quickly her pretense dissolves.

"I wanted to see you for you, Nicky. I got makeup. *Cheap* makeup that my mother would disinherit me for if I weren't already disinherited. I wanted to look pretty so you would like me like I like you. I thought things were different between you and Rebecca."

"Things are different between us, despite how it looked today."

"I'm not convinced."

I just sigh. There'll be a time for this conversation, and a time for one about her boyfriend. But this isn't that time. "Don't do this, Zora. Don't try to figure this all out right now. And please, don't come to dinner at my parents' house."

"Why not?"

"They don't deserve to know you. They already think you're something I know you're not."

"Myth of the black whore?"

I can't bring myself to tell her what she knows is true, and then she starts blaming herself.

"I bought right into it. The restaurant comment and flubbing the name. Saying you stopped by last night."

"No, Zora. It was me. I'm the one with the bad reputation, famous for running around, trying to see how many women I could conquer. I laid the groundwork for that one. But you shouldn't have to be a casualty of my past. Let me take you home. That's why I didn't want Rebecca to come with us. I just wanted to tell you not to come. And I wanted to hear why you walked to church. That amazes me, Zora."

"The things you put on my door amazed me. *You* amaze me, Nicky."

"Let's get out of here. Nobody but Rebecca will miss me."

"Don't let this be the day she misses you. Please don't do that to her. Do you love her?"

"No. I mean, I do, but only in a 'love thy neighbor' way. Not in the way she needs me to. I'm not in love with her at all."

"She's in love with you."

"I know."

"And now they all think you have jungle fever."

I snicker. "I may really have it, God help me." Then I give her a shy look. "Any ideas about what to do about that?"

She starts singing the *Jungle Fever* theme song, only she changes the words to match our alleged pairing.

"I've got jungo feeeva, heeee's got juungo feeva, we've got jungo feeeva. We're in love!"

"You are so wrong for that."

"She's gone white boy craaazy, heeeee's gone black girl haaaaazy, ain't no thinkin' maaaaaybe we're in love!"

I know she's clowning, but the lyrics convict me. Not the white boy crazy, or the black girl hazy part. The part where she says, "We're in love."

"Cut it out, Zora."

"Are you trying to get sensitive on me now? Did that one ethnic-sensitivity training class you took at Berkeley just come to mind?"

"It might surprise you to know that maybe the fever I have burning for you is not about sex. And maybe I want to take you away because I don't really want them to think you're my little black plaything."

She narrows her eyes, but they're sparkling and playful. "Are you sure you just don't want them to know you got you a little chocolate swirl to go with that vanilla *ice*."

I tease her back. "I would never have guessed such a sweet girl, a bishop's daughter like yourself, would have such a wicked sense of humor. The stereotype that white women are frigid—I'm appalled by your lack of sensitivity, Zora. I shouldn't encourage you."

"You didn't encourage me."

"Maybe that's because you aren't my chocolate swirl."

I want to add, "but you *can* be. Have mercy!" But I don't say it aloud.

"I'm not your *anything*," she reminds me.

"Then you probably shouldn't be singing that we're in love."

"Oh, come on, Nicky, your parents and girlfriend didn't hear me."

"I heard you."

"Did it bother you?"

I take a long and very serious look at her. "Maybe it made me reflective."

"And what did it make you reflect on?"

"The possibilities."

"Is falling in love a possibility?"

"You just convinced three people that it is."

"Three people, or four?"

"Three. One person standing there already knew he could love you."

In a bit of shock that I'd just said that, I put one hand on the steering wheel and turn the key with the other. "We'd better get going or Rebecca's going to be knocking on the window."

"Trying to climb into the truck."

"Lying across the hood."

"You suck as a boyfriend."

"Maybe I've just got the wrong girlfriend, Zora."

I glance across the parking lot, and I can see that my parents have stayed to speak to a few more people, but Rebecca, to her credit, has gone on. I wonder if she went somewhere to compose herself. Pick up some heavy artillery? Get a passel of girlfriends for reinforcements?

Like I'm really deeply concerned. Zora is right. I do suck.

"Hey, Zora."

"What?"

"Thanks for coming to church."

The truth is, I'm really glad she's here. I put the truck in drive and we pull out of the parking lot toward my parents' place. When I reach out and take her hand, she lets me hold it.

God, what are we going to do?

CHAPTER FIFTEEN

ZORA

Nicky and I have families full of odd contrasts. He is the product of generations of genteel Southern Baptists, now Northern bred, and we are first generation Word-Faithers from a crop of the independent Apostolic heretics that grew out of organic slave religions, whatever we could piece together. We are from one of the oldest black families in Ann Arbor, a largely white, liberal community. Nicky grew up in Ypsilanti, which now is known for having the larger black population of the two cities.

The Parkers live in historic Ypsilanti in a house built in the 1800s, a breathtaking masterpiece of Americana they show off each year in the historic homes tour. When Nicky pulls up to the house, he is obviously horrified that he didn't remember the wide-eyed, jet-black lawn jockey greeting us with huge, smiling red lips.

"I forgot about that."

"I'll bet you did."

"I'm sorry, Zora."

"Anything else I need to know about, Nicky? Got a mammy in there? Couple of slaves?"

"They don't have slaves, Zora."

"Not since it was outlawed."

"You didn't have to accept their invitation."

"But I did. You should have told me I'd find soul brotha here upon arrival."

"My parents are mostly nice people. They're kinda scary, but they're … I don't even know how to describe them."

"Let's just go in."

"I tried to get you not to come. And now you're feeling defensive."

"I'll be a good Negro, boss."

"That's not nice, Zora. I'm not your enemy."

"You look like them."

"I can't change my skin, Zora. If I could, I'd make it real easy on you today. I'd go for something kinda Wesley Snipes. That African American enough for you?"

We sit there for a few moments. I don't even know why I'm acting this way. I can handle his parents. If I know anything, it's how to work a room. I'm just nervous. I was stupid enough to want to be liked, and now that I'm the whore anyway, I may as well shoot for high-class whore and hold it down for the next sistah he brings home. You know what they say. Once you go black, you can't go back.

What a dumb saying. God, what's the matter with people? I decide to take a teeny little risk.

"Nicky?"

"Yes?"

"I've had a few bad days, that's all."

He chuckles. "I'll say."

"I'm feeling really defensive. I just wanted to be with you."

"I should have just knocked on your door last night. I didn't want to … I don't know, Zora. I didn't want to do anything unacceptable. I'm actually trying for gentleman with you. "

"It was probably late when you left your *girlfriend.*"

"I know it doesn't look like it, but I'm not a player. I *was,* but I'm not now. And believe it or not, I want to tell you what I'm feeling for you, but I don't know. It seems wrong what I'm feeling. I mean, beyond wrong in some ways. I'm feeling a lot toward you, Zora. I didn't expect you. And I have no idea what to do with you."

"You don't have to do anything with me, regardless to what either of us is feeling."

"Somehow I don't think that's true. You're already meeting the parents."

"I don't think I've impressed them."

"You impress *me* every time I look at you, Dreamy."

"Let's just go inside, Nicky. The lawn jockey thing threw me off. Among other things. I'll make this work. I'm good at that kind of thing. Well, my last dinner with my parents was a bust, so if tomorrow your apartment is empty, disregard what I just said. Deal?"

He grins. "Deal."

He opens the truck door for me. Together we pass Jocko. Nicky whispers "I'm sorry" to me one more time, and I accept his apology. Before we go inside, I stop.

"Did you ever hear the legend of Jocko, Nicky?"

"Jocko?" he says. He has no idea what I'm talking about.

"Your pal here? The lawn jockey."

"I'm sorry, I don't know anything about him. I'm ashamed to say he's something I just took for granted. Never thought to ask."

"Don't feel bad. A lot of people don't know, including black people. In fact, there's no evidence that it's really true. It's a legend. You wanna hear it?"

He shugs. "Sure."

"The legend goes that Jocko was the twelve-year-old son of a free black man named Tom Graves. During the Revolutionary War, Graves joined George Washington's army. Jocko wanted to go to war also, but he was too young. Little Jocko was a spunky kid, however. He went anyway."

Nicky shakes his head. "That was some twelve-year-old. I sucked at twelve."

"Me, too. I was totally self-absorbed, much like now, God help me. Anyway, according to the legend, just as Washington was about to cross the Delaware River for the battle of Trenton, he realized there was no way he could transport his horses by boat, and his steeds would have to be waiting on the other side. Young Jocko volunteered to hold the horses and make sure they were ready when the troops arrived."

Again, Nicky shakes his head. "Why do I have a feeling this is going to end badly?"

"Because it will. Here comes the hero part. During the night, vigilant Jocko froze to death, and the poor kid never let go of the horses' reins. General Washington was so touched by his sacrifice that he erected a statue in Jocko's honor. That statue was the precursor to lawn jockeys."

"Which would later become racist symbols of slavery."

"Yes."

"And that truly sucks."

"It truly does, Nicky."

He takes my hand. "I'm so sorry, Zora."

"On the bright side—"

"And you would find a bright side in this."

"Lawn jockeys were also used in the underground railroad to alert runaways to safehouses. A lit lantern in his hand or a bright ribbon tied on his arm meant the house was safe."

"Uh oh," he says. "That one doesn't have a lantern or a ribbon. I think we should turn around. Let's blow this pop stand, baby."

"Your parents are expecting me. I wouldn't want to disappoint them."

The smile, if one could call it that, he pastes on his face is so full of bitterness and irony it's almost frightening. "It'd be me they'd be disappointed in. As always. Not to worry." A sigh escapes his mouth. "I guess I'll have to keep you safe today."

He squeezes my hand, and the gesture makes me feel as safe as a little girl holding a grown-up's hand.

I tell myself I'm ready. I can do this.

I tell myself one more time for good measure, "You can do this, Zora." I take another look at Jocko. I don't think he's smiling at all. I think that's a grimace on his face.

NICKY

You'd think I'd have remembered Jocko in the yard, wouldn't you? I'd even read Flannery O'Connor's *The Artificial Nigger* in college. But no. I didn't even think about it until, to my horror, there he was, smiling at Zora with those big red lips. I wanted to drive far, far away, but I couldn't.

You know, I never think about these kinds of things. I never think about Aunt Jemima or Uncle Ben or the myth of the black whore or the BET video girls, pimps, hos, and the hundreds of negative images that must assault Zora every day. No wonder she's so freakin' sensitive. I see a hillbilly image and I laugh, but I don't think about hillbillies again unless I see Jeff Foxworthy on TV or something, and there are a million positive images to reinforce that I'm good and right and beautiful. Zora didn't laugh at the lawn jockey. And it's not funny. I see why she says it's hard for her to turn it off, and the lawn jockey is just one thing—that I've noticed, that is.

I remember when I first saw her, and how I mused about how I'd have to marry her, and then I dismissed the idea when I couldn't figure out why black people pronounce chitterlings the wrong way. And who's to say the way they say it is wrong? I said to myself then that it's too complicated. I've known her for almost a week and already I don't see the world in the same way. And the complications haven't even begun. But they're about to. I don't doubt that at all.

I open the door, and we're in white people's paradise. There's a flag in the corner and a gun rack and early American furniture, and I'm embarrassed it's so freakin' white.

"This is a lovely old house," Zora says.

"Ummm."

"You grew up here?"

"Um hmmm."

"I'll bet there are all kinds of nooks and crannies you played in."

"I could tell you stories."

She looks at me with those brown doe eyes. "I'd like that." And it looks like she means it when she says it. "Show me your room when you were a kid."

"It's my mother's sewing room now."

"Please."

This woman absolutely delights me. I can't deny her anything she asks. And much of what she doesn't. My folks aren't here yet and neither is Rebecca, so I take her upstairs and show her what used to be my bedroom. I can't stop talking.

"Everything is different now. The whole house is different. Back then this was just a crappy, drafty old house. We had this awful wallpaper." I laugh, remembering it. "It had these big, horrible flowers. Like huge cabbage roses."

I wonder if she can see cabbage roses where hunter green walls are now. Then we walk down the beige hallway. "This had bad wallpaper, too. More awful flowers from, like, the thirties or forties."

Zora laughs. We reach my mother's sewing room, a shrine to *Martha Stewart Living*. It's all white, glass jars, buttons, and notions.

"This is it."

"What color was it?"

"Blue. Cowboy theme."

"Nicky the cowboy. Did you sleep in here alone?"

"Yep."

"You have brothers and sisters?"

"Nope. I'm an only child. All bets are on me."

"Is that why you're on Prozac?"

"Nah. That's why I *need* Prozac though."

"Were you lonely?"

"All the time. Especially at night."

"I had two brothers and a little sister, but I used to be lonely too. If we were neighbors, we could have strung two cans from out our windows and talked even though I lived far away. Mine would have once been a can of collard greens." She winks at me.

Princess probably didn't even have canned goods. We did! "Mine would have been a string-beans can. And we could have talked a lot because I'd have had plenty of those cans."

I lean against the doorway. I like the thought of us being kids together. I take her hand again, and she lets me. "What would we have talked about, little Miss Zora?"

"Horses, since you were a cowboy."

"And what would you have told *me* about?"

"I would have told you all about princesses, of course."

"I so wouldn't have talked to you anymore after that."

"You would have if you were lonely."

"No, I wouldn't have. You probably would have made me pretend to be the prince. I can tell."

"Whatever. I would have thought you had cooties anyway."

I rub her hands and am struck by the contrast. Her skin is so dark. Mine so fair. But we keep holding hands. Dr. Martin Luther King's dream. I don't want to let her go. I don't want to stop seeing this black and white of us together, the stark contrast of our intertwined hands.

I can hear my family come in with Rebecca. "They're here." I have an impulse to snatch my hand out of hers as if we've done something wrong. I resist it.

Her voice sounds full of longing, the same longing stirring within me. "It was so nice just being kids up here, wasn't it?"

"Maybe we could stay. I really do know places we can hide. I could tell you some of those stories I mentioned."

"They'd think we found a bedroom and were gettin' busy."

"Yeah, especially with *your* reputation."

She hits me with her free hand.

"This is going to be all right, Zora." I know it's a lie, but I want to believe it.

"Okay, Nicky."

I don't think she believes me. "I'm with you, okay?"

She smiles at me. "You be here for Rebecca."

But I want to be here for her. Rebecca has her team.

And at that, she lets go of my hand.

I lead her back downstairs, and everybody glares at us, especially my grandfather. What? Do they think we got a quickie in since we left the church fifteen minutes ago? I just want to get her out of here. I can tell by the obscene way they look at us together this is going to be even more of a nightmare than I imagined, and I'm beginning to get the feeling she knows it too. That lawn jockey knew what was coming.

I didn't get to introduce her to my grandfather at the church. Now he's standing there with my parents, freakin' leering at her, the old pervert.

"Who's this, Nick?"

"This is my friend."

Rebecca offers her up like a lamb to the slaughter. "Her name is Zora."

He gives me this look. It's the look he gave my cousin Robbie when he shot his first deer.

"Where've you two been?" he asks.

"I showed her mom's sewing room."

"You mean your old bedroom?"

Dirty old ...

"It's not my bedroom anymore."

Mom whisks Zora off for a tour of the house, and I follow them, even though I know Rebecca wants to ask me what Zora and I were up to. I'm trying to scope out any more signs of white supremacy in the house, and I don't have a clue how. Now I'm freakin' hypersensitive, and worse, I don't even know what I'm supposed to be looking for. We don't have lawn jockeys in the living room. I feel a little sick to my stomach, and the smell of the pot roast gnaws at my gut.

Can't they ever serve chicken for heaven's sake? Spaghetti? Veal? Turkey? I'd take a can of Spam! A bologna sandwich on stale bread with no condiments.

After what seems like six weeks, we finally settle into the dining room, and my grandfather parks himself right across from Zora. I sit beside her. Rebecca beside me. Of course.

I don't think this dinner could feel more ill at ease if we were all trying to sell each other Amway. There are a lot of uncomfortable silences between awkward questions like ...

"So, Zora, what do you do?"

"I'm unemployed."

Endless silence.

"So, Zora. How are things going over at Light of Life?"

"I don't know. I'm not going there anymore."

Pindrops. Crickets. Silent screams.

Then Rebecca gets nosy. "So, uh, Zora. You and Nicholas went out to a restaurant Friday?"

Oh, man.

"Yes. He took me out after he went shopping for me. He bought me a lot of things." She sees Rebecca's stunned expression and becomes more nervous and information pours out of her. "I mean he just got me things I needed mostly. He got me some outfits. I guess I didn't need the jewelry. That was just kind of him. It was innocent."

And of course my dad says, "It sounds innocent. Nicholas buying you jewelry."

"Then he came over late Saturday with art supplies for me."

Rebecca squeaked. "After you left me you went back to her with *more* stuff? And all I got was this necklace?"

I shove a fork full of pot roast in my mouth to keep from speaking. Don't even bother to look at Rebecca because what Zora described *sounds* far from innocent, regardless of the real facts.

My father gets interested. "Why, you certainly have taken an interest in Zora, Nicholas."

"She's had some losses, Dad. She needed help. She and some other Christians I know have been helping her. Zora lost everything. We've helped her."

"It's true, Reverend Parker. It's all been Christian charity."

He snorts at her.

"I don't think a man buying a woman jewelry is charitable. Neither is giving her *art supplies.*"

"It is if she's an artist. Zora is a painter. She did an amazing sketch of me. I happen to think her doing her work is healing—and good for her soul."

My dad gives me the contemptuous look I'm so accustomed to. "What would you know about what's good for the soul, Nicholas?"

"Good point, Dad. Not much. I wasn't taught about that, was I?"

He opens his mouth to say something to me, but must think better of it. After all, we have company. He turns to Zora.

"So you're an artist?"

"Yes, sir."

"She's very good," I say.

"Nicky's quite an artist in his own right," Zora says.

My mother chimes in. "What do you mean by that, Zora?"

"Nicky is a wonderful writer."

Rebecca seems to find the way Zora says my name bothersome. "Why do you call him Nicky?"

Zora leans over me and looks her in the eye. "Why do you call him Nicholas? That sounds rather formal for his girlfriend."

Of course my mother comes to Rebecca's rescue. "We find the name Nicky rather juvenile."

I wonder if Zora is going to be rude to my mother. My mouth goes dry. But she sits back in her seat. "Really? To me it's playful and charming, as delightful as he is. He was introduced to me by older, wonderful people as Nicky, and he seems to prefer it. I like it. I think he likes it. I certainly don't mean any disrespect to any of you, but if Nicky enjoys it, that's what I'll call him."

My mother clears and touches her throat as she does when she is losing control of a situation. My father comes to her aid.

"You were saying something about Nicholas's writing."

"I think he has a wonderful sense of joy and sorrow, whimsy, reverence, and beauty in his work. And I've only seen one thing."

"And what was that?"

"It was a poem."

Rebecca huffs. "I've never seen any of his poetry."

"I have," my father says, his face reddening. "It's a waste of time. He spent all that money writing poems and short stories when he should have been going to seminary, or at least getting a degree that could prepare him for the real world."

"Isn't being an artist real work?" Zora asks.

"They don't think so," I say.

My mother speaks. "I think creating art is one thing, like what you do, Zora. I think God can use that, like that wonderful painter—what's his name, honey? We always see his work at the Christian bookstore."

Oh, no. Don't let them say it.

"Thomas Kinkade," my father says.

Dear God. They said it. Rebecca squeals. "I love his work. Are you familiar with him, Zora?"

I can't even look at her.

"Yes, I am. The painter of light."

"He has light," I say.

"And paint," Zora adds.

That's it. I'm really, truly, madly in love with her.

Zora goes on. "But Nicky makes art, too. When he writes poems, or novels, or even his own version of Psalms, he enters into the human drama and records the beauty and terror, all of it. Unflinchingly. He's going to turn the world on its ear."

Rebecca adds, "I think he will too. He's going to be just like Max Lucado."

I think I'm going to have a heart attack when she says that.

Zora looks over at Rebecca. "Max Lucado?" She actually laughs. "Girl, my father is a preacher. He's got nine books out, and hasn't written any of them. Max is a preacher. Maybe he writes his own books. I hope he does, but whether he does or doesn't, those aren't the kind of books Nicky's going to write. Nicky isn't a Max Lucado. He's a J. D. Salinger, full of righteous anger and sadness and longing for authenticity. He's a Rilke, full of beauty and God hunger. He's a King David, singing his prayers, his praises, his penance."

I'm astounded at what I'm hearing. Because of one bad poem, she's standing up to my family on my behalf, and I have had no such courage in a lifetime. My heart is so overwhelmed I don't know what to do with myself.

My father looks angry. He stabs at his potatoes. "You're talking nonsense, young lady."

"That's the kind of writing he's made for, Reverend Parker. It's not nonsense. It's his gift."

My grandfather, who has been blessedly quiet the whole time, mumbles some bit of profanity, but we all hear him. He follows it with, "Uppity gal. I remember when niggers knew their place."

Silence.

My parents gasp. Some unintelligible protest escapes from my throat. Rebecca says, "Oh my gosh, Zora." Everything seems to happen in slow motion. Zora's back straightens. She stands with the grace of the dancer she is.

I feel truly ill. I have never been so completely ashamed of my family in my life, and I feel completely at a loss as to what to say or do to right this terrible wrong.

I expect her to throw her water, pot roast, or potatoes in his face. Smash the freakin' plate on his shining bald pate. But she doesn't. She simply says to my parents, "Thank you for having me, Reverend and Mrs. Parker. I should be leaving now."

My father stands. And I stand too. No one apologizes. Not in my family. No, we Parkers can deny like Peter on Good Friday. Only we're less vocal with our denial. Had not Zora stood, my grandfather would have probably asked her to pass the peas after calling her a racial slur. My mother looks like she doesn't know what she's going to do. Get up? Keep eating? Go upstairs and sew? Rebecca looks like she's going to burst into tears. Dear God, what a mess. And my grandfather does keep eating, still mumbling to himself.

I take Zora by the elbow, and she gently pulls her arm away from me. She heads toward the door on her own.

"Zora, wait."

I hear my father's voice. "Nicholas." And then Rebecca shoots up like a dandelion on the lawn.

"Where are you going, Nicholas?"

"I'm taking Zora out of here before he puts on his white sheet."

My mother stands and defends the creep. "Nicholas, that wasn't fair. Your grandfather is from a different time."

"There's no good time for a racist, Mother, including today." I try to catch Zora, but she's well on her way to the front door.

"Nicholas, just let her go."

"How is she supposed to get home?"

"Well, she walked to church."

"What is the matter with you people?"

I jet into the living room and catch up with her just before she gets out the door. "Wait."

She yanks the door open and is out of there before I can stop her, slamming the door on me.

I have to fumble to open it. "Zora, wait."

My eyes have to adjust to the bright sunlight, and by now, she's running away. I'm calling her, and she's running. I don't even want to think about what we look like.

Finally I pull even with her. I have to grab her arm and yank her to me, and when I do … she's crying. Aw, man. "Oh, Zora. I'm so sorry."

"Why did you let him … you let that man …"

"I'm so sorry, Zora."

"You were right, Nicky. I shouldn't have come. I shouldn't have been involved with you. *At all!*"

What was I supposed to say? Both of us knew it would be a disaster no matter what false hope we cloaked ourselves in. What else would it be? I let her rail on.

"You're all racist. All of you."

"No, we're not. I'm not like that, Zora."

"Yes, you are."

"I'm not."

"You ever use that word, Nicky?"

"No."

A flat-out lie. I've used it, as flippantly as my grandfather had and worse.

"You're not a very good liar, Nicky."

"Okay. I've used it."

She nods her head. "I thought so."

"I didn't want to admit it right now while you're upset. But I would have told you eventually." I can tell she doesn't believe me, and why should she since I just *lied?* "Look. I grew up with *them.* But I've changed."

"Why, because you went to California? Got a black friend or two? Do you have black friends, Nicky?"

I don't want to answer her.

"Do you?"

"Just you, for now."

"But you're not a racist?"

"I don't have a lot of friends *period,* Zora. And how could I be a racist if I'm crazy about you?"

"You think because you're attracted to a sistah now that's special? What about your friend Pete? That *racist* is attracted to me."

"I think I've shown you I'm a cut above Pete."

"Oh yeah, Nicky. You're a regular Thomas Jefferson."

"Thomas Jefferson?"

"Yeah, the slave-owning, freedom-talking Founding Father. You remember him, don't you? He had this slave, Sally Hemmings. He didn't rape her, like most of my great, great grandmothers got raped by their masters. Not a nice, upstanding Christian guy like Thomas Jefferson. But he sure did have some pleasant *visits* with her, Nicky. The kind that produced children who his white descendants still don't acknowledge. That's the kind of white man you are, Nicky. 'I like you, Zora, but not enough to fight society to be with you. Not enough to make my life uncomfortable for you. Certainly not enough to let my *real, white,* acceptable-to-the-parents girlfriend go.'"

Is this the kind of man she thinks I am?

She's not done hurling accusations at me.

"But you'll go tiptoeing over to the slave cabin at night. Bring ol' Sally some poetry and art supplies. And I was stupid enough to—"

A sob escapes her mouth.

"Zora. I'm—" I go to her, all the while asking myself, am I that white man she just described? I try to hold her, and of course she resists.

"Stay away from me."

"I'm sorry."

"You're not sorry."

"I am. I truly am."

"Look at me, Nicky." She starts furiously wiping her eyes. I'm looking. I can't take my eyes off of her.

She only has to look up a few inches to see me. I love that she's so tall.

"I don't want you to forget this moment for the rest of your life, okay?" she says.

"Okay."

"Nicky?"

"Yes, Zora."

"Whenever you hear the word *nigger*—"

"Please don't say that, Zora."

"You didn't say that to your grandfather. Don't say that to me. Whenever you hear the word *nigger* ... "

I nod.

"Are you looking at me?"

"You know I'm looking at you, Zora."

"I want you to remember *my* face, okay, Nicky?"

Her statement takes the wind out of me. "Stop it, Zora."

"You think I'm pretty, right?"

"You know I do."

"Well, *I'm* the nigger who came to dinner. I'm *every* nigger you ever uttered and ever will. I'm every nigger in the world, Nicky. They're all me. Every nigger you've ever known is me. Do you understand?"

I don't understand and I do. I can't stand to hear this, but she won't stop.

"If there is one nigger in the world all black people are niggers."

That word tears at me, and I just want to stop her.

She keeps assaulting me with it. "And all niggers are Zora Nella Hampton Johnson, the nigger you *think* you want. You got that, Nicky? All niggers are me. Every single nig—"

I scoop her into my arms and kiss her. I don't even try to be gentle. I'm a freakin' beast with her. And she is all sweetness. Man. She's amazing. She starts beating the crap out of me, but it's so worth it.

She finally gets out of my grip and pummels me with blows to my chest.

"That was a very *white man* thing to do, Nicky Parker!"

And I don't even care that she's kickin' my butt on the street in front of the neighbors. I'm totally short-circuited because I kissed her so good I blew my own mind. Then she surprises me and comes back at me with a kiss of her own.

Holy cow! I'm about to have a coronary my heart is pounding so fast.

Only this kiss isn't a she-beast kiss. It starts that way, and then she seems to go shy on me, and turns soft. I give Zora every bit of tenderness I have inside of me, every bit of it. I pour all the love I have and some of the love I don't into tiny little kisses and the gentlest caresses I can muster.

I will remember her face all right. I will remember this moment. Always.

If I could stop time right here, I would, and I would hold onto this woman. Honest to God, I would never let her go. I would spend my heaven kissing Zora on the sidewalk on this spring afternoon. She would be my heaven. But I can't stop time any more than I can pick my own heaven.

"Nicholas!" Rebecca screeches behind me

I let Zora go.

My father stands next to Rebecca, stern looking, crimson faced, and ramrod straight. Rebecca lacks his restraint, but his eyes scream to me everything I need to know. I've disappointed him. Again.

He clears his throat. Gestures to the side of him. "We called a cab for ... your friend."

It kills him to call her that—my friend. I can only imagine what he wants to call her. Rebecca is looking like a statue of a martyr. And Zora is trying to walk away from all of us.

"Wait," I say to Zora.

"I don't need anything else from you. Thank you."

"Please, it's too far for you to walk."

The cab, windows rolled down, pulls up to the curb.

Dad and Rebecca stand behind me like a Greek chorus, only they're silent, but I can sense them urging in harmony, *Get in the cab, get in the cab, get in the cab.*

But not Zora. "I can walk."

"Please. Take the cab. I promise you can be as proud as you'd like while you ride."

The cabdriver, a black man, steps out of the car, takes one look at Zora, me, my dad, and Rebecca and says to Zora, "I think you should take the cab."

Zora seems to war with herself. She looks from him to me and back to him. He nods his affirmation to her, and she sighs and relents.

Dad reaches for his wallet, but not this time—I take my last forty dollars and hand it to the driver. It's twice what the fare would be or better, but I really need a little help, and as far as I'm concerned, he is Christ to both Zora and me in that moment. "Take care, man." I shake his hand.

He snickers at me. I don't care. She gets in the cab without so much as looking at the rest of us.

I should be taking her home but he does. She leaves with the black guy she doesn't know. Although maybe she knows him better than she knows me.

And who am I trying to kid saying Zora doesn't know me? She just laid my soul out like the bone china on the dining room table right in front of my family. She knows more about me than they do. A few things she said made me wonder if she knows more about me than I know about myself.

Am I an artist? Can I dare to listen to my yearnings?

Am I racist?

But I can't explore these things with Zora. She wouldn't even let me take her home.

I don't think she's ever going to see me again, even though for some crazy reason she kissed me. Maybe it was just her way of saying good-bye. The thought of her not being in my life anymore makes me unbearably sad.

And angry, and I'm not sure why.

I don't understand anything that just happened.

Nothing.

I look at my dad and at Rebecca.

I'm sure *they'll* have a lot of explaining to do about my behavior, as usual.

CHAPTER SIXTEEN

ZORA

Because I have broken into a million pieces. Because I have shattered like glass and pieces of me are scattered all over the sidewalk. Because I am not flesh and blood, only glass and dangerous dust that can burrow in your eyes and cause you to bleed, I try to remember that my broken soul is em*bodied* and no one can see that only some shell of a soul is nearly all that is left.

Embodied, this shell I am makes a move toward the cab. The body of Zora has hands, and one of those brown and barely responsive hands takes hold of the handle of the back passenger side door, and somehow I enter the cab. I sit down inside. I watch Nicky give the driver what looks like more money than he should. I see them shake hands.

It is this Zora that still feels Nicky's hands at my waist while the pieces inside of me slide downward. I still feel the sensation of my stomach dropping to my knees. Oh Lord, oh Lord, oh Lord. Could he hear those pieces of me shifting to my toes, sounding like falling water? Like a rain stick turned upside down again and again?

I put my hand to my mouth and press my lips to my open palm. I can still feel the pressure of his lips, in turn fierce, firm, gentle. I can still taste him on my tongue, and I savor him.

"Let him kiss me with the kisses of his mouth: for thy love is better than wine."

No wonder that mysterious book of songs starts that way. I understand this now.

Nicky's kiss was a song. A poem. It was like that crazy earring falling in front of us—something strange and beautiful, silly and senseless in the middle of our painful thrashing. I don't understand it, but I can't get out from under the awful beauty and mystery of it.

The cabdriver slides inside the cab. He takes a look back at me.

"You all right, little sistah?"

"Yes," I lie. Then, "No."

"Where you goin'?"

I rattle off my address. He leaves me be with a warning. "Buckle up. Wouldn't want you in harm's way."

I laugh.

I'm already in harm's way.

It wasn't supposed to be Nicky. Miles was supposed to give me my first kiss. Maybe when he asked me to marry him. Or at the altar when he kissed the bride. And even if for some miracle or accident it was Nicky, it wasn't supposed to be like that. Not that nightmare. Not that mess.

Oh, God. I think I'm going to die right here in this cab.

Everything has fallen apart. Nicky Parker gave me my first kiss right after his grandfather called me a nigger. And why would he do that? To shut me up? I don't even know. And the worst part? As much as it infuriated me, I took it in like a life force, let it energize and awaken me.

Oh, God. I'm disgusting. I'm like Sally Hemmings. Next thing I know I'm going to have a bunch of little tragic mulattos Nicky Parker doesn't claim. I've got to fix this. Fix me. Everything has fallen apart, and I've got to get the feel, the scent, the taste of that white boy off me.

I run my shaking hands through my hair. "God, I'm not gonna make it. I'm losing way too much here."

"You'll make it," the incarnational cabdriver says. I take it. Sometimes all you need is a little gift from God.

"Thank you, brotha." I make sure I say "brotha" because I need to sound—to feel—as black and proud as possible.

"You're welcome, little sis. Was that your boyfriend?"

A hollow, empty sound, rises from my throat.

"Sure did look like it," he says. "That was some kiss."

"That, my brotha, is an understatement." I shake my head. "He's not supposed to be my boyfriend. He's supposed to belong to the white girl that was behind us. My boyfriend, in the words of the guy I was kissing, sucks. But my father took all my stuff, and my boyfriend went with my father. And Nicky—that's the one I was kissing—he started giving me my stuff back—but not the stuff I lost. He started giving me the stuff nobody took. The stuff I had to give away myself, but I didn't know it."

"Sounds complicated."

"Yeah, it does."

"You were kissing him like you meant business."

"At the time I did."

"Which one of them do you love?"

"Love? How should I know? What do I know about anything? I asked Jesus to teach me what He meant by 'blessed are the poor,' and then my daddy took all my stuff. And then these white people came along. *White people!* And I don't do white people. At least I didn't think I did. And that one I was kissing? He's a real cutie, and a good kisser. And I want to kiss him again. In fact, I could spend a good long time kissing him, but I don't go with his lifestyle, if you know what I mean. So don't go asking me anything about love. Not at this moment. Cause, like Tina said, 'What's love got to do with it?'"

The cabdriver didn't say anything else to me. I sat back, my spine bumping softly against the seat, flushed and aching, reliving my kiss with Nicky all the way home, and wishing he hadn't opened something terrible in me. Something unthinkable.

Desire.

I wanted—no needed—more of him.

NICKY

My father gives me "the look," full of disapproval and recrimination. With a sideways glance of his eyes, he tells me that before I even begin to deal with him and my mother, he wants me to talk with Rebecca. On this, I actually agree with him. And if she wants to beat me like Zora did, I deserve it.

I wish she were angry. She should be angry, and maybe she is, but all I can see on her face is how much I've hurt her. I've been a coward since our first date when I realized she'd bore me numb, and if I'd have just owned up to it then, I'd have spared her this senseless pain.

Man. I suck.

Her blue eyes—beautiful blue eyes—are full of her readiness to forgive me my trespasses. I take a few tentative steps toward her. She ought to slap a back molar loose on me, but she doesn't. She makes a very simple statement.

"You told me you loved me."

I don't speak.

"Do you love me? Because your dad said sometimes guys do things, and they don't mean—" Her voice breaks.

I don't know how to comfort her because I don't love her the way she wants me to. All I can do is offer her the truth, something I didn't do from the beginning.

"It's not like that, Rebecca. It's not some thing I'm doing."

"Are you just friends with her?"

"I don't know. I don't know what we are."

She takes a deep breath and asks what I know she doesn't really want to hear the answer to. "Do you love her? Is it her? Is she *the one*, Nicholas?"

I can't bring myself to say the words to Rebecca that we both know are true. If I say I love her, it will hurt Rebecca more than saying I love someone should hurt anybody. I just say, "It's her."

She nods slowly, and a tear slides down her cheek. I wish I could wipe it away, but I don't think I should.

"How long has this been going on? You've been taking her to restaurants. Buying her things. Going to her apartment."

"Honest to God, Rebecca, I met her Wednesday. It hasn't been a week. I know that sounds crazy, but—"

"But it's her. You know that in less than a week?"

"Yeah. I think I do."

She lets out the most pathetic little laugh—a heartbreaker of a laugh. "Any chance you could be wrong?"

"You deserve better than me. Don't waste another minute with me."

"Nicholas, I love you. I want you to be sure about this."

This time I take a risk and grab Rebecca's hand. "I'd say I'm sure, but I'm not. The only thing I'm sure of is that I'm the biggest screw-up around. I'm not going to be what you want, and if you really took a good look, you'd see it. You need a man like my father, and that's not me. Rebecca, I don't really like pot roast that much."

She laughs. "I don't have to make pot roast, Nicholas. I can cook chicken. And I can call you Nicky."

"You don't say Nicky the way she does."

For a moment she's quiet. Then, "I'm really going to miss you."

"You're a really amazing person, Rebecca. Don't give me another minute of your time."

"Is she worth it?"

"Yeah."

"I can tell by how she fought for you." She pulls her hand out of mine. "Try to be happy."

"I will. You too."

She nods. "I'll try, but I don't think I will be for a while."

"I'm so sorry, Rebecca."

I could have left then, but my keys were in my jacket in the house. I was tempted to walk home, like Zora wanted to, but Detroit is a bit of a ways from Ypsilanti. I trudge behind Rebecca, trying hard to surrender to my fate.

A million thoughts and feelings compete for my attention, but I want to stop and dwell on the feel of Zora. And dear God in heaven, I felt. Too much. More than I've allowed myself to feel in the past three years.

Now what am I going to do?

If only I were so smart. But no. I go inside my parents' house to face the abuse I know is coming.

My mother is God only knows where. Maybe sewing what I'll wear in my casket once Dad kills me. Maybe she's weeping into tomorrow's pot roast. Or maybe she's somewhere trying to figure out why I broke her heart this way.

I go into the living room, and there's my dad and grandfather. Their sober expressions tell me to sit down. It's the look I got when I said I wanted to go to Berkeley. The look I got when I said I got a girl from youth group pregnant. The look they seared into me, not much later, when she had an abortion I didn't want her to have.

I sit down, my own expression, third-generation Parker, equally grim. "You shouldn't have said that, Grandpa."

"That gal had no right coming in here talking all uppity."

"She was only defending me. Something nobody else around here does."

"Nigger doesn't know her place."

"Grandpa! You've stretched my patience today. I'm going to ask you not to call her that."

He stands up. Raises his hand to me. "Boy, just because you got yourself a taste of black tail—"

Now it's time for me to stand, and when I do, something in me—something I need, some restraining force—snaps, and I snatch my grandfather's collar. He doesn't expect this—this sudden surge of violence, and neither do I. I see the fear in his eyes, and I like it. I hope he sees the anger in mine.

"Listen, you filthy old—"

My father grabs me, pulls me away from the old man, but I lunge at him. I want to fight him, and neither of them are a match for me.

"Nicholas, have you gone insane?" Dad yells.

I have. I want to snap my grandpa's bony neck.

I start yelling back. "You don't know her. You don't know anything about her. She's not a piece of tail. She's more than any of you can begin to think. *I'm* more."

"Calm down, Nick," my father says.

"Crazy nigger lover," my grandfather says.

And I go after him again. I'm a lot stronger than my father. And just to slow me down, my father sucker punches me. It wasn't bad, either! Before the end of the day I'm going to have to go to the emergency room.

I hear my mother scream.

"Call the police, Anne," Dad says.

"I can't call the police on my child."

That's when my grandfather does what he does. He gets his gun. My grandpa is an expert marksman. He points it at me, right at my head, and for a moment, I think he's going to kill me. I can't say that I'm not scared. But I'm more than a little relieved. Part of me wants to go.

Mom is losing her mind. She's screaming and crying like crazy, and the only thing that keeps me from tearing the house down until he shoots me dead is her tears and the thought that she doesn't want to see me lying dead on her parquet floors.

"I'm sorry, Mom."

And for the first time in a long time, in forever, I hear her call my name through her sobs. *"Nicky."* She reaches her hands toward me, and I want to go to her, but if I do, I'll cry with her. I realize Grandpa isn't going to kill me. I'd be dead if he was.

If I go to my mom those men will mock me until the day they die.

I do what I have to do. I get out of there like hell on wheels before my grandpa and my dad see me cry.

ZORA

The cab drops me off, and when I step up to the entrance, I see Miles getting out of his BMW. I have no idea what he's doing here, and in true Miles fashion, he makes it to my house with absolutely nothing but Miles.

"What are you doing here?"

"Where have you been in a cab?"

"I went to church. And to dinner."

We walk up the stairs to my apartment, and I let us in the door with the key I got the super to charge to next month's rent.

"What church did you go to?"

"One where they don't think I'm a witch." They think I'm a nigger and a whore. But who's keeping track?

Oh, man. Stop it, Zora.

"Come on, Z. We love you at LLCC."

"Yeah. I'm overwhelmed with it."

"We're all praying for you. We just don't want you in rebellion. That's the sin of witchcraft. Don't you understand that, baby? I want to protect you, and I can't do that if I'm aiding and abetting the problem."

"What do you want, Miles?"

"I'm here because Pamela called me. She said you were walking the streets at night."

"Yeah, Miles. I'm a two dollar hooker now, trying to earn money to buy stuff again."

I lock the door even though there's no reason to, and for lack of anything else sit on the floor. Again.

"Pam said you needed to go to the store. I came to talk to you. Call your father, Zora. This is crazy. You can't be out walking around at night."

"I wanted to do something to my hair. You may have noticed I don't have a car to jump in and go to the beauty supply store. You may have noticed I don't have much of anything, except for what a few kind souls, including Ms. Pamela, have been good enough to share."

"You have a Lexus."

"Apparently I don't. *He* has a Lexus."

"Do you want to go to the store?"

"So you can aid and abet my sinful lifestyle? I don't want you to dirty your hands on the witch, Miles."

He sits down on the floor with me. "I wish I knew what to do for you. I feel like I'm stuck in the middle of this. I love you, Zora. I just want to hold you and make all of this go away."

I shoot a look at him. He almost looks sincere.

"Will you let me hold you, Zora?"

"Sorry. I'm not feeling the love, Miles."

"That doesn't mean it's not there. Come here. You've got to be so tired."

He's right. Nicky's right. I'm exhausted.

And Miles says he wants to make all of this go away. It's beginning to sound like a good offer. He reminds me of my daddy in the good way sometimes. I miss my daddy. I want a strong man to hold me. I do.

Something inside of me says yes. Make all of this go away.

"I'm so confused, Miles."

He reaches out and strokes my hair. "Don't confess that, baby. God isn't the author of confusion. You have to speak life into this situation."

And he's off. The moment seemed so hopeful. Does anybody challenge this stuff at LLCC?

"But I *am* confused, Miles. My faith is raggedy at best. If God doesn't know that, I need a new heavenly Father." A new earthly one sounds good, too.

"Zora, baby, that's not right to say."

"Why is that wrong? God already knows I'm confused, so I really don't need another one, Miles. And I don't feel right. Everything is wrong. If I've got anybody's sympathy, it's God's."

He reaches for my hand, but I don't want it. I want Nicky's hand. Nicky would say, "Me too" instead of "That's not right." And I'm angry at myself for wanting Nicky's lily-white hand instead of Miles's.

I should want Miles. Miles is black and beautiful. Miles's grandfather is not going to call me an uppity nigger. Miles is a dreamboat. Miles is the fantasy of every single woman at my church—and a few married ones. I'm blessed to have him. And he's still here. He's mine despite the craziness of our situation.

Just try with him, Zora. Maybe count this all as a really bad day.

"Miles. Did you know when you first came to LLCC, all us ladies had a crush on you?"

He chuckles. "I knew a few of you were interested."

"I was."

"You didn't let on."

"Mac knew."

"She never told me."

"She's my best friend. Why haven't you kissed me?"

He lets out a big, boisterous laugh. "You really want to know?"

"Yes."

"For real, Zora?"

"Yes, tell me."

"Your father threatened everyone in youth group with bodily harm about you."

"You mean he really did that?"

"Baby, he told us …" He shudders. "Let's just say, you will not be kissed by an LLCC man who fears God."

"That's too bad. Because I need my man to kiss me right now."

Miles looks around like somebody is in my apartment taping us so this conversation will get back to Daddy and ruin his future. He actually looks conflicted. Almost tempted.

"I'd like to kiss you, baby."

The memory of Nicky's kiss assaults me once again. I can't stand it. I'm not sure about this, but I say it. "Maybe you should."

No. Please don't. I don't really want that.

But maybe if he kisses me I'll stop thinking about Nicky's kiss. Maybe I can go on with my life and everything will be all right, eventually.

Oh, man. I've started something.

Miles leans over and cradles my face in his hand. I close my eyes and feel his lips touch mine.

This is awful.

I want it to be like it was with Nicky. I want to feel the anger and outrage and passion. I want to feel the fire of it. But there's no fire.

There's nothing but want of Nicky, Nicky, Nicky. Tears spring to my eyes.

God, this is so not fair.

I push Miles away, gently, but it's unmistakably a push away from me.

"What's wrong?"

"I don't want *The Bishop* to hurt you."

"I'm not going to worry about that now. Come here." He takes me back into his arms and finds my mouth again. This is terrible. It's too! Too much. Too wet. Too smushy. Too horrid. And he doesn't taste good.

Okay, how do I get off this ride? I don't really want to hurt his feelings since I started the conversation that got this going, but this isn't working out for me.

I try to talk myself into it as he jams his tongue down my throat. Ewwwww! This is really, really awful.

But maybe this bad feeling is better than all that good Nicky feeling. Maybe I should just roll with this.

So, I do. We kiss and kiss and kiss until I'm nauseated. I think maybe he's getting sick from it too, because he asks me to lie down.

"Lie down? Why?"

"I want to make you feel good."

That'd be an upgrade from how the kissing is making me feel.

"I want to feel good."

I should be kissing Nicky.

I feel unbearably sad in Miles's arms. My tears flow. Miles wipes

them away, but I'm afraid they won't stop. Being around Nicky has
opened a well of grief that's always been there. Then again, maybe it
wasn't Nicky opening it at all. Maybe it was just time for all the
cracks and fissures in the walls holding me together to shatter and for
me to break open and let all that misery inside of me out. Right now.

Yes, Miles. Make me feel good.

He takes off his jacket. Balls it up and gives it to me. I'm confused.

"It's for a pillow."

I nod. Put it under my head.

He starts unbuttoning his shirt.

Oh, no. Wait a minute. I just wanted you to kiss me so I could
erase Nicky's kiss from my soul. I mean, I don't even like kissing
Miles. I certainly don't want clothes to come off. Oh, no. What have
I done?

My mind starts shutting down.

I don't want to think about what this man of God, this bishop-
in-training is trying to do. I can't handle this right now, God. I start
thinking in parts so I won't have to put the whole of this together.
While he touches me I think:

Miles has on a blue button-down shirt. He must have worn it to
church. I've seen it before. He wears it with the camel-colored suit.
It has pale yellow pinstripes. He has on jeans, but for now, he's only
unbuttoning his shirt. He has a solid, strong build and a surprise of
a curly tuft of afro hair on his chest. For a brief moment, I wonder
if Nicky has hair on his chest then banish the thought.

Miles has his shirt wide open, but the last few buttons remain. He
stops unbuttoning to kiss me again. I wonder if he thinks I think his
chest is sexy.

Finally, I find a little voice. Something inside that can't let this happen. "Please stop."

He doesn't stop.

I close my eyes and tell myself I should marry him. It's sensible. My mother would think this is a good decision, marrying Miles. This touching he's doing will only hasten the day. I think of all the people at church who are dishonoring each other with bad touches. Good Christian people in churches all over have done and are doing this. I tell myself that it won't matter. That Jesus will forgive us. That no one will know. And the fact that I feel nothing but afraid and confused is secondary to what I really need. I have to get what I really need.

I have to fall out of love with Nicky Parker. And I have to do that right now.

NICKY

I pull into the nearest parking lot, and no one comes after me, including the police. Despite my concern of what the men in my family would think if they drove by, I can't help myself—I put my head on the steering wheel and cry like a baby.

I'm so confused. I feel like a stranger to myself, and today I'm even more of a stranger to my family than I usually am. I don't want to be a white man today. And I don't want to be the color of water so you can see right through me like my family does. I want to be a Vincent Van Gogh, *Starry Night,* full of color. Zora would understand that.

I want to write. Literally. Right now. I keep a notebook in my glove box. I yank it open and fumble around for a pen. Some writer

I am. I can't find a pen to save my life. After rummaging around under the seats, I finally locate one and begin a poem for Zora.

> I wish I were the color of the sky
> because you love the sky
> maybe you could love me, too—
> my distant winking stars,
> my nameless constellations
> my strange new worlds to explore.
> Most of all I wish you would love
> my impenetrable darkness.
> Could you love me if I'm black,
> but only on the inside?

Before I have time to censor myself—and God knows I should—I take it to her.

ZORA

His touches have become tentative, as if he is warring with himself. I don't think his higher self is winning. He keeps touching and kissing.

My lovely white dress with the circle skirt. Circle like a wedding ring. It's getting dirty on the floor. This morning I loved this dress. I took a few moments after I dressed and danced around the empty living room in it. The whole place is one big studio now. Good, hardwood floors just made for dancing. I twirled around thinking of how happy I felt. How I wanted to see Nicky. Meet him in the house of God, even if I had to walk. I danced, thinking of him.

I'm going to hate this dress from now on, the way accident victims hate the clothes they were wearing when tragedy struck. I will not associate this dress with Nicky standing at my door trying to give me the box, saying it was from Jesus.

Mr. Incarnational Christian.

Where is Jesus now?

Oh, no. Don't you start crying anymore, Zora Nella Hampton Johnson. Miles isn't listening anyway. It's like MacKenzie always told you. Once you get a man going so far, you have to just let him have it. You can't just say no.

Is she right?

Can I say no, Lord?

Where are You?

I need an incarnational Christian to show up right about now, because I'm in trouble, and the trouble is about to get worse. This man who says he wants me to do what's right, who says he's been praying for me, who says I'm cursed and he doesn't want to make it worse, is about to do something I don't want him to do.

I start sobbing. "Miles?"

"What? Why are you crying so much?"

"I'm a virgin."

"I know that, Zora."

"Are you a virgin?"

He doesn't answer right away.

Dear God. He isn't. What's the matter with us Christians?

I cry even harder.

"Baby, that's in the past. I've respected you. We can get married as soon as you'd like to."

"You promise?"

"We can get married as quickly as we can get a license."

"What if Daddy doesn't approve?" I don't ask with an attitude. I'm serious.

"I'll talk to him. He listens to me, Zora. He loves you. He wants what's best for you too."

I try to force myself to believe it. "I love you, Miles."

That's not me. I've fallen in love with someone else. That's the youth group girl who's seventeen with the crush on the guy who looks like a young Denzel. Because the real me—the one on the floor of an empty apartment with the man who is supposed to love her— she's not feeling this guy who has given her nothing in her time of need. She's not down with the one who doesn't think she has any real painting talent. She's cursed as it is, and if she thinks about all this, she's not going to declare her love to him. She's going to start swinging on him like she did the guy she really loves, the one who gave her the white dress, poetry, art supplies, and forty dollars to catch a cab that cost thirteen. And the driver gave back change.

"I love you too, baby," Miles says.

"Stop touching me, Miles."

"Come on, baby. You got a brotha all worked up. We can get married in a few days if you want to."

"I don't like this. I don't want it, and I'm scared."

"I won't hurt you."

"I'm not ready for this."

"You're not going to take me there and just say stop."

I try with all my strength to get up. He struggles with me. I want to knock his head off. I try to remember that this guy is supposed to be my boyfriend. I'm supposed to love him. I don't care what Mac says about not getting a guy started. I'm going to do everything I can to finish this my way. I may not be the strongest between us, but God help me.

I give him another push, and if that doesn't work, I'm gonna start scratching, kicking, and screaming.

On the second push, he responds. "What's the matter?"

And all I can think of to say is, "You're getting my white dress dirty."

And that says so much. God, have mercy.

"Zora, it's just a dress. Relax. I'll make this good for you."

The buzzer sounds, and it's as if he puts on an I'm-a-really-great-guy-who's-not-about-to-date-rape-my-girlfriend persona. I see him change personalities before my eyes. I get up and run to the bathroom. If that's my father at the door, this is all I need, God!

I hear Miles buzz the person in. He didn't ask who it was. And a few moments later, there's a knock on my door.

Before I can get to it, Miles swings it open.

My mouth opens with the door. Nicky Parker is standing there.

NICKY

Surprise!

The door opens, and she's not standing there. The Lion King is. And he's the freakin' king of the jungle! Zekora has got to be six-foot-four or -five. I look up to him, and I'm six-foot-two. He's annoyed that I'm there, and because he's buttoning his shirt, I can figure out why he's so annoyed.

I had her wrong, and I don't usually call 'em wrong. I pegged her for a virgin. Shoulda known. She's too sensual to be a virgin. And here I am, with a poem in my hand, now wondering if someone else is going to smack me around today.

He sizes me up. A white boy at his girlfriend's door. And it occurs to me that I don't know anything about Shaka Zulu. I don't care how racist I sound, or am, either. Maybe I'm not the one I should be concerned about him hurting. I don't know if me showing up is going to be a huge problem because I didn't factor him in this equation. Every freakin' "black men are dangerous" fear I've ever had seizes me. And my reflexes are about as sharp as marshmallows right now.

"Can I help you?" he says. He ain't smiling.

I look crazy. I've got a big bruise where my dad hit me, I just tried to beat up an old man, and I've been crying profusely, but I'm a white man in a suit. And I'm a Baptist.

"Good evening, sir. I was wondering if I might share with you the good news of Jesus Christ."

A part of me wants him to please say no. I think if he has any good sense whatsoever he will say no and slam the door on me, no matter how much I want to keep her safe. God, let her be okay. I just *feel* like I need to get in that apartment.

I'm being paranoid.

"Oh," he says. "Come in."

And I do.

But I do it with an attitude, and not of gratitude. I want to see her. I want her to look me in the face after she kissed me and then did the wild thing, literally, with him.

What kind of hypocrite am I? I took her to dinner with my freakin' girlfriend. I'm trapped with Zora in an existential nightmare.

I step into the apartment, and she is standing by the bathroom door, totally shocked to see me. I'm still trying to wrap my brain around the idea of their shared intimacy. Her man says, "Z. He's a brother in Christ."

She just nods and stares at me like she's never seen a Christian before.

Miles sticks his hand out. "I'm Miles Zekora. This is my wife, Zora."

I shake his hand, trying not to react to the fact that he called her his wife. He takes that one flesh thing seriously. "Nice to meet you, Mr. Zekora."

"Call me Miles," he says.

I turn to her. Nod. "*Mrs.* Zekora."

He waves off my formality. "Naw man, just Zora. What's your name, brother?"

"Nicky Parker."

Miles offers a witty little remark about my name. "Nicky Parker? Brother, you got the same name as the character that comedienne chick Monique plays on that TV show, *The Parkers.*"

I knew the show, but honestly, no one, even Pete "I love all things black" Greene has ever said that to me.

"Your name reminds me of something, too." I look like I'm struggling to think of what. "Can't remember," I say. "Oh, well. *Hakuna Matata!*"

Zora intervenes before I get punched again. Or give a punch. "He's been here before, uh, witnessing."

"I did witness here before," I say. It wasn't really a lie. I may not have been proselytizing, but I did try to truly be Christ to her.

"I've had a very hard day, and God knows I need Jesus right now," she says.

Does she need Jesus after the lovin' like some people need a smoke? I certainly need Jesus after she's been with Miles, and this is one instance I truly want nothing to do with incarnational Christianity, but I actually care too much to let her statement go without throwing her a bone, even if it's an Ezekiel one, all dead and dry.

"We all need Jesus, Zora. Today seems to be a big day for needing Him. At least for me."

Miles looks at my face. "Looks like you been needing Him bad today, man."

"That's true, Miles. I've had a very hard day as well."

"And you're still out here being a soldier for Christ."

"Soldier?" I chuckle. "That's apropos, especially with my war wounds."

"You can learn something from him, Zora. About perseverance."

She gives him a beatific smile. "I'm sure he'd have a lot to teach me, Miles."

I don't touch that one. But God, I want to. And I want to touch her, despite how sick I feel being around the two of them. Is this how she felt today around Rebecca and me? And nobody has called me racial slurs standing here.

My eyes catch hers. There's a world of emotion in those eyes, including one I know well: shame. She's safe, and now I'm not. I'm getting so angry at the thought of the two of them together, I am capable of saying or doing anything. I need to get out of here. She needs me to leave.

"I just thought I'd stop by to say God loves you and has a wonderful plan for your life. I'll be going. I hope you and your wife have a great rest of the day, Miles."

Zora steps forward. "We're not married yet, Nicky."

"It'll be a matter of days," Miles says. He sounds defensive, and if I were him, I would too. "Might as well say it's done."

I can't help myself. Nastiness flies out of my mouth. "Really? Days? No wonder your apartment is empty. You're *moving*. Hey, where's your engagement ring, Zora?"

Miles looks a little ticked off at me. "I've got that taken care of."

"Of course. It's probably with her other stuff. What was I thinking? Forgive me. I just find it odd that your fiancée isn't wearing a ring."

"I'm handling it," Miles says.

I want to keep up the nasty, but it will only make matters worse. And it won't change anything.

I've lost her.

What am I, crazy? I'm not pursuing her. Just hanging out with her for a few days has got my life totally twisted. I've lost my head, she's just gotten cozy with Simba, and I need to get out of here.

Suddenly I'm drained. I take another look at her. She's so beautiful she takes my breath away.

I reach out to shake Miles's hand.

"I wish you and Zora every happiness."

"Keep in touch, man. I'll invite you to our reception. Let us get your number. Take his phone number, Z."

"Miles, he probably doesn't want to come to our reception."

"I wouldn't miss it, Zora. Let me give you my phone number. Do you have a pen?"

"As you can see I don't have *anything*."

"You have Miles. I'm sure he can at least give you a *pen!*"

"I'm not so sure," she says.

Miles gives her a very unpleasant look, but he takes a pen out of the pocket of his jacket on Zora's floor. He gives it to me. I write my name, address, house and cell phone number, and e-mail address on the folded paper with the poem I wrote. I even write my work number and put Linda's name in parenthesis. Try to hand it to him.

"Just give it to Zora. She'll probably be the one sending out invitations and stuff. You know how that kind of thing is, man. You got a girlfriend?"

"Not anymore. She broke up with me today."

He actually laughed. "She dot that eye?"

"It's actually just under my eye. And, no, that was my father."

"Whoa, say it ain't so, Nick. Sorry to hear it. What did you do?"

"Long story, but let's just say I was really into another woman. Everybody could tell. Nobody approved."

"She must be something else if nobody approved."

"Something *else?* Now that is an apt description, Miles. She was something *else* all right. But regardless of who or what she was, my *girlfriend* didn't like me being obviously crazy about her."

Miles nods. "True that. Any way you can work things out with your girlfriend?"

"We weren't a good match. Frankly, the other woman is better for me."

"Why don't you hook up with her then?"

"I *just* found out she's getting married."

"Dang, man." He shakes his head. "I hope you find somebody. Maybe you'll be blessed and find somebody like Zora."

"Now *that* would be something."

"Yeah, man. I'm blessed."

"You sure are, Miles."

He pauses. Seems to strain that pea brain of his to think. "Hey, maybe *I* can hook you up with somebody. Would you have a problem going out with a sistah?"

God, you've got to be kidding me.

I feel Zora looking at me, and I fight not to look back. "*Problem? Why on earth would that be a problem?* It's not like this is the fifties or something, Miles, sheesh!"

"Yeah," Miles says. "Things are different now." He rolls his shoulders back in smug self-satisfaction. "Then it's settled. We're going to hook you up with a sistah."

"I'm excited." I shift my attention to Zora. "Zora, do you know anybody I'd be interested in?"

"Maybe one person."

"Would it help if I told you what I want in a woman?"

"I don't think so."

"Oh, come on. It'll be fun." I glance around at the sapphire walls that she said match my eyes. I love her. I'm mad at her. "May I sit, please?"

"We don't want to keep you, Nicky." But her *husband* waves away what she's said with a flick of his hand.

"Naw, it's cool. Take a load off. We're brothers in Christ, right?" He holds out his fist, and for a moment, I'm confused. I wonder if this is some kind of precursor to aggression, but then I realize he just wants me to pound it. This is just a guy thing.

I pound. Sit. And he sits with me.

"Sit down, Zora," he says. He just orders her. He's not really asking. She sits down obediently, in a way Rebecca would if I said, "Sit down!" Didn't even challenge him. This isn't the Dreamy I know and love.

Miles leads the questions once Zora sits with us.

"So, what kind of woman do you want?"

"I dunno, Miles. Somebody kinda *dreamy*."

"Okay." He looks at Zora. "You know any dreamy chicks, Z?"

"Maybe one."

"And I'd like her to be artistic. Somebody with little dots of paint splatter and residue on her clothes and shoes she can never quite get out because she paints so much, and so passionately, she just keeps messing up her clothes. I want a sistah who cares more about art than her clothes."

Miles rubs his chin. "I don't know about that one. I mean, she would sound a little flighty to me. Are you sure that's what you want?"

"I'm sure, Miles."

He seems to consider this deeply. "What else are you looking for?"

"A woman who loves books. Maybe not as much as I do, but enough to engage me in passionate conversation about them. I'd want to share every novel I love with her. And know all the novels she loves." He seems a little bored with me. I don't like this Miles. "Do you know your wife's *favorite* book?"

He doesn't even look to Zora for help with this one. "The Bible."

For a moment, I think he should go to my dad's church instead of Zora's dad's. He should be in love with Rebecca, because that really is her favorite book, including her favorite novel.

"I meant her favorite novel, Miles."

The question seems to take him by surprise. He scratches his head. "I don't know, man."

"A woman like Zora. Classy. Most likely educated. Her freakin' *name* is Zora. I'd guess it's *Their Eyes Were Watching God*."

I look at my Dreamy. She seems to be like a flower wilting in the heat of too much sun. "What's your favorite novel, Zora?"

"That's it."

I shot a viciously triumphant look at Miles. "That's what I mean. I'd want to know my woman's favorite novel. I'd want to know who she is, and not just who she's been constructed to be by somebody else, including me."

Miles seems to consider this. "That's deep."

I pull myself up from the floor.

It's hard to breathe. My cheek is swelling by the moment. I hand her my information and the poem she doesn't know is a poem.

She takes it and locks eyes with me. "Thank you, Nicky. Thank you for stopping by."

"You're welcome. I'm sorry you had a hard day."

"I'm sorry *you* had one. Why don't you and Miles head out together? Miles was just leaving."

Miles doesn't look like he wants to leave, but she gives him a look full of fire and determination, and I'm glad to see the Zora I know back.

"Keep me posted on your wedded bliss. Good-bye, Zora. Good-bye, Miles."

She stands, as does Miles. She doesn't even say good-bye to me.

Miles slips on his jacket. "I'll be back soon, baby. I'll bring you back some things you need." His gaze shifts to me. "Hey, I might call you so we can double date or something."

"You do that, Miles."

I will jump off a building first. On fire. With a noose around my neck.

We finally get out of that apartment. But I don't say a word to him on the stairs. I suddenly no longer exist for him. Obviously, she's the only thing on his mind.

Mine, too.

I've got one thing on my mind to do. I need to get drunk. And I have no money for that kind of thing.

My new best friend, Richard, comes to mind.

CHAPTER SEVENTEEN

NICKY

By the time I arrive at Richard's apartment, I'm so ready for a drink, I can taste it. I'll have what he's having, thanks! I was never very discriminating when I was drinking anyway.

Three years of sobriety down the drain, but the payoff—something to numb the thought of him being with her in that way, of him touching her; the thought of her making love with him—

Man.

I've never kissed anyone with lips so full and soft. And I've never been with a tall woman. Why, I don't know. Maybe I felt so small myself, I wanted all those petite cuties to make me feel bigger. I only know that everything about her in my arms felt right and perfect and it just didn't seem to matter when I held her that her skin was darker than mine. Everybody else thought it mattered. Maybe not everybody, but all the people in my little world.

I knock on Richard's door, ready for my foray back into the wonderful world of alcohol abuse. Richard opens the door, looking a little more frail than usual. He's got a smoke in his hands.

"Nicky," he says. His green eyes light up. "It's good to see you, son. Come on in." He still smells of booze, but he doesn't seem drunk. He invites me in, takes my jacket and hangs it up. "Come on in and have a seat."

Despite the fact the apartment smells like a smokehouse, I like Richard's place. It's cozy. It's neither fancy nor ostentatiously austere, if you can believe that kind of oxymoron, but God knows I've seen it in action. Just a welcoming place, a place to entertain the stranger. God knows that's me today.

I take an annoyed look at him puffing away. He's often asked if his smoking bothers me, and I always lie and tell him no. He eventually stopped asking. Now I have the nerve to be ticked off because he doesn't ask this time.

"Richard, do you ever actually breathe in between the constant, unrelenting, endless inhaling and exhaling tobacco?"

He doesn't seem to notice my rudeness.

"I'm sorry. I should have asked if this bothered you." He ambles over to an ashtray by his sofa, and I follow him so I can sit down. I watch him crush his cigarette and finally beckon me to sit.

Guilt pricks me. "I'm sorry I hung up on you earlier."

"I'm sorry I wasn't there for you. At least not all the way there. Something on your mind, Nicky?"

"Yeah. We can talk about it over drinks."

"Of course. What would you like?" He stands, ready to serve.

"Whatever you had earlier. Make it a double."

Richard chuckles. "You don't want that, son."

"That's exactly what I want."

He tugs his trousers up and sits on the couch beside me. Turns to face me before I blast him.

"Richard, your hospitality is slipping, man. I asked for a drink."

"I'd be happy to get you something. I've got some great tea. I get that nice Harney and Sons tea from Barnes and Noble. Got this great African Autumn infusion."

"No thanks. I've already had my African infusion today by way of Zora and her boyfriend, or husband, or whatever he is. Apparently

I'm a racist, and you know what, I'm really starting not to care. So please. If you're going to offer tea, I'd like something European. English Breakfast, or Earl Grey, or something white sounding, but quite frankly, I'd rather have booze!"

"Why don't you tell me about that? What happened to your face, Nicky?"

"I'd be happy to share over drinks, Rich."

"Nicky …"

I stand up. "I don't need a sponsor today. I didn't come here for you to walk me through the steps or ask me if I'm hungry, angry, lonely, or tired and to H.A.L.T. Because you know what, Rich? I'm hungry. For Zora. I'm angry because she did the wild thing with her big black buck promptly after giving me the most amazing kiss I've ever had. I'm lonely because who on this freakin' planet gets me? *She* gets me, without even trying, but we had *Guess Who's Coming to Dinner?*—the new millennium version—only unlike the one with Ashton Kutcher, I didn't get the girl or the happy ending. And I'm tired, Richard. I'm bone weary in my dead freakin' soul. I want a drink. I want alcohol."

For a moment he's quiet. And then, "Nicky. I just want to be the heart of Jesus to you in your time of— "

"Dude! You want to be Jesus to me? Be Jesus at the wedding in Cana. Turn some water into wine, Richard, because what I want is a drink."

"You've been sober three years, Nicky. I know what it is to give that kind of time up, and I don't believe I'd be serving you well by helping you do that."

"But you were drunk this morning. You were lit up like the

Christmas tree at Rockefeller Center on the eve of the Lord's birth-day *today,* Richard."

Tears shine in his blue eyes. "You don't want to be like me, son. You love Jesus so much."

"You love Him too. And you had a drink."

He sits on the sofa while I stay standing. I don't think I've ever seen a more weary soul than Richard. He clears his throat, which does nothing to relieve it of its alcohol and smoke-weary rattle.

"Kid. You don't want to be me. You don't want to be anything like me."

"I just want a drink, Rich."

"And then you'll want another one. One is too many. A thousand is never enough."

"I know the rhetoric."

"Let me tell you what you don't know, son. You don't know what it is to be me. You don't know what it is to fail so often, son, and have other Christians—some you thought were your friends—dismiss you without a second thought. And the worst part is, you know you could have been so much more. Yeah, lots of people buy my books, but that's a mercy. I'm grateful that God's messy people read them, but sometimes I just want to be a nice guy, Nicky. I don't want to be a drunk. I don't want to be the guy who tells people God loves them despite themselves. Sometimes I just want to get it right. And I can't, Nicky. I preach grace because I don't have a choice. I wish I did. Don't be like me. Don't take that drink, because drink-ing is what made me lose my wife, and she was the best thing that ever happened to me. I want you to have a better life than I had. I don't want you to be a lonely, sick, crusty old man who can't stop drinking and smoking to save his life, literally. Let me be clear on something. At this moment, I'm not talking about God's love. God is going to love you whether or not you drink. God is going to love you if you're the biggest drunk on skid row. You can't earn God's love, or lose it, whether you're perfect, or a rebel, rascal, or whore. But I'm going to tell you a little something about Richard's love. I love you too much, and I'm too selfish to let that first drink—the drink that will turn you into me—come from me."

I finally sit down. "I love her. And she's going to marry him."

"Let's pray, Nicky."

I run my hands through my hair and try to breathe.

Richard puts his hand on my shoulder. "Nicky?"

I want to break something. I want to destroy something.

He begins to pray something from the Psalms in his whiskey tenor voice, over and over for both of us. Richard loves this prayer so much he's turned it into his own. He said it's supposed to be a prayer of deliverance from your enemies, but he loves it for its poverty.

Make haste, O God, to deliver me, make haste to help me, O Lord.

I am poor and needy; make haste unto me, O God: thou art my help and my deliverer; O LORD, make no tarrying.

I love Richard for this. I want this deliverance he prays for, but it eludes me. God does tarry, and my need feels urgent. He's silent, just like He was when my grandpa was so vocal at the dinner table. Where was God when Richard needed the strength to say no to that drink this morning? How could He give Richard the grace to minister to me, but not himself?

And my need for a drink has passed. God, will You be with

Richard later on tonight? When he's hungry, angry, lonely, or tired? And what about me? Because I don't want a drink, Lord, but my need for Zora has increased exponentially.

I hug Richard and go home.

I want to go back to her. I don't care that she's been with him. I love her. At least I think I love her.

God, I'm so confused.

No. I can't love her. It's only been a few days. I just want her. It's just lust. She doesn't want me anyway. She slept with him.

Maybe she's easy. Maybe I can just go back and have a turn too.

No. I know she's not like that.

Then again, I don't know anything.

Again, I run my hands through my hair. By now my eye must be a sight—no pun intended.

Just go home, Nicky.

But I want her. If she kissed me and went right to him, maybe I can have a chance.

To do what?

If I can make love to her, just once, I can make her love me. I know I can.

And then God finally decides to chat.

It didn't make Brooke love you.

Richard and I have revival, and God says nothing. Want to go have a little feel-good time, and then He talks. And that's what He says.

"Thanks a lot, God."

But it worked. As much as I wanted to try to find her alone and seduce her, I take my rascally, rebellious, whoring self home.

And I ain't happy about it, but I do it. Who I do it *for,* I can't even say.

ZORA

Incarnational Christianity.

I have to admit, it's a little annoying but looking good today, Lord. My mind keeps going back to Nicky showing up at my door the first time with the clothes. What he said that day:

"You're in trouble. Will you take this package from Jesus, and not turn Him away because He happened to come to you looking like a ticked-off white man today?"

Jesus came again, looking like that same white man, still angry, but wearing a cloak of sorrow even his scowl couldn't hide. And he came just stopping me from disaster right on time, dear Lord! What a mess I found myself in. He came, Nicky Parker, that is, protecting me. Never letting on the day's events, how his kiss had ruined me for Miles.

Miles said he was going to get some things to make me more comfortable. I'm glad he's gone. I need to process.

Maybe I overreacted. Would Miles have raped me? *Rape* is a very strong word. Miles wants to marry me. We could be married within days. Men that marry you can't rape you, can they?

God, what in the world is going on?

Am I in love with Nicky Parker?

I am, aren't I?

I'm not sure. I've never been in love before. What does it mean if I can't stop thinking about him? Or if I relive kissing him over and over? And if Miles's kiss was totally disgusting?

The buzzer sounds. He's come back way too soon. I hoist myself off the ground and shuffle over to the door to buzz him in. I open the door and wait, but it's not Miles and his stuff that meets me. It's Linda and Billie.

I don't know how I feel about this at first. I'm still a little leery of my white brethren and sistren. But they keep showing up for me. Where is my own family? Has anyone told Zoe or the twins? What is my mother thinking? I think about the words of Jesus.

Who is my brother and sister and mother?

There's Ms. Pamela and her widow's mite. And now Miles has gone shopping. Maybe all of this will end soon. I don't know.

They're carrying flowers. Linda has calla lilies. She's wearing some bright Mexican-looking skirt and peasant blouse and looks like a little less stylized version of someone Diego Rivera would paint. Billie is beside her. She's got a bunch of Shasta daisies, in completely unnatural but wonderfully silly rainbow colors. They hold the flowers out to me like they're some kind of peace offering.

"For me?"

And Billie is so blunt. "Yeah. We were hoping you don't hate whitey now." Then she laughs. "Hey, do you remember that Garrett Morris skit from *Saturday Night Live* where he's this convict? And he did this audition or something, he sings this song that goes—" and Billie actually starts singing, "'—I'm gonna get me a shotgun, and kill all the whiteys I see.' And then they dragged him off." She cracks up. "Remember that?"

My mouth flies open. I know it only because I saw my father watching a rerun and laughing hysterically, but I'm not sure I should admit finding it funny in mixed company.

Linda turns beet red. She speaks to her compadre like she's a small child. "Billie. Please don't. And I'm sure that was before Zora's time."

Billie waves it off. "It was funny, and it's from a *comedy* skit. Now I can name a few people singing that and it wouldn't be funny. But Garrett made it funny."

"Billie."

"Okay. Sorry, Zora," she said. "We're supposed to be reconciling, and here I am inciting hate crimes. Can we come in?"

"Sure." I step aside. Billie really is funny. I can't help but find her interesting. It's like she missed some important social-skill-gathering phase in her life, but her inappropriateness, even though she's old enough to know better, is somehow hilarious.

"I'd offer you a place to sit, but as you can see, not much has changed."

"That's one reason why we're here," Billie says. "Oh, yeah, read the cards on your flowers."

I slip out the first card tucked into the green tissue paper holding the lilies. It says, "Not all whites are bad."

I groan. "That's cute."

Linda smiles. "I've got a box of white towels and washcloths, white pajamas, a white terry-cloth robe, a white china tea cup, and some white tea in the car for you. And we have some other things too."

"Now read mine," Billie says.

I can't imagine what hers will say. I find it tucked between an electric blue and hot pink daisy. She kept it simple. "We love hue. Don't leave us because of this."

"Richard sent you a box too. It's in the car."

"What is it?"

"It's a surprise."

"I can't take any more surprises today. Nicky gave me more than enough."

Linda looks reluctant.

Billie looks bored. "Oh, for heaven's sake, just tell her."

Linda shakes her head. "I can't."

Billie howls with laughter. "Richard sent us to Zingerman's Deli for you. We got you, like, ten different kinds of crackers. He said to tell you 'not all crackers leave such a bad taste in your mouth.' And we got you some tasty spreads, cheeses, and jams to go with the crackers."

Now it's my turn to laugh. Boxes of crackers. I laugh so hard that I start to choke. Billie bangs on my back until Linda says she's going to beat me to death, and then I can't help myself, I start to cry. Just as quickly, Billie's arm draws me to her and she holds me like she was my mama.

"Aw, sweetie. It's okay."

"It's not okay. I'm feeling totally white-people weary right now."

"That's completely understandable," Linda says. "What Nicky's grandfather said to you was horrible."

"And that's not all. Nicky ended up kissing me."

"We heard about that, too." Billie says, with way too much enthusiasm. "Is he a good—"

Linda clears her throat. "You were saying Nicky kissed you."

"And I ended up kissing him back. And I sorta lost my head because I had never kissed anybody before. Not even my boyfriend. And …" I'm talking too fast. I sound like a lunatic.

"Are you supposed to feel numb and tingly at the same time? Or get chills and warm—well, maybe *warmer* than warm?"

"Yeah." Billie grins at me. Linda gives her another look.

"Anyway," I say, "I didn't think I should have enjoyed it so much, considering, and then when I got home, Miles showed up."

"Did you tell him you kissed Nicky?"

"No. Not yet. It kinda creeped me out. No offense, but Nicky is ... you know. He's not like me. His grandfather made that clear. Should I have told Miles?"

Billie shakes her head vigorously. "No! I don't see any need for you to add that drama to your life right now. Anyway, what else happened?"

"I ended up trying to make Nicky's kiss go away. I mean, I feel kinda guilty telling you this, but I just didn't ... I don't know. I'm confused. It wasn't supposed to be Nicky giving me my first kiss. What am I supposed to do with that?"

Billie can't seem to help herself. "Get another one! Nicky's a doll! Are you nuts? And he loves Jesus. He's a mess, but you can work with him."

Linda seems to have the patience of Job. "Billie, Zora has to find a job so she can keep her apartment. She really doesn't need the complications of adding Nicky Parker and a confusing interracial romance to her life right now."

"It's always time for romance. Unless you're married or something and it's just wrong, but she's not married, and neither is he."

Linda says, "What about Miles and Rebecca?"

"They both need to be deleted," Billie answers.

Linda sighs deeply. "What else happened, Zora?"

"I kissed Miles. A lot. And he just doesn't kiss the way Nicky does. And he doesn't … he doesn't taste right."

"That's because you're in love with Nicky now. Did you know that biologically speaking, only the people you're compatible with taste good to you?"

Linda shakes her head. "Billie, can you bring something helpful and *Christlike* to this?"

She gives Linda her own annoyed glance. "This is Christlike. Jesus wants her to dig Nicky. It's obvious. And I'm not afraid to say so."

"You're not afraid to say anything, Billie."

"This is true. Go on, baby."

I shake my head at the two opposites. "Anyway, I got Miles all excited, and he said he would make me feel good."

"Oh, sweetie," Billie says.

Linda just lays her hand on her heart.

"He started touching me all over my body. He had his hands all over my … I feel so ashamed. I have to marry him."

"Oh, no, baby. I don't like him for you. You can't marry him. He's an a—"

"Billie," Linda says, raising her voice without raising it.

She shoots a frustrated look at Linda, and then gives her attention back to me. "Okay. I'm going to try not to cuss because I'm working on that, but he's a jerk. You know that, I'm sure. You're smart, Zora. Your instincts have gotta be telling you he's not right for you."

She releases me enough that we can have a conversation. "I know."

She plops down effortlessly on the floor. "Sit down, baby. Let me tell you about my man."

This I have to hear. Linda sits down with us. She crosses her long legs and swings her hair behind her back. She's a crazy hippie, and I just love her despite my misgivings about white people.

Billie starts her story with, "I was a hooker, sweetie, with a drug habit and a bad man. I wasn't a high-end call girl, either. I was workin' the streets for this idiot named Rodney, and believe me, I was a bigger idiot than Rodney if I was workin' for *him*."

I look in her face. She's beautiful. I mean, really pretty. I wondered how long ago this was. As if she could read my mind, she told me.

"This was years ago, when I was about your age. I was twenty-three. And I meet this guy. He's passing out condoms and sandwiches to us girls. And he called us 'ladies.' He was just plain good to us."

I nod. What kind of guy passes out sandwiches and condoms to hookers and means it when he calls them ladies? Her eyes light up with love and memory.

"One night, it was freezing. Rodney didn't make enough money that night because it was thirty below or something crazy. Three of his girls had the flu, and I was one of them, but they were throwing up and had high fevers. I could still stand up. So he put me out on Woodward Avenue to do what I did."

I shake my head. Imagining a young, wisecracking, cussing Billie freezing up and down Woodward.

"I couldn't get a boyfriend if I paid *him* that night. And that's when I saw John, the condom-and-sandwich guy. Ironically, his name is John."

I laugh.

"He became my boyfriend that night. He went to his ATM

machine and took out three hundred dollars, the most he could get. Took me to a diner and got me some chicken soup. I couldn't get warm enough. And he just kept giving me hot liquids and asking me to tell him my stories. And baby, I had a lot of them."

Her eyes fill with tears, and she brushes them back. "I'd never had a man listen to me. Not since my daddy died. And John listened and never said much about himself. He didn't even preach to me, and I knew he was some kind of preacher. He just took me off the street, gave me soup, money to keep my pimp from sending me to the hospital, and kept me warm until the next time. And there was a next time. And a few more."

"Oh, Billie," I say. "That's so sad."

"Yeah. But it's my life. I gave it all to Jesus eventually. 'Cause you know what, baby? John kept giving out sandwiches and condoms. Saint Francis said, 'Preach the gospel, and use words if you have to.' Sweetie, that man preached to me every day without saying one thing *about* Jesus. He just acted like Jesus. Protecting me. Looking at me. Truly seeing me. Not trying to take what he could get, and I offered him some, for free. He's a cutie!"

She laughs, then has that satisfied smile I've seen on women truly in love. "And pretty soon I asked him to start telling *me* stories. About Jesus. About the Samaritan woman. About Mary Magdalene. And he told me about the desert harlots. Now those were some changed whores, Zora. And Jesus loved them! He excited me."

"Wow." I want to tell them Nicky excites me, but I'm so confused right now. Billie goes on with her story.

"He kept coming back, asking for nothing, just giving, until one day, I said, 'Hey, remember that water you were tellin' me about?

That water that'll make it so you ain't never thirsty again?' And that cutie smiled at me, and I told myself I was gonna marry him. Anyway, he said, 'I remember.' And I said, 'I'm pretty thirsty. Can I have a drink of that?' The rest, as they say, is history. We fell in love."

"Amazing," I say. "Now that's a story."

"And that's a *man*. Seems like the one that shows up with the clothes, and the food, and gets you a cab, and fights his family for you is the one—"

Linda clears her throat.

Billie rolls her eyes. "I can't help it. I'm a romantic."

Linda rankles. "She's got a crisis, Billie. She's not trying to get a man."

"I know she's not. She's got two of them. I'm just sayin' only one of them is worth a—"

The buzzer sounding again interrupts her. Speaking of men....

I get up off the floor and think to actually ask who it is in case I get another surprise and find the pope standing there. But it's just Miles.

"It's my boyfriend."

"Oh, joy," Billie quips.

This oughta be interesting.

I buzz him in, and he's surprised that I have company. He turns on the charm. He is truly my father's protégé. He's got a big Wal-Mart bag in his hand.

The ladies stand.

"Miles, these are my friends. This is Linda."

He reaches out and gives her what I know is a firm handshake.

"And this is Billie."

He extends his hand to Billie but she doesn't take it. "Hey," she says. Linda gives her a subtle glare.

Billie looks at him up and down and starts in. "Somebody's been to *Wal-Mart*. Whatcha got there, big spender?"

I think that woman has a spiritual gift of flustering people.

He stammers. "Uh. I got her uh, a …"

He pulls out of the bag, of all things, an *air mattress!*

Billie stares at him. "You gotta be kiddin' me."

"She's sleeping on the floor," he says.

"Yeah, what else is new? Where were you Friday with your little air mattress?"

"I don't have to explain myself to you."

"No, you don't, because I wouldn't buy what you're selling, pimp. You've got to explain to *God* why three whole days after your girlfriend loses everything you show up with an air mattress and that box of condoms you think I don't know are in that bag. And why you do this only after you spent the afternoon feeling her up."

His ire rises like my father's. Daddy's taught him well. First he looks at me. The looks says, *Zora, did you tell them our business?*

"Don't look at her like that," Billie says. "I know what you're thinking. I'm prophetic."

"I don't know who you are, *woman*. But I suggest you watch what you say to me."

Billie gets right in his face. "I could have you for breakfast without a burp, sweetie. Bring it on."

Linda pulls Billie to the side. "We're going, Zora. I'm very sorry."

"I'm not," Billie says to me. "Come with us, baby. I don't trust Romeo here."

I look at her and Linda, and then Miles, and all the emptiness. Blue walls. Red walls. It still feels too lonely. Frankly, I'd rather go with them no matter what color they are. I think. But I'm not sure.

I'm surprised Linda doesn't tell Billie to mind her business. I think she wants me to go with them too. In his anger, Miles must sense my hesitation.

"Zora, you'd better ask your friends to leave."

"I think everybody needs to calm down," I snap back at him.

I've never seen Miles so angry. His left hand is shaking. He reminds me so much of the worst of my father that I feel afraid.

His voice is controlled rage. "As the man you are about to marry, I'm telling you right now to ask your little friends to leave or I'll put them out of here myself, and you won't like it."

"I've met more compelling pimps," Billie says.

"I'm sure you have," he replies.

"You've got to come stronger than that to break me down, my friend."

Miles looks at me. "Zora ..."

I feel like I can't take any more. "Can you all just leave? I just want to be left alone."

"Zora. You're my woman, and I don't have to take orders from a female."

"Feeling me up doesn't make us one flesh, Miles. Just let me have some space. Take your air mattress and condoms and go."

"Fine," he says.

"Miles?" I say. "Wait."

He looks angry. "What?"

"Do you really have condoms in that bag?"

He doesn't say no. I look at Billie. She's harsh and crazy, but she knows so much more about life than I do. Linda just looks at the floor.

"Why didn't you bring me a Bible?" I asked.

Linda says, "We've got a Bible in the car. We'll get the things we brought for you and just leave them by the door. It's just the stuff we told you about and some clothes, personal items, and a few quilts and pillows. We're so sorry we didn't get these things to you sooner."

Billie adds, "The House of Hospitality and The Beloved Community rely on donations. I've been looking for furniture for you since Friday, but we have to dole out our resources according to priority needs. I'm sorry, baby. Take the air mattress. We'll get you a bed soon. I promise."

Miles doesn't say anything. He just sets down the bag with the mattress in it, condoms and all, and walks out. I don't try to stop him.

I do follow Linda and Billie down to the car they came in—an old-fashioned hippie VW van. I can only imagine who it belongs to. Miles is long gone, even though he heard them say they had some things for me.

They have two big boxes, and that doesn't include Richard's stuff from Zingerman's.

Billie takes the braggin' rights. "Look, baby, we didn't shop at Macy's for you, but lemme tell you, I got a good eye. I didn't let Linda pick out *anything*. I know nuns who wear more interesting clothes."

Linda doesn't even look fazed. "I know that I'm beautiful in Christ, and I happen to love my modesty and my personal style."

"I love it too." I say. And oddly I mean it. But I like Billie's style more.

Billie laughs. "Not that there's any leather in here for you. I just figured you got a classy yet bohemian kinda vibe. Am I right?"

"That's exactly right."

"I got ya good stuff. Even us needy God-broads like to look good. Right, baby?"

"I think so. I don't know."

She laughs again. "Trust me on that one."

Once again, Jesus has shown up, this time looking like two crazy white women. Maybe He looks like Miles, too. With an air mattress so I wouldn't have to sleep on the floor, despite Miles's agenda. But what if he returned? Could I handle him?

"Can I go with you two after all?"

"Of course," Linda says. "We'd be honored to have you, either one of us. Do you want to go to my place or The Beloved Community?"

"What's The Beloved Community?"

"That's the community of Jesus where Billie and her family live. I live alone. I'd love to have you."

"I'd love to come, but I've got to see a place called The Beloved Community."

A wide grin creeps across Billie's face. She thrusts her fist in the air. "Yes!"

"The Beloved Community it is," Linda says.

We put the boxes in the apartment, and I take a moment to go through them. Billie is right. She has a great eye and scored some wonderful things for me. I grab a few necessities, including Nicky's phone number, a sketch pad, and some pens, and head out the door.

NICKY

I get home and I feel like I've got freakin' posttraumatic stress syndrome or something. All I can think about is Zora, and I don't know what to do about that. I've got exactly four friends. Three of them go to Bible study with me, not including Zora. The other is Pete.

I do *not* want to talk to Pete. I do *not* want to talk to anybody of the female persuasion from the Bible study, except for Zora, and I can't decide whether I'm mad at her, depressed, or both. I just drained Richard, I'm sure, so I'm on my own.

I don't have much furniture. Just a cheap futon I got for a hundred bucks at the Meijer in Ypsilanti, and a floor lamp and end table. In the corner is a bookshelf, but I haven't put many books on it. I feel guilty about reading the books I want to read, and even more guilty about not reading the books Dad gave me to prepare me for seminary.

I sit on the black futon. It matches my mood. Pull out my cell phone. I'm going to have to torment Richard again, because God knows as much as I want to have a little talk with Jesus, I need to hear a human voice.

I punch the numbers. He answers on the first ring.

"How are you, son?" he says.

"I suck, Richard."

He chuckles. "You're all right, Nicky."

"How do you know when you're falling in love?"

"I think one of the first signs is that you start asking people that question."

"She came to our Bible study four days ago. Five days ago I didn't know a Zora Nella Hampton Johnson existed in this world."

"Sure you did, Nicky."

"I did?"

"Sure. Maybe you didn't know it was her, but you knew there was somebody out there who'd want to see you for who you really are. Who'd want to know you. Somebody you'd want to know as deeply and intimately as you can know another person."

"That's exactly how I feel, Richard. She's going to marry Simba."

"You should stop saying things like that, Nicky. I don't think they're helping you."

"I'm not going to get any help here, Richard. God made my dream woman black. He puts me in the most racist family imaginable and makes me fall in love with a black woman."

"You sound very self-pitying. And you're not even being honest."

"I am being honest."

"First of all, there are families far more racist than yours. Second, God didn't make you do anything."

"Are you saying I'm choosing to feel what I feel?"

"I'm not saying that there isn't a little magic and mystery happening. It's springtime. You and Zora are two young, attractive people. Love is in the air. But the truth is, yes, you are making choices, many of which you didn't have to make at all."

I think about what he says. Can't even deny the truth of it. "I can't help myself, Richard. She captivates me."

"I know, kid."

"She's gonna marry that guy."

"I hope not. She'd miss out on you. I'd hate that."

"I don't understand those people. They took everything from her. He's supposed to be her boyfriend, but he didn't stand up for her. I didn't see one thing in her apartment that I didn't give her. Well, Linda said she and Billie took her some food and stuff, but that was it. He probably made love to her on the floor, Richard. He didn't even spring for a hotel room. How could he watch her be stripped to nothing, and then keep taking from her?"

"You don't know what happened, Nicky."

"Yeah, I do, Rich. He was buttoning his shirt when he came to the door."

"Don't judge her, Nicky."

"Why not? I've been celibate, trying to follow Jesus. Trying not to sin."

"But you have sinned. You may not have been with a woman, but you've sinned, even sexually, haven't you, Nicky?"

I don't say anything, because of course he knows I have. "I'm so sick of everything. I'm sick of pious lies. Everybody cleaning up real nice, and all of us full of filth on the inside. I'm full of filth, and you are, and Zora. But we all say we love God."

"Nicky, I know you're upset today. But don't lose perspective. We all sin. I'm not crazy about being an alcoholic, losing my wife, making a mess of my life and reputation. I'd rather be a good guy, but the fact is, I'm a mess, and the best thing I know about God is that He loves people, even messy ones. So even when I sin, I have an advocate with the Father. Don't go all legalistic, Nicky, just because you're hurting."

"I don't want to be legalistic. I just want to be right with God. I want to live a good life. Why is that so hard? To live a good life and maybe be myself. Find somebody that can love me for me—all of who I am. Dude, Rebecca thought I'd be writing like Max Lucado. *Dude!*"

"Do you want to pray again, Nicky?"

"Just pray for me, Rich. I've got a raging headache. I'm going to bed."

"Okay, son."

We hang up. I get some ice, even though my eye is swollen underneath like crazy by now. My dad has never been much for hitting, even when I was a kid. While my grandfather was a real "spare the rod, spoil the child" kind of guy, Dad never did seem comfortable with corporal punishment. Maybe I really am like him in some ways.

Nah.

I don't give that another thought because my mind goes right back to Zora and those sad-looking doe eyes. She doesn't even have a phone to call me. And I wonder if she will. I wonder if she'll give me a chance to plead with her not to marry the Lion King.

How can he be good for her? If she were mine I'd be her father's nemesis right now. Nothing would keep me from taking care of her. As it is, I've spent almost all of the cash I have available to buy her things I thought she both needed *and* wanted.

I should have done more. If I had, maybe she wouldn't have walked to my church, and none of this would have happened.

Again, I think about her sad eyes. I want to go to her, but she's probably with him.

You're crazy, Nicky. She's somebody else's woman. You knew that all along.

But it doesn't change how I feel.

I hear a knock at my door. Nobody comes to see me. It's after ten on a Sunday night now. I don't know who could be at my door.

I get up from the futon to answer it. The knocker is insistent.

"Who is it?" I yell to the door.

"Yo, it's Pete."

I don't bother to mask my sarcasm from the God who knows all things, except apparently how much I *don't* want to see Pete. "How nice."

I open the door. God must be really happy with me. Pete's standing there with my dad.

I let them in.

Pete shakes his head when he sees my face. "Yo, man, what are you doing?"

"Shouldn't you be asking *who* am I doing, Pete? Because I'm thinking that's what this little visit with my dad in tow is about."

I close the door, and they go right over to the futon and sit down. Now I wish I had furniture. I drag a chair out of the two feet of space that passes for my dining room. Slam it in front of the futon and straddle it for bad-boy effect.

Why do this to me, God? Why tonight?

Pete tries for peacemaker.

"Yo, Nick. Your dad is upset."

"Yeah. Me, too."

"We didn't come all this way for you to act all ticked off."

"Then I suggest you go back to Ypsi, 'cause I'm ticked off."

My father clears his voice. "Nicholas, I'm not happy at how things went today either. I called Pete because I'm frankly bewildered by your behavior."

"*My* behavior?"

"You attacked your grandfather."

"I collared him. Then I got attacked."

He holds his hands rigid on his lap. "I've never seen you in such a state. I had no idea what you'd do."

"Well, it looks like you figured out how to get the situation under control pretty fast."

"I'm not pleased that I hit you, son."

For a moment I'm confused. The only person who's called me son in years has been Richard. "What?"

"I said, I'm not pleased that I hit you."

He didn't repeat the son part. Figures. "Well, it's done. What do you want now, Dad?"

"I want to talk to you about that woman."

"Her name is Zora. Don't call her *that woman* like she's a White House intern that I did naughty things with."

At this he looks at Pete who takes over.

"Yo, Nick, man."

"Pete," I say, "didn't I tell you not to say *yo* to me again?"

"Look, I know she's hot."

"Pete—"

"Your dad and I talked about this."

"You really don't want to go there, Pete."

He puts his hand up with a "stop" gesture. "Yo, just listen, Nick. Okay? I'm just keepin' it real."

"Why don't you keep it *white,* which is what you are, Pete."

"It's what you are too, Nicky. Look, I've seen Zora. I totally feel you. She's hot, man, but you don't bring her *home.*"

"First of all, I didn't invite her to dinner. Dad did."

My dad steps back in. "I realize now that was a mistake. I didn't recognize you were having relations with her. I should have, based on the things she said."

I run my hand through my hair. I can't believe him. "I'm not having *relations* with anybody. She was nervous. Everything came out wrong, but nothing is going on between Zora and me, meaning, we are not having *relations.*"

"I'm not naive, Nicholas. Rebecca and I saw you kissing her in public."

"Dad, you make it sound like we were on the JumboTron in Madison Square Garden."

I'm getting sick again. The people in my life literally make me sick.

Pete gets straight to the point. "Look, Nick, what your dad and I are here to say is, if you haven't, just do her already."

I get up from my straddling position, turn my chair around, and sit straight as a judge to face them. "Excuse me?"

My dad nods in agreement. "My father always told me white men have had a certain fascination with women of color. I know you've been keeping straight, Nicholas. Maybe you just need to experience this so you and Rebecca can move on with your life together."

I stare at the shell that looks just like my father, but surely some alien life-form has overtaken him. My mouth goes dry. "Dad? Are you saying what I think you're saying?"

"I'm not proud of myself. But I can't stand by and let another incident happen."

Incident. I know what *incident* he's talking about. The one that drove the biggest wedge between us.

"You think I'm going to get someone else pregnant? Dad, I promise you I will never have another abortion on my conscience for as long as I live. No, thank you."

"I can't decide what would be worse, Nicholas. *That woman* having an abortion, or you having an illegitimate half-black child."

I'm astounded. My heart pounds so hard I think I'm going to have a freakin' heart attack. My ability to speak abandons me.

"Yo, Nick. Think about it. A little half-black baby would totally scandalize your family. Your family has worked too hard to let your lust for some black chick ruin them."

I'm still struck dumb.

Dad speaks. "It's not just the fact that she's black. It's *who* she is. Her father is one of the most heretical preachers in that community. The only reason I tolerate him at all is because his is one of the few local ministries that is actively involved in campaigning with me against abortion. Their family is tacky. She doesn't have any class."

"Tacky?" This from the people with red-lipped, tar-black Jocko in the yard. This is the abortion rights activist and politician, who just said that he can't decide if an aborted baby, which he abhors, is better than a living half-black one that I fathered. And I won't even get into the horrific racism implicit in his comments. And to top it off, he makes a sweeping judgment on another man's ministry. And he called Zora's family tacky!

"Dad, unlike Rebecca, Zora graduated magna cum laude from a top, historically black university."

"That doesn't impress me."

"She's an amazing artist. A dancer. She's got more class on a bad day than—"

"Nicholas, I've put up with all your irresponsible choices. But this is the worst of all. You're only doing this to lash out at me, but you've hurt Rebecca and your mother terribly. I'm pleading with you, Nicholas. Stop this foolishness before anyone else gets hurt."

I can't take any more of this. My voice modulations rise with my blood pressure. "What makes you think I'm trying to hurt someone? What if I just really like her?"

"Do you honestly think I'd believe a handsome, intelligent young man like you would choose someone *black* when you can have your pick of white women?"

"Are you suggesting black women are somehow inferior, Dad?"

He looks flustered. His face blanches. "Of course not. I'm only saying that you don't have to needlessly make your life difficult because you're sexually curious."

That again. Sexually curious. Is that what this is? How am I supposed to know? I want to ask him. This is my dad. I'm supposed to be able to go to him and ask him how to know if I'm falling in love. How to know if her brown skin is an issue.

"But what if she's *the one,* Dad? Like Mom was the one for you?"

My dad stands up. I've never seen such an expression of outrage on his face. He steps over to me, and I think he's going to punch me in my other eye. He points his finger at me, and he's shaking in rage. Pete gets so scared, he stands up too. Like he's gonna help if Dad suddenly lunges at me, but Dad doesn't. Not physically.

"You selfish, sorry, spoiled-rotten brat. You've never cared about anyone other than yourself. You're weak. Always crying. Sensitive. Too much like a woman. I'm giving you an out here, Nicholas. Go and have a—whatever you want to call it—with your black girl, and come back to reality and have your life. She's *not* the one. She can't be. Not in this world, and you know it. You're doing this to get at me."

"Dad—"

"Shut up, boy! Look at yourself. You are smarter, more handsome, and far more charismatic than I ever have been or ever will be. And I watch you make choice after choice to throw it all away. I could have been the governor, Nicholas. But you, you surely will be, if you just listen to me. But not with a black wife. Not with a bunch of half-breed kids. The world isn't ready for that. I want you to succeed, and you are determined to fail. And I hate you for that."

And now he does hit me. A backhanded slap across my mouth. He follows the slap with an assault of furious blows. For a moment I look into his eyes, and I see passion there. It reminds me of how that word *passion* is rooted in pain. Suffering. My dad is *feeling* something for me. Finally. I've looked into this man's icy blue eyes so many times and found nothing staring back at me, and now in this moment there is something. Hate. It's not love's opposite. It's better than the apathy I've gotten most of my life.

I actually prefer it.

He unleashes blow after blow upon my face until Pete pulls him off of me.

It all happens quickly. I'm stronger. I could take my father, but I won't. His words "I hate you" drive a stake inside of me, pinning me to the chair.

I hate you.

The words seem alive, mocking and challenging. Demanding

me to do something about them. *I hate you* pokes and prods me, whispers, "You don't have to be the good son." Says, "Go and get your woman. Your fine black woman."

My ears ring. My face stings. I don't feel the pain, but I taste blood inside my mouth. I swallow it.

I knew he hated me. I've always known.

He'd never said the words before now, but I've felt him despise me through a myriad of indignities stacked upon each other for years, like a miser stacks his coins.

I will not let him see this destroy me. Just let him have this moment. This release of righteous anger of his. When I can gather my wits about me, I nod to let him know I understand what he's said to me. And to disappoint him more, I will *not* cry.

He will not cry either.

I have never seen my dad cry, but I don't think I've ever seen him so emotional. His eyes are almost as red as his face, and they shine with tears I know he will not shed. Not in front of Pete and me. He yanks away from Pete and rushes, nearly running, out of my apartment. Pete looks bewildered. His torn gaze shifts from me to the door and back to me.

"Go with him."

"Nick, man. I'm sorry."

I don't say anything, just gesture with my head toward the door, and Pete scurries out to my dad.

The words *I hate you* keep swelling, permeating the room. It's one thing to know your father hates you. Another to hear it. Another to know it's growing like fungus on your walls.

I can't stand this apartment. It was where I tried to hide from the knowledge that he abhors me in the first place. Now my little sanctuary seems contaminated with his loathing.

I grab my jacket. I gotta get out of here. I try to tell myself that I don't know where I'm going, but I do. If I could just see her. She knows me. God, I promise I won't do anything wrong. I won't do anything like what people keep suggesting to me. I don't want to just do her. I love her. If I could just hold her and have her tell me it's going to be all right.

I get in my car and head to I-96. Won't be long, and I'll be lost in those brown doe eyes.

ZORA

We drive to Linda's house, and I'm surprised to see the hippie van isn't Linda's but Billie's, and even that really isn't a surprise. We drop Linda off, and I can tell she's a little disappointed, but we promise not to have too much fun without her, and I get very excited because it just feels like Billie is going to take me on some big, wild, crazy adventure, and I can't wait to go.

We drive all the way to Detroit, and I wonder why she motors all the way to Ypsilanti for a small, informal Bible study.

"It's the people I come for."

"But it's just a few."

"Yeah, but what a few. But you oughta know that by now."

"I'm beginning to see what you mean," I say.

She takes a peek at me, and puts her eyes back on the road. "Okay, Linda is so gone. You gotta tell me. The kiss? Spill it."

I laugh. "You sound like a teenager, Billie. How old are you?"

"Too old. So you gotta tell me. Humor a senior citizen, will ya?"

"You really are a hopeless romantic, aren't you?"

"Oh, baby. I'm not without hope, glory to God. Now about that kiss?"

I sigh from deep inside. "I shouldn't talk about it, Billie."

"If you didn't want to talk about it, you'd have spent the night with Linda. Or your boyfriend, God have mercy!"

She's right. "Okay, I want to talk about it."

"So talk."

"How do you know if you're falling in love?"

"Tell me how you're feeling."

"When I think of Nicky, I feel like I'm standing in some wide open place, and I've been living inside a mason jar. I feel like breathing, and dancing, and singing, and stretching. I feel like doing and being *everything,* all at once. And that's what his kiss felt like. I wanted to just breathe him in. Take him into myself like sometimes in church I want to take God into myself. It made me feel all those things. Does that sound awful?"

She literally screams. "That's awesome!"

"I just met him."

"Just because you're feeling a lot right now doesn't mean you have to rush. For some people, there really is love at first sight, and then they grow into loving one another with a mature love that's very different from what you're describing, but it's still really nice, baby."

"I'm so scared. He wasn't supposed to be white. Shoot. He was *supposed* to be Miles."

"But he isn't. What are ya gonna do?" She shrugs even as she drives.

"I think Linda is right. I don't even have a job. I don't know where I'm going to be living after three weeks if they put an eviction notice on my door."

"When was the last time you paid your rent, baby?"

"First of this month."

"You won't be on the street any time soon. But I hear ya. We're gonna work on the job thing. But right now, you're in love with a white guy. Are you gonna let yourself feel that?"

"His grandfather called me a nigger to my face, like I was nothing. Like I didn't have a feeling worth sparing. And this wasn't somebody hurling insults at me from a mob. I was an invited guest at the dinner table."

"Nicky stood up for you."

"But how long will that last? Nicky is a black sheep that wants to be the favored sheep. You think he's going to keep bringing me to dinner?"

"Have dinner with other people."

"I will. My own people."

"Zora, I know how you feel."

"How, Billie?"

"That guy John I told you about? His parents hated me. Of course they didn't call me that awful thing Nicky's grandfather called you. They called me a white-trash whore. To my face. They didn't think their beautiful Princeton-educated son should have fallen in love with a hooker who would never amount to anything."

I looked at her. She kept her eyes on the road. She cussed. Then said she was sorry. "I agreed with 'em. John was a dreamboat. I could think of four or five women from his church—good, educated, hot-looking women who his parents would love—and I set about trying to get that going, girl."

"No way."

"I loved him. And I wanted him to be happy. More happy than he'd be with a whore."

"Former whore."

"To some people, if you were once a whore, you'll always be one. I knew I'd never make the cut with them, and he loved his parents. I didn't want him to give them up for me, so I let him go."

"Wow."

"Yeah," she says sarcastically. "Wow."

"So what ended up happening?"

"He became a priest."

"Really?"

"Yeah."

"How did his parents feel about that?"

"Hated it."

We both crack up. It was the *way* she said it. Billie is hilarious.

"Girl, you made that poor man turn into a priest, and he still didn't get his parents' approval. You might as well have married him."

She gives me a wicked grin.

"What's that smile about?"

"Anyway," she says, ignoring my question, "I know what it feels like to be despised by the parents. At least you have no control over your skin color. I felt like my life was all my fault, whether or not it actually was."

Time seems to fly by as Billie and I talk about everything. We whiz down 96 until we hit the downtown area. Finally, we pull up to a lovely old Arts and Crafts house somewhere near Grand Circus Park.

"Welcome to the Beloved Community," she says.

"It's smaller than I thought."

She shakes her head and laughs. "Well, this is just one house of many that's part of our community. This is a kinda modified House of Hospitality. You familiar with those?"

"Not really."

"It's a Catholic Worker thing." She thinks about it. "No, really, it's a Jesus thing. We wanted to offer hospitality to the stranger. Remember how Jesus said in Matthew 25:35, 'I was a stranger, and ye took me in'?"

"Yes. So, you help who? Poor or homeless people?"

"Not always. In our community, a stranger is a person who, for whatever reason, is disconnected from love. Sure, if you don't have a place to lay your head you're certainly most likely disconnected from love, but people who seem to have everything can be 'the stranger.' You can have the best designer clothes and drive a fancy car and live in the biggest mansion but feel like nobody is listening to you. Or you can be just lonely for some reason you don't even know. We give meals and clothes, a place to sleep, and a little hand up. We even give a handout or two. But sometimes a cup of coffee and a bowl of soup with somebody to listen to your story is what people need most. And we give them that."

God knows I need that. If that's the criteria for being a stranger—being disconnected from love—I've never been more strange in my life.

Billie keeps talking. "Sometimes, a girl just doesn't want to sleep on the darned floor again and look at those blue walls, no matter how pretty the blue is. And she doesn't want to sleep on the air mattress her boyfriend bought for makin' whoopee. We'd like to make her feel welcome too." She shakes her head. "Makin' whoppee! I'm showing my age now, baby." She chuckles, but I don't get it. "Anyway, some of our houses are more for the homeless. We welcome the stranger, but some strangers are stranger than others. Even with hospitality there are issues. Sometimes it just gets darned—" I can tell she really wants to cuss. "It gets darned hard, Zora. Hosts get tired. Guests get crazy. We try to be Jesus to them, but we're not. God knows I'm not my husband. I'm always ready to give a smackdown. I have to apologize to somebody every day. But I love this life. It's the hardest grace to come by, and I love it."

We get out of the van and walk up to the house. Before we even get on the porch the door opens and Billie runs into the arms of a man and gives him a fierce kiss. The kind I gave Nicky.

He's a black man. A good one. Tall. And fine. Brotha is into her like he's gotta serious love jones, and when I see them together it feels like someone takes a pair of vice grips to my heart and tightens it. And not because I'm lonely.

Billie's husband is black! She didn't let on one bit after all our talk about what's happening to me.

Few things rankle me like brothas passing over sistahs for the prize of a white woman. And for a moment, I think about all the *worthy*, beautiful, intelligent sistahs I know who couldn't get a date with a good black man if they paid for one, and this former hooker—

Oh, this isn't feeling good inside of me. Didn't we just have this conversation? And despite *me* kissing very blond and white Nicky

Parker this very day and loving it, I feel angry that Billie has herself a brotha.

She practically purrs at him.

"I was bad today," she says to her husband.

"What did you do, Ma?"

Ouch. He called her Ma in that sweet way the brothas do.

"I was mean to Zora's boyfriend. He was trying his game on her. And I called him on it."

He pulls her into a hug. "Baby, you can't judge people."

I can't judge people either, but I am. I am!

"I know," she says. "I'll apologize. But he bought her an *air mattress* and some prophylactics! You know I couldn't let that go."

Her husband shakes his head. "Air mattress. Lord, have mercy." He kisses her again. "Now stop smooching and let me meet Zora."

He finally disengages himself from Billie long enough to come up to me. I try to hide my disappointment, but it's all over me like God's handwriting on the wall. "Hello," I say, but it sounds cold, though I don't mean it to. Billie notices, and her own crestfallen gaze finds mine. She's so tough. Such a broad. I wait for her rebuke, but she doesn't say anything hard to me.

She takes me by the hand, and it nearly kills me. "This is my new friend, Zora, who I've already told you everything I know about. And as you can see she's as fabulous as I said. And Zora ..." She looks at him with such love and admiration. "This is my husband, Father John Jordan, priest, husband, father, and former condom-and-sandwich guy."

I utter a feeble, "I thought priests were celibate."

"With a woman like Billie? I'd have changed religions."

She howls in laughter, like she's never heard that joke, although she's probably heard him say it a million times before.

"I'm an Orthodox priest. As in Eastern Orthodox. We're allowed to marry."

"Billie's told me all about you. In a very sneaky way. You two have quite a story."

"So do you, I hear. Now come on in the house. Let us show you around."

I step into the house, and everything is simple. The furniture is simple. It's just the kind of place that invites you to come on in and sit a spell. Nothing is too nice or too shabby.

Billie quips, "It ain't much, is it?"

"I kinda like it," I say.

"We've just got beige walls, but I long for color. I think color is soul feeding, but John is afraid to let me paint."

"I can't imagine why," I say, and the three of us crack up.

John rubs Billie's arm. "I let her paint once, and we ended up with a Day-Glo pink family room."

"I didn't realize it was Day-Glo until I got it home. It seemed like a really good deal, and I saw why when I got it on the walls." She looks at her husband. "But you have to admit. It did brighten the place up."

"Billie, it brightened *Chicago* up."

She gives him a playful punch.

"After that we had to take her off the decorating committee, and she's been mourning the loss ever since."

I keep thinking how weird this all is. He doesn't seem like a priest. Not that I've ever seen a black priest, Eastern Orthodox or otherwise.

He seems like some kind of college professor. I try not to think about how much it bothers me that a catch like him is with Billie, who I just reassured in the van. *Former hooker,* I told her.

I've always hated it when white people cry reverse racism. I figured the odds were stacked up so far against us whatever we thought or said about them was a trifle by comparison.

What do You think, Jesus?

An ache in my heart tells me.

I don't think He likes it. But I don't want to think about it tonight. I just don't want to be alone, and if that means hanging with Billie and her brotha man, I'll take it.

I should have gone with Linda. I'm certain Linda wouldn't have had a black man hiding in her closet.

God help me. Nicky was right. I am a racist.

I suck.

We get to the dining room, and there's a huge oblong dining table. It must seat sixteen. Father John says, "This is where we share meals. I don't think there are many things in the Christian tradition more important than shared meals."

"Really?" I say. A procession of shared meals I have known come to mind. I think about the pharisaical Sunday dinners we had at home after church, all elegant and refined, complete with our black servants. We only invited the best of the best; we only hung out with those who had the shine of God's prosperity on them. And then there was the dinner with Daddy, Mama, and Miles on Thursday night where I gave my father back the Lexus and got in exchange this nothing that is changing everything. The lunch I had with Nicky ended abruptly with him insulting my work. Then the disaster at Nicky's parents' house today. "What's the hype about eating together? The last three shared meals I had left a lot to be desired."

"I heard about the last one, Zora, but it may have been an unexpected grace."

"I know people have a lot to say about my father's church, but even there we've got the right definition of grace. That's God's unmerited, undeserved favor. I didn't see any grace being passed around today."

"Your definition is basically correct, Zora. But grace is much more then that definition can contain. It's much more than our language can contain." He pulls out a chair for me. "Have a seat, Zora."

Billie seems to know the drill. She hurries to the kitchen and comes back with bread and a bottle of wine.

"I don't drink," I say.

"Are you an alcoholic?" she asks.

"Uh. No. I just …"

"I don't think God is going to strike you down just because Father wants to make a point."

"Uh, okay."

Billie sets the wine and basket of bread on the table and disappears once again.

"Let's go back to the upper room when Jesus instituted the Eucharist."

"Is this some kind of Catholic thing? Billie said something about the Catholic Worker Movement. At our church we don't—"

"I know what your church teaches, Zora. I've seen your father on television many times. But you take communion, right?"

"Yes, but it's not the same way that Catholics do it. And I don't know anything about your church, Father John. In fact, doesn't the Bible say that Jesus said, 'Call no man father'? I don't even know if I should call you that."

He winks at me. "Call me John then."

"Okay, John."

"In the Holy Orthodox Church we believe that we partake of the mystery of the body and blood of Christ each and every time we share in the mystical supper."

I don't know what to say to that. All my life I'd heard that teaching was wrong, and I wasn't interested in a theological debate I couldn't offer anything to. I didn't want to be converted either. I didn't come here for that.

Again, these people seem to be psychic or something.

"Don't worry, Zora," John says. "We're not trying to convert you. We want to share with you something vital about hospitality. So you can understand why we do this."

"Don't you do it because Jesus said, 'When I was a stranger you welcomed me,' like Billie said?"

"Definitely. But there's more." He looks at his wife. "Billie, could you get us some water and the pitcher, dear?"

Billie returns with a single wine glass in one hand and a basin of water balanced in her arms. She sets the glass and water on the table in front of John. He picks up the glass and pours wine into it.

"A long time ago," he says, "on one of the worst nights of His life, Jesus sat with His disciples. He wouldn't be long in this world after that." He pauses as if lost in memory. As if he had been there himself. "They sat at a table that I like to think was much like this one. It was there He showed us what hospitality is about."

Father John holds up the glass. "But first," then he sets the glass back down again, "He humbled Himself. He put on the garments of a slave and became a servant to His own disciples. Zora, will you please remove your shoes so that Billie and I may serve you?"

"Excuse me?"

Billie places her hand on my shoulder. "We want to serve you as Christ did His disciples. May we, please?"

How can I say no to that kind of request?

Father John and Billie kneel down before me, and oddly, I feel so sad. I don't even know why. Billie slides off the black leather ballet slippers another servant of Christ gave me. I feel nervous and my heart palpitates. I've read about these kinds of services at Spelman but never participated in one, not even at my grandfather's church. Daddy abandoned so many of the old traditions. Tradition is almost a dirty word at LLCC. And this isn't church. This is some weird shelter or halfway house. I don't know what it is.

"You have beautiful feet, Zora," Billie says.

I start chattering like a fool. "I get a pedicure every week. Or at least I used to. I go to this Korean lady, and I always leave her a good tip because she does a great job." I jabber on and on because I start feeling choked up because she's cradling my feet reverently. As if they are sacred. This white lady is about to wash my feet.

"I'm so sorry, Zora, for all the hateful burdens you carry that my people placed on your beautiful back."

I try to pull my feet out of her reach. I don't want to deal with this stuff right now. She put me on the spot. But she eases my feet so gently into the warm water. And then she starts to cry.

"I feel that pain you have. I'm so sorry," she says.

"You can't feel it," I whisper.

"Not like you do. But I feel it a little. Jesus is giving me just a little bit of it. But He feels all of it, Zora."

She keeps dipping her hands in the warm, soothing waters and pouring it onto my feet. Dear God, it feels good. And she's telling me she's sorry.

"And I'm sorry for taking one of your men. I know you're angry at me for it. I just fell in love with him. How could I not? He gave me so much love. And nobody loved me like that before."

And then she really begins to weep. And I start crying too, because everybody needs love. The world is so messed up. John dips his hands into the water, and he begins to wash my feet too.

"You must feel like I betrayed you, sister Zora, marrying this white woman. But she made me love her. She's so wild and beautiful. She was like a daisy growing between the concrete, but loving her never meant that I don't love you. Or my mother. Or my other sisters or myself. But forgive me for hurting you with my choice. I never meant to, sister. I believe my African American sisters are dark and lovely Shulamites, just like the Song of Solomon says."

"You nailed me," I choke. "I'm so sorry."

"Sister," John says, "the only nails here are the ones on the cross. And that's where all our sins belong. We are all sinners. But we all belong to God. Let's allow Him to begin this work of welcoming one another."

We sit there crying as they wash my feet, until I'm so tired I don't think another tear can come out of me. Billie realizes she didn't bring a towel and jumps to her feet.

She returns and hands the towel to Father John, and he dries my feet while she puts the basin away. When Billie returns, John informs me our sharing isn't over.

He picks up the wine glass again.

"And now for the best part." He smiles at me. "You didn't think I forgot about the food, did you?"

I answer him with a smile.

He lifts the glass. "This is where hospitality began. Jesus lifted a single cup and gave it to His disciples. Then He took a cup, and after giving thanks He said, 'Take this, and divide it among yourselves: For … I will not drink of the fruits of the vine, until the kingdom of God.'" He pauses. "Have you ever celebrated Kwanzaa, Zora?"

"Yes. We used to every year, but it kind of fell out of favor."

"You know how there's a unity cup that everyone drinks from?"

I chuckle. "We never really drank from it. We just did it symbolically."

He nods. "I understand. But the Eucharist Jesus instituted here was no mere symbol. It's the foundation of the church. It's the feast that we are all to continually share. Without it, we cannot worship. We cannot be hospitable. I know we're far from real unity, just like with the Kwanzaa unity cup. But we're meant to drink from it. All of us. From one cup like Jesus said."

I don't understand. This is nothing like anything I've ever known. What about germs? How can we all drink from one cup in reality?

John holds the cup of wine in his hand to his lips and takes a long drink. He gives the cup to Billie, and she drinks, and then he offers the cup to me.

For a moment I hesitate. What's it gonna be, Zora? Think about how you're going to live your life. Symbolically? Or will you get down to the messiness of being involved with something real for a change? I take the cup. I take a drink as long as the one Father John took. The wine is sweeter than I imagined it would be and, though it's cold, the alcohol warms my throat.

John tears a piece of bread from a single loaf in the basket.

"At that same table, Zora, Jesus said to His disciples, 'This is my body which is given for you: this do in remembrance of me.'"

He eats the bread. Father John lifts the basket and extends the loaf to me. "Please. Break bread with me."

He asks with such sincerity. I don't even know if I'm having some kind of Orthodox communion or not, but I want to share with them. I take the bread and pull a small piece from the loaf. I thought it'd be bland, but it tastes better than I expected. I pass the basket to Billie, and she too eats.

John surprises me and takes the wine again. "Finally, Jesus passed the cup, once again. He said, 'This cup is the new testament in my blood, which is shed for you.'" He pauses for a while, as if this is a marvel to him. He drinks deeply of it. I'm so moved by his passion, I take another long drink, and I pass it to Billie, and we all sit quietly for a few minutes.

"What does this all mean?"

"It's full of mystery, baby," Billie says. "We don't even know what it all means. We just know it begins with Christ. Him becoming our feast and telling us to share Him with each other, and we all come to one table where we can partake of Him. At least that's how it should be. It's not yet. Christ's body is broken apart. Every time I serve communion, I weep for all the people who can't partake of it with me. But I do what I can. I leave it to God to bring us all back together.

We're His body, broken or no."

John seems to ponder what she says. He adds, "But I believe regardless of what we believe about the Eucharist, we are all to feed off Christ. Because we all must feed off Christ, He is present inside all believers, so the stranger is always Christ, and Christ is always welcome."

"But what about crazy people? What about sociopaths? What about people who don't take communion at all and who haven't fed off Christ?"

"Seems like to me, at that very table where the Lord instituted the Eucharist, a sociopath sat among them who would sell the Son of God for thirty pieces of silver. And Jesus washed his feet. It's Jesus who said, 'Judge not.'"

"He also said, 'Ye shall know them by their fruits.' How can you protect people in your community who are vulnerable?"

Father John answers, "Love is the biggest rule here, Zora. We have houses that are more equipped to deal with mentally ill people. And homeless people. People who could harm children. Part of living in love is making room for everybody. Sometimes love is asking someone predatory to leave. It's hard, but we have to do it sometimes."

Billie nods. "I'm not sayin' we've got it down perfect. We take a little wisdom from the Romanian Orthodox monks, and some from the Benedictines, and some from the Catholic Worker Houses of Hospitality. And we pray, and screw up and try again. But we give coffee. And soup. And love, wine, and bread."

"I like it."

"We like it too," John says.

"Sometimes," Billie says. He shoots her a look, and she winks at him. He smiles despite himself.

"How do you get money?"

"Donations. And what we earn using our skills and talents. We don't get any government grants or assistance," John says. "We trust God and His people. We seem to get by."

"It's not easy," Billie says.

"You probably noticed my wife speaks her mind."

"I noticed."

Billie gets up. "Then let me speak my mind and say how shabby this place looks. I'm hoping Zora can give me some decorating tips so we can fix the place up without scaring Father John half to death with Day-Glo colors."

"Please, Zora. Don't let my wife's colorful personality sway any good ideas you have. We'd love to get any insights you want to offer that will make our home more inviting, but not any concepts with the words *Day-Glo,* or *hot,* or *screaming* in front of them."

"You can count on me."

"Be careful what you say, Zora. I just may do that," he says.

And I smile, because somehow, I don't think I'll mind him counting on me at all.

NICKY

So, it's eleven thirty at night when I get to her apartment. I sit in her parking lot another freakin' half hour because I look like a monster, and I don't want her to see me like this. But I gotta see her, or more to the point, I gotta see her see me.

I think about Jesus while I'm in my truck. The Good Shepherd. I wonder if He's calm when He goes after the one. Does He whistle a psalm or something and walk with slow ease? Does worry crease His brow? Does He think about any of the bad things that could happen? Or does He hurry, like disaster could strike at any moment if He doesn't get there in the nick of time?—pun intended.

And the worst thing? My father did come after me. He came with my so-called best friend to save me from the black woman he thought would ruin me. Like Zora was some kind of she-wolf out to destroy me. My father who doesn't like to hit has done so twice in a single day to get my attention. He came with the sternest of warnings today, sparing not the rod for his spoiled-rotten child. Maybe that's his version of love and it's as real as it's gonna get for him—or me.

I can't think about this. How small is his world if I can't fit one black woman in it? I have to see her.

I tell myself how amazing she was to walk what—seven or eight miles?—just to get to my church. How brave she was to have dinner with me after she saw Rebecca connected to me like we're conjoined twins. And how sassy and courageous she was at the dinner table, the way she stood up for me, how classy she was when she dealt with my family's ignorance.

I tell myself that I need to see her badly enough that I can push her buzzer, even if Miles is in there and his arms are curled around her and he's whispered to her that he loves her after he's made love to her maybe better than I can, because everybody knows what they say about black men and—

Man.

I don't know where this courage is going to come from. I'm just a lust-filled sinner. I don't even know for sure if I'm in love. But I know this: It enrages me that he hasn't done anything for her. And she's not wearing a ring. And he doesn't think she's an incredible artist. I don't want anything but what is best for that angel.

Just thinking about him enjoying the full benefits package ticks me off. And I'm getting smacked around because I kissed her. I don't think so.

I get out of my truck, march up to the door, and press the buzzer long and hard. Anger and adrenaline surge through me, and I can feel a manly urge to do something destructive. A good old-fashioned brawl is in order, and not with my father or grandfather.

Nothing.

I nearly lie on the buzzer this time. Then I press on all the buzzers, which doesn't please the occupants since by now it's after midnight. I press on Zora's buzzer again and again until it finally dawns on me. Zora isn't home. She isn't lying on the floor amid the blue and red walls. He's taken my Zora home with him.

I pull my cell phone out of my jacket pocket and dial 4-1-1.

"Information. City and state, please."

"Ann Arbor, Michigan, I think. Do you have a listing for Miles Zekora?"

"Hold for the number."

I hold all right. I tap my foot and ball my free hand into a fist and when she comes back, I say, "Yes, please," after she asks if I'd like for her to connect me to that number.

The phone rings nine times. I would have waited if it had rung nine thousand. I would have waited if it took nine days for him to answer it.

He sounds sleepy, no doubt from a vigorous session of love-making to Zora.

"Hullo," he says.

"Miles!"

"Who is this?"

"Where is Zora?"

He pauses. "Who is this?"

"Put Zora on the phone."

"Zora isn't here."

I don't have the patience for this. "Don't play with me, Miles. I'll come over there and get her if I have to."

Now Miles sounds ticked off. Really ticked off. "Who is this?"

"This is God's soldier. You shouldn't be having sex with God's handmaidens." Man, what a freakin' hypocrite I am.

"I'm not having sex with anybody. I'm going to marry—I don't even know who this is."

"This is the voice of prophecy. You can't keep having sex with Zora. You don't deserve her. You don't even have a ring for her. You suck, Miles."

"Is this that white boy?"

"What white boy?"

"That white boy that was at … this is Nicky. The white boy with the comedienne's name."

"Yeah, this is Nicky Parker. And you still suck."

"Man, why you callin' me?"

"Because you don't deserve her. You don't know her. You don't even think she can paint, and that's just crazy, Miles. How can you not think she can paint?"

"I don't have to explain myself to you. You don't be calling me, white boy. I don't know who you think you are, but you don't know me like that."

"No, I know you like *this*: I know you were at the dinner at her dad's house, and she ended up walking to the bookstore, and it was me who gave her a ride home that night. I know you left her in pajamas on Friday, and it was me who brought her the white dress you took off of her today. I know it was me that fed her Friday. And it was me that gave her cab fare, and if she were in my bed, I'd have a ring on her finger, unlike you. That's what I know about you, Miles."

"I'm gon' say this one more time, white boy. You don't know anything about what's going on with Zora and her family. You need to keep your white nose out of black folks' business. And here's another thing: I think what you're most upset about is that it *ain't* you taking that white dress off Zora, and it ain't never gon' be you. So you need to step off. Don't call me no more, and stay away from my wife."

"Is she there? Because if she's there I'm coming for her."

"Yeah. She's here. Come and get her."

"I'm on my way."

I call information again and find out his street address. I'm in such a rage I don't know what I'll do. I'm a lot worse off than I felt earlier. I feel like I'm going to both implode and explode all at once.

I keep thinking I should call Richard. I don't want to bother him again, but the desire becomes so insistent that I can't ignore it anymore. It's late, but Rich is a night owl. I'm so frustrated I pull over and get out of the car. I punch in his number. He answers on the first ring.

"Nicky, hey."

"Rich."

"You okay, son? You sound upset."

"I'm on my way to beat up Zora's boyfriend and take her out of his apartment."

"What are you talking about, Nicky?"

"I called Miles. Zora is over there. And they're probably making mad, passionate love. I'm going to go get her."

"Nicky, are you certain?"

"He said she was there."

"Did you speak to her there?"

"He wouldn't put her on the phone. Why would he let me talk to her when he's making mad, passionate love to her?"

"Zora is not at her boyfriend's house making mad, passionate love, Nicky. She's at the Beloved Community."

"What?"

"I talked to Linda fifteen minutes ago. Zora went home with Billie."

"Richard, are you sure?"

"I'm positive."

"Could Billie maybe have taken her over to Miles's?"

His laughter explodes into my ear. "Are you kidding? Billie Jordan?"

I have to laugh with him. What a clown I am. "She's at The Beloved Community? And I've probably gotten her into a lot of trouble with her boyfriend."

"Go home and go to bed. It's after midnight."

"I can't. I've got to see her. I just need for her to look at me. That's all. If she sees me, I'll stay together, Rich."

"You've got it bad, Nicky."

"I need her."

"I guess you'd better go see her then."

I hang up the phone, say a prayer of thanksgiving, turn around, and head back to Detroit.

ZORA

After Father John and Billie's impromptu lesson on hospitality, Billie pulls out a photo album and shows me pictures of her children. She and John have a whopping eight of them. They're a house of hospitality unto themselves. Again, questions about entertaining strangers plague me.

"The Beloved Community is all our kids have ever known, baby. They've seen Christ in the stranger from the time they've seen me, and they've always shared all they had. Of course, as you can imagine, it's hard on them when they get to be teenagers, and they want the trendy clothes. I had to get real creative about knowing what to look for in the donations, especially for my girls. But sweetie, it ain't always easy when people give clothes that should be recycled into rags. We're grateful for it. But it's hard to explain to a teenager why she can't have Baby Phat."

"Baby Phat isn't all it's cracked up to be. I had all those things, and I found out later they affected other people in my life—namely my best friend, MacKenzie—in ways I never dreamed of."

"I'll bet."

"And you know, Billie, I'm still trying to sort out how I feel about that stuff. I know I can get it all back. This is just a taste of what disenfranchised people go through, but Mac was right. One call and this can all go away."

"But you haven't made that call. Why not, baby?"

"I don't know. I'm not trying to play games. Trying to see how the other side lives. Not with people who have less money than we Hampton-Johnsons, and not with Nicky Parker. I don't know what's going on with me, quite frankly. All I know is that life as it was just seemed unbearable one day, and I walked out of my church. And then I came to your Bible study, and it's been all upheaval ever since."

"Sounds like God is moving."

"I remember when I thought God moving felt good. It just feels scary now."

"Baby, who said God was safe? We've got this warm fuzzy image of God in our heads, and don't get me wrong, God is loving. But He's also mystery. And He's sovereign. Does exactly what He wants and isn't real invested in explaining Himself."

"I feel like I'm one big paradox."

"The kingdom of heaven is full of paradoxes. To live you gotta die. To win you gotta lose. The last are gonna be first, and the first last. It goes on and on."

"I always thought it would be easier. My dad's preaching makes living a life of faith sound so easy. You say the right words and God gives you everything you need."

"Is that how it's worked out for you?"

"If it doesn't work out you don't have enough faith."

"I guess that covers everything then."

"Thanks for letting me come here, Billie."

"Just like Jesus, you're always welcome here, baby."

"John is great."

She nods, and for a moment she's quiet. "Zora? I didn't mean to embarrass you. I saw the look you had when you saw he was black. I just didn't want to act like I didn't know what was going on. I didn't think that would serve any of us. I couldn't do anything toward reconciling with you by pretending it didn't exist, and I'm glad I took that risk."

"I'm glad too."

We hear the doorbell ring. I look at Billie. She doesn't move. "We let one of the men answer the door this late at night."

"I see."

John welcomes whatever stranger in. Voices are muffled, but I hear John say, "Can I help?"

And maybe ... something, something, something.

John sounds surprised. "Zora?"

I startle at the sound of my name and bolt upward. "Someone is here for me?"

Billie stands. She looks all tough and ready to brawl. "Did you tell anyone you were coming?"

"No. I don't have a phone."

"Well, who would know you're here?" She doesn't wait for my answer and goes charging out to the foyer with me on her heels.

"Nicky!" she says. "What are you doin—you came for *Zora*?" She puts her hand on her hip like she's about to tell him off and then softens. That same hand goes over her heart. "Awwww. That's sooooo romantic. Isn't it romantic, baby?"

She calls me so many endearments I can't tell if I'm baby or her husband is.

"It's romantic," John says, answering at least that question.

If I could just get my stomach from off my feet where it's dropped. If only my heart would slow down a few thousand beats per minute so I can give Nicky a proper greeting.

The poor baby. He looks a hot mess. His face is a little more swollen now, and his eyes have such shameless misery in them my body moves on its own accord until I'm closer to him.

"Hey," I say. It's not poetry, but he accepts my greeting as if it were.

His eyes take me in as if I'm bread and he's a starving man. He whispers, "Dreamy, hey."

I can't help myself. My fingers graze his red, swollen cheeks.

"What happened? You get hit again?"

"I wanted to look like that lawn jockey. The black skin part didn't work out. But what do you think about the lips?"

"I think that's a terrible joke."

"It's better than what really happened."

"Who did this to you?"

"My dad. And I didn't get to tell you my grandfather pulled a gun on me. I thought he was going to shoot me. I won't even mention what he called me."

He just stands there looking at me. I think I hear Billie say she and Father John will let the two of us have a few minutes alone, but I can't say for sure that's what she said. They leave us. I only know I can't take my attention off of him. I have to work hard to find those model good looks in his face.

"Your lips don't look as big as the lawn jockey's. They're not even like Angelina Jolie's. This is nothing," I say to make him feel better.

He doesn't respond. Just whispers my name. "Zora?"

"What is it, Nicky?"

"Can you still see me?"

I gaze at him, confused. "What?"

"Can you still see me, Dreamy?"

What kind of foolish question … "Of course I can. I'm—" Suddenly, understanding dawns. It's not a foolish question at all. It's simply a strange one—a question a stranger, someone cut off from love, would ask.

I take a deep breath. It's like Nicky is tiny particles floating around in the air and I want to inhale him into myself. I feel if I could make him a part of me, I could keep him safe and loved inside of me. And happy.

"I see you."

I stand very close to him. Lift up just a bit on my toes and put my forehead against his. His forehead meets mine and for a moment we stand like that. His breathing is labored.

"Are you okay, Nicky?"

"Do you ever feel like you're going to implode and explode all at the same time? Or like maybe it'd be okay if your grandpa shot you?"

"Is that what you're feeling right now?"

"I feel sick."

He doesn't feel feverish. I put my hand in his hair. It's soft and loosely wavy, conjuring images of me touching my mother's auburn mane. I loved the silky texture of her hair and her almost-ripe peach skin, but I was never allowed to have a doll that looked like her. She looked too close to white. There was a study done about black and white dolls. And little black girls kept choosing the white dolls over the black ones. My parents didn't think I'd love myself if I had white dolls. But I just liked my mother's hair and skin. I just loved my mama. I felt guilty about that for a long time.

All these strange ideas about race—these cut-off-from-love ideas. I didn't want Nicky to spend one more moment feeling like a stranger anywhere in this world.

"Welcome home."

Now he looks confused. "What did you say?"

But I don't repeat it. I put my arms around his neck. If he inclines his head, he can kiss me, but he doesn't. I tell him again what he asked me to. "I see you, Nicky, and you are very beautiful to me. Your soul isn't black like your poem says at all. It's as bright as one of the stars in one of those constellations. Even brighter than that, Nicky. Your soul is like the sun because God made it that way."

"Where've you been all my life, Dreamy?"

"I've been wandering around, a stranger just like you."

"I can't cry anymore," he says.

"That's okay. You don't have to."

"Did I tell you I feel sick? I get sick when I feel this way."

"You told me. It's okay, Nicky. I'll help you."

"I told God I wouldn't do anything bad to you. I just wanted to come so you could see me. I knew you'd be able to see me, and I'd be all right then."

"You were right, Nicky."

I don't know where this boldness comes from. "Your lips are swollen." And I put a little kiss on them.

He blushes and laughs. "That hurts."

"I'm sorry."

"I liked it though. You can do it again. But softer."

So I do. His shoulders slump. It's like he collapses into me.

"I got you in trouble with Miles. I called him. I thought you were with him, and I told him he doesn't deserve you. I was going to go get you from his apartment. He's probably mad at us."

My heart catches, but just for a moment. "You called Miles?"

"Yeah. I'm sorry."

"You told him he didn't deserve me?"

"I told him he sucks."

I can only imagine how that's going to ripple. He's going to tell my father. "I'm going to be in trouble."

What does it matter? Can my father be any more disappointed in me? Nicky must read the concern on my face.

"I'm sorry. I'll just let him beat me up. My dad already gave him a head start."

That reminds me. "You have a black eye for real, now." I plant a delicate kiss just under his swollen eye. I try to push the thought of my father out of my head. Didn't my father marry a very fair-skinned woman? What could he say about this?

Nicky pulls me closer to him. Oh, Lord, a flame flares up within me. He buries his head in my neck. And I can't stand it. I don't know what to do with myself.

"You smell good," he says. "Is smelling you bad? I told God …"

"I don't know what's bad or good, Nicky."

"Me either."

I want to tell him that I want him, but this wanting is so very unfamiliar that I'm afraid of my own body. I simply tell him, "I think I need you."

He breathes into my neck. "Don't tell me that."

"I can't help it. I don't know what else to do. What are we going to do, Nicky?"

He pulls me flush against him. "I can't do anything but this right now. It's all I can figure out, and I'm confused about this."

We stand there for a long time holding each other, and in some ways we're saying everything, though none of it in words. After a long time, he whispers, "I'm going to try to let you go now," but he doesn't. Not for several more minutes.

Finally, Billie walks back into the room. She clears her throat. "Nicky, you're welcome as a guest, but I'm afraid I'm going to have to see to it that Zora gets to bed now."

He releases me, though he seems reluctant. I want to kiss him so badly it hurts me.

"Thank you, Zora." He sounds so brave.

"You're welcome, soldier in the army of the Lord."

For that, he rewards me with a tiny smile from his sore mouth.

Nicky seems to find his peace and gathers it about himself. He reaches out and touches my face, then with those long, beautiful fingers, sweeps my hair back with his hand. "I knew you'd get me in trouble," he says.

He leaves without saying good-bye at all.

CHAPTER NINETEEN

NICKY

I go back to my apartment and can't sleep at all. From my bed, I watch the pink-and-orange-sherbet perfection of the Monday sunrise and wish I could serve those colors on a golden spoon to Zora. The paradox of a happy lamentation creates a simple song in my soul.

Because of the Lord's great mercies we are not consumed, for His compassion never fails. They are new every morning. Great is Thy faithfulness.

Somehow I lived through the night. The image of my grandfather pulling the gun on me flashes in my mind, and with that sunrise and new mercy, I whisper "Thank You, Jesus" for my life. Last night, I dreamed I was with Zora. I'd gone to her, and in those blissful moments of unconsciousness not only did she see me, she held me. She kissed me. My grandfather and his gun were not there. My father was not there. My mother was not there. Rebecca was not there. Prejudice was not there.

I take a deep breath. I know it wasn't a dream because I can still feel her waist in the circle of my arms. Her scent still fills me. Her hair, that intoxicating blend of textures, soft spun wool and silk all together, still lingers beneath my fingertips.

I've barely slept at all, because most of my thoughts have been dreams of her, but those flights of imagination are soul fuel, energizing me. I take a look at my watch. I can go into work early. I hear my cell phone ring. I hope against hope it's Zora, flip it open, but the caller ID says it's Linda calling from home.

"Good morning, Nicky."

"Oh, hi, Linda."

"Well, thanks for your enthusiasm."

"No offense. I thought you were someone else."

"I'm sure Zora is sleeping right now."

"How did you …?" I don't even know why I bother. Linda just knows things. Our little Bible study is just like a family in the worst way. We're in each other's business like crazy. "I didn't do anything wrong, other than make a late visit."

"I didn't say you did anything wrong." But she adds, "Except make a late visit."

"I was desperate."

"So I hear."

"Why are you calling, Linda? I'm on my way to work. You can interrogate me then."

"I'm calling to save you the trip," Linda says. "As romantic and heroic as you were last night, Billie said you looked like the Elephant Man. Are you okay?"

"I just have some swelling and bruises. I'm better now."

"I'm not talking about your bruises, Nicky. She said you were very unlike your usual self."

"Well, it was a very unusual day."

"Take the day off, Nicky. Regroup."

"I'm fine, Linda. I missed work on Friday."

"Consider it a long weekend."

"But Linda—"

"Nicky, your physical wounds are small, but your psychological and spiritual wounds are massive. Don't make light of this. I'm also calling for an emergency Bible study and prayer meeting tonight. We're going to take these matters to God together. All five of us."

"Okay, Linda."

"Okay. I'll see you at my house at seven."

"I'll be there."

"I'll make sure she's there too."

"You just ensured that I'll be there."

"That's good to know. Seek God today."

"I will."

"And call me if you need anything."

"I will, Linda."

She takes a deep breath. "I love you. You're my little brother."

And this actually makes me feel like some tears are going to come. "Hey, cut it out. Are you trying to make me go all mushy?"

"Have a nice day, Nicky."

"I love you, too, Linda."

We hang up, and I tell myself that—even if only for this woman who loves me despite myself and refuses to give up on me—I'm going to be a good boy today. That's what I tell myself. And I believe it.

ZORA

Monday morning, Fred Hammond wakes me up. Not the real Fred. No, in real life, Billie's little girl wakes me up because she's sitting on the bunk bed telling her sisters how pretty I am, but even before I knew they were there and before I could hear their voices, Fred sang in my soul.

I know it might be tough to get yo'
  praise on
Devil been messing with you all
  week long
If you don't have a reason to praise
  Him let me give you one
He gave you a brand new mercy
With the rising of the sun, say....

Oh, yes, my brotha, I'm ready for my blessing. I'm ready for my miracle. And even though this song makes me miss LLCC fiercely, especially MacKenzie, I decide I've got to get up out of bed and see what life holds for today. Nicky came back to me last night. He kept fighting for me. I think of the contrast between him and Miles. When I needed protection, Miles protected me in the way he thought was best for me. And Nicky protected me in the way *I* thought was best for me.

Which was better? Honestly, I don't know, but someone acting in a manner that made sense to me, at least one that I can understand. Someone who didn't think I was cursed and "uncovered." I feel like Nicky gave me a little more to work with.

But what will Miles be up to today? Because surely he and *The Bishop* will confer.

I open my eyes. Three striking golden children stare at me. I'd gone to a conference at Spelman about being biracial in America, and one of the speakers said she called herself a "golden" person. I thought that was the dumbest thing I ever heard. I went home and made a running comedy monologue out of the poor woman's thesis.

My mother is a "golden" person whose white mother would have nothing to do with her. My father made sure we were spared the nonsense of such romantic thinking and drilled our mother's blackness—despite her mostly white looks—into us from the beginning of our preschool confusion about race. But looking at Billie and John's children, with their heads of wild blond or brown manes, their pairs of blue, hazel, and brown eyes, I see a room full of golden kids. Gorgeous kids. Not that I think all biracial children are gorgeous— and I know some people who do. God help us, but these kids really are as good-looking as their parents.

She looks like she's five or six. She smiles. "Hi, Miss Zora."

"Hi, pumpkin. What's your name?"

Her brown eyes light up. "Monica." Her golden skin has warm red and peach tones just like my mama, and she's chubby and round like a little peach, too. She's going to have her father's solid build. She's got his dark hair and eyes. Her springy sable hair is standing straight up on her head.

"You got a comb, kiddo?"

"Uh huh." She jumps off the bed and goes scavenging for a comb.

The other is seven or eight. Her coppery hair is a finer, wavier texture than Monica's. And she's got the psychedelic hazel eyes that seem to change colors every moment. She seems quiet and reserved. I sit up on my elbow. "Hi there."

"Hi." Her eyes look cast down.

"What's your name, pretty girl?"

"Clare."

"Monica and Clare. Those are pretty names." I point to another one of Billie and John's doll babies. "And what's your name?"

"Frances." She favors Monica very much.

Their older sister has a mess of blonde Afro curls. She's got Billie's wiry body and face. She's about sixteen. "They're saint names," she says. "We all got saint names. It's an Orthodox thing."

"What's your name?"

"Perpetua. My mom calls me Pet."

"You're going to need therapy for that, aren't you?"

She throws back her head and laughs, very Billie-like. "Uh. Yeah."

"Nice to meet you, Perpetua."

"Nice to meet you, too. At least a cool story goes with my name," she says.

Clare and Frances protest, with Clare loudly proclaiming, "We got cool saint stories for our names too."

"Everybody knows Saint Francis and Clare of Assisi lame-o," she says.

I realize then that all preachers' kids the world over are alike. Little Saint Monica returns with the wrong kind of comb. "I need a big comb. Do you have a wide-tooth comb?"

She looks bewildered. I look to Perpetua for help.

"Don't look at me. Our mom is white. We've been looking like this all of our life."

I don't mean to, but I can't help but laugh. "I sympathize. My mom has the straight hair. If she didn't send me and my sister Zoe out to get our hair done, we'd have been nappy, but not happy."

Perpetua sighs. "I feel you."

"Is there a store around here? My African roots are definitely showing. If I don't get an afro comb and soon, I'm going to be sporting a 'fro whether or not I want to."

"I think you'd look cute in a 'fro. I like my 'fro most days. But sometimes I wish I knew how to do more with my hair. We get a lot of visitors, but not a lot of people stick around long enough for me to really get the trick of doing my hair."

"I'll show you some things."

"Really? Are you planning on staying awhile?"

"I don't know how long I'll be in this house, but I can definitely guarantee that your mom won't be getting rid of me too soon. I think I'm falling in love with the Beloved Community."

Perpetua gives me a wide smile. "That's good news."

"Amen," I say.

The girls are all dressed, so I get myself together, and when I get back into the bedroom Perpetua is waiting for me.

She gets up from her bunk bed and takes me by the hand. Her kind gesture startles me, just as it did when Billie held on to my hand as she introduced me to John. Perpetua and I walk with our hands joined into the kitchen, and I remember being a little girl and holding hands like this with Mac. And it makes me want to talk to her.

We get into the kitchen, and Billie is cleaning up a mountain of dishes.

"Let me help you," I say.

"Not a chance, baby." She makes kissy lips, and I go to her for a kiss on my cheek and a hug she doesn't use her sudsy hands to give me.

"How did you sleep?"

I sigh. "Impossibly."

"I bet."

Pepetua lets out a big sigh. "You are soooooo lucky. Nicky is totally gorgeous."

I shoot a look at her and then Billie.

Billie shrugs. "Well, she's sixteen. And come on, there hasn't been much excitement in this particular house in months. Not since this woman named Tina stayed here and her boyfriend came here trying to shoot everything."

"He was shooting at people? A crazy man with a gun just came in shooting?"

"No, he was an idiot with an air gun and those plastic pellets. He didn't shoot anybody. He shot stuff. A lamp. A big stuffed bear. Stuffy sustained multiple gunshot wounds. I didn't appreciate that. John won that bear for Monica at Cedar Point when she was three. She loved that bear, and she was traumatized when he got shot."

I laugh because Billie is salty about the *bear* getting shot.

She must realize how she sounds. "Well, you know what I mean."

"So you saw him, huh, Perpetua?"

"You can call me Pet, Zora. It's not that bad. And I've seen him before. He dropped off some donations from his church. He's way hot."

"Okay, not hot," Billie says. "You can call him a lot of things, but not hot."

"Maaaaaaoohhhhhm."

"Men can be a lot of things, but never, ever hot. Not until you're married. And only your husband can be hot. So make sure you marry a hot guy."

"Well, how can I marry a hot guy if I can't think any of them are hot before I marry one?"

"It's a paradox, sweetie." She looks to me. "So you didn't sleep thinking about your true love?"

"I don't know about that."

"Oh, sweetie. I saw the two of you. If I've ever seen two people in love.... He wanted to know if you could see him."

Perpetua starts piling food on a plate for me. "Do you love him?"

I go quiet. I think Billie is going to answer for me, but she doesn't. Perpetua doesn't push me. Instead she puts a plate of eggs, grits, fresh fruit, and toast in front of me. She pours me a glass of orange juice.

"We already prayed over the food," she said. "And we pray for about an hour so it's way blessed."

Billie laughs. "Yeah. We gotta bless, and say the Lord's Prayer, and about twelve Lord Have Mercies. It's blessed all right."

The food is good. Pet starts helping her mom. I think about Nicky between bites of eggs. How I felt touching his face. How I saw him hours ago, but I miss him. How I want to hear his smart-mouthed remarks and hear him laugh and see everything—that whole world—inside of his eyes.

"I love him," I say.

I feel so happy saying it. And so sad.

"I know, sweetie," Billie says.

Pet says, "I so could tell. Are you gonna marry him?"

Billie looks horrified. "Perpetua Jordan!"

"What?" she asks. She is truly her mother's child. "I just want to know if she's going to marry Nicky. He's adorable, and he's totally into her."

"That's crazy," I say.

"Marrying him, or that he's into you?" she asks.

"Both," I answer.

WE DO SOME cleaning around the house, and I dream of colors for the walls. I think of my family's timeshare in the Bahamas and all those island-inspired colors. Ocean and sand. Shells. The sun rising and setting. Nothing Day-Glo. All colors from nature. From the beach. And maybe in the bathrooms I can use a bit of a nature theme too.

Lord, where is the money going to come from for that? And who cares?

Billie would care. And probably Pet. Those kids. Would the stranger feel less welcome if he came into a house of beauty? Not ostentatious beauty. Simple beauty. Something a few coats of paint could bring? Nicky would like it. I can make a wall to match the blue of his eyes.

What am I thinking? I'm acting like I'm a part of the Beloved Community. Maybe I wish I was. I wish I was a part of something.

Or is it someone?

I wish I could see him today.

I'm afraid to see him. I just told two people that I love Nicky Parker. I just told *myself*, and unfortunately, I meant it.

Now I want to tell him.

I have to distract myself before I start calling a certain phone number written on the back of a poem.

Zora Parker. That sounds so much better than Zora Zekora.

I'm losing my mind.

"Pet, is there a corner store around here?"

"Sure. Wanna walk over there?"

"Yeah. Billie, can I put cornrows in Monica and Clare's hair?"

Billie looks up from sweeping the kitchen floor. "Really?" I can tell she's excited about it. "Can you do Frances's hair too?"

"Sure."

"And can you put some beads in my dreads?"

"I think I can manage to get some on the small ones. I can give you an up-do too."

She grins. "John had better get ready!"

"Just don't get *pregnant* again, Mom," Pet says.

We're in a black neighborhood. I know I can find the right kind of comb in the 'hood. I'm going to get some hair oil and some rubber bands and make an offering out of doing all kinds of pretty little golden-girl heads around here. I don't have any paint, but I can cornrow some hair like any sistah from around the way. I can give God that before I head back to that lonely apartment and wait for the gauntlet to come down.

FIVE CORNROWED HEADS and one up-do later, a finer version of Billie reluctantly takes me home. She's still worried that Miles is going to get his "paws" on me.

"Don't forget," she says. "Just because you had a bad moment doesn't mean you have to make any lifetime commitments to him."

"I feel so tainted."

"It's a feeling. Yesterday was a colossally bad day, sweetie. What you felt is gonna pass."

"And what about all these feelings I have about Nicky? What about those, Billie?"

"Those aren't going anywhere anytime too soon."

"The feelings I want to have for Miles, I have for Nicky."

"Just allow yourself to feel what you feel."

"What if he's just playing games with me?"

"Which one of them?"

"Nicky?"

"Nicky is totally serious. It's Miles that's playing games. And his games are far more dangerous."

"Miles has been seriously interested in me for a long time. I knew he would ask me to marry him. I mean, I expected something more romantic, but I knew it was in the plan."

"I'm sure he has plans."

"Billie, that's not fair. Miles is just ambitious. There's nothing wrong with that."

"Maybe it's not. Maybe it is. But Zora, I haven't heard you say a thing about being in love with him, or even wanting him, but I did hear you say you loved Nicky. I did see you with him, and all I saw was grace and tenderness between you two. But when I saw you with Miles, he had an air mattress and a box of condoms."

"That was my fault."

"Somehow I doubt that, unless you asked that man to go get you those things, and I know you didn't."

"Maybe my actions asked him for it."

"Oh, sweetie. Please don't do this to yourself. This is why you don't need to be alone."

"I can guarantee that if Nicky called Miles, Daddy is going to come around and see me today. And he's probably going to be bearing gifts."

For a few moments Billie is quiet. "We've got a couple that's moving on. What if we made room for you at our house? You can stay with us. You wouldn't have to worry about finding a job right away. All your needs would be met."

"But don't you guys share everything?"

"Yes."

"That's a pretty radical move. I don't know if I'm ready to live in that kind of community."

"I understand that, Zora, but we are just crazy about you. And I don't like the thought of you being on your own. Community has its challenges, but it has its joys. And it has its safety. You can leave when you want to. We're not a cult, Zora. We're a family of God. You can take some time to seek God and find out who He wants you to be. And who He wants you to be *with*, and we'll help you so you avoid the kind of situation you had with Miles yesterday."

My heart actually feels a little torn. I've been asking Jesus what it means to be poor in spirit. And here I can give up everything and live in community and dedicate my life to service. I can free myself from being a slave to possessions and what someone else believes God made me to be. Now Billie is offering the opportunity to be a part of the Beloved Community. Even the name stirs up longing inside me.

I slump in the seat of the VW bus. "I'll have to think about it, Billie. Either way, I'll still have to go to my apartment. I know my family is going to want to contact me."

"Don't make any decisions when you're feeling this way. Especially bad ones."

"Miles is all stirred up, Billie. It's just like the Song of Solomon says. Don't awaken love before its time."

"What you awakened in Miles wasn't love, baby. Love doesn't go to Wal-Mart to shop for what he got. The other 'l' word does."

"He wants to correct it. He said he'll marry me."

"Zora, you're going to make me have a stroke if you say that one more time. You can't marry him because you let him take a few liberties. Don't you see how confused you are? This is precisely why you need to let us love on you and protect you. And you'll have to forgive me for saying this, but I don't think your family has been protecting you. Not lately."

"I don't know what they're doing. I don't know anything."

"Will you let me know if you need me, Zora? Please?"

"I promise I will, Billie."

I meant it when I said it.

NICKY

I go to the bank early in the morning and get the last bit of cash I can spare. I need the rest to make it through until I get paid again. As it is, I've missed two days of work. That's going to bite into the budget. Plus, I've burned up the road and a whole lotta gas going back and forth between Detroit and Ann Arbor. I knew I couldn't afford Zora. I could never do this. I have very little cash to work with as it is, and what I do have I try to be smart with, and keep something on hand for emergencies.

I have no idea what's going to happen to me. I saw myself as playing the good son, going on to seminary and eventually bringing my father's ministry into the postmodern world.

I guess that won't happen.

I would have never thought that when I walked out of church Sunday, it would be the beginning of me walking away from my family again. Because after that conversation last night, I don't think I can go back.

I hoped my dad would guide me, like a shepherd. The fact is, I hoped he would be a dad to me, and I guess in his own way, he was. He actually came to me. Gave me what he thought I needed to help me. What he didn't realize is *she's* what I need.

And what am I supposed to do about *her*?

I end up getting a hundred and fifty dollars. I try to strategize about what this will get me. Not much. I have no idea when I'll see my folks again. Or if my gun-wielding grandpa is going to go Charleton Heston-NRA on me if I show up at their house. I wonder how fast I can shower and change so I can get over to Billie's to see her. I just want to get her in my arms again, in the light of day, when I'm not feeling so fragile and looking so desperate.

I HURRY AND get myself together. My cell phone rings again just as I'm getting back into my truck. God, I want it to be Zora, but it's from my parents' home. I don't know if I should answer, but I can't help myself.

"Hello."

"Nicky?"

It's my mom, and she's calling me Nicky.

"Hey, Mom."

"Can we meet somewhere?"

I can hear in her voice that this is killing her. This is as bad as the "abortion incident" years ago. "Mom, I don't want to cause you any more pain."

"Please."

"Dad won't like it."

"I don't care. I just want to take you to breakfast, unless you have company or something."

I know exactly what she's asking.

"Mom, I didn't spend the night with her. I'm not going to get her pregnant. We're not doing anything, I *promise*."

"Your dad said—"

"I don't care what he said. I've never touched her. You don't have to give me any credit for that, but I wish somebody would at least give her some, because she's one of the coolest people that I've ever met, and she doesn't deserve to be treated like the whore of Babylon just because of stereotypes she has nothing to do with."

"She certainly didn't represent herself very well."

"I don't want to argue with you, Mom. Zora and I are just …"

"Just what?"

I don't answer her.

"Nicholas?"

So much for calling me Nicky. "Yes, Mom?"

"Will you have breakfast with me?"

"Sure. Where do you want me to meet you?"

"At Denny's on Washtenaw."

"I'll be there."

An hour later, I'm in Ann Arbor settled into a booth at Denny's.

We used to come here every Friday evening, me, my mom and my dad. I think about the lawsuit against Denny's and all those allegations of racism. I never thought much about them before. I used to think black people were too sensitive. That they had to be imagining some of the racism they cried so frequently, but now I'm not so sure. Nothing is what it seems to be. Not even my own heart.

My mother comes into the restaurant just when I expect her to. She is a prim and proper Parker through and through, fifteen minutes early, which she considers right on time.

I stand up to greet her, and she looks so frail. When I gather her into a hug, it feels like I could break her.

"Hi, Mom."

"Hi, Nicholas." She pauses. "Nicky."

"Mom, just call me whatever you feel comfortable with." We settle into the red vinyl booth. A waitress comes over and introduces herself as Catrina. She's a short, gorgeous, freckle-faced redhead, and she's making eyes at me. I know I'm in love because I don't give her a second glance. Okay, I do, but not a third.

"I miss calling you Nicky," my mother says.

Catrina asks if she can take our order. My mom orders a Grand Slam for both of us.

"I'm not hungry, Mom."

"Why not? You love their Grand Slam breakfast."

"Maybe I don't want to support this racist institution."

"Nicholas, what in the world are you talking about?"

"What about those lawsuits, Mom? All the allegations of racial discrimination." Frankly, I'd rather say this than "I'm so lovesick I can't eat." But my mom knows me.

"You're sick over *her,* aren't you?"

I don't answer her.

"If you're sick, this isn't good."

Catrina looks disappointed that I'm obviously smitten with someone else. To keep her from knowing all my business, I order. "Okay, Catrina. I'll have the Grand Slam breakfast too. With orange juice."

She nods, takes my mother's drink order, black coffee, and off she goes.

"Come on, Mom. I'm always sick when I'm upset."

"You're serious about her, aren't you?"

I don't want to get into this with my mom. If she tells me to "experience" Zora and come back to my senses too, I think I'll give up on humanity as a species.

"Well, are you?" she presses.

"Yes."

My mom shakes her head. "I don't understand. Saturday, Rebecca called me so excited. She said you got her a present from Eddie Bauer and you kissed her for the first time since you've been dating. She thought you were finally getting serious about her. She's brokenhearted, Nicholas. I liked her for you."

"I didn't mean to hurt Rebecca, Mom. I did kiss her. I wanted to see if I could feel with her a fraction of what Zora makes me feel."

My mother's eyes, the same blue as mine, search mine. "Are you sure what you feel for her isn't just—"

"Please, Mom. Please don't say it. Because what if I do feel *that?* Yes, I'm attracted to her. I'm freakin' bowled over by her beauty and sexiness. But that's not all, Mom. She's funny. And she's intelligent.

She's sensual, and I feel a little more alive when I'm around her. I feel more like myself when I'm with her, and there are very few people in the world I feel that way with anymore. That I happen to feel sexually attracted to her is a little low on the scale of why I love—"

My mother raises an eyebrow.

I rub my hand over my mouth.

"You were going to say you love her."

I pick up the menu promoting the featured pies. I don't want to talk about being in love.

I don't look at Mom. She makes a sound like a balloon deflating. *Almost* saying I love Zora has taken the wind out of her. I guess she'd fall dead if I admitted it.

We sit quietly until Catrina returns with our beverages. Mom sips on her coffee and I gulp down my orange juice in three big gulps.

"I think I've only heard you say you were in love twice before."

"Yep."

"With Leslie Shanoski. Remember her?"

"Yes. She was the only fifth grader in our class with breasts. All of us boys were in love with her."

"And you were in love when you came back from California. What was her name again? You said very little about her."

"Brooke Bennett."

"Was she white?"

"They were all white, Mom. Every girlfriend I've ever had."

"Why a black girl now, honey? Your dad thinks you're just acting out."

"I know what he thinks."

"He said you may need medication."

"He may have a point about that."

Mom looks frustrated at me. She gives me "the look." Then takes a sip of her coffee. "That's what I mean. We never know when you're serious."

"You didn't think I was serious when Grandpa was about to shoot me?"

"I think that's very serious. That's why I'm here. I want to know if you love this woman. I want to know what your intentions are."

I settle back into the red vinyl. I no more know what I'm going to do with Zora than I know what I'm going to do with Nicky. I only know what I wish. But Mom thinks it's as simple as that. Just make some kind of freakin' declaration.

When I don't answer, she advances "the look" to another level. She's getting serious with me. She wants to know my position.

"I think she's the one, Mom."

"What makes you think so?"

"Because I can't imagine living without her."

My mother takes what must be a scalding gulp of her coffee like it's a shot of whiskey. She throws her head back and swallows.

"Your life is going to be so complicated from here on out."

"It's been complicated before now."

"You haven't seen anything, Nicky. You're going to grow up now."

At that, Catrina returns with our Grand Slams, and I can't help but notice the irony.

CHAPTER TWENTY

ZORA

Billie drops me off at my apartment and I see Daddy's Bentley and my Lexus in the parking lot next to each other. He's in there, and someone else is, too. Probably Miles.

I tell Billie, and of course she wants to go in there with me. She feels like I'm about to be thrown to the dogs, but I have to remind her that this is my family.

"Yeah, but I'm your family, too. And I think I treat you better."

"I'm going to be fine, Billie. Just let me handle them myself. I don't need to bring them any more surprises."

"Are you sure, sweetie?"

"I'm sure."

"Tell me my phone number again."

Billie actually made me memorize her telephone number, and I rattle it off for the twentieth time or so.

"Okay. Just let me go in with you."

"No, Billie. I'm fine."

"Oh, fine," she says. She's in a snit about it. But I kiss her on the cheek and promise I'll call when it all blows over, and I'm hoping it does soon.

I try not to tell myself that I'm "dead sistah walking" going up the stairs and into the building. I dig into the backpack Billie gave me for my keys, thankful for the copy I got from the super, and that I don't have to buzz a half-dozen people to get into my own place. I get inside the building and walk down the corridor, which seems unnaturally long today. There seem to be too many stairs. I almost wish Billie had come with me after all. I haven't seen my daddy since Friday when he took everything I owned away except the pajamas I wore. And now I'll face him. My heart drums inside of me.

I miss my daddy. I don't know the man who did such a terrible thing to me. I don't understand him. I knew Daddy to be controlling and manipulative, but not with me. Somehow I had thought I'd be exempt from his games now.

I finally reach my door and put the key in. I don't even turn the knob all the way before the door opens, and my mother pulls me into her embrace.

"Oh, baby," she says, squeezing me. "I promise you that as soon as I found out about this I raised heaven! And Jack and I have been arguing ever since. Me and several ladies from the church have stopped by. We never catch you home. And he wouldn't tell me where he'd taken your stuff. Baby, I've been praying, and if the Lord hadn't assured me you were in His hands, I'd have lost my mind. I refused to go to church on Sunday. I told Jack *and* Jesus that LLCC wouldn't see the First Lady again until he brought every piece of furniture in this place back. Where on earth have you been?"

When Mama lets me go, I see that my stuff is back. The buttercream colored sofa. The Cheryl Riley chairs. The prints. Everything is as it should be, except MacKenzie is gone. The nightmare is over, I suppose. I close the door behind me. I also see my dad.

"Hi, Mama and Daddy."

My mama squeezes me again. "Zora, baby, I can't believe Jack took your things. I was absolutely sickened."

Daddy is sitting on a funky wooden Cheryl Riley chair looking grim. "I told your mother that I never expected to keep it. I expected you to call and apologize by Friday evening. How was I supposed to know you'd be so stubborn?"

My mother puts her hands on her hips. "She's always been just like you, Jack. What else would she do?"

"She's got plenty of you in her too, Liz."

My mother looks me up and down. I'm wearing the black pants and white shirt Nicky gave me. The silver cross and hoops. My mother is horrified. "Oh. Those cheap clothes. We need to get you out of those."

"I like this outfit, Mama."

"And where is your gold jewelry?"

"What's wrong with sterling silver?"

"You're a daughter of the King. You can wear gold. Your Father in heaven owns the cattle on a thousand hills."

"He also owns sterling silver. And my daddy, who does *not* own the cattle on a thousand hills—but probably is claiming them—took my gold, he, and the overseers with him, took everything but the pajamas I was wearing. They'd have probably taken those too, but I don't think Daddy would have wanted them to see me naked."

Daddy protests. "That's precisely the kind of insolence that caused this mess. I don't know what's gotten into you, Zora. Or who."

"Who?" I say. Daddy is never crude with me. Ever.

He stands up. He wouldn't want to let his baby girl have a height or psychological advantage or some such thing. "I know I took your promise ring, but I didn't mean for you to go crazy."

"I dunno, Daddy. That one led me to believe all bets were off. What did Miles tell you?"

"He told me a white boy has been calling him. What do you have to say about that, Zora?"

"I'd say he's a white *man.*"

"A white *man?*"

My mother almost seems amused by my answer. She sits down on the sofa but doesn't ask any questions about him. Dad has enough for the both of them.

"Miles says his name is Nicky Parker."

"It is."

"Please tell me that your *white man* Nicky Parker isn't the infamous skirt-chasing son of Reverend Nicholas Parker."

"That's him."

"Zora, do you know what kind of reputation he has?"

"Yes. I heard he's a rebel, rascal, and whore."

"What did you just say? Are you using profanity?"

"I don't think the word *whore* is profanity, Daddy. In fact, I'm really good friends with a former whore. And now that I think of it, Jesus seemed really fond of whores. And since we're on the subject, Nicky's family thinks *I'm* a whore."

I've watched my father's face since I was a little girl. I love his face. The rich, dark skin like mine. I look in his face and see in living color the sharp angles and lines of a Benin bronze sculpture. I've memorized that face singing lullabies to me, laughing, praying, preaching, telling stories, yelling, eating. A lifetime of expressions I've watched for twenty-two years, but I've never seen this face—a morbid mien of sorrow, anger, and horror—that says, "I've failed at what has meant the most to me."

I turn away from him. I've never regretted saying something so much in my entire life.

Daddy's voice becomes a hoarse whisper. "I don't want you to ever see that boy again."

"But, Daddy—"

"I understand that you were upset with me, Zora. I understand that I may have overreacted, but this has gone too far. My daughter is not—"

"I'm sorry, Daddy."

"Come in the bathroom with me."

My mother gets up from the sofa. "Jack, what are you—?"

His withering glance silences her.

"Come with me, Zora."

I follow him. I think he's going to take me in there and give me a spanking. Or some kind of beating. He used to spank us when we were little, but he hit us so hard Mama told us that if he ever hit us again, she was out like a ghost, and he'd never see us again. In that way, he had too much of his own father in him.

Mama grabs his arm. "Jack, if you lay a hand on her—"

His voice turns to ice. "Don't touch me, Elizabeth."

He takes me by the arm, yanks me into the bathroom, and turns the light on.

"Look into that mirror Zora Nella Hampton Johnson."

I don't want to look at myself.

His voice demands. "You look up in that mirror, girl."

I take a quick glance and look down again.

"I said look!"

This time I fix my eyes on my image.

"I want you to see what I see." He grabs me by the chin and keeps my face toward the mirror.

"I see the crown jewel of creation in that mirror. From the time you were born, I have spoken God's Word over you. I have told you that you are the head and not the tail. You are above not beneath. You are more than a conqueror in Christ Jesus our Lord. You have dominion over the earth. I have not raised a whore. Do you understand me, Zora?"

"Yes, Daddy."

"You will not walk in fellowship with *anyone,* black or white, who believes you to be a whore. Those people, they are not worthy of you, and if in any way you have misrepresented yourself, if in any way you have behaved in a way that may have led them to believe you are a whore, then you have lost your mind, little girl. And you are far from the woman of God I have raised you to be. Do you understand me, Zora?"

"Yes, Daddy."

"I want you to say to that young woman in the mirror. 'I am nobody's whore.' "

I wanted to say it. I wanted to say it loud like James Brown telling the world he was black and he was proud, but I had let Miles put his hands all over me. I didn't feel like I wasn't a whore. I didn't know what I was.

"I can't, Daddy."

His voice becomes steely with controlled rage. I think my heart will come right out of my chest as he nearly hisses, "Oh yes you can."

I feel like a tiny toddler. "No, I can't."

"Say it," he yells. It feels like his voice could shatter the red walls in the bathroom. Tears spring out of my eyes.

"I can't, Daddy. I'm sorry."

My mother stands behind him. "Leave her be, Jack."

He turns his rage to her. "My daughter is nobody's whore."

"We know that, Jack. It doesn't matter what they think."

"It matters!" He is nearly screaming now.

And then some monster comes into the bathroom that isn't my daddy at all. That man grabs me by my shoulders and throws me against the door. He slaps my face so hard, my cheek goes numb. "You don't let no white man violate you. Didn't I teach you about what they did to our women? That's what I sent you to Spelman for. To study your history. You knew better."

He shakes me by my shoulders, banging me against the door while my mother screams at him to stop. "You brought shame to us. We didn't raise no whores."

Bang. Bang. Bang. I slam against the door.

"You don't let no white man violate you."

I can't let this go on anymore.

"It wasn't Nicky."

"What?"

"It wasn't Nicky. It was Miles ... it was Miles who touched me. It was Miles who violated me."

Finally he lets me go, but my mother is so angry she hits him all over his back. "I told you not to hit my baby," she says. I want to call the police, but I don't even know where my cell phone is. I don't know why I'd even bother at this point. He doesn't hit me again and doesn't do a thing to Mama. He just goes into the living room and leaves us in the bathroom. That's when I hear the most God-awful sound I have ever heard in my life. Some deep, terrible noise of soul travail.

My mother and I go into the living room when we hear it. That's when I see Daddy with his head in his hands. For the first time in my life, I see he is crying.

NICKY

I say good-bye to my mother and leave the restaurant more frustrated than ever. While she doesn't share my father's abject horror at the thought of me being with Zora, she certainly isn't giving us two thumbs up. Not that I have a relationship with Zora. We kissed. She looked at me. We held each other. I'm thinking that may not mean we should start picking out china patterns, which makes me wonder why I'm getting roughed up, fighting with my family and friends, and calling a black man I don't know in the middle of the night threatening to come and get *his* girlfriend.

Maybe I'm doing all this because none of this is fair. It's not fair that my family won't acknowledge the dreams I have. And Zora's won't acknowledge hers. And it's not fair that we had to find each other at the worst time. And I ended up hurting Rebecca, who I should have never been with in the first place.

And it's not fair that Zora is with the Lion King and he sucks. Or that her father took all her stuff. And now I'm in love with her. And maybe she feels something for me, too. And people who don't even know her think I can just take her to bed at will because they watch too many rap videos or have outdated ideas that should have been left behind when Lincoln freed the slaves, if not before.

What's the matter with all of us? I want the apostle John's revelation. The one where he looks and sees a great multitude that no man can count, from every nation, tribe, people, and language standing before God's throne. And every one of those people is in a white robe—and they aren't Ku Klux Klan white robes either. Everybody holding palm branches saying in loud voices: "Salvation to our God which sitteth upon the throne, and unto the Lamb."

Why aren't we living right? Why are we all looking the part, but are nothing but a bunch of whitewashed graves? Dead on the inside?

At least some of us are. Most of the people I've been dealing with are, though not all. God, what a mess Your people are.

I have never been to a church that resembles that multitude in the book of Revelation. I have never been to a Christian conference that looks that way. Even the Beloved Community doesn't look that way. Not yet.

I'm so tired. Of everything and everybody. Second to You, God, she's the only one that makes me feel better. I just need to see her. I'm going to her.

Right now.

ZORA

We sit in silence for a while in our own unholy trinity. My father is on the sofa. My mother is beside him, and I'm at the peak of this triangle, ignoring the perfectly good chairs, sitting, ironically, on the floor. We sit there as if a bomb has detonated, and we're devastated, unable to the move ourselves away from the ruins.

Daddy breaks our silence first.

"Miles will correct this. He's asked to marry you right away. I've agreed."

I knew it. I knew he'd side with Miles. Miles is the black man. I look to my mother.

She nods. "He's a good man, Zora."

"What if I don't want to marry Miles?"

"You've been dating him for six months," she says. "How could you not want to marry him? Grow up, Zora. What did you think was going to happen if you kept dating him?"

I want to tell her that I don't like the way he tastes, and that's a biological sign that we aren't compatible, according to Billie. I want to tell her that he's not the man I thought he was. That when I said he violated me, I meant he nearly forced himself on me. And that we won't discover the mystery of one flesh for the first time together because someone else already knows him. And it's not that I could have that with Nicky. But at least I'd know what I had to work with from the start instead of being surprised like I was with Miles. I want Mama to know Miles got me an air mattress and condoms instead of a white dress. But this doesn't seem like the time or place. God, what am I going to do?

"Mama, I don't want to marry—"

My father stands up. "Miles is going to honor you. He's going to pay for whatever he did and marry you. Don't think that white boy is going to do right by you just because he didn't make whatever mistake Miles did. At least not yet. No matter how you look at it, you've shamed us. Do you think the Reverend Nicholas Parker is going to welcome you into the family? He will never accept you! I can hear the gossip buzzing among their friends at their country club." His face is a mask of disgust. "*No!* You will *not* shame us."

Now I stand up. "I'm sorry I've really caused an uproar at the

Parkers' country club, Daddy, but according to your son-in-law to be, I've caused quite a ruckus with the faithful at LLCC. They're telling Miles how cursed I am. Can you see them at their little social clubs, Daddy? 'The Bishop's daughter is *crazy*. She doesn't want her golden Lexus cage lined with our offerings anymore. She wants to fly free with a paintbrush in her beak. What a wretched, poor, naked, miserable sinner she is.' Looks to me like I'm the object of gossip regardless, Daddy. What difference does it make if the people are white?"

"At least they don't think you're a whore."

"I'd rather be the whore. At least the whore would have fun."

Once again, he raises his hand to me, but this time my mother grabs him. "You hit my baby one more time, Jack Johnson, and it will all be over today. Marriage. Family. Ministry. Everything we have will be over right here, right now. I promise you that."

Daddy looks at Mama. I don't know what he sees. I don't know what is going on between them, but he backs up. He turns to me.

"You get married in the next few days, or I'm cutting you out of my life completely. I will never say another word to you again for the rest of your life, Zora. I don't care what your mother says."

At that, he storms out the door.

For a moment, my mother and I stare at the door. I feel as if I'm waiting. I don't know what for. Maybe I'm waiting for another dramatic turn of events, but nothing happens. He's said all he will say. He's done all he will do.

Maybe I'm waiting for some spark of courage to fire inside of me, but everything within feels cold. Maybe I'm waiting for my wings to unfurl at this moment. Maybe I'm waiting to fly far away from here, but those big black wings stay tucked inside, and I can't seem to move them.

I give Mama a pleading, desperate look. "I don't want to marry Miles."

"I don't want to have to worry about you, Zora, I really don't." She shakes her head. She opens her mouth to speak, but nothing comes out.

Oh, God. Let me fly away from here.

"Zora. In some ways you're so young. I wish I could say I think you're going to be fine, but you're so fragile in so many ways. You don't need to be alone. Even if you were with MacKenzie I wouldn't worry about you."

"I'll be stronger, Mama. Look, I've been on my own without my stuff. I can go on without him."

She shakes her head at me. "Oh, honey. You really don't know a thing about this world."

She steps up to me and places her hand on my cheek. She covers with gentleness the place still sore from Daddy's slap. But her words are hard. "You're going to have to sell your soul so many times to make it in this life. You'll do it if you have a career. You'll do it in a marriage. But if you marry well, at least you'll do it in a comfortable bed wearing a pretty gown. And you'll be lying down in that bed inside of a house you built from the ground up to your exact specifications."

"That's what *you* did. I don't want your life, Mama. That was good enough for you. It's not enough for me."

"You haven't suffered enough. We've kept you from experiencing any of the bad things of life. You don't know what it is to have it hard. You go off on your own chasing after that white boy and you'll lose everything, sweetie. He'll leave you behind as surely as my mama left me behind. You'll wish you had a Miles Zekora when that Nicky Parker is through with you. You'll see. Love is overrated, honey. At least it is with the Nicky Parkers of this world. And he doesn't love you. He's a playboy, and you're just some brown sugar."

"You don't know him, Mama."

"It's you that doesn't know him, Zora."

"I think I do."

"You think you know a lot that you don't, honey."

Mama takes me in her arms and kisses my forehead.

"Mama, Miles is way too ambitious for me. He just wants what Miles wants. I'm just secondary to the plan. Just another item on his agenda. I can't live like that. He's the one who doesn't love me."

My mother gives me the saddest look. "Zora. You won't want for anything with him. If you marry him, his ambition will make sure you have all that you need. And by the end of the week you'll be a woman. God help you."

"I'd rather be a woman in God's time without a man like Miles. Without Daddy if need be. I'm going to paint. I'm going to be the woman God created me to be. I'm in love, Mama. I want to see what God wants to do with me and Nicky. I have to try. God made me for more. And I'm going for what God made."

"It won't work out, baby. And your daddy will never approve."

"Maybe it won't, but I'm going to see, and I'll live my life without Daddy's approval. And without his stuff if need be. I choose poverty and the Beloved Community with Nicky over all this. Don't abandon me too, Mama."

She slips her arms around me. "You're my little girl. I think you're making some very foolish choices, but I'm not going to abandon you. I know what it's like to lose your mama. A house divided can't stand, so I guess my house is going to come down. It wasn't built on much anyway. You pray for your mama. I may be choosing poverty with you, baby. And I don't want to do that. I'm too old for that."

"Mama, it looks like you've figured out how to handle him. I don't think you're going to have it too hard. Just try to listen to Jesus. I don't know what that is going to sound like, but try, Mama."

I hug her. My mother is the opposite of Ms. Pamela. She's the poorest wealthy woman I've ever known.

NICKY

I'm embarrassed by how badly I need to see her. I wish she'd left something in my car or in my apartment, but she's only left something in my heart, so I tell myself that I'm going to go to her, and when she opens the door I'll tell her she's left her eyes on my heart, and that since she sees inside of me all the time, I'm afraid I may be forced to keep her. But that sounds stupid, not to mention psychotic. So I think I'll just show up and try not to look like a dork until she makes me leave.

I buzz the buzzer, and my lungs feel like they want to jump into my throat. Man, she makes me feel like a little boy in the best and the worst ways, all at once. I consider how I'll say my name when she asks who it is, but she doesn't ask. She's expecting someone. I'm thinking it's not me.

I trudge up the steps wondering how soon it's going to be before the Lion King is behind me clobbering me. I can't help it. I've had a lifetime of negative stereotypes stored in my head. The fact that Miles has already threatened me doesn't help. But he's going to have to do what he's going to do. I need to see her.

I get ready to knock on the door, but it's already ajar. I feel a little worried when I see that. I tell myself that this is irrational. She's expecting someone, probably Miles, and she's opened the door for him. I almost turn around, but push the door open instead, and she's standing there staring at me with those big Bambi eyes. I can see that her apartment is full of furniture. The princess is back. She won't need me anymore because, from what I can see, her stuff is way better than anything I could give her.

It's over. It's all over.

"Hey," I say. I wonder if she can hear how my heart sounds like African drums, just for her.

She looks so surprised to see me. How can she possibly be surprised when nothing can keep me away from her? Nothing at all.

"Nicky? What are you doing here? I thought you'd be working today."

"I should be working. I would have called you, but—"

"It's good that you couldn't call. My parents just left. In fact, I thought you were them coming back. If you had called while they were here it probably would have been trouble for both of us."

"You got your stuff back. Congratulations."

"Would you like to come in?"

She waves me forward and I walk in to Black American Princess world. It's a freakin' awesome place to be. I don't belong here.

Zora doesn't look good. I mean, she *looks* good. She looks incredible. She's wearing the black pants and white shirt. Oh, man. She'd look good in anything, but those long legs draped in that flowing fabric! Still, in this princess paradise my outfit from Janelle's isn't good enough for her. *I'm* not good enough for her. Zora's out of my league. My dad may think she's tacky, but she's got more money, style, and class than we lowly Parkers ever had. I knew when I first saw her I couldn't afford her. Not snack-machine guy.

"You look really beautiful today, Dreamy."

"Thank you, Nicky."

She's been crying again. I want to ask her what happened, but then again, I don't really want to know. She's no doubt had her own version of the nightmare I've been living. I just want to take her in my arms and get her out of here.

"Zora, let's go."

"Go where?"

"I'm taking you home."

"I can't go home with you."

"Sure you can. Let's go."

"That's what they all expect. You to take me home. You to bed me down. My parents told me to marry Miles. Miles tried to rape me, Nicky."

"He tried to rape you?"

"I told him no, and he thought I shouldn't have gotten him worked up."

"Had you ever … you know … had you been with him before?"

"I'm a virgin, Nicky. I'd never even kissed Miles. You gave me my first kiss yesterday."

"No way, Zora."

"Way, Nicky. You gave me my first kiss."

Her words weaken my knees. I sit down on her leather sofa. "Dreamy, baby, you should have told me."

She sits beside me. "Does that change things?"

"I thought you slept with Miles."

"No wonder you were being such a jerk. But you stayed."

"I didn't know if he would hurt you because I showed up. Something told me you were in trouble, but I didn't trust my instincts. Not completely. Man, Zora. I'm sorry."

"You came back to me, even after you thought I slept with Miles. That's why you called him, isn't it?"

"Yeah. I thought maybe you were ... I don't know. I just didn't want you sleeping with him. You can't marry him, either. Even if you slept with him, and thank God you didn't, I'd still protest you marrying him."

"That's not what you said at first."

"Well, I changed my mind. You can't marry Miles."

"You don't have to worry. I told my mother I was going to marry you."

I have a mild heart attack, but I get over it fast. "You told your mother that?"

She looks embarrassed, because she can't know how lightheaded I feel. How I think I just grew four or five inches taller. But surely she can see I can't stop smiling.

She tries to take it back. "I realize now that sounds presumptuous."

"Not so much. How did that go over with your mom?"

"She doesn't think you'll have me."

"I'll have you, all right. I'm going to take you home with me right now."

"That's not what I had in mind when I said you'll have me."

"I want to have all of you, Zora. May I have all of you?"

She just nods her pretty head with a smile, and says, "Yes."

Oh, man. I think I just asked Zora to marry me. Or did she ask me? I don't even know. I just know suddenly my stomach is doing cartwheels, and she's grinning, and she looks so freakin' happy.

"We'll fly away together." She stands up and spins around. Dear God, she's lovely. Her voice is music. A song I feel like I've always known. "Wherever our wings lead us, Nicky."

"You and me. Free as birds." I want to believe it.

"Free as birds."

She starts singing. Right there in my arms by the door. She throws her head back, and what comes out of her mouth is so ethereal and haunting it almost scares me.

> *One of these mornings bright and fair*
> *I want to cross over to see my Lord*
> *Going to take my wings and fly the air*
> *I want to cross over to see my Lord*

Oh, man. Zora is singing Negro spirituals. I don't do that. I may do a rousing rendition of a hymn on a good day—and it'd have to be a real good day—but this is way out of my league.

I don't know if I can handle a wife that sings Negro spirituals.

Or is it me wondering if I can handle a Negro wife?

I release her. She kisses me one more time and runs to grab her backpack.

We leave quickly. Zora forsaking her princess possessions to go away with me. I don't tell her how afraid I am. I don't tell her that I come from a family of hunters, and that birds get cut down in flight and come hurtling down to earth again wounded or dead, and sometimes those birds get stuffed and put on display so their murderers can enjoy their beauty long after they've crossed over to see the Lord.

CHAPTER TWENTY-ONE

ZORA

We decide to take my Lexus to Nicky's apartment. He wants to ride in style. He says he's never driven a Lexus. He's really getting into it.

I don't like this. It feels wrong. It has an exaggerated quality about it. Like Nicky is a cartoon caricature version of himself. I can't escape the feeling that he's somehow mocking me. My defenses soar.

Before we got in my car, he grabbed a bunch of CDs out of his truck. His music is appallingly white. He listens to people like U2. I mean, I know Bono does a lot of work for Africa, but I'm not really feeling U2. Or Coldplay, and his other music that sounds suspiciously country. I don't do country music.

He has the driver's side window down because we've got another stellar unseasonably mild spring day.

"Can you just turn the air on, Nicky?"

"Why?" he says. "Its beautiful! Don't you think the fresh air is nicer?"

"That's a white thing. Always needing air."

"What? Black people don't need air? You don't have lungs or something, Zora? Did I miss some detail in anatomy? I knew we didn't have the same amount of melanin. I knew the hair was different. But what is this lung thing?"

"I just mean you don't see us hiking, and mountain climbing, and doing extreme cold weather sports."

"Come on, Zora. You know that's not true."

"Oh, really? Name some black athletes that do those things."

"I'm not that well versed in black hikers or mountain climbers. White ones either, Zora. But I'm sure that's not the problem. Is it the music? Are you embarrassed that black people may think you're listening to U2? What would *you* like to listen to, princess? Shall I put in Fred Hammond for you?"

"Maybe I'd like for you to stop calling me princess. Not that you mind driving the princess's Lexus."

"I'm sorry. Does the princess have trouble sharing her toys?"

"Does the cowboy have to come in, conquer, and take what he wants like all white men do?"

He doesn't say anything. Just stares straight ahead, but he turns off his music, puts the windows up, and turns on the air.

I end up complaining because now I feel too cold.

"Is this a sign of things to come, Dreamy? Are you going to be hard to please?"

"What difference does it make? Everyone says you aren't going to stick around."

"And you'll give me good reason to go exactly like you're doing. Is that how this works?"

"I don't know how it works. You tell me. Are you taking me home to have a little taste of brown sugar?"

"Brown sugar? I haven't heard that one. I heard the whole darker-the-berry thing. I thought maybe I could just taste your sweet berry juice. I don't know. Maybe you can give me a taste of *all* your flavors. We can explore the whole gamut of racist stereotypes. You can put Baskin Robbins out of business today."

"You know, Nicky, I've been defending you, and now I'm not sure why. You suck."

"I've been defending you, too. You might want to take a look at my face, Zora. I've been fighting for you. For your honor. I'm on my way to a freakin' jewelry store to buy you a ring that I can't afford so I can marry you, which we both know neither of us is ready for. I'm not a Thomas Jefferson, despite your eloquent speech. I broke up with Rebecca, the acceptable-to-the-parents *white* girlfriend. I told her I'm in love with you. I told my mother I'm in love with you."

"You told her that?"

"What does it matter? I'm not sure you really believe in us. Nobody believes in us."

"Billie does."

"Yeah, Billie. That and five bucks will get you a venti latte from Starbucks. You may even get some change back. Oh yeah. Let me taste your *coffee,* too."

"Stop it."

"You started it, Ms. *Brown Sugar.*"

"I believe in us, Nicky. I wouldn't be here if I didn't, but that doesn't mean I don't have my doubts and fears. Miles was my first relationship. And I totally got him wrong. I have no idea what I'm doing. Are you sure about any of this, Nicky?"

"I'm not sure about my own name most days."

"Do you *think* you might love me?"

"I'm thinking I might. How 'bout you? Do you *think* you might love me?"

"My father slapped me today. I'm not just taking a little ride with you, in case you didn't realize it. I've walked away from everything I lost, as far as I'm concerned. It wasn't taken. I walked away from it. I'm thinking I might love you very much, Nicky. I'm thinking I might want to spend my life with you, but I don't know how. You're white. And I don't know how to be with a white man."

"We'll figure it out."

"You promise?"

"Yes. I promise."

"Can we just skip the ring? I'm tired. I'm tired of fighting. Of everything."

"I'm not Miles, Zora. If we're going to get married, I want to get you a ring."

"I just want to go home with you for now. Can we just go home?"

"Sure, Zora. We can go home."

He doesn't argue with me. He just takes me home.

NICKY

I get her to my apartment, and before I open the door, I'm thinking of all these differences between us. I don't have sapphire and red walls. I'm going to open the door, and she's going to be disappointed, and that look on her face, however subtle, will burn into me like a brand, no matter how she'll try—if she is as kind as I think—to reassure me. And if she's not as kind as I think, it will be worse.

We get inside, and her Bambi eyes look for some sign of life or color but find none. My apartment looks as soulless as my inner life. The princess is appalled by my cheesy apartment. She doesn't offer me any consolation. No insincere "Nice place" tossed in my direction to soothe my wounds. She gives me nothing. Rebecca would.

What did she expect? I'm not a freakin' engineer like Miles. But I can give her all the Tom's potato chips and pretzels and M&Ms she can stand. Can Miles do that? I think not!

I tell her she can have a seat, and she tells me she wants to see where I write. Of course I write in my bedroom, and if I'm not mistaken, I told her that. The thought of Zora's presence in my room seems like a delightfully bad combination, but I'm strong in the bedroom. I'm the king in that domain. I can right this slight I feel if I can get my hands on her. And if I can get her in that room, I can. She's asking for it.

"Right this way, Dreamy."

I lead her past my poor excuse for a dining room and living room. Past the shabby black futon. I open the door to my bedroom—the monk's cell where I haven't taken a woman since I've tried so hard to do the right thing. And now I don't want to do the right thing so much.

"There's nothing in here but my bed and my laptop," I say. "I don't even have a chest of drawers. My clothes are stacked in my closet, and my socks and underwear are in freakin' plastic shoeboxes from the dollar store. And you suck to make me talk about where I put my draws, Zora."

She laughs.

"What?"

"I didn't know white people said 'draws' for underwear."

"What can I say? I'm *urban.* Sometimes I say 'drawers.' "

"You did go to Ypsi High."

"Yeah. And you went to Pioneer?"

"I went to Sankofa Shule."

I don't even attempt to say that. "What is that?"

"It's an Afrocentric charter school. Very revolutionary."

"I thought you Word-Faithers thought stuff like that was of the devil."

"Most do. But we have strong AME-Church roots. We had to know who we were as a people, plus my grandfather had lots of converted Black Panther cronies. Our blackaliciousness is an LLCC distinctive, hence the Spelman, rather than the Rhema, education."

"You are so in trouble for slumming like this, and with po' white trash like me."

She sashays into my bedroom, that rear end swinging from side to side in those black pants. I should have stuck with skirts. Then I'd have just been tormented by the endless calves, but that would be more manageable by far.

I stand in the doorway while she glides inside with the rhythm of a sonnet. I'm captivated by her melodic voice, even though she's judging my stuff. Or I feel like she is.

"You're right. All you have is a bed. And a computer."

"I live a Spartan existence, but I can compensate by making your stay here most enjoyable."

She sits down on my bed, and the look on her face is innocent. Childlike. She bounces up and down on it like she wants a test-drive that evil Nicky is more than happy to give her. Good Nicky is terribly weak right now, but he tries to make an appearance despite my attitude.

"This is where I write. Come on back into the living room, if you could call it that."

God, what was I thinking bringing her here? I just wanted to go away with her. I wanted to get us away from all the ugliness around us, and now all this ugliness is cropping up inside of me. And now she wants to interrogate me.

"Tell me about your first kiss."

I decide I won't tell her. Ever. The thought of it makes my palms sweat. I clench my fist. "You don't want to know about that."

"I do. Tell me."

I feel a little claustrophobic. I lean against the doorjamb. I try to think about kissing Zora. I remember her taste that first time. My mother's gravy still lingering in her mouth. Peas. Something minty. Something tangy. "Tell me about yours."

"I don't have to. You were there."

"I only know what *I* felt, Zora."

"What was that?"

I don't want to deal with *my* feelings like we're in freakin' therapy. Frankly I want her to tell *me* something that will be about as close to her talking dirty to me as she's going to get, and I know that won't be very far. "What did *you* feel?"

"Do you remember that part in the Song of Solomon, when her beloved comes to her and she's sleeping? And he knocks. It says, 'I sleep, but my heart waketh.' That's what I felt. Like my whole life I'd lived inside of a strange dream, and with that kiss you awakened me. It was like being a princess. In the best way. In the 'my prince has finally come and kissed me' way."

"I'm no prince."

"Yes, you are."

"You think too much of me. I'm going to disappoint you."

"No, you won't."

"I will. I suck."

"Kiss me again."

"I told you I don't want to play *the prince* for you."

"Then kiss me like a cowboy."

Ah. I see. She may have asked to see where I write, but she's not in my bedroom to sample my rhymes. And the thing is, I know she doesn't really know what she's asking for.

I go to her. Sit on the bed. Everything inside of me screams, *Nicky, don't do it.* But I'm not an engineer. I don't have the *stuff* Miles does. She wants to see where I write? I'll put my signature on her body. Let my hands create a language meant only for her. I'll make a poem of effleurage, starting with light touches with the pads of my fingers on her face.

We begin. I stroke her cheeks, eyes, nose, lips until she sighs with pleasure and relaxes into my hands. She trusts me completely.

My, my, my. Zora is magnificent. So soft. I lean in for the kiss that will elevate us to another realm of possibilities. A place where neither of us is thinking. There are no first kiss questions. Just feeling. She touches my face in turn, giving herself to me.

We could stay here in this little empty room and fill it with whatever we have right now. Let that be enough. Never leave this room again.

Then God speaks.

Though I speak with the tongues of men and of angels, and have not charity—

Not now. That sounds like the apostle Paul. You let a little Paul in, and the next thing you know, you'll be fleeing fornication and marrying rather than burning. I'm better at burning.

I am become as sounding brass—

I take a breath. God is asking me to *love* her. He wants real love, not my cheap horizontal imitation.

She stops. I assume God is speaking to her, too. I don't even bother to ask. I just push away from her and wait for her to tell me what God is saying to her like she's some kind of prophetess.

"I want to wait," she says.

"Of course you do."

"Don't you?"

I want to say very bad words in front of *no*, but I don't want to scare my wife-to-be. I just smile at her like a good Baptist and lie like a rug. "Yeah. I wanna wait."

"I'm a virgin, Nicky."

"I know."

"I'm scared."

I feel unreasonably angry. I'm not even sure exactly who I'm so ticked off at.

"You might want to keep that in mind before you go bouncing on a man's bed, or whatever your little seduction ritual is. What'd you do to Miles? I'm beginning to feel a little sympathy for him."

She slaps me for that. And lemme tell you, she can hit. I get up and charge out of the room. "Screw you, Zora."

She yells after me. "Looks like you're mad because that's what you *didn't* get to do."

"I don't need this. Why don't you take your sleek black carriage and head back to your pampered princess palace? You don't want to be here anyway."

"Is this your way of running away, Nicky? Are you going to go write? Where you off to this time? New York City? Gonna write the great American novel in the Big Apple?"

I stride, trying desperately to keep my cool, into the dining room like I actually have a reason to be upset. I'm beginning to see some really bad similarities between me and Miles. What's worse, she probably sees them too. I wish I could get out of here, but I don't even have my truck. Not that I'd know where to go. Where do you flee to escape your own shame?

ZORA

He leaves the room angry, but he comes back in a little while. I think he's going to apologize, but he just gets his laptop and goes back out into the living room.

I want to tell him that I didn't mean what I said about him running away to go off writing, but I'm afraid I did mean it. And I don't like that I did.

I hear him typing. He's probably drafting my walking papers. There's a phone by his bed, and I don't ask him if I can use it. I figure I'm his fiancée, at least for the next few minutes. That ought to be good for a phone call. I call MacKenzie. I need my best friend.

She answers on the first ring.

"MacKenzie, I'm in Nicky's bed."

"Giiiiiiiirl? What's up with that? Hold on while I have somebody revive me. I just had me a heart attack."

"Don't waste your heart attack on me. Nothing happened. I didn't want anything to happen. I don't think he did either. He stopped before I asked him to. But he still got mad."

"First of all, stop trippin'. If you in his bed he *did* want something to happen. That's why he mad. But they all get mad if they don't get any. That's how they're wired."

"Something bad like that happened with me and Miles yesterday. I thought he was going to do what Jordy did to you back in the day."

"What?"

She sounds like she's going to have a heart attack for real. I try to calm her.

"I got him going, and he didn't want to stop."

"Girl, I leave you alone for a few days, and you get in all kinds of trouble. You got Miles, who never even kissed you, 'bout ready to date-rape you, and now you in Halle Berry's white boyfriend's bed. Lord, have mercy. I'm coming back home."

"You don't have to come home. I'm getting married."

"Oh, Lord, I'm having a big one. It's like Fred Sanford on *Sanford and Son*. Girl, you 'bout to kill me. Who you talkin' 'bout marrying?"

"Nicky."

"Did you do it with him? I thought you said nothing happened! Do I have to tell you the definition of sex? I know yo' mama and daddy didn't teach you nothin', but I thought at least you knew the basics."

"We haven't done anything but kissed, but we're in love and we're going to get married."

"When did you meet him?"

"Last Wednesday."

"It's only Monday, heifer! You've known him for five days. That ain't even a week. I'm about to get in my car—"

"MacKenzie, I'm in love. Have I ever said those words to you?"

She gets quiet on me. "Baby, you *have* said those words. But I know you never meant 'em. What scares me is that you mean 'em now. I can hear it in yo' voice. I knew when I looked into that white boy's face he was going to be the one that turned you out. I'm comin' home, Z. We gon' work through this. Don't marry, or have sex with *anybody,* and please get out of his bed. Get out of his apartment. Girl, get off the same planet as his fine self."

"I'm going to marry him, Mac."

"You may just do that, but not right now, baby. It's way too soon."

"What if I ask him to wait, and I lose him? What if I'm already losing him? He's mad at me. He's in the living room writing me a Dear Jane letter."

"Let me tell you something, Zora. You ain't no Jane. You don't get those kinds of letters, and you're not the girl to ask the kinds of question you're askin'. I am. You're the girl the good guy waits for. You're the one he gives everything he has for. You hear me?"

"What if he's not as good as I think he is?"

"Then he ain't the one."

"I've gotta go, Mac."

"I'll see you in like, eight or nine hours."

"Don't come home, Mac."

"I'll see you soon, Z."

I hang up. I don't know what I've gotten myself into.

NICKY

Though I speak with the tongues of men and of angels.

Paul won't let me go. Love won't let me go. She won't let me go.

I really am in love.

I suck.

I want to do right by her, and I've never done right by a woman. I've never had to. Don't know how. Paul said when he was a child he spoke as a child, but when he became a man he put childish things away. How am I supposed to do that, Lord? I don't want to lose her, but I feel like bolting here.

Though I speak with the tongues of men and of angels.

I grab my Bible from off the floor by the side of the futon. It's been sitting there since Friday when I'd read it, planning to spend the day just me and Jesus, and instead He sent me on a clothes-shopping mission and the journey to falling in love with her.

I turn to the New Testament. First Corinthians, the thirteenth chapter. Read Paul's infamous words about how to really love and know I've missed the mark big time. I want to write. I need to absorb these lessons in that way, with a prayer as I write, that the gruff last apostle will give me roots deeper than Alex Haley's.

Help me, Paul. Heavy my feet long enough to get myself a real job. Make it to the altar and the wedding night with my spotless bride, and to stay for the babies, the spreading waistline, gray hair, and death do us part.

I read the passage again, put the Bible down, and pick up my laptop and begin to type:

> If the words I write
> broke the hearts of men,
> and staggered angels
> and I did not love

I am mere noise, needing
grace to silence me.

And if my prophecies, opened
the fragrant bud of mystery
and my faith made mountains bow
and leap, and I did not love
what is the use of me?

If I emptied myself of myself,
and gave all I had to the poor,
and if I yielded flesh to fire
willingly, and on my knees
and I did not love
I should be pitied for my poverty.

Love stays.

Love cares for others more.
Love doesn't ask for
what is not for love.
Love bows,
and love gives way.

Love doesn't think too highly
of itself, nor does love
violate. Love doesn't insist
that it has its way.

It doesn't remember sins.
Love doesn't make you beg.

It just lets it go.

Love loves when truth blossoms
like lilacs and gardenias
swollen with scents
sweet as a mercy.

Love allows.

Trusts Abba always.

Love opens wide eyes
to see the best
and shuts them tight
to what is behind us;
It doesn't comprehend
the past.

Love never,
ever
fails.

Like God,
Love stays.

I decide to stay where love is. I'll fight whatever demons I must to be with Zora, even if the demon is me.

She comes out of the bedroom and passes by me without a word. Goes banging around in my kitchen. I don't know what she's doing, short of looking for the sharp instrument she'll kill me with. I only hope she stabs with less power than she slaps with.

CHAPTER TWENTY-TWO

ZORA

He's calling out to me from the living room where he's stopped typing. When I passed him, he had that contented look about him, and I know despite what I said, he's just written something wonderful. I can't wait to read it.

Nicky has a dismally ill-equipped kitchen, not that I know my way around a kitchen. But Mac did show me a few things. My collard greens have come a long way, and I can make a box of Jiffy cornbread sing. My chicken is melt-off-the-bone good. A sistah's got to do chicken right. But I'm not here to cook for him, at least right now. I pray we'll have plenty of time for that later if we can make it through this awful right now.

I've got the cans. He doesn't have collard greens but he has string beans. Abundant string beans. I'm going to have to learn how to cook fresh string beans for him. Show him what a string bean is supposed to taste like. But if that man thinks I'm going to make him a chitlin, he'd better get himself another black woman.

I don't care how he pronounces it.

I just need rope. I open all kinds of drawers, but I don't see any. I have to call MacKenzie again. That means I have to cross the living room. It also means I have to go back into the bedroom. Even if I use my cell phone, my purse is in his bedroom.

I take a deep breath, throw my head back like a runway model, and catwalk out of the kitchen like I own his apartment and he's annoying me just being there.

He looks up at me. "Hey."

I ignore him. Communication at this point would completely defeat my purpose. I get my cell phone out of my purse in the bedroom, just in case he makes me get off his landline. Hit MacKenzie up. She answers on the first ring, sounding frantic.

"What now?"

"I need to know where he might keep his man stuff?"

She fires questions at me like her mouth is a machine gun. "What kind of man stuff? Girl, what you need man stuff for? What are you about to do? Don't do nuthin', okay? I'll walk you through this all, but you got to take it slow. You ain't ready for man stuff."

"I just want some rope."

She moans. "Oh, Jesus! Jesus, stop her! That freaky white boy done broke her down and she talkin' 'bout rope, Lord! I knew I shoulda stayed. I could just look at him and see he was trouble."

"Mac, what are you talking about?"

"What am I talking about? You're talking about rope and man stuff."

"I just mean where would he keep tape, and nails, and that sort of thing."

"Oh, Lord, what are you tryna do, girl?"

"I just want to make a tin-can telephone."

I can hear MacKenzie take several breaths. She seems calm for a moment, until she starts yelling. "*Why would you need a tin-can telephone?! Are y'all having vacation Bible school?! What is the matter with you, Zora?!*"

"We had a talk once. It would be sweet and meaningful. I think it would be a good way to end our argument."

"I just had a stroke because you want to do something sweet?"

"I told you I'm not going to do anything."

"Zora, you drivin' me crazy."

"Stop worrying about me, Mac. I just want the chance to grow up, just like you're doing. I'm worried about you, too, all the way in New York, alone. But I had to let you go. Why don't you just let me go, and take the call when I need you? You don't need to come back home for me."

She doesn't say anything, and I know she's thinking it over.

"Mac?"

"Yeah, baby?"

"You can let Jesus take care of me."

I hear her sigh. "I guess I have to."

"Are you really on your way here?"

"Girl, I'm so on my way."

"Turn around and go back to New York."

"Just ask him if he has any rope."

"Just ask him?"

"He's a white boy. He'll think you want to do something freaky. If he got some, he'll tell you."

"You're gonna have to work on your racial profiling, you know."

"Oh, no. Now you 'bout to turn in to *that* sistah."

"The one who is trying to lay her racism at the cross?"

"Yeah, that one."

"Bye, Mac."

"Bye, Z. Stay good. Okay?"

I tell her I will stay good, and I pray that God will give me the strength to, and I mean that. I try to act like I've got some sense and go out of Nicky's bedroom, and actually say something to him when I get to him sitting on the futon.

"Nicky?"

"Your highness is speaking to me now?"

"Do you have any rope?"

"Will you be tying me up and torturing me before you kill me? I'm assuming you were in my kitchen drawers looking for knives."

"Are you still mad because you couldn't get in *my* drawers?"

A wide smile spreads across his face. "You are way too clever. And it hurts when I smile. It hurts when I laugh. It also hurts when I kiss you. You've been tormenting me all day."

"You don't have to smile, laugh, or kiss me anymore. Now, about that rope. *String,* Nicky."

He goes to his living-room closet, of all places, and pulls out a roll of string. Gives it to me as if it were an offering. "Zora?"

"Have a seat, Nicky."

He sits on the futon.

I go into the kitchen to finish the telephone. I'd already punched the holes in the can, and make quick work of adding the string. I didn't want to be in another room to talk with him. I just wanted it to be a simple peace offering. It was silly, but I wanted it to be something innocent. This may be the last childhood thing we'll do.

I come into the living room holding the tin can telephone.

He grins when he sees it. "I'm assuming you're not about to kill me."

"I'm not going to kill you, cowboy."

"I would have recommended you shooting me, anyway. It's less personal than stabbing. You don't want to get close or personal with me, do you?"

I hand him a can. He takes it reluctantly. "No sparring, Nicky. You can talk about horses though. Or cowboy stuff."

"Guns are cowboy stuff."

"No guns."

"Are you going to be controlling when we grow up?"

"Yes."

"Good. I hate making decisions," he says after he puts the can to his mouth. I put mine to my ear. "Hello, Dreamy."

It doesn't sound good. He notices I'm not thrilled by the sound quality.

"Why don't you pull out your blackberry and text message me, princess?"

"Do you have a Blackberry, Nicky?"

"No."

"Then shut up.'"

"Do you?"

I don't answer him.

He says, and not into his can, "You have one, don't you? You have every freakin' thing."

I don't say into my can, "That doesn't mean I'm not lonely, cowboy. Just like you. Despite what I have, I can see you're lonely, and here I am. I'm the one trying to talk to you through a stupid can."

I take my can and throw it across the room. His sails along with it.

He doesn't look upset. He looks delighted. "Hey, Dreamy. Are black women in general violent, or is this unique to you?"

"It's just me, and only when I'm with you, Nicky."

"So I make you a she-beast?"

"In more ways than one."

"I wrote you a poem, she-beast."

"I don't care."

"Come and read it anyway."

"I don't want to read your poem."

"Please read it, Dreamy. It's a love poem."

The dreamy way he calls me Dreamy, the lulling timbre of his voice when it's full of sweetness and play, his words, they all conspire to tame the wild thing he rouses inside of me. I remember why I love him.

I think maybe we'll make it.

NICKY

We sit on the futon together, Zora curled into me. I ask her to go for a walk with me, mostly because Zora is curled into me and we'll be safe this way for another two seconds or so.

It's going to rain. We've had so much good weather, and now, finally, the heavenly mood seems to have shifted. The sky looks angry, and though clouds haven't spilled their furious waters, the cold moisture in the air is enough to dampen the bones.

I give her one of my jackets and the sight of her in it makes her look more womanish to me. We walk around my building, talking about living at The Beloved Community while I get a better job and she can go to the Center for Creative Studies. CCS is my idea. She hadn't even thought to dream of anything so big. We talk about how we can make a life that's perfect for us.

Despite the ease of our conversation, each step I take feels like a funeral march to the end of our relationship because I've got the princess in the heart of Cass Corridor with it's worn brown buildings sidled next to ruins. We're in the cultural center, but not the bright and shiny part that houses the museum and the art school she's dreaming of. We're where I'll worry about her getting mugged, raped, or hounded by crackheads.

I try to beat back my thoughts with the hope of love and the God who's bigger than my fear.

I tell her I'm called to be a pastor, but I don't know how that's going to work now. I tell Zora I want to be a writer, mostly, but sometimes I want to be the guy that does it better than my dad. She just says God told her once she'd marry a pastor, and she didn't believe Him. I said we'll follow God and figure it out. I'm so in love I don't know if I can be any happier. I didn't think what I feel was possible a week ago.

Her hand in mind. Her beautiful hand, dark and lovely, intertwined in mine. I look at the stark contrast of us as we walk along. Black and white. But it doesn't seem so much with all this love I feel. It's just some color. I won't let anything come between us, even though I'm scared. We'll make it somehow. I'll take care of her. If I can get through my fear and be willing to stick with this for real, a little color and a whole lot of life isn't going to get the best of us.

I hear voices, "brotha" voices behind us, directed at Zora because no one would mistake me for a "sistah."

"Wassup, sistah? What you doin' wit da white boy, girl?"

Another one. "He ain't got nuthin'. Baby, come on over here. Let me give you some Mandingo love."

Zora, this woman I plan to marry, without breaking stride, or looking back, pulls her hand out of mine.

I'm stunned. I can't look at her. I feel this aching void along with the chill where her hand was. I thrust both hands into the pockets of my jacket. I won't give her another opportunity to hold them. Not again.

Our hecklers like what she did. Start cheering for her, though she doesn't give them anything else. They follow us for another block, talking trash. Asking for her phone number, until one of them says something lewd.

I turn around.

He rises to the challenge. Tall as me. Dark, like Zora. Has a diamond stud in one ear. Bald head. "What you gon' do, white boy?"

"I'll show you, black boy."

His friend walks up on me. This one shorter. Heavy, fair-skinned, and boyish looking, but his eyes are as black and hard as flint. "You call him boy? Huh, honky? We got yo' boy."

I ready my fist. The two of them can take me, but I'm going to give them a hard time of it. That's when Zora lets out a scream like we've been plunged into a scary movie and she is the person about to get the ax across the head.

She scares all of us. The "brothas" back up. Look at each other. One says, "Man, that sistah is crazy."

His friend says, "She into white boys, anyway." Just turns and walks away. One calls her a foul name. I lunge at him, but she grabs me. They don't even get to see my burst of chivalry.

But I yank away from her grasp. "Don't touch me *now,* Zora."

"You shouldn't have called him 'boy,' Nicky."

"Why not? He called me a boy. I just called him the same thing."

"You didn't call him the same thing. You called him a lot less.

You've got four hundred years of history behind what you said. You stripped him of his manhood. He was a lot less than a boy to you. You're a *white* man."

"I don't know what you're talking about. Did you hear what he called you?"

"I heard him, Nicky. It's not the same. You'll never understand."

"I understand you pulling your hand out of mine. I understand you'll always feel your solidarity is with him. The *brotha*. Not me, the *white* man."

"I just didn't want them to give you any trouble."

"You're the one who didn't want the trouble."

"That's not true, Nicky. I mean it is, but what's wrong with not wanting any trouble?"

"You were ashamed of me."

"I wasn't."

"You were. You pulled your hand away because you wanted to distance yourself, way too late might I add, from me. You didn't want *brotha man* and his friend to know you love a white boy."

She doesn't bother to deny it this time. It spares me having to flat out call her a liar.

"You're a racist, Zora. You and your calling me 'white boy' and being ashamed of letting the outside world hear you listening to my 'white boy' music in your car. You and *your* stereotypes. You want all of America to be the big bad racist, but what about you?"

I stride ahead, spittin' mad. I don't worry about her keeping up. Not with those long legs of hers. Of course she catches me. Tries to link her arm in mine.

"Don't touch me, Zora. Keep your racist hands off of me."

Her anger comes down with the rain. Words pour out of her like droplets from the sky.

"What about you? What about your racism, Nicky? You think because you're funny and charming it's not there? Or that I don't see it? You think because you kiss me, or even love me, you're not infected with the disease we're all infected with. You're a racist. I'm a racist. We were born with it because we were born here. The soil is seeped in the blood of its African and Native American ancestors. This is a sick land full of sick people who don't remember how sick they are. Well, sometimes I remember, and that's why I pulled my hand away. I didn't want to hurt them. I didn't want to hurt. I didn't want you to hurt, or be hurt—"

"I don't want to marry you, Zora."

"Wait a minute, Nicky."

"It's over, Zora. This is way too heavy. I'm just one *white boy*, as you're so fond of reminding me. I can't change America. I can't change my family or yours. How long are we going to have to fight racism? And I'm not even sure you want to fight if you're more concerned about two thugs who walk up on us than you are me."

"Nicky, I'm sorry."

The rain pounds us, which only angers me more, triggering the memory of something I saw on television.

"Do you think I smell like a wet dog?"

For a moment she looks confused. "What?"

"I said, do you think I smell like a wet dog?"

She's not confused anymore. Her words ask a question but her hooded eyes reveal her shame. "What are you talking about?"

"You don't know what I'm talking about, Zora?"

She doesn't answer.

"Do I?"

"Who told you that, Nicky?"

"I saw a comedian talking about it on Comic View. He said black people think white people smell like wet dogs, and nobody in that mostly black audience was surprised. And I thought that was the meanest thing. I want to know since we're laying it out there if that's what you think."

"Can we just go back to your apartment? It's raining hard now."

"Answer me."

She doesn't even sound angry. More resigned. "No. You don't smell like a wet dog, Nicky. And white people didn't have to drain their pools when one of us got in. And they don't have to spray their lawn furniture with Lysol, like a neighbor did when she realized my fair-skinned sister was black when I came to pick her up. We needed our wet dog thing because white people had so many things like that. And it's ugly. And mean. And it's sin. And I'm sorry. You don't smell like a wet dog. You smell like a wet man because we're standing here getting soaked."

She tries to touch me again.

"Don't."

"Nicky. Let's get out of this rain. I said I'm sorry."

"I'm sorry, too. I don't need this. I don't want this, Zora. I can't do it."

"No, what you needed—what you wanted, was an excuse. This is you running away. Just like you ran off to Berkeley to run away from your father. I'm glad I could be your excuse before you had to run off to Paris to write or something. That would have been pretty expensive. And we both know you don't have that kind of money, which you seem to enjoy reminding me of."

And that was that.

CHAPTER TWENTY-THREE

ZORA

Sopping wet, I drive back to my apartment, and I realize I'm homeless. All my stuff is back, and none of it is mine. I know Daddy won't take it again. Mama will see to that, but I feel separated from love. I'm a stranger here. My name is on the lease, but I can't possibly *live* in the truest sense of the word here.

I get showered, warm and dry, and call Billie. I tell her I've got a lot of clothes and furniture to donate. I decide to do what I told my mother I would, only I'll do it without Nicky.

In the morning, with the new mercy God gives with the rising of the sun, I will become a servant for the first time. I will give my whole life away.

Tonight, I will cry out all the tears I've got inside of me.

The buzzer rings. With all my heart I pray it's Nicky, but his truck is still in my parking lot. I doubt he could get to me so fast.

It's not him. It's Miles.

I buzz him in.

He comes to me, and in his hands he's got a bag of groceries he doesn't know will go to the poor and needy, distributed through the Beloved Community.

I take the groceries and tell him to have a seat. He looks like he's been run through an old-fashioned washing machine wringer. His slick veneer is gone.

"What's going on, Miles?"

"I've been talking to your father."

"Have you."

"He told me you talked to him about what happened. And I've been thinking."

"I don't know if you should think, Miles. It might be dangerous."

"That's not funny, Zora."

"You're right. It sounds suspiciously like someone else I know. I apologize. What were you thinking?"

"I was thinking about what that white lady with the dreads was saying when I came here with that stuff. And your father. And how I just let happen what I've been doing in my head for a long time. I mean, what good is all this positive confession if you really aren't thinking positive thoughts?"

"I agree."

"Will you forgive me?"

I don't want to. I don't like Miles very much, but I haven't been the most likeable creature God ever made lately, either. "I forgive you, Miles. Forgive me. I sincerely mean that. I've been pretty awful, too."

"I don't want to rush into anything if you're not ready. I just want things to go back to how they were."

I reach over and touch his hand. Just briefly. I don't want to stir him up and have to give him a beat-down. If I slapped the man I'm in love with today, I'm liable to put a real hurt on Miles.

"Miles, forgiving each other doesn't mean we're going back together."

"Are you serious? You can't tell me you want that white boy?"

"Can you describe people using adjectives besides *white?*"

"Zora, he's—"

"Miles, I don't care what he is or isn't at the moment. That has nothing to do with this. You're not the man for me, Miles. But there are dozens of women at LLCC plotting to get you as soon as they think 'ding dong the witch is dead.'"

Just like that, Miles slips back into his smooth, cold bishop-to-be suit. He gives me the full length of his veneer smile.

"You'll be back."

"Keep on confessing that, Miles. I'll see you out."

And praise the Lord, I did, with nary a hitch.

NICKY

I lasted three weeks.

I thought the first one would be the hardest. That was the tearful one that made me feel like a girly man. That Tuesday I didn't answer my phone, not even when Linda called repeatedly because I was a no-call/no-show for work. When I missed Bible study for fear that she'd be there, they started calling me. Linda, Billie, and Richard. That night, I asked Pete to take me to get my truck. And when she got back from Bible study she'd see that I'd been there and of course she'd be devastated by the mere thought of me.

Yeah, right.

Zora wasn't calling. She wasn't leaving messages on my machine or cell phone. Finally, to escape the lack of messages from Zora, and the excessive messages from Richard, Billie, and Linda, I finally called the job to tell Linda I quit. Of course Linda wanted to know the scoop on what happened with Zora and me. I told her she could ask Zora.

In typical Linda fashion, Linda said, "Zora has only Zora's story. What's your story, Nicky?"

I got off the phone.

I spent the rest of the time at Pete's, job hunting in the daytime, and kickin' it with him to stave off my Zora hunger. The last week, I was too exhausted by my efforts to keep pretending. I got a job offer as a teaching assistant at, of all places, Sankofa Shule high school. I think they hired me because I'm white. Maybe they needed to fill some kind of reverse affirmative-action quota. I know I applied because I want to know everything she knows. It isn't possible with me just being a teaching assistant there, but I wanted to be where she'd been. I missed her.

I spent the next-to-the-last day so sick with love I thought it'd kill me.

I spent the last day of that three weeks with her dad.

ZORA

Three weeks. I didn't know it could hurt so much to love someone. Billie and Pet try to cheer me up, but I can't be consoled. Even Ms. Pamela noticed my sorrow when I finally got through to her and took her to the hospital. I couldn't even be consoled with the thought that I may have saved her life. I just keep painting golden people on the big canvas Nicky gave me, and one golden child in particular with sapphire eyes I paint with painstaking detail. I'm working on the tin-can phone the child is holding in his hand when Pet comes running into my room with her mother. They're holding hands. They're grinning their fool heads off.

My heart pounds because they are two of the most hopelessly ridiculous romantics I know, and every bit of paint on this huge canvas is the hope of love. Oh, Lord, could it really be?

"You got company," Pet says in a singsong voice.

I put the paintbrush down. "Who?" I say, knowing. I don't know what to do with myself. I look a hot mess with paint all over my cut-off overalls and T-shirt. My hair looking like Billie combed it.

I wipe my paint-smudged hands on my shorts. Billie and Pet each grab an arm and practically drag me to the living room, ready or not.

Oh, my. He's more beautiful than I remembered. The bruises and abrasions on his face are healed. He looks a little paler than before, a little sadder, much thinner, but the light in those gemstone eyes sparkles when he sees me.

He still loves me. And that crazy man is holding the tin-can telephone in his hands.

John is standing with him, like he's Daddy and he's gonna be watching us carefully. He beckons me over like I'm his little girl.

"Here's my baby," he says. "And I'm more than just her father confessor now, Nicky. You catch my drift?"

He gives John a very serious look, but his eyes are full of mischief. "Yes, sir."

"And you may talk with her right here in the living room. They'll be no being alone, young man."

"That's not a problem."

"All right, then. Billie, Perpetua, and I will just go over to the table and pretend we're not listening to every word."

"Thank you, sir."

John opens his arms, he and Nicky embrace, and he and the ladies file into the dining room, which would be out of earshot to most, but they are well-trained in nosy.

"Hey," I say.

"Hey yourself."

"It's good to see you."

He extends a can like it's a gift. "May I speak to the little princess?"

"Come on over to the sofa and sit with me."

He follows me to the sofa, and it feels like he's unleashed a thousand butterflies inside me. All kinds of flying is going on inside of me because he is here.

We sit. Side by side. I hold the can to my ear.

"Tell me about your first kiss?" he asks.

I don't know what he's done to it, but the sound quality has dramatically improved. He puts his can to his ear, and I respond.

"You already know about mine. But I can tell you I fell, deeply, irreversibly in love, and it was just the beginning. I used to see myself as a tiny shoot on a great big brown tree. And I used to think that tree was my history. My people. But that's only part of the tree. I realized the tree is all God's people. That tree is a body like His Body. All of us are nourished by the river that is His Word. His Spirit. His Life. And we're all connected. You were right about me being a racist. My first kiss scorched me and sent me to find the shade of that tree. And when I found it, it didn't look like I remembered it. There were blossoms of every color on it, Nicky. And one particularly beautiful white blossom. I knew I could love every flower blooming on that tree."

I put my can to my ear.

"Wow," is what he says. Then, "I guess I should tell you about my first kiss."

NICKY

"Put the can down, Zora. This isn't a children's story."

She lets me take the can from her and set our childish phone on the floor. I anchor my soul to the tempering kindness in her eyes.

I take a deep breath. Once Zora said to me the Sankofa bird looked behind itself to retrieve something from its past it may have left behind. I never wanted to dredge anything up from there, especially this. I have to.

"I got my first kiss at my friend Pete's family's summer house on Lake Superior. Both our families vacationed there in the summers. I already told you about how much I loved to go there when I was a kid."

She nods to encourage me, staring at me, eyes wide in rapt attention, brow a bit furrowed, lips slightly parted. She's concerned. I go on.

"He's got this aunt, Jerri. A real hottie. Redhead. In her thirties. Wildly inappropriate."

She takes my hand.

"She sent Pete to the store. It was Tuesday afternoon. June thirtieth. A really ordinary day, Zora, and I wanted to go to the store with Pete, but she said she wanted me to stay and help her with a few things. And I'm twelve, and dumb as a bag of nails."

She squeezes my hand, and I squeeze hers back.

"Don't tell me any more, Nicky."

"No, you wanted to know. Jerri gave me my first kiss, and then she gave me more. And then she took every bit of innocence I had. Every bit of it, Zora. And I never again saw that boy I used to be. I've been looking for him for thirteen years. I don't care who calls me Nicky, I haven't been able to find the glimpse of the good in me, or even the *me* in me, until you gave me that sketch, and I saw me."

Oh, man. Tears well in my eyes. "I'm sorr—"

But her kisses stop me from speaking. She rocks me and lets me weep for the boy I lost. She said Sankofa means "Go back and fetch it." What I went back and fetched was the little Nicky. I didn't know I couldn't go on to be a man until I rescued him.

ZORA

Nicky is spent, but he asks for a pen and some paper. He writes while I sketch him. When he's done, I hand him a drawing of him writing, and laugh at the irony because both of us were so stalled when we came together. He gives me his poem.

Beautiful Mosaic

I use to think I could fix
broken people.
I made a mess.
Broke a few
more than they were
before they met me.

Still, I'm drawn
to shattered people.
Their lovely sharp edges,
their exquisite, cutting shards.
I just don't try
to fix them anymore.
I got tired of bleeding
more than I already do.

Instead, I take
my splintered pieces
and scoop them into
a scarlet bag.
I place myself
at their feet
spread myself out before them
as a love offering.

Sometimes this works.
Sometimes they walk
all over me.
Oh well.
I did say they were broken.

But sometimes
they'll take all their pieces
their many, hard-edged pieces
and pour them out

of black leather

or white velvet

right at my feet.

And God will put His fingers—

carefully now! Be careful, God!—

on all our sharp and shining places.

Make a beautiful mosaic

out of all our brokenness.

He will bind us together,

by the bright, white strength

of love that never fails,

even though we are broken,

even though we are tiny little

fragments of what we used to be

or what we should be.

He has the face of an angel, and surely he writes like angels wish they could speak. I place my hand on his cheek. "I'm going to marry you."

"Do it now."

"How am I supposed to marry you now?"

"Zora, I never told anyone about Jerri. I've carried that for all those years."

"I know. I'm so sorry, baby."

"I've hurt a lot of women. Really good women, who I should have been leading to Christ. I've been a slave to lust. Even after I was celibate I remained a slave—this broken thing Jerri left behind. She ruined me."

"Nicky, she victimized you."

"I want to belong to Jesus, Zora, and I want to belong to you. I've missed you so much."

"I missed you too, Nicky. I didn't know you could miss someone you haven't known forever so much."

"That's the thing. You have known me forever. I don't know how, but you have."

He reaches into his pocket and pulls out a circle of gold. The earring God gave us. He holds it out to me.

"Did you know that in biblical times a Hebrew slave, in his seventh year of servitude, could declare his love for his master and refuse to go free?"

"I didn't know that, Nicky."

"But you can appreciate this from your own cultural experience. A slave is lowly, and despised. Above all things a slave wants freedom, right?"

"Right."

"So you gotta really love that master if you refuse to be free when you can be, right?"

"Right."

"I'm not saying I don't want to be free of the lust, and the pain. And I'm not going to be a perfect man because I've made this resolve, but I've got to be a real man. A better man. A loving man. Your husband. I want to be all those things. Christ's slave. In biblical times, if a slave declared his love for his master and refused to go free, the master took him before God and pierced his ear, and he remained his slave for life."

Nicky takes my hand, and places the earring in it. "I want you to pierce my ear, Zora. I want you to see I am declaring my love for Jesus. I want to be His slave for the rest of my life. I want to be His servant."

I can't even speak. The beauty of his act steals my words.

"Please, Zora, pierce my ear and make me God's slave. And make me yours. I am your servant."

He drops to his knees and his head goes to my lap. "Make me your man."

"I can't, Nicky. I'm afraid I'll hurt you."

Billie's voice calls from the dining room, "Like *heck* you can't!"

A tear slips from my eye as I get to my knees beside him.

"My hands are shaking too much."

Billie and Pet come out and Pet's got the ice tray in her hand. Billie's got a tea towel. They both join us on our knees. "Okay. I'm the queen of self-piercing. We'll numb him up with the ice and he won't feel a thing."

Nicky's head shoots up.

"You guys can't bring ice. That's going to ruin the moody beauty of the whole thing."

"Whatever," Pet says. "Besides, the ice will give Zora a chance to calm down. The way she's shaking you'll end up being Swiss cheese by the time she's done with you."

John comes in the room with the bread and wine. "Might as well go for the full effect."

"Including the footwashing?" I say.

John shrugs. "Slave making blood covenants, dubious communion, why not wash each other's feet? We'll just make a party of it. A big Jesus party."

Nicky takes my hand. "Can't have a party without a song."

Nicky opens his mouth and a song so sweet and familiar begins to pour out of him that tears stream out of me with every soaring note.

He sings, *"Let us break bread together on our knees."*

Voices swell in song around me. I look at Nicky. "How did you—?"

"I asked your dad." And he goes right back to singing as if saying "I asked your dad," doesn't tell me everything I need to know about him. I'm going to marry him. I'm going to give him a house full of golden children.

John tears Christ from a single loaf and passes Him around.

> *Let us break bread together on our*
> *knees.*

I put Christ in my mouth and begin to chew on Him, sweet and spongy in my mouth. Christ is holding my hand, looking just like her mother, crying just like her mother. I'm in love with Christ singing my favorite spiritual. Christ is scurrying around the kitchen readying towel and pitcher and bowl for our foot washing. Christ is all around me, loving me, and being loved by me. We all sing:

> *When I fall on my knees*
> *with my face to the rising sun,*
> *O Lord, have mercy on me.*

... a little more ...

When a delightful concert comes to an end,

the orchestra might offer an encore.

When a fine meal comes to an end,

it's always nice to savor a bit of dessert.

When a great story comes to an end,

we think you may want to linger.

And so, we offer ...

AfterWords—just a little something more after you

have finished a David C. Cook novel.

We invite you to stay awhile in the story.

Thanks for reading!

Turn the page for ...

• **Discussion Questions**

• **A Conversation with Claudia Mair Burney**

• **What's Next for Mair?**

DISCUSSION QUESTIONS

1. Zora and Nicky meet at a home Bible study. What do they see reflected in this community that they haven't found in their home churches?

2. Billie tells Zora that at the Beloved Community a stranger is someone who "is disconnected from love." In what ways are Zora and Nicky strangers at the beginning of the novel?

3. Richard, the author of *Good News for Rascals, Rebels, and Whores,* is perhaps the most missional character in the novel. Do you think his brokenness makes him easier or more difficult to relate to?

4. When Nicky is struggling with feelings of lust, Richard tells him to think about whether the love of God wants him to defile Zora. What does this question say about the way that Richard views God? How does Richard's perspective differ from the way Nicky views God?

5. Have you ever experienced a relationship or community where you knew that you were loved at the core of who you are, regardless of your past? If so, how did this knowledge change you?

6. Zora and Nicky are immediately attracted to each other. How does this initial attraction grow into a more mature love by the end of the novel?

7. Zora's father doesn't want Zora to lack for anything. How is this desire a reflection of his past?

8. The Sankofa bird's head is turned back to symbolize that what we've lost is in our past, and only in going back can we truly go forward. How do Zora and Nicky come to terms with their pasts in this novel?

9. At the beginning of the novel, both Zora and Nicky are quick to point fingers at each other. How are they forced to confront the pride and racism in their own lives?

10. Do you think that racism is an issue in our culture today? In the church? Why, or why not?

A CONVERSATION WITH
CLAUDIA MAIR BURNEY

Zora and Nicky **is about two of the subjects held most sacred in America: race and religion. How do you see racism reflected in our culture and the church today?**

I think racism is alive and well in America in both blatant and subtle ways. How could it not be? We've got a painful legacy to contend with—the shared soul wounds inflicted on us through the experience of chattel slavery. I'm forty-three years old. If my great-grandmother could tell me stories about her mother being greased and placed on an auction block, we aren't far removed from the horror of those days.

Martin Luther King Jr. said, "It is appalling that the most segregated hour in Christian America is eleven o'clock on Sunday morning." I don't see that things have changed much. If I go to my black church, I'm comfortable. Everything is familiar—the music, the preaching style, even the way we worship. I'm not a minority there. It's the same for white Americans. Go to a predominantly white church and you're likely to have a distinctly European experience of church. I've gone to several predominantly white churches where I never saw a black person on the ministry staff or heard a black gospel song during worship. I was completely excluded culturally. It wasn't intentional; it just showed what was culturally important to them, what was comfortable.

I've seen these same church leaders deeply hurt that black people would not come and stay. I know why they didn't stay. It's because they didn't find anything there for them. They had a European church experience in those churches, and they weren't European.

Doing what is familiar isn't inherently wrong, but it keeps us separate. We don't have to deal with the messy issues of our biases when we stay with the people most like us. We don't have to confront our fears, or our hate. But it's still there, and until we can meet at the foot of the cross and say, "I've got this wound, but I'm willing to give it to Jesus to heal," and then say to our brother or sister who is not like us, "Hey, show me *your* wound and we'll take that to the cross too," we aren't going to make any progress.

We also have to make a commitment to stop hurting one another. And we must create safe places to share our pain, fissures, and scars, or we won't take that risk. And it is a risk. That's why so many of us are trapped in our little segregated dead ends, every bit the pious deniers, which in many ways, is not much different than being pious liars.

Can you tell us a bit about your faith background?

In a word, my faith background has been *messy.* I started off having my "born again" experience at the age of fifteen in a fiery Church of God in Christ. From there I went to what is now called Word Faith or Word of Faith churches. I went to a variety of independent charismatic-friendly churches, black and white, some having very little accountability. I saw a lot of abuse during those years.

I left the church as a young adult. I did a lot of running from God. I chanted with the Hare Krishnas, wanted to be a whirling dervish, got all new-agey. I blew through a whole range of religious experiences seeking the love I'd left behind in Jesus. And then I spent years making my way back to Him. Although I'd returned, I was unable to articulate or honor the deepest longings of my heart, which I believe were put there by God. I wanted a very multicultural experience in worship, and I don't mean only black and white together. I'm closer to having that now than I've ever been, but I'm not quite there yet.

Now I'm Eastern Orthodox. I like it because it's pretty much the same everywhere. No matter what Orthodox church I go to, we're going to be celebrating the Liturgy of Saint John Chrysostom. It isn't personality driven. You go to worship God and receive the sacrament of the Eucharist. We aren't driven into emotional frenzies. We don't have a preacher who is a superstar. It's just one long prayer service until we receive the Body of Christ. I love it. It feels safer than the madness I've been through.

Zora and Nicky are both changed by what you would describe as incarnational Christianity. What does this mean to you? Is it something you've experienced in your life?

I got a real "incarnational Christianity" bug as I wrote this novel. I'd heard the term, but it didn't click until I began asking myself questions as I wrote. What does it mean to have "this treasure in earthen vessels"? If I were to take being the body of Christ seriously, how would that affect how I lived? Christ loved. He healed. He delivered. I asked myself: How do people heal? How do they love through Christ? I put the characters in situations that challenged them to make Christ real to one another. For example, Christ is concerned about our needs. If we need clothing, He's probably not going to drop a few outfits out of the sky. It's more likely that He'll provide through community. He provides for His body through His body. I believe if we caught on to this we'd change the world. People like Saint Francis of Assisi and Mother Teresa of Calcutta changed the world through incarnational living.

I'm still trying to find my footing. This is all new and exciting, and it's turned everything I thought I knew about being a Christian on its ear. I can't be the same old self-obsessed, apathetic slug if it's up to me to be Christ to "the least of these." There goes my worldly ambition! My desire for success and fame falls to the wayside when I think of all the need out there. And it's up to me to do something. So, now I say, "Amen!" I'm trying to empty myself like the Virgin Mary did and let the Holy Spirit fill me, and use me for service that goes way beyond what I thought I was capable of giving. But it's still a challenge. It goes against the grain of all the selfishness I've absorbed because of the fall, because I'm American, and because I'm an unwitting victim of the disease of affluenza, no matter how much or how little money I possess.

WHAT'S NEXT FOR MAIR

My next book, tentatively called *Wounded,* is about a young African American woman who is sitting in her Vineyard church and receives the wounds of Christ—the sacred stigmata. I'll explore some very personal issues, particularly a question I've asked myself many times: What does it mean to share in Christ's suffering? In that novel I explore what makes an individual more receptive to accepting his or her personal cross. The main character, Gina, has lived much of her life as "the least of these." And now Christ wounds her in this peculiar and extraordinary way. And she doesn't fit the profile of one who'd likely receive such a grace. She's a black protestant single mother who is not particularly devout, but she knows something about suffering.

The theme of poverty of spirit seems to be woven into all my work, and from what I see in the Gospels, poverty of spirit is something we definitely need to pay attention to, whether we understand exactly what it is or not. I don't think you can live out any of the other Beatitudes without being poor in spirit first. Poverty of spirit is deep. We don't particularly raise our hands high to be chosen for that blessing. And blessed are they who mourn? Ewww! No thanks, unless you're the one who's in deep mourning. Then you need that blessing badly.

Christian community will also play a key role, and in my books, community is often found outside of one's "home church." Many of my characters have been alienated from church, or they have had experiences as messy as my own. I want to give messy people like me hope.

Jesus loves us, meets us exactly where we are, and grows us through His great love and unfathomable mercy. If somebody closes my book and feels like no matter what kind of hot mess they are, God still loves them, then I've done my job. I trust God's love to draw them to Christ, and then the Holy Spirit can begin to make them more like Him, but I really believe they have to know the love is there first. The John 3:16 stuff. Love really does cover a multitude of sins. I think we need a new revelation of that. We tend to forget, and that is truly a shame.

Thanks for the chat. May God have mercy on us all.

Pax et Bonum!
Mair